a hostage

a hostage

CHARLOTTE MENDEL

Toronto, Ontario, Canada
www.inanna.ca

We gratefully acknowledge the support of the Canada Council for the Arts and the Ontario Arts Council for our publishing program. We also acknowledge the financial support of the Government of Canada.

Cover design: Val Fullard

A Hostage is a work of fiction. All names, characters, businesses, places, events and incidents in this book are either the product of the author's imagination or used in a fictitious manner.

All trademarks and copyrights mentioned within the work are included for literary effect only and are the property of their respective owners.

Library and Archives Canada Cataloguing in Publication

Title: A hostage / Charlotte Mendel.
Names: Mendel, Charlotte R., 1967- author.
Identifiers: Canadiana (print) 20230447678 | Canadiana (ebook) 20230447686 | ISBN 9781771339247 (softcover) | ISBN 9781771339254 (EPUB) | ISBN 9781771339261 (PDF)
Classification: LCC PS8626.E537 H67 2023 | DDC C813/.6—dc23

Printed and bound in Canada

Inanna Publications and Education Inc.
210 Founders College, York University
4700 Keele Street, Toronto, Ontario, Canada M3J 1P3
Telephone: (416) 736-5356 Fax: (416) 736-5765
Email: inanna.publications@inanna.ca   Website: www.inanna.ca

To Rouane Susie Mendel, the most loving and generous of sisters.

chapter one

CONSCIOUSNESS SEEPS AROUND the edges of my brain. I try to ask my husband for water, but before I can open my mouth, exhaustion overtakes me again.

The second time consciousness knocks, I stay awake long enough to wonder why my eyes won't open and again demand water from my husband in a parched croak that doesn't belong to me.

"The only reason I stay with you is because you're a great nurse when I'm sick," I want to tell him, but it's too hard to unglue my tongue from its arid nest. Before I can gather the energy to pinch viciously at the inert mass I imagine snores beside me, I'm already asleep.

The third time, the fact that sleep keeps reclaiming me, as though it were my master, fills me with rage. I'm determined to stay awake. I struggle to open my eyes; complete darkness rewards me. I peer toward the skylight in the roof of our bedroom to check whether cloud cover is obliterating the light of the stars, but I can't even see the outline of the skylight. Have I gone blind? A frisson of fear courses through me, and I quickly close my eyes again. For a while I lie there, carefully probing the various parts of my body with my mind. A raging headache throttles my brain, and my dry lips stick together; I slide my hand across the mattress and reach the end of the bed. Where the hell is my husband?

Of course, I'm not at home. I am... focus... my brain feels so heavy and stupid.

I sleep.

The next time I wake up, reddish-yellow shapes dance behind my lids and there is a moment of joy as my eyes spring open and see sunlight streaming through a large window. Of course, I'm in a hotel room. Like, duh. I guess that's what they call a blackout; how much did I drink, anyway? Yesterday had been a great day: hanging out in Dahab in the Sinai, swimming in the Mediterranean, getting stoned with tourists (predominantly white) and locals (predominately brown). Relaxation and meditation. My memory floods back as my brain comes to life.

I HAD LEFT MY FAMILY in Israel and grabbed a few days to do a solo trip in the Sinai. It was wonderful to escape. Our yearly holiday is always spent with my husband's family in Morocco; the problems started on the first night and deteriorated from there. His mother circled around the table, serving us, her other two sons, and her husband. I don't judge; different folks, different strokes. Making us happy made her happy. The problem started when Adam forgot he was Canadian and launched a whisper-hiss competition in bed.

"I can't believe you didn't help my mother; she's getting pretty old."

"You help her."

"You know she won't let me."

"The kids can help her."

"I'm asking you to be an example to Rebecca."

"By reinforcing Moroccan sexism?"

This was the point when whispers escalated to hisses. There was no resolution; of course I ended up helping my aging mum-in-law and exemplifying misogyny. But this year I actually convinced Adam that I deserved compensation for two weeks of cooking and cleaning, while he sat around smoking and playing cards. So we made an extra stop in Israel, because I'd lived there for a decade and have a lot of friends.

Adam thought a side trip to the Sinai was too dangerous, so I popped over by myself for a couple of days. I love the Sinai—you can sleep in a cheap hut for a few dollars a night, the weather is always good, and the dope is great. After the first night in the cheap hut, my middle-aged back began to ache, so I opted to pay a few more dollars for a hotel. I remember lying against the carpets in the restaurant last night, realizing that whatever happened in my life, I would never be happier than I was at that moment. Two wonderful children, a good husband, a brother, a sister who was also my best friend, my ninety-year-old mother. Double gratitude that I still had my mother at that age. Fear about her eventual death occasionally overwhelmed: a third of the adults who really loved me would be gone. Nobody loves you like a mother. Surely her death would end happiness... for a while.

But right now she was alive and compos mentis and full of love, so I lay there on the carpet, focusing on my happiness. A fucked-up, miserable human being surrounded by love and fortune. How did that happen?

And then the Jewish part of my mind kicked in: when will the other shoe drop?

I SIT UP CAUTIOUSLY, pressing the pain in my head with my palm to hold it at bay. Praise my guardian angel and the thoughtful hotel maids, there is a big bottle of water and a glass by my bed. I fill it and drink, and then drink again and again. The horrible throbbing in my head seems to recede a little. It's weird that I still feel so groggy; I try to remember what happened after my stoned bliss on the carpet. Obviously, more imbibing. Still holding my head, I rise cautiously to my feet and look around the hotel room. It doesn't look the same as I remember. Surely there'd been a queen-sized bed? My single bed stands in the corner of a square, plain room. There is a door beyond the foot of my bed with a sliding door beside it, and another door in the corner opposite. The window dominates the fourth corner. A desk and chair squat in front of the window, supporting my carry-on. The usual TV takes up a chunk of the wall, but I'm surprised to note that there are also several shelves of books. I totter to the door at the foot of my bed and open it to reveal a small bathroom equipped with toilet, shower, sink, and mirror. Just what I need.

Perhaps not. The mirror reveals a ghastly face, with black mascara streaking my cheeks, failing to hide my puffy eyes. I retrieve my toiletry bag from my carry-on and wash thoroughly. It is wonderful to rinse the nasty taste from my mouth. The headache has receded to a dull throb, unless I move my head sharply, and I begin to feel more cheerful. I check out the sliding door beside the shower, which hides an empty closet. The third door, oddly, is locked.

I can't get out.

I walk over to the window, catching my breath against the force of the sun scorching through it.

Dunes and large hills covered with sand-coloured rock stretch in every direction.

Below is a parking lot–sized cement floor, surrounded by a high, wire fence. Buildings dot the area, and a group of men march in formation toward my building. They are in army uniform. They have brown faces and black hair. Moustaches.

A tremor of fear sweeps through my body. The pain in my head resumes its thudding blows against my frontal lobe.

What is going on?

I close my eyes tight, wishing myself back in bed, 'round about the time before I woke up properly. Wishing that I was still washing my face in the bathroom. Wishing to be at any other moment of my life, rather than this one.

Where the fuck am I? Childishly, I scrunch my eyes shut and begin to pray. "Please make me be with my mother in Canada. Please, when I open my eyes, let me be holding my mother's hand in the goat pen. Lilah and Willow will be eating our clothing, and we'll be shoving them back and laughing. Please."

While these foolish thoughts course through my brain, I observe the fact that I am panting like a dog. I try to slow my breathing, even as it accelerates. Focusing on breathing has always proved effective as a means to control my anxiety. I chivvy myself along like a little girl.

There's no need for this anxiety, you know, it's all in your head. Just relax.

But it doesn't work, because whatever the hell is going on… *damn this breathing*… it's like it's got a mind of its own. I turn toward the shelves of books, seeking answers, or comfort. All my favourites. Jane Austen. George Eliot. The Brontës. Dickens.

A Hero.

Turn Us Again.

Reversing Time.

My books. A wave of panic rears its ugly head and strikes at me; I rush to the second door and pull frantically at the knob, knowing already that it's locked. Somehow I'm on the floor, struggling to breathe.

I don't know how long I lie there, fighting with my breath like it's a mortal enemy. It seems like a long time. It seems like minutes. I lie curled in a ball on the floor, underneath the books.

Is this a nightmare?

My fingers caress the skin of my earlobe, then pinch viciously. Ouch. So not a nightmare. Have I gone crazy? Is it possible for a person who is crazy to know they are crazy? Am I still in the hotel, and this is a normal consequence of alcohol poisoning?

There is a gentle knock at the door. I freeze, no longer aware if I breathe or not.

They are coming for me. I am in an army camp somewhere in the Middle East. They know about my Israeli passport. They'll think I'm complicit in Palestinian suffering. I will be tortured and raped and murdered.

The knock comes again. What the fuck are they knocking for (are they waiting for me to invite them in so they can torture and murder me)? I leap to my feet and begin to search feverishly for a weapon, grabbing and discarding the plastic water bottle, darting into the bathroom and seizing my face-cleansing lotion, which happens to come in a relatively hefty glass bottle. Positioning myself to one side of the door so it will hide me as it opens, I raise the bottle, ready to smash it over a head.

There is a final, peremptory knock, and the door opens slowly. My body tenses; I wish I'd taken karate classes with my children back in Nova Scotia. At least it would've taught me the most effective place to smash the bottle.

Whoever it is doesn't advance into the room, although he's saying something in Arabic. One becomes infinitely more aware of tone when the language is incomprehensible, and this tone is definitely soothing, perhaps a little nervous. Tantalizing smells waft through the open door, and my resolve to kill wavers. Food today, torture tomorrow? The edge of a tray inches beyond the open doorway. The soothing voice says something that sounds to my ignorant ears like "Isha hama blah blah, okay?" I keep silent, my glass bottle suspended.

"Hama Bama shey blah blah, okay?" asks the voice again. The tray advances a couple more inches. The few Arabic words in my possession are mostly swear words, served up during Hebrew language lessons along with *please* and *thank you*. Curse words stolen by the Israelis, along with everything else. Hey, if you're going to resurrect a 3,000-year-old language, you've gotta revamp it a little bit. I weigh my options. I could say "Shukran" to thank him for the food, or "Coos emek"—your mother's cunt, to curse him for my captivity. It really is an impossible decision.

The tray advances another inch, and my stomach rumbles in response. My traitorous arm trembles, proclaiming its desire to descend. I eyeball the bottle of lotion, recalling how very expensive it had been and how unlikely it is that I can obtain any more here if the bottle were to break.

The entire tray appears beyond the door and takes a sharp right in the direction of my bedside table. The long arm it's attached to seems to be trying to reach the table without actually entering the room. I jump out from my hiding place, brandishing my bottle, and the tray guy leaps about a foot into the air. The tray slips from his hands, clattering onto the table directly below, luckily landing right-side up.

"Ishy hatay blah blah!" yells the man, who doesn't look very frightening. He's just a kid, really, around eighteen or so. Then he tries to close the door. I spring forward and wrench it open, and a little tug-o-war ensues. To my delight, I seem to be winning, but the guy opens his mouth and bellows something, and, in an instant, two more men appear carrying truncheons, which they use to thrust me back into the room. Within minutes, they've turned the lock on me again. You'd think I'd be relieved because they'd obviously tried not to hurt me, but no, a kind of madness seizes me. The desire to insult. My brain sifts through Newfie/Polish/any-race-you-want-to-be-rude-about jokes from my childhood (*How many Newfies does it take to change a lightbulb? Three, one to hold the bulb and the other two to turn him around and around*).

"How many Arabs does it take to vanquish a Jew?" I scream through the keyhole. "No, wait; how many young, male Arabs does it take to vanquish a middle-aged Jewess?"

Utter silence. Just as well, because I hadn't thought up the punchline yet.

And they hadn't really tried to vanquish me.

And the food smells so good.

A little deflated, I pick the tray up off the floor and settle cross-legged on my bed to explore the surprises under the dome-like covers. Humus and fresh pita. Salad. Boiled eggs. Salt and pepper. Butter. Coffee and mint tea. Sugar and cream. Baklava for dessert. And wonder of wonders: a pack of Benson and Hedges. Light. Extra long. The kind I never get because they're too expensive.

Everything is delicious. Whoever my captor is, they certainly know my preferences. Books, cigarettes, lovely food. They obviously care. Maybe torture and murder aren't my destiny after all. Maybe everything is going to be all right.

It's amazing how optimistic you can get with a bit of nice food.

WEIRD THOUGH IT SOUNDS, the rest of the day is reasonably okay. True, I don't know what the hell is going on, and whenever I focus too much on that, my breathing goes wonky again, but most of the time I manage to talk myself into calm. Is it likely that a murderer would thoughtfully supply my favourite cigarette brand, complete with ashtray and lighter? My kidnapper wants me to feel comfortable. Probably figures he can get a good ransom out of a Canadian (poor bastard, he doesn't know how broke artists are).

But why are your books here?

Calm yourself. Focus on the positive. Is it likely that a murderer would fill the room with nice books?

What about The Collector by John Fowler, where the madman kidnaps a girl and puts her in a room with lots of nice things, and she gets sick and dies?

Breathe deeply. That won't happen to me. I'm as strong as a horse. I'm never sick.

At some point, I remember my laptop and boot it up. There are two electrical outlets in the room, but they have too many holes for my plug. The laptop still has some juice left, and I immediately try to access the internet. No luck, of course.

Twice more throughout the day, which I trace by the position of the sun outside my window, there's a gentle knock at the door and the same guy fearfully holds out a tray. Both times, I grasp it firmly with a cheerful "Shukran." I've decided it's best to make friends, not enemies.

Dinner is curried goat. Which I happen to *love*. The best thing about my pet goats Lilah and Willow is chowing down on their babies. Instead of the cigarettes, there is a little wad of tinfoil. I can't believe my eyes when I unwrap it to reveal a delicious little clump of marijuana.

After that, there are no panic attacks or breathing struggles. I take a shower, revelling in the hot water and ignoring the anxiety about whether I'm using too much water here in the desert. I dress myself in a light cotton robe and nothing else; I hate underwear and bras and there is absolutely no reason in the world to burden my body with them here. Then I lie on my bed, journal in hand, and make a plan, quelling a rush of affection for my captor. He must be a kind, thoughtful man.

> I might be here for a while, especially if the ransom is too high for my husband to pay, but does that matter? This place is an introvert's wet dream. I just need to create a life out of a small space. I'll do an hour of exercise every day. One hour of meditation. Two hours reading. Seven hours writing. I'll show the food guy my laptop and ask for an adaptor. I bet I can write 5000 words a day. My next book will be done in a month. The only downside is I'll probably be let out before then.
>
> *Hah hah.*
>
> Seriously. For the last fourteen years, I've been an introvert who's never alone. Resentment simmering gently as others gobbled my time: kids, demanding husband, work colleagues... even the goats bleating every time I went outside the house or the cats mewling for food every time I went back in. When our cat Pooty got senile and began to mewl constantly, forgetting that she'd been fed, I contemplated theriocide. I resented the friendly

neighbours who stopped to chat as I marched to the school bus stop with the goats in tow. Bless Nova Scotians; they are so nice and I'm such a bitch. How can you convey your need for solitude in the five minutes remaining before you meet your excessively extroverted children off the school bus?

Not to mention the list of unanswered emails staring at me reproach-fully, that never, ever decreases.

And now, for an inestimable period of time, there is nobody. I am alone, with myself. It's amazing.

Yeah, probably best to be delusional in this situation.

Did I mention this annoying voice in my fucking head that pipes up the minute the kids have been put to bed and the husband finally installed in front of the television with a cup of tea?

And when you're alone in the house all day while the kids are at school and Adam works, you ungrateful bitch.

I am grateful. How many times have I wrenched my mind from sliding into the abyss of negativity and depression through gratitude? A mental countdown of my blessings, the first of which is that I don't work full-time, and every day I wave goodbye to the kids and eat my breakfast in solitude and feel grateful.

And I feel grateful right now, so I take a moment to close my eyes and give thanks for this gift of time. For this hiatus.

Maybe He did it on purpose. So I could appreciate how wonderful my kids are instead of moaning about the lack of a room of my own.

That's likely. Thousands dying all over the world from war, Ebola, starvation, COVID, but you—you're special. God is busy concocting plans to help you appreciate your kids.

You have a minor point.

Plus, you don't even believe in God.

True, but I like to have someone to pray to when I'm desperate.

I CLOSE MY JOURNAL, masturbate, and fall asleep. My usual stoned ritual.

Another knock at the door. My eyes open reluctantly. I might have to up my exercise routine to two hours a day if they're going to feed me so much. "Entrez," I say grandly. Find out whether the kid speaks French; a lot of Arabs do.

The door opens more forcefully than before, and a man stands in the entrance. I rub the sleep from my eyes and perch myself on my elbow. He comes in, takes the chair, and places it beside the head of my bed. He's very tall and slim.

I rub my eyes again.

But it's still him.

President Kassem of Syria.

Absurdly, an intense desire to check my face in the mirror overcomes all other thought. Somehow, crusty sleepy-dust doesn't jive with this meeting. To tell the truth, I got a little obsessed with him while I was writing A Hero. Some harmless fantasies, that type of thing. I realize he's done terrible things. I'm not an *idiot*.

"Excuse me," I mutter and skid on my bottom to the end of the bed, so as to avoid passing too close to him on my way to the bathroom.

I rub my eyes and fluff up my hair a little. My hand hovers over the makeup bag. For God's sakes, what's the matter with me? It's a good thing my comfortable cotton dress almost reaches the floor. Perfectly modest.

Makeup-less, I march out of the bathroom. The kid is placing a tray of tea and delicacies on my bedside table. I note his obsequious manner as he bows out of the room.

Sitting primly on the edge of my bed, smack-dab next to the bottom rail, I wait for Kassem to make the first move.

He gestures elegantly toward the tray. "Would you like me to pour?"

I shrug inelegantly.

He squeezes a lemon and spoons honey into a cup, then pours hot water over it. I watch his long, delicate fingers. I wish I hadn't smoked the joint; although the stone is gone, the head's still heavy. And filled with an intense desire to scarf every one of those little cakes.

He sips his tea. "You must be wondering why you're here."

"Mm-hmm," I reply, leaning irresistibly toward the cakes. It's important to play this right. The other person will say more if you're quiet. And I want him to say a lot.

"I suppose the quick answer would be that you're here because you wrote *A Hero*."

A Hero? How does he know about A Hero? Nobody except your friends and family have read that book.

I raise my eyebrows, partly to prod him to further speech, but mostly because my mouth's full.

"I want to assure you that there is nothing to fear. I enjoyed your book. I have no intention to hurt you. You are my honoured guest."

My whole body seems to give a sigh of relief. I hadn't realized how tense I'd been.

You believe this psycho?

If I don't believe him, how will that help me? No point ruining the present with futile worrying.

Kassem is waiting for an answer, so I nod. Man, the cakes are delicious.

"Anything you want, anything at all, you just need to ask." There is something genuine about the way he says it, which comforts me.

He's a psycho mass murderer.

Yeah, but he doesn't want to hurt me.

I expect he doesn't really want to hurt Syrians either, but that didn't prevent him unleashing chemical weapons on them.

Yeah, well, they're pissing him off and I intend to suck his ass. Possibly literally.

"*A Hero* is based on Syria?"

I swallow quickly. Every word I say might be used against me, but what might the right answer be? How was Kassem portrayed in *A Hero* anyway? It's really annoying that I always forget the last book I wrote as soon as I'm into another one; worse that I can never read them again because they invariably produce a gag reflex. So really a waste of time adding my books to this library.

"A simple question," he prompts.

I'm pretty sure the actual hero in the book supports Kassem. More or less. Until he starts poisoning his own people and stuff. I eyeball the real McCoy with interest. A bona fide madman. "It was inspired by the Arab Spring, really."

"But it's obviously based on Syria."

Why's he asking if it's so obvious? "I guess I was particularly interested in the events here."

"Why?"

Because you were the sexiest of all the Middle Eastern leaders?

Grow up.

"Because you were a leading figure in America's axis of evil, and I wanted my readers to hate my hero. If he supported an evil leader like you, that would be another strike against him."

careful.

I've never managed to acquire the art of pondering one's words. What I think, I say; I call it verbal vomit. Surely fear should curb verbal vomit? But I don't feel afraid. Call me stupid.

call you a pothead.

Kassem sneers. "The Americans label so many Arab leaders as evil."

"I guess it depends on your perspective."

"You will see that I am not evil."

I take a sip of tea. It is deliciously sweet. Today he's playing good cop, thank God. And tomorrow... is unfortunately another day.

"You said I just needed to ask to get what I want, so, can I go home?"

He leans forward anxiously, blue eyes fixed on mine. Large blue eyes fringed with abundant dark eyelashes. "Are you not comfortable here?"

Love the accent. Hope stupid questions don't indicate idiocy. "I have kids," I say as gently as I can. "They need me."

Instantly, ridiculously, tears threaten. The image of my worried children rises up before me; they don't like me to be away. Their father doesn't understand kids, and he always equates undesirable behaviour with bad intent.

"You are only here for a short time. Just to answer some questions."

He hands me the platter of cakes, but suddenly I'm not hungry. "Can I answer them all now and go home tomorrow?"

"Perhaps not tomorrow."

That damn panic, rising up and clutching my chest. "When?"

"Soon. Very soon." He takes a cake and pops it into his mouth. I hate thin lips. He's got a weak chin, too.

He dabs his mouth fastidiously. "I want to talk about... Kassem's... death."

I nod furiously. Kassem—the dictator in *A Hero* who was brutally murdered in the end. Pile on the questions as fast as you can, and let me answer them all and go home.

"Are you psychic?"

"Are you a psycho?" *Damn.*

"No," he says, and a crease of annoyance appears between his brows.

"Likewise. *A Hero* is a work of fiction, inspired by the Arab Spring. It's based on Syria, but Kassem's death is based on Gaddafi. I was taking bits and pieces, which I'm allowed to do because it's fiction."

"So, you don't think I'm going to die like that?" He watches me intently.

"Of course not."

"Then why did you write that?"

Anxiety writhes in my intestines. "I already told you, it was based on Gaddafi's death. Listen, how did you even hear about *A Hero*? It's not like anybody's read it. My first book is crap and it won three prizes, but *A Hero*? Nada." I lean forward on the bed. "I thought it was such an important book. Contemporary, enjoyable. There is a wave of Islamophobia sweeping the West and every page of *A Hero* reinforces the commonalities existing between humans: we share massively more than we differ, in terms of culture."

He leans back in his chair, releasing me from the penetrating gaze of those blue eyes. He's probably bored, but I'm on a roll. "And do you know why *A Hero* didn't do well? Probably because Canada is too PC to read a book about Muslims unless it's written by one. Know any Muslims writing books that foster mutual understanding lately? Neither do I."

That's because you're an ignoramus. There's plenty.

Probably, but I bet he doesn't have much time to read.

He looks around the room. Taps his fingers on the arm of his chair.

I take a deep breath. "Do you mind if I smoke?"

"Perhaps you are afraid I will be angry if you admit that you foresaw my death." He launches himself forward in his chair again, enveloping my eyes with his own.

"I am not psychic," I say very slowly. "The only reason *A Hero* is based on Syria is because it was on the CBC a lot when I began to write, and as a result I was marginally more interested in Syria than anywhere else. The CBC is Canadian radio; I wouldn't know a thing about the world without it and *The Guardian*."

He is silent, scanning my face like it's a book.

I stare back, praying he can see the truth shining from my eyes. Is that really all he wanted to know? Whether I foresaw his death? Please God, please God... breathe. Relax.

Kassem picks up the lighter and courteously lights my cigarette for me.

I take a deep, comforting drag. "Is there any ventilation in this room? For the smoke to escape?"

"Certainly there is. You can open the window too, you know." He gets up to demonstrate. The window only opens a few inches—not enough to push a fist through, let alone a body—but if I put my nose up close I can smell the outside. Under pretense of blowing my cigarette smoke out the window, I smell and smell.

He stands beside me, looking out into the night. "I wish I could read your mind," he says.

Oh no.

"I'll let you in on a little secret," I whisper, like we're not all alone in the middle of nowhere, like I'm not juggling balls without knowing which one spells *death*, which *life*. "I always tell the truth."

He gives a short bark of laughter. Then, surprisingly, he slips the cigarette out of my fingers and takes a drag. "Nobody always tells the truth."

"All right, point taken. I can lie, but there's got to be a solid reason; I never lie lightly. Please believe me: I'm not psychic."

Bullshit! You can't lie because you always look guilty.

He looks right into my eyes again. "It's not just the death of the dictator. There are other things in the book..."

Damn.

He glances at his watch. "I will visit you again tomorrow. Is there anything you need?"

"What other things?"

"Tomorrow."

He turns to leave. My mind races frantically—what do I need in order to remain sane for the next twenty-four hours? "What time is it here?"

"Nine p.m."

"How long will I be here?"

"We'll talk about it tomorrow."

"Can I have an adaptor so I can use my computer to work?"

"Certainly." He continues to stand there. "I wish I could see into your soul."

Oh no.

I DON'T SLEEP WELL. Nightmares.

When I wake up the next day, I can feel tendrils of depression curling around my stomach. I hang my nose out the window and wonder how long I'll remain sane, shut up in this room. Strict adherence to routine is sure to help, so I launch into mine with a vengeance: one hour workout, including push-ups, sit-ups, leg exercises, and some cardio stuff which involves jumping jacks until I feel sick. I keep looking at my watch desperately; never has an hour elapsed so slowly. The only thing I enjoy doing for exercise is walking. Preferably with my goats next to water.

Don't think about that.

I choose *The Count of Monte Cristo* to read during breakfast, then open my laptop to use up the last of its battery. During a two-year segue during which I wrote a children's book, the characters of *A Hero* battered at the doors of my mind, wondering how the silly child in my kid's book could compare with the complex characters they had become. So I began again, taking up with my beloved characters two years after the events of *A Hero*. Ahmed was working and fighting inappropriate feelings for Zaynah. The formidable Rana still ruled her family with an iron grip; she had finally confided her suspicions about Mazin's homosexuality to Fatima, who had been unhelpfully horrified. ISIS had reared its ugly head and the family lived in fear that their border town would come under attack. As I flip through what I've written, the horrid depressed feeling retreats to the background. Throughout my entire life, writing has dispelled the uncertain fears of the outside world. Dope is the only other thing that accomplishes this. As I enter the world I have created, the looming panic recedes. I launch in right where I left off.

Rana heard the kitchen door close gently behind her, but she didn't lift her eyes from the speckled rooster—the monstrous fellow wreaking havoc among her poor hens. She hated him passionately.

"He's got to go," she announced to her invisible companion. "Today. I can't stand his raping any longer."

Fatima giggled softly as she slipped forward and threaded her arm through her sister-in-law's. "How can you hate a simple animal, one of God's creatures?"

"Henny Penny won't even come out of her coop," Rana spat venomously. "She sits roosting all day on that tiny stick because if she steps outside this brute..." As she spoke the speckled rooster grabbed an unsuspecting hen by the feathers of her neck and leapt astride her. Rana aimed a kick in his direction, and both hen and rooster squawked away.

"Really Rana," admonished Fatima. "He's just doing what comes naturally to him. The hens expect it. It's not like they're resisting."

"That's all you know," shouted Rana. "Do they look like they're enjoying it to you? He's holding them by force!"

"What on earth's the matter with you?" Fatima stroked Rana's cheeks. Her sister sometimes got this way when she read too much on the internet. She had become much angrier with the roosters since the #MeToo movement. She was also incensed against the West because of the money they were pouring into COVID to protect ninety-year-olds, while young men died on the streets here.

Rana ran into the shed and came out brandishing an axe. "I'll do it right now, the lecherous bugger. You hold him."

"Certainly not. Wait until the kids get home from school. The twins will be happy to help you. Why don't you go and lie down for a bit? You're obviously in a state..."

"I'm not in a state," bellowed Rana, brandishing the axe furiously. Fatima looked anxiously up at the windows of the houses that backed onto the same courtyard. Sure enough, animated faces were watching the show.

"Come inside," she wheedled, holding her hand out to her sister, gently maneuvering the axe out of her hand and leading her into the kitchen, where she busied herself making tea.

"Sorry," said Rana after a brief silence.

"That's okay. You need to meditate, perhaps?" Fatima meant it kindly, but Rana's irritability flared up again.

"My place of meditation has been transformed into a Place of Rape!"

"Now you must be consistent, Rana," Fatima said, stirring extra sugar into the mint tea. "You always say that the chickens help you think more clearly—you're not thinking very clearly now, are you? The roosters are doing what they're supposed to do, and the hens are fine with it."

Rana lowered her head and sipped her tea. It was delicious. She wasn't sure what to say next; so many conversations led to this feeling of discomfort between her and Fatima. Her sister, whom she loved so dearly. If the conversation brushed on sex, then the image of Mazin drove between them like a sword. She glanced at Fatima and saw that she looked uncomfortable too. Irritation conquered her hesitation. "Perhaps you think females are supposed to be submissive? Sexually, I mean. If you don't mind my using that word."

Fatima reddened. "Unless you want to argue that our urges are the same…"

"Mine are."

"Mine certainly weren't." If there was one advantage to widowhood, it was the end of those nightly obligations. Offering her body to fulfill a need, no matter how tired she was. And Fatima was always tired. Yet, she missed Mohammed's warm arms around her, the length of his comforting body pressed to hers as they slept. She missed that very much.

"You're not like other women, Rana. We're naturally submissive— you said so yourself. You said that was why nobody had sent death threats to the inventors of Viagra, that wicked invention. Preventing women from attaining their well-deserved rest after years of service."

Rana grinned, fishing out a bit of mint from her glass and popping it into her mouth. "Did I really say that?"

The kitchen door banged, and the children glided in, obviously immersed in an argument of their own.

"You know I'm ten times as smart as you two," Zaynah was saying to the twins. "I could easily be a doctor. Why shouldn't I be?"

"Because you're a giirrrlll," drawled the twins in unison, evoking Zaynah's ire to such an extent that she grabbed them both by the hair and tried to bang their heads together. "You stupid little…"

"Zaynah!" Rana spoke sharply. "What type of behaviour is this?"

Zaynah released the black heads and turned toward her. Rana saw that she was almost in tears, and the reproach died on her lips. She opened her arms. "How about saying hello?"

Zaynah hugged her fiercely, struggling for control, while the twins piled into Fatima's arms behind her, instantly forgetting the quarrel.

"O'mmy, we did very well in our tests…"

"We both got the same mark—eighty-eight percent…"

"That's very good, isn't it O'mmy?"

Fatima, full of love, wondered briefly, as she had done a thousand times before, how they always thought the same things at the same time, how they always got the same marks. So bizarre. She looked over their heads—she was still just capable of doing that—and caught Mazin's eye as he came through the door. She smiled and nodded, but the comfortable feeling of love dissipated. It was sad; a part of her knew it wasn't right, but she simply felt uncomfortable with Mazin. Ever since Rana had told her what she'd felt compelled to tell her. How Fatima wished she'd kept it to herself!

SHIT, THE JUICE IS RUNNING out on my computer. I've only been writing for two hours. It's like pulling teeth, forcing myself to keep going. Did I say writing has always helped me to control my panic? Yeah, well, I never tried it while being held hostage by a deranged dictator. I keep losing track, agonizing over my current situation in an unhealthy way. What if I can't write anymore? Rana, don't desert me! How shall I fill my days if my focus goes?

chapter two

BY FIVE-ISH I'M READY FOR HIM, glancing at my watch and wondering if he'll come at 7:00 like last night.

Pathetic.

Fuck off.

I stand defiantly in front of the mirror—bathed, scented, and absolutely slathered with makeup.

contemptible.

I'm *aware* that negative minds might construe it that way, but as it happens this is a logical, thought-out strategy. So you're totally *wrong*. I'm like Scheherazade in *One Thousand and One Nights*, doing my best not to get executed. Maybe I should start a story every night, ending at a cliffhanger to ensure my survival to the next night. Don't you think this Persian chick tried to look her best too? Tried to please, in any way possible?

Your descent into sexism has been terrifyingly fast...

When in Rome…

And into racism. Just focus on your goal.

Which isn't to cure misogyny. It's to wring a release date from Kassem. Otherwise, I'll go mad. It's quite simple. I return listlessly to the window, running through my accomplishments during the day to raise my spirits. Big pat on the back for having stuck to my self-imposed routine—typing until the battery was completely dead, meditating, exercising, reading, eating. Standing by the window and breathing a lot. I'm not used to so much time in a day, but it didn't feel like it stretched out endlessly in an impossible-to-fill way.

Always look on the bright side of life!

There'd been a couple of panic attacks in the midst of my virtuosity where my children's faces rose before me, triggering bouts of uncontrollable weeping. There'd been a little daydream in the middle of a meditation session where Kassem had penetrated every orifice in an excess of uncontrolled passion.

What is wrong with you?

What? It's not like I'm attracted to him or anything; this is an unfortunate side-effect of an over-sexed imagination—I mentally shag practically everyone I meet.

Shame you don't masturbate mentally.

I'm just saying, no need to imbue this train of thought with special significance.

This is not everyone you meet. This is someone who has complete control over your life and death.

Well, it's not like he can read my thoughts.

He's probably listening right now.

That causes another panic attack.

After the usual battle between mind and matter, I climb wearily to my feet and check every nook and cranny of the room for hidden cameras. I don't find any, but they could be behind the wall. Stands to reason they'd keep an eye on their prisoner, in case I decide to off myself or something. But my eighteen-year-old friend and his mates don't speak English, so no worries. Still, I'll avoid saying words like *shag* out loud. Just in case.

I check my watch: 5:30.

Time *is not* my enemy.

When Kassem comes, I will focus on him completely, fulfilling his every desire. After I've extracted a release date, of course. But during the day, left alone with my own miserable brain, I must construct a life that will hold insanity at bay. I've done well today. I'm still in control of my own emotions and behaviour, and nobody can take that away from me.

Grit your teeth and remember you're British, as your mother used to say.

Says still.

It's important to analyze each feeling as the day marches along: what makes me feel good? Sticking to my self-imposed routine produces a sense of virtue = good feeling. Not smoking dope, ditto. I'll try to limit smoking to days when I feel like crap. But right now, with him coming, it's good that I'm compos mentis.

If he comes.

Nasty waiting = bad feeling. This is no good; I need to reconstruct my day. Smoke in mornings as soon as I get up. That'll take care of mornings. Then after lunch, launch into my routine. Then when he comes, I'll feel irritated because I'll have to stop my work, rather than waiting here like some love-shorn sheep.

Who are you kidding?

I throw my journal to the floor. Six p.m. Uncertainty drives me nuts. I pick up the little tinfoil wad of dope and regard it. If I knew he wasn't coming, I could smoke a joint and enjoy the evening instead of waiting around like a Stepford housewife. I want a cigarette, but there's nothing to drink with it. Wearily, I pick up my journal and add to the growing list of "things to ask for":

1. A kettle;
2. Tea (Tetley's?)
3. A mini-fridge
4. with juice
5. and milk.

And isn't my captor secular?

6. Gin and tonic.
7. Two long, shapeless cotton dresses.

I have several lists on the go already. Lists keep one sane and create an illusion of control. I enter the bathroom and sit on the toilet with my journal.

8. Subscription to the weekly *Guardian*.

Dream on.

9. *Calvin and Hobbes* to read in the bathroom.

Isn't my captor rich?

10. Every issue ever created.

I check myself for the umpteenth time in the mirror. Definitely present the head-on view, not the side.

There's a knock at the door.

Joy!

For fuck's sake.

I can't help it, that's what I feel. The first human I've talked to all day.

The knock sounds again. Am I really jabbering at myself instead of answering the door? "Come in," I shout, and just have time to arrange myself prettily on the bed.

"Why Charlotte," he says, looming over me and holding out his hand to shake. I flush, idiotically, because I know he's looking at me with admiration. Makeup is magic.

A different guy comes in with coffee and cakes. Just as obsequious.

Kassem's long, slender fingers flutter over the spoon, measuring and stirring.

"What did you do today?" he asks.

"I wrote almost 1000 words, but then my battery ran out."

"Ah yes," he says and pulls an adaptor from the pocket of his suit.

I try not to let gratitude beam from my give-away face as I take it. "How was your day?" I ask. "Kill many people?"

"Do you think that's what I do?"

"Of course not. You order others to kill people."

He stirs his coffee with little jabs. It's the black, thick, spicy stuff they call Turkish coffee in Israel. I gauge whether annoying him = good or bad feeling.

"I see we have to talk about what I'm doing and why. You are prepared to listen to me?"

"Do I have any choice?"

He puts down his coffee and leans .toward me, blue eyes staring intently into mine. "I don't want you to listen because you feel there's no choice. Are writers not truth-seekers? All the information you have

24

received about me is false. The Western media lies. I hope you will listen to me because you want to know the truth."

He's touched upon one of my passions. "I believe that in order to approach the truth, you've got to listen to as many different people as possible, preferably from varying perspectives."

"Exactly."

I sip my coffee. I'd prefer fair-trade coffee with cream. "If the people I'm listening to are rational human beings, then the reasons behind their perspective will probably make sense. So even if I don't agree with their conclusions, I will understand how they arrived at them. So yes, I'll listen to you."

He's leaning toward me with a spellbound expression. "You are wise."

Shit. I'm doomed if it's wisdom he wants. Please remove expectant-puppy dog expression from face.

Kassem nods and leans back, sipping his coffee. He jumps a little when I snap my fingers.

"No—I remember where the idea comes from! You've got to read Ari Shavit's book *My Promised Land*. The perspective of every single group's in there: the religious, the settlers, the Arabs—even the younger generation." I wave my hand impatiently at his puzzled expression. "He's an Israeli writer."

His expression changes to contempt. "Let me guess the solutions *he* came up with."

He almost spits out the word *he*.

"Actually, he didn't come up with solutions. It was basically a cry for help. An SOS for wiser leaders, wiser people, dialogue."

Kassem's sneer hasn't disappeared; I try to mimic it. "Yeah, I agree with you. Good luck, right? But what impressed me was the objective way he dealt with every group. He just listened and recorded. Everybody always has such strong opinions about Israel—I have such strong opinions. If we all had superior minds like Ari Shavit..." I sigh.

The contempt has been replaced by amusement. I bite my tongue to stop my rambling. Lord, what a day alone can do to one's tongue!

"So can I deduce that you will listen to me objectively?"

I can deduce you've been to a snooty English school, I almost say, but luckily my inner voice kicks in.

Remember your goal.

Like I'd forget, Voice.

"I can't—I won't—listen to anything you have to say while I'm being held captive."

"And how exactly will you listen to what I say after your release?"

Yeah, curb the heavy sarcasm, will ya? It's not like this is a level playing field. "What do you want from me? You've only got to tell me. You want me to listen to your side of things? Sure, no problem, but first let's figure out how long it'll take, so I know approximately how long my… visit… is going to be."

"I don't know," he says with a trace of irritation.

Fuck his irritation.

"That's too bad. Try to listen to my perspective for just one moment. I'm your prisoner, for fuck's sake. My focus is on self-preservation, period. So you tell me exactly what you want from me, and I'll do it. Anything at all. You want me to tell you the truth? Fear undermines my ability to figure out the truth, okay? I don't give a shit about the truth, or Syria. I want to see my kids." My voice has risen to a shriek. It had been like that all day; one minute I'm feeling good, the next, suicidal. I wish I could see a psychiatrist just long enough to ask if this is normal under the circumstances, or the first step on the slippery slope toward insanity.

What the… he's kneeling in front of me and reaching for my hand.

"I told you there's nothing to worry about. I just want to talk to you for a few days. Please, you must believe me. I will release you very soon."

I grasp his hands, kneading and stroking them. If I talk about my kids I will cry, and that will make me ugly, but who remembers now why I wanted to look pretty? "When my son has nightmares, I have to place my hands on either side of his head, press my forehead against his, and say: bad dreams go away, good dreams come to stay." The tears are flowing now. I realize I've avoided thinking about my family all day. To keep despair at bay. No point despairing when you're all alone. Possible point in despairing in front of your captor. "That's the only way to stop his nightmares. Only *my* hands work. For my own sanity, I have to know how long, precisely, I will be here. And you also have to communicate that to my family, somehow. They have to know I'm all right. They'll be worried..." And the thought of their misery and fear overwhelms me. I release his hands and cover my contorted face.

He tries to encircle me with his arms, but I don't want him to touch me and jerk sharply away. I don't care whether it's better to antagonize him or mollycoddle him. I can't think of anything except the sad, anxious faces of my children. My husband. He must be going mad. Such a controller, and this so far out of his control!

There is utter silence beyond the safe haven of my hands. I spread my fingers to peek. He is squatting in front of me, observing me dispassionately. "I do not want you to be unhappy, but I need you to stay with me for a few days. Your kids will be fine; I'm sure you've been away longer than a few days before."

"What do you want from me? I'll give it to you, right now. It won't take a few days."

Kassem smiles at me sadly. "It is already time for me to go and we haven't begun to talk about all the things I'd like to talk about."

"What? What?"

"First, what were you writing about today?"

I groan. "It's a continuation of *A Hero*. Rana, Fatima, Ahmed, the kids. Their life goes on."

"And who is leading Syria?"

"Chaos. I'll probably lean on Egypt for that one: everyone they elect will turn out to be power-hungry or have hidden religious agendas or both. So they keep overthrowing their democratically elected leaders and someone worse takes their place. No offence, but I don't think you Arab people have quite grasped what democracy is yet, but kudos for trying."

while you white people have nailed your inviolate right to vote for The Donald.

I smile at Kassem. "Democracy isn't all it's cracked up to be, so if you want to prevent it, that's fine by me." My hand itches to reach for my journal to start another list: Interesting Things to Discuss with Kassem during His Visitations to The Prisoner.

"Yes, but among the people here. The wannabe leaders. Who do you think will seize power if I die?"

I look at him incredulously. Does he really think I have the foggiest about who leads the rebels? That there's enough Western interest in his rinky-dink little country for that amount of detail?

keep focused on your goal, or there'll be another twenty-four hours of anxiety to get through.

I reach forward and grasp his hand. "I'm happy to discuss what might happen in the future, even though my guess will be much less educated than yours. I'm happy to listen openly to why you're really a good person and not a psychopath murderer. But I can't do any of these things unless you give me a deadline for my stay."

"I don't know," he repeats.

"Well, I can't talk to you until you find out."

He looks taken aback. "Do you mean that you don't want me to visit anymore?"

"I can't stop you visiting, but I won't talk to you unless you give me a solid date and let my family know the date too." I lean toward him, conscious again that he is a man and I am a woman. "But Kassem, if you give me a date, then I will talk to you and listen to you—I will do anything you want."

"I don't want you to do that just because you are a prisoner.'"

Then maybe you shouldn't have kidnapped me, asshole. You're like a rapist who wants his victim to have an orgasm. Still, that's a lot better than a rapist who just wants to hurt. "If you give me a date," I say softly, "then I will enjoy the time I have here and do the best I can with it. I will listen to you and try to predict what might happen. I will focus entirely on you while you're with me. Happily, from my own will."

His eyes careen over my lips and back. I'm glad I put on makeup now. Surely a man bends to a pretty woman's will more easily? Or is it better to be plain, if one wants freedom? If only I knew!

"All right," he says finally. "I understand your need. Let us say one month from today?"

"Two weeks," I interject, and instantly regret it when he shakes his head.

"One month."

I jump to my feet and rush to my carry-on, pulling my paper calendar from the front pocket. My husband wanted me to get an iPhone, but I resisted. I couldn't stand the thought that anybody could contact me at any time.

"What day is it today?"

"November 12th."

"So you will release me on December 12th?"

"Yes," he says simply.

I want to do something dramatic, like kiss his feet. "Thank you," I say.

"I have to go now," he replies.

"You have a war to run," I joke. I want him gone, so I can relish the intensity of my relief, privately. "But wait!" I open my journal and tear out the list of "Things to ask for." "I'd like these, if possible…"

"Certainly," he says without looking at the list.

"And will you let my family know the date of my release?"

"Would you like to tell them yourself?"

My heart starts to pound against my ribs. He's going to let me phone my family?

"If you give me an email address for your husband, we could videotape you and send it to them."

"Yes," I say, "but then I wouldn't know how they were doing."

He smiles, picks up his coffee cup to take a last sip. "They could send you back a videotape," he says.

Now I really want to kiss his feet. Gratitude and affection course through my body.

He's your kidnapper, idiot.

Right, right. Got a little carried away there. I wave him off demurely and immediately roll a joint. For the first time since I woke up here, there's no background of anxiety pulsing behind my brain. One month is nothing.

Everything's going to be okay.

I WAKE UP IN A cheerful frame of mind. The month stretches before me: I will exercise fiercely, until all my cellulite is swallowed by muscles. A yearly resolution, but I've never had a free month like this. I will write 3000 words a day, even if they're crap. I will meditate. I hook up my computer to the adaptor and sit down purposefully.

Rana waves the last child off to school and sits at the kitchen table, relaxing for the first time since she rose two hours previously. Then... then...

Hmmm; 3000 words a day? Easier said than done. I'm as jumpy as a jack-in-the-box. I stare at the page, willing Rana to tell me what's going to happen next.

A rat-a-tat-tat at the door makes me jump, and I leap to my feet in relief. Breakfast!

I'm glad to see it's the same guy as usual. A familiar face.

My little eighteen-year-old puts the tray down on my bedside table, but instead of leaving immediately, he stands grinning at me. Then he raises his hand to his shoulder and I see there's a black strap there. I watch with a touch of trepidation as it slips down his arm and advances toward me, until I see what it's towing. I reach for the video camera, smiling. He tries to back out of the room, but I grab his hand. A look of alarm crosses his face.

I point at myself. "Charlotte." Then I point at him.

A wary look.

Triumphantly, I remember the word for *me* in Arabic. "Ana Charlotte," I insist, thumping myself on the chest. I point to him. I don't know the word for *you*, so I try Hebrew. "Atta?"

He looks puzzled for a moment, but then he brightens. "Anta," he crows.

Atta, anta, same difference, c'mon already (is he a bit thick)?

He points to himself. "Sami."

I grin; I used to know a Sami in Israel.

I'm about to try another word, but Sami backs away and closes the door. The thickest kid around here has more decision-making power than me.

For a moment I feel despondent, but the boiled eggs, cheeses, salads, and fresh pita provide pleasant distraction. As I munch, an idea occurs to me. I will ask Kassem for books to learn Arabic. A vague remembrance of reading something about German-speaking Jews faring better in the prison camps than those who didn't speak German. It's harder to treat people like animals if they speak your lingo. At least I can spew recriminations if they do end up torturing and killing me. Meanwhile I can chat to Sami.

I allow myself an hour for breakfast and meditation, the same amount as if I were at home. Then I sit and stare at my computer again.

Rana waves the last child off to school and sits at the kitchen table, relaxing for the first time since she rose two hours previously.

Come on, come on—spit the next sentence out.

But it eludes me. There are days like that, when forcing yourself to write is like pulling teeth. I punch at the keys angrily.

I don't feel like writing this story. My head's not with Rana right now. I couldn't give a fuck about Rana, all right? I'm in a fucking prison.

So write about that.

Umm, what?… mmmm…

November 13, 10:30

Sami brought a video camera with my breakfast. He always knocks on the door after I've returned from the bathroom. How does he know exactly when I wake up, especially since it differs from day to day? One of the things my schedule doesn't include is a wake-up time. For the past fourteen years—ever since my first child popped out—I haven't slept in once. I used to love it more than anything else. Now I know that I'm getting out of here in a month, I'm determined to treat this like a holiday. Not an ideal holiday, I'm an outside person and the walls close in horribly, but nevertheless the first time in my life where there's ample time for both self-discipline and indulgence, all in the same day.

Sami knows when you wake up because there's a camera.

Have I really been reduced to writing whatever crap my inner voice is dispensing? That's *more* interesting than Rana? Apparently. It's a riveting fucking conversation, me and Voice.

Hey there, Voice, please don't say shit like that about cameras. It just makes everything worse. If I start thinking about the fact that there's a camera trained on me 24/7, it'll be hard to enjoy anything.

Why?

Relentless self-consciousness. I won't be able to eat with the same gusto.

Nobody's watching you, Ms. Self-obsessed. They just glance at the camera now and then to make sure you're alive.

That's true. Of course that's true. It would be dead boring to watch someone for five minutes. Sami probably cranks the volume up around the time when I wake up to make sure he knows when to prepare my breakfast. Kassem has ordered him to meet my every need, that's all.

Keep all flesh covered. Just in case.

chapter three

I dragged the table over and propped the video camera on books, rushing back and forth and peering through the viewer until it's focused on my face when I sit in a certain place on the bed. Then I activate it and rush to my position, planting a happy smile on my lips. It doesn't matter if it looks fake, I can re-do the video again and again.

You're mixing your tenses.

"Look, thanks for the great idea about discarding Rana, but I'm the writer, okay? I've done the video already, and now I'm writing about it. So it's past tense."

I glance at what I've written. Damn. I've always been crap at tenses.

All right, I snap, *I'll write in present tense all the time. Satisfied?* What's more, I'll follow the advice I've given to countless creative writing students, and read what I've written out loud to make sure it sounds okay.

What for?

Because. I'm not writing a frigging detailed diary for seven hours a day. This is my work.

For public consumption? Oh, this desert of egotism men call life...

The public will eat it up. Lots of ex-prisoners have written of their experiences.

And you've read them?

Nah, non-fiction ain't my cup of tea.

There is a short silence, during which I was probably expected to dwell on my own hypocrisy.

You can't write your obscene, childish fantasies about Kassem.

I'll edit those bits out.

What about just writing for the joy of writing?

Fuck that, it's hard work. Now shut up and let me write—in present tense—about that lovely videotape I ~~just made~~ am making.

"HELLO MY DARLING FAMILY," I say, beaming steadily and hoping the imminent tears won't spill. "Today it is November 13th, and on December 12th, I will be with you again. Just one month. As you can see, I'm perfectly fine. They're treating me really well and the food is like a 5-star hotel!" An anxiety crosses my mind. "Nobody is forcing me to say this. Look, I'm completely alone!" I get up from the bed and grab the camera, showing them every corner of my room. "They've even given me shelves of books." I aim the camera at the packet of Benson and Hedges. "They've even supplied me with my favourite vices."

Returning the video camera back to the table, I seat myself on the bed. "I'm not sure whether I'm allowed to say who has kidnapped me and I don't want them to cut out pieces from the video because then you'll worry that all the content has been tampered with—but my captor is treating me very well and he doesn't intend to hurt me. He... he's got this crazy idea that I'm psychic and he wants to talk to me. That's all. Just talk." I will them to believe I've not been hurt. What can I say to reassure them? "I love you so much. My heart aches when I think that you are suffering—please don't feel sad; I *am not* being mistreated. I love you, love you, love you, my dearest family. Now, sweet children, you must spend at least twenty minutes a day with the goats. Take them for walks on the weekend, and make them do their tricks once in a while so they don't forget."

I am not sure how much time Kassem will allow me to ramble on, but I might as well make it as long as possible. If I go on about the animals they'll know I'm fine. I wouldn't be chelping about the need to walk the goats if I was being coerced into creating a "happy" video, would I?

I go on for over an hour, as though I'm really talking to them. It almost feels like that. I show them their photos that I always take on my trips, because even though I spend most of our shared time trying to do my own stuff, when I'm away I miss them terribly. I tell them every detail of my routine. My husband will want to know, even if the children phase out after a while. I read them the 1000 new words I wrote on the Rana story, with a few edits. "That's all I have so far," I tell them. "But I might give the Rana story a rest, just for a bit. Instead of writing in my journal, I'm going to type everything that happens to me on the computer, every little detail of this time. Every word that I'm saying to you right now," I joke. I don't mention that my surroundings have apparently killed my imagination, that I'm not capable of writing fiction.

"How often," I ask my children, "have I wished for the time to record every passing thought for a day? You should do it too; write down just a couple of lines every day, and see how much pleasure and amusement you'll get out of them in ten years' time. Wouldn't I just love to have a detailed record of my thoughts at thirty? Won't my fifty-year-old mind fascinate me at seventy? How often have I wanted to compare my current mind with past ones? But I never had the time."

Luxury.

I launch into a lively rendition of the Monty Python "Four Yorkshiremen" skit—"You lived in a rolled-up newspaper? Luxury!"—and imagine my children giggling as they watch, maybe checking out the original on YouTube.

It's as good a place to end as any. I grin furiously at the camera, blowing kisses and naming the parts that will receive them: the nape of the neck; the soft curve where chin meets neck; their supple cheeks; the armpit, which renders my son hysterical with both laughter and anguish. Asking them to imagine that those parts are truly receiving my kisses, as I am imagining their soft flesh under my lips as I blow. Finally, a brisk "don't worry; I'll be home soon," to my husband, and I stand up to switch the camera off.

I watch the video obsessively several times, to make sure it's okay for other eyes. To visualize how my children will see it. A loving, happy mother. Missing them desperately, but completely confident that it's only for a month. Longer than I've ever been away, but still manageable.

Deep breathing. Trust that it will be okay. There's no point in not trusting. It doesn't help.

I do an hour of exercises, mixing cardio with muscle toning; now here I am sitting, writing. Trying to record "my mind at 50." It's not going well. My mind bores me almost as much as the exercises. I start to feel bad, but there's a remedy for that too.

I roll a joint. Enjoy my lunch passionately. Cover myself with the sheet and do my stuff, turning my face to the corner, just in case there is a camera somewhere. There are cracks in the wall that resemble a stick man running.

Sleep.

I AM WAITING FOR HIM, determined to keep my promise. I will set out to amuse and soothe, like clever Scheherazade in *One Thousand and One Nights*. If that's not what he's looking for, I'll probe until I understand what he wants. I can fulfill any role.

The videotape is tucked under my arm, ready for delivery. It has succored me all day. The vision of my children's little faces, watching the video and beaming with joy.

Oh—if they should send me a video of them!

There is a gentle knock at the door. Kassem enters with his usual courtesy, closely followed by Sami carrying an armload of stuff, which he dumps on my bed. I can see a kettle and some *Calvin and Hobbes*. That was quick.

"Salaam Aleichem, Sami," I say to show off, but immediately wish I hadn't when Kassem shoots a mistrustful look at the boy.

I decide to postpone the launch of my brilliant idea to learn Arabic until later.

I push myself to the end of the bed, ready to do the honours with the tea and goodies, watching him out of the corner of my eye; perhaps he prefers to wait on me? He's probably pampered rotten; he leans back without even noticing the reversal in roles.

The aroma of the tea wafts toward me as I bend over and instantly one of those abrupt changes of mood occurs. From happy to crappy, from bliss to pissed, from...

"What have you accomplished today?" Kassem asks me.

Right, no self-indulgence allowed. Focus on him. The man. Not so different from what I've been doing all my life, actually. "This smells just like Israeli tea," I say.

"Have they stolen our tea as well?"

"Wish they'd stolen Tetley's instead," I mutter, squeezing lemon into his cup. Israeli tea is never strong enough to mix with milk. He accepts his cup graciously and raises his eyebrows at me.

"Ah yes; well, the most important thing I accomplished was this." I hand over the videotape proudly. He gazes at it, bemused.

"Don't you remember you promised to send this to my kids? And also that you'd allow them to send me a videotape in return?" A tinge of desperation, uninvited.

"Of course." He pockets the tape without looking at it. "Thank you. Now what else did you do?"

"Will you let them send me a video in return?"

"Yes. I said so, didn't I?"

I quell the tremulous gratitude in my heart. "I tried to write about Rana, but gave up; my present situation is too... absorbing."

"And?"

"That's it." I shrug irritably. What the fuck does he think I've been doing?

Aren't you trying to be nice?

Oh right. Shit.

Kassem clears his throat. "I want to ask you a few questions, if you don't mind."

Yeah, yeah, the psychic bullshit.

"There are hours in a day. The video took maybe two hours? So what else happened? Are you trying to develop a routine of some sort?"

I gaze at him blankly. What is his game?

Who cares? Soothe and amuse—tell him you spent your day doing the three M's: Meditation, Masturbation, and Moping.

37

Very funny. "Umm, I meditate. Exercise. Write."

"And does this make you happy?"

"Huh?"

"Are you satisfied and content with staying here one month?"

He's leaning forward, looking all anxious and everything. I wrack my suspicious brain for possible evil motives, but nothing clicks. So... the guy just wants me to be happy?

"Yes, I'm ecstatic that we reached an understanding about my time here. I feel much better now it's limited to a month." I smile as happily as I can. He must really care. Perhaps Sami has reported tears.

"I'm kind of a manic-y depressive-y type, Kassem. In any situation. And let's face it, my future lies in the hands of a..."

Don't say it.

"A stranger. So there's bound to be a bit of anxiety there. Plus, I hate being cooped up in one room."

His face is falling by degrees.

"But really, I'm totally satisfied with our arrangement. It is the best it could be in the circumstances. And I totally trust you."

Not.

"Totally. Please believe me."

"I am glad. In one month, you will go home to your family. I appreciate your agreeing to stay here one month with me. It means a lot; thank you. Anything that you want or need, anything at all..."

I decide not to respond to his statement that I've agreed to stay here, though I wouldn't have put it quite like that. Instead, I gesture to the pile of stuff on the bed. "Thank you. You've been more than kind."

He leans back, relieved. We sip our tea. I feel like my soothe-and-amuse role has been played to perfection.

"I'd like to tell you a little bit about myself today, if that's okay," Kassem says after a moment. "You've really got the wrong end of the stick."

"I suspect both ends are equally pointy."

He doesn't smile at my joke. I must remember to compliment his English at the earliest opportunity. Flatter him. Plus it's good.

"I was never a political man; I had dreams of becoming a doctor. You know I had a Western education?"

Actually, I had known that, but he doesn't stop for my answer. "My elder brother was supposed to take on the role after my father, but he died tragically in a car accident. So I returned home from my carefree, medical student life and was pushed through the ranks of a military academy, achieving the rank of colonel in just five years."

I peek at him through my eyelashes; is this supposed to impress? He could have been a complete dolt and still become colonel.

"When my father died, the people voted me in with ninety-seven percent of the vote."

He looks at me with an element of pride, which annoys me. "Lot of competition, was there?"

He shoots me an indecipherable look. "Don't you think ninety-seven percent indicates that the people were happy for me to be their leader?"

"I'm sure they were. Even Mugabe was democratically voted in once upon a time, I suppose."

What the fuck's wrong with you?

Indeed. Can't I be like Scheherazade for two minutes? Can't I at least *pretend* to be a nice, admiring woman? Lucky Western men don't have access to Arab women; none of them would look at us twice.

"I dreamt of making Syria a modern state. Don't you remember my public statement—and private belief—that democracy is a tool to a better life?"

He is so sweet, imagining that I know so much about him. Men always surprise me with their innocent egocentricity. I nod; of course I remember, as if I ever fucking knew, as if I ever had the remotest interest in Syria before I wrote the book, and even then I did the absolute minimum of research.

'cause you're a lazy pothead.

Kassem continues to speak; he's set his tea to one side and has leaned forward to penetrate my eyes with his own. "In many ways, I have succeeded; as soon as I got in, I released hundreds of political prisoners. I introduced reforms. Because of me, Syrians enjoy cell phones, satellite television, internet cafes. But it's not that easy... it's not easy." His gaze falters and he looks down. I worry that my goal to amuse and soothe is a failure. Then he's looking into my eyes again, and his voice has ratcheted several notches up the irritation scale. "You think I'm the big guy here and can do whatever I want? It doesn't work like that! There were many people more experienced and older than me when I started, and they 'advised' me to go slowly. Economic reform in a state-controlled country isn't the same as in a democracy!"

His chin really is weak. He looks like a weak sort of man altogether, really. I'd always thought so, even when I only knew him through internet images.

"It's difficult for a private sector to develop when there's so much bureaucracy..."

"Which you control," I interrupt.

"Do you think I'm alone here? Do you know how many people make decisions with me? I'm not a dictator; I work with my governmental colleagues in the same way your prime minister does."

There is a pause. He watches me intently as I sip my tea.

"So why haven't you held elections?"

"What do you mean? I held elections in 2014!"

Yeah, well, I'd already written *A Hero* by 2014 so I wasn't following Syria anymore. Sorr-ee.

For your unbelievable ignorance.

I hazard a few guesses. "The rebels didn't vote, did they? The millions of Syrians who have fled didn't vote. So they weren't real elections, representing the majority of your people."

He leaps to his feet, agitated. I'm certainly doing a crap job amusing and soothing. I offer the plate of baklava in a belated gesture of conciliation.

"No, the rebels didn't vote. Instead, they tried to kill the people who did vote." He spreads his fingers over his chest. "I am trying to introduce reforms, I believe in democracy—but these things aren't done in a day, you know, especially in a country like Syria. You think that was the only thing on my plate? In 2002, the U.S. listed Syria in its 'axis of evil' list. What had Syria done to deserve that? Nothing."

Maybe nothing, maybe something. We ignoramuses don't know enough to tell—but that doesn't stop us from judging. Oh no! But even though the abrupt change of subject makes me suspicious, at least we agree on something. "That axis of evil bullshit has caused so much harm. Bush was an idiot."

"So was Obama."

"I liked Obama, but it's true that he had a lot of problems pushing change through, with a Republican-controlled senate blocking his every move. People who didn't care about making the country better, only about getting into power themselves," I say clearly, looking him directly in the eye. "I'd thought presidency was an all-powerful position, at least in comparison to our prime minister's powers, but it's shackled to bureaucracy too."

I look at him speculatively. Perhaps it isn't so easy for him to implement democracy. Especially with such a weak chin.

"In 2004, the U.S. imposed sanctions against us; in 2007, Israel bombed us for no reason."

I hold up a weary hand. "Let's not get into the subject of Israel. We're bound to disagree, and as it happens, I have a small modicum of knowledge in that area—shoved into my head against my will during my ten years there." I sneak a glance at him; had he known about that? Is he aware of my tainted blood? His expression doesn't change. "So if you spout a bunch of lies in that area, I'll know, and that will throw suspicion on everything else you've said." I try to smile into his tight face in an amusing, soothing fashion. "And that would be a shame, since you're doing so well explaining your perspective."

He searches my face for sarcasm, but evidently finds none. I take a baklava and try to bite into it in an attractive way, but you can't do that with baklava. Honey drips down my chin and mortifies.

"Did they teach you lies over there?" he hisses, his voice dangerously quiet. "Did they teach you that we attacked them, perhaps?"

"No, they taught me that they'd bombed your nuclear facility and..."
Don't say that.

I bite my tongue. Thank God I stopped before declaring what a good thing that had been—kudos to Israel for preventing another unstable menace from attaining the capability of wiping Israel off the face of the earth, and didn't he think it was a fucking amazing country, if he could just dig down past his racism and be honest for once?

"That is untrue," he says with dignity, and I wisely let it go. But it sours something for me, because I want to hear his perspective; for some inexplicable reason I want to exonerate him from the wrongs he's been accused of. I can already tell that he's not the evil monster the West depicts. There's something very gentle about that wobbly little chin. But now I know he can lie. Unfortunately, there's this little looney-tunes part of my brain that can't seem to differentiate between truth and deceit, so once it discovers you in a lie, it worries that you're lying all the time. Basically, there's no point in him talking anymore.

Little extreme or what.

Well, my little Looney-Tunes you know, nothing I can do about it. 'Course I won't tell him. I'll let him burble on for another twenty-nine days.

"Am I boring you?" Kassem asks in an icy tone, and I realize he's been burbling for the last few minutes.

I'm totally failing at this amusing, soothing stuff. Then his strange questions at the beginning come back to me. It doesn't matter if I'm soothing and amusing or aggravating and exacerbating; he just wants me to be happy. For whatever reason.

"Actually, you're convincing me. I can see how hard it must be to move forward with reforms if your political advisers are resistant. But... if I may ask a question without annoying you... why didn't you give your people democracy right at the beginning, when they first started demonstrating?"

"There weren't many peaceful demonstrations of the people; we have been facing terrorism since the very first days. I must defend my people against terrorism, no? Even you must see that."

My foot starts to jiggle. "But you're just calling anyone who disagrees with you a terrorist. Everyone is bandying that word about these days. Since when do citizens demanding change constitute terrorists?"

"Since citizens use weapons to demand change." Kassem jumps to his feet and starts to pace the room. I bite my lip. Really, what's my motivation?

"Do you think if Canadians decided they wanted a change in the status quo and took up arms to achieve that change, your government wouldn't counteract like I have done?"

"Actually, no. Or do I mean yes?" My mind gets bogged down in grammatical issues for a minute, until I catch a look at his chin, trembling with impatience. "I mean that my government would never counteract like you've done."

"What happened when the Quebec terrorists kidnapped the government officials? Your government immediately invoked the War Measures Act, throwing hundreds of people in prison without charge and without the right to talk to a lawyer. What happened when your Natives set up road blocks to dispute a golf course? The army was called out again. Every time your citizens have risen up with violence, the government's response has been to meet the violence with military force. They do this to protect their citizens and to enforce law and order, as I have done—this is the mandate of all governments."

Shit, he's done his homework. Pity my head's like a holey sieve; otherwise, I might remember the details. "Is there any chance that I could get access to the internet?"

"No."

It's the first time he's refused a request. So naturally, I push. "You could sit beside me, checking what I'm doing. I only want to look up that old Quebec thing. Jog my memory."

He sits down again, shoots me a placatory smile. "It isn't possible. Please don't ask."

We sip our tea. In the sudden silence I hear him swallow. It makes him seem very human. A powerful leader of a country who, for some weird reason, wants me to think well of him. So convince me. "Did you use chemical weapons on your people?"

He sighs, puts down his cup. "Do you remember what you read in your papers?"

Ahh, he's cottoned onto my crap memory. I nod vaguely.

"They claimed a couple of hundred people died. Tens or hundreds of thousands of people would have died if I had used those kinds of weapons. Syria is not Canada; there aren't acres of wilderness here. Most people live crammed together in cities. Of course we didn't use chemical weapons."

My face must be registering doubt. Despite sieve-like quality of brain, I distinctly remember Obama trying to convince Congress to go to war because Bashar had used chemical weapons against his own people.

"How do you know that Farouq didn't use the chemical weapons? They blew up Homs hospital, because it had been treating soldiers. They are animals."

"Yes, but everyone says you did it," I say weakly. As if I knew who the fuck Farouq was.

"And I am telling you that they paint me in a black light for their own purposes. Who do you think the rebels are? Peaceful people driven to war because they want democracy?" He gives a bitter laugh. "That's why they're all joining ISIS, because they're so peaceful. Are they teaching you how peaceful ISIS is in Canada?"

I hate talking politics. I hate the feeling of my own ignorance, preventing equal dialogue. If only he'd give me access to the internet, I could dig around, instead of probing the innermost reaches of my Sieve-Brain for any remnants of information I might have retained. "There are lots of moderate Islamist rebels fighting against you..."

"Even they join ISIS," Kassem interrupts.

"If that's true, it shows how much they hate you."

"Or who they're more frightened of. Most of all, it's indicative of the chaos that would exist in Syria without me."

"More chaotic than now? At worst, everyone will still be fighting everyone else, like now." Please, let's not talk politics. Is this what our visits are going to be like for the next month?

"Without us, the extremists would take over. Why do you think so many of my people support me? The women, the ethnic minorities? What will happen to them if the extremists take over?"

I wrack my brain for an answer. "I read that there's no longer any Syria—just a bunch of different areas of control."

"How can you trust your own media and your own leaders so completely? They say that I am evil; you believe it. Just like you believed it when all your Western leaders swore that Iraq had vast stores of weapons. Justification for war. But they didn't find any weapons, did they? Because of their intervention, there's now a gaping hole instead of leadership in Iraq. And out sprouted ISIS. Now they want to do the same thing here. How can you be so innocent?"

There is a brief silence as he watches me.

He has a point. Or am I simply desperate to believe him? I give a faint nod, and Kassem relaxes and settles back in his chair. Does this mean we're done? Thank God; I don't want to talk about what he's done or hasn't done anymore. Avoiding conflict is a no-brainer, so politics isn't a good subject. Why is he going on and on about this stuff? Who cares whether one ignorant little head believes he's a good guy or not? Unless… my opinion is important to him. The way he nervously inquired as to my welfare when he first came in… Hey, if he needs to convince me that he's a good guy, then I'm here to serve. And be convinced.

"Thank you for explaining things. I do see your point of view."

He smiles. Picks up his disregarded tea and sips. I weigh the wisdom of sharing my belief that there'd be a lot less terrorists if Arabs fucked more. Providing beautiful women here on earth would remove the allure of beautiful virgins waiting in heaven. Wouldn't those same women who are supporting the Kassem regime through fear be willing to sacrifice their primitive attitudes toward sex in order to end the war? Use your Pussy Power, girls! And if not, then I've another brilliant idea. Get them all hooked on marijuana—dope quashes violence. Hookers and Hookahs! I could *totally* solve the Middle East's problems if I was in control.

Did you slip in a few tokes while you were out of my sight? Haha.

Suddenly, Kassem stands up and in one stride he's beside me, sitting down on my bed.

"Charlotte. Is there anything I have said today that doesn't make sense?"

Phew; relief. We're still on politics. I think for a second. How best to answer? "I think that you believe everything you've told me today. You think you're a good person, trying to do the best for his country. And that's good news, because it means you're not a psychopath." His smile

45

wavers and I smile encouragingly, to assure him that that's a good thing. "If you were a psychopath, you wouldn't have enough empathy…"

His face continues to darken, so I change tactics quickly. "What I'm not sure about, is whether every human being, except psychopaths, justify their actions in similar ways to what you've just done—painting the other side as the terrorist, which essentially justifies every action one takes against them. The Americans do that as well; it's human nature. So the only way for you to really prove what you've been saying… that most of your country supports you, or you didn't use chemical weapons, is to give me access to the internet."

He leaps to his feet again. I'm relieved; sexual fantasies are a pleasant way to pass the time, but I've just discovered they don't translate into reality. The inch between his knee and mine only created fear.

"I told you not to ask me for access to the internet," he barks. "It's not possible."

"Why? Is there stuff that you don't want me to see? Stuff about my kidnapping?"

"Yes."

I light a cigarette and go to the window, leaning on the sill to blow the spirals of smoke out into the dark night. Like before, Kassem slips the cigarette from my fingers and takes a drag, watching me.

"You are beautiful."

"Thank you."

You're not a patch on his wife.

He pushes the cigarette between my fingers; I feel his skin against my hand. Again, that frisson of unpleasant fear. My fingers stay rigid, unyielding to the gentle pressure. I stare fixedly into the night, as his fingers rest lightly on mine. Repressing the urge to jerk away. A month alternately seems short and endless. If that's what he wants, I won't be able to survive.

Yes, you will. Like so many women before you.

Tears pool and I open my eyes wide, willing them not to spill. Why has this happened to me? Why me? I'll slit my fucking wrists, I swear to God I will. I'm not like other people. I get suicidal even when my life is ideal, fighting an almost daily death wish. Driving by a particular tree on the highway and thinking: *I only have to swerve the wheel and this desert of egotism men call life will be over.*

"I'm not a bad person," he whispers.

A second for his words to register; then my body sags in relief. I must relax; he's not going to hurt me. Not yet, anyway. Not today.

Day by day.

I straighten up and turn to look into his pleading eyes. For some weird reason, this fellow wants my good opinion. This fellow, who is responsible for millions of lives. Suddenly, an epiphany erupts in my mind. I know why I'm here! For some reason, fate/destiny/God/chance has given me the opportunity to make a difference. I am here in order to influence this human to do right in this horrible war. Fearless now, sexual innuendoes forgotten, I grasp both his hands in mine.

"I know you have goodness in you, but I don't believe you've always done good. You won't let me research past actions, so at least let me judge current ones. Let's make a pact. Over the next month you'll tell me honestly what's going on, what actions you're taking and why, and we'll decide together if that's the best thing for you to do, for your people."

Are you fucking nuts?

Doubt pierces my arrogance—do I really expect this dictator to consult with me over his actions? His blue eyes gaze steadily down into mine, earnest and waiting. No sign of disbelief or amusement.

"Good people do bad things. But if you truly want to be a good person—and you're not just bullshitting me—then you don't want to do harm, right? That should be your guiding principle. You mentioned your advisers and how your decisions are sometimes swayed by them, but if you just keep that one aspiration in your heart at all times, Do No Harm—or perhaps in the case of war, it's Do as Little Harm as You Can, and Only for Justifiable Reasons—then that's the best we humans can do."

Who decides what's justifiable?

Nothing is simple, but shut up anyway. We're having a moment here.

I raise my eyebrows and wag my head from side to side, to lend amusement to what I say next, in case it's ludicrously arrogant. "And if you want help, of course I'm here. Got lots of time to consult and I don't charge much."

He smiles and squeezes my hands. "I have to go, but I will be back tomorrow."

I gaze at his face, trying to determine his reaction to what I've just said. Closed. But my epiphany dances around my head to the rhythm of "you are right, you are right." This is *not* senseless. I am not a puppet jerking on Random's strings. There is a reason I am here. And if I'm wrong, then I can still try to influence this man. Perhaps it'll be the only worthwhile thing I do in my entire life. However long that might be.

"Is there anything that you need?" he asks.

I come back to myself and glance at the pile that Sami dumped on my bed when Kassem first came in. I didn't want to waste the precious people-time hour looking through it, so I'm not sure what's there. "Could you get me some tapes and books so I can learn Arabic?"

"Why?"

I know better than to say I want to communicate with Sami and the other non-English speakers. "I like languages. I've got lots of time. Why not?"

"I'll think about it."

I repress a pout. The past hour has made me realize how important it is to mask any hint of flirtiness.

"Thank you."

"I must go now." My hands are still caught in his. He raises them, one at a time, to his soft lips, bracketed by the graze of his moustache. I lower my head in order to hide my sudden flush.

Then he's gone.

I keep to my routine. I read that day's journal out loud, ignoring the retching sounds of Voice.

Just before I get into bed, I pick up my calendar and cross off another day.

chapter four

Going through the little pile that Sami dumped on my bed = instantaneous pleasure. Everything that was on my list is there: shapeless dresses (for sexless comfort during the day), a kettle, Tetley's tea, juice and milk, gin and tonic—praise the Lord! Endless alcohol at my disposal will definitely make me smoke more, but somehow imprisonment undermines those little obsessions about health that used to attack me occasionally, a very long time ago. When I was free. Somehow, it no longer matters in the slightest how much I smoke. Especially since *it's* free!

There's also a pile of Calvin and Hobbes books, more than I've ever seen in one place. I haven't even read all of them.

"This is really living," I murmur to myself, staring at my riches. My father used to say that when he was happy. Absurdly (though I'm getting used to it), the thought brings tears to my eyes.

I arrange my new possessions: the dresses in the closet; the tea things and drinks on the table, which I drag close to the only electricity outlet in the room. I pile most of the Calvin and Hobbes neatly beside the toilet in my bathroom, keeping one beside my bed. I survey my tiny kingdom, deriving satisfaction from the orderliness. It's neater than I ever kept my house at home.

Filling the kettle in the bathroom in anticipation of my first cup of "homemade" tea—there is no tea like Tetley's—I realize that I've forgotten to ask for sugar. Impossible to enjoy Tetley's without sugar!

"Fuck!" I scream as loudly as I can. "FUCK! FUCK! FUCKITFUCKIT FUCKIT FUCK EVERYTHING SHIT MOTHERFUCKER." My own screams rile me up further and I begin kicking the wall, the curses deteriorating into harsh sobs, which seem to belch from my throat of their own volition. I listen to the noise, marvelling at my own pain, thinking: *I can stop at any point. I'm allowing myself to have hysterics.*

"WHY THE FUCK NOT?" I scream into space. There is no reason to control anything. No terrified children's faces, no disgusted husband. Perhaps Sami is watching, but probably not; anyway, I couldn't care less about dim-witted Sami. I'm all alone, and I can behave however I fucking want.

And then suddenly it's not possible to control anymore. Nobody is watching me, not even myself. I'm rolling around on the floor like an animal, snot and tears pouring from their respective orifices, pinching chunks of flesh so the simple physical pain will overtake the misery within.

Only with exhaustion does control return; my sobs subside and I listen to them, unwilling to stop them too suddenly, as though that would somehow make them fake.

what an ungodly sound.

Ah yes: Hello, Control. Immediately, it feels a little silly to be lying here on the floor, and I'm seized with the irresistible desire to look at my own face in the bathroom.

My eyes are swollen into slits.

All the better to see him with.

There are red welts where my nails have scraped down my cheeks.

All the better to repel him with.

My nose is bright red and shiny. I am fascinatingly ugly. Does everybody's face span such a massive range between attractiveness and hideousness?

Making lists = feeling good. In control.

1. SUGAR!!!
2. Creams for my face, preferably Yonka;
3. Chocs
4. Ecstasy or acid or cocaine. Actually make that cocaine.
   ~~To help me live through this godawful month.~~

Yes, cross it out; you don't want to hurt his feelings. He's such a nice man.

5. Fucking sugar;
6. Lemon for gin,
7. CD player. List of music to dance to attached.
8. A Qur'an
9. Lesson books and tapes for beginners to learn Arabic
   (please, please, with sugar on top—if I had any).
10. I ASKED for a FUCKING MINI FRIDGE.

11:30: MEDITATION. The only way I know to bring my mind under control; to stop—even for one blessed second—its eternal twirling and whirling.

Breathing in, I smile.
Breathing out, I relax my body.
Living in the present moment.
The present moment is a wonderful moment.

12:00: DONE MEDITATION and feel calmer. It's strange how often human beings repeat the same crap habits. How many times have I been in a nasty argument with my husband, letting rip unpleasant things about his family or his character? I always think I'm in control and can stop any time, until I'm not. Maybe he's ignoring me and looking at the computer and I start to poke his shoulder, purely to irritate, convinced that I'm not really upset. Until I'm pounding on his head with the sole desire to maim him for life.

Afterwards, I'm always shocked by such behaviour, hardly believing that it was me. Is this what murderers feel?

Wicked, in front of the children too.

Yes, but there are no children here. Relief! I can act as badly as I want! Who cares?

Unless letting go of control will lead to a decreased ability to control in the future.

Damn.

What about this destiny crap? Helping Kassem do good?

The right thing to say, for once. A pleasant, fuzzy feeling envelops my heart. If only there was a reason for my bizarre incarceration!

Or even a reason for your bizarre behaviour.

If I could actually do some good! Whatever Kassem's interest in me, it certainly exists and therefore it's not completely crazy to wonder how to exploit that interest for the good of the Syrian people.

How noble.

Hey, he wants me to think well of him. There's only one way to do that.

Let you go?

Yeah, well, that'd work too. You know what? Screw the Syrian people. Still, if I have to be here for a month, the idea that I might do some good is wonderfully comforting. Much better than agonizing over whether he'll keep his word about December 12th.

1:00: SAMI COMES IN with the food.

"Salaam Aleichem, Sami," I call out cheerfully, to mask my need to talk for a few minutes.

He bobs his head and smiles.

"Ana…" I pull my lips into a gruesome smile. "Happy. Ana Happy."

He stares at me like *I'm* the idiot. I pull my lips down into a grimace. "Sad." Up again: "Happy. Bay Arabi?"

Bay is Hebrew for *in* and Arabi must be close to how you say Arabic in Arabic, mustn't it?

Like espanol is close to Spanish or francais for French?

Why can't you just shut up sometimes?

My changing expression has alarmed Sami; he's backing out the door. NO!! I resist the urge to yank him back in; in any case he's already closed the door in my face.

So then I resist the urge to smash the door down.

I collapse on the bed, kneading my chest. What's the matter with me? I just meditated for fuck's sake; I'm supposed to be CALM.

Breathe. Breathe.

Oh my God, I'm going insane. That's the reason for these mood swings. It's obvious Sami is terrified of me; he can see the insanity.

Going insane?

You're right; I've always walked a thin line.

What's insanity, anyway?

I ponder.

It's when you have a certain way of looking at the world, and you make everything that happens conform to that view. And you're sure you're right, regardless.

So you think your situation is shit—and it really IS shit! So you're okay.

The worldview you create doesn't have to pertain to the entire world. It depends on your level of insanity. You could be sane at work, for example, but insane about a certain person. If the insane person decides that a certain person is lazy, then everything they do is perceived as lazy, even if it's obvious to everybody else that they're hardworking.

You thinking about a certain person here?

I giggle nervously. It always pisses me off when my husband calls me lazy. He has no idea what I do all day; he just says it because the house isn't clean enough for him. Because I refuse to do more than an hour of house-related work per day. Hoping insults will bend me to his will and the house will morph into spotlessness.

Laziness is relative, like everything else.

Your point?

You spend half your life stretched out on the sofa stoned. He works way harder than you.

I dither for a moment but decide against attack.

You digress. The point is, if that's the definition of insane, then I'm not.

I thought the definition of insanity was doing the same thing over and over and expecting different results?

Well, it's the same thing really. Adam nags and nags in the same critical way, presumably expecting a miraculous transformation in the form of a spotless house. After all these years.

The fragrance of the food drifts toward my nose. I lift the cover and inhale. Skewered lamb on a bed of rice. Salad. A bowl of dates. Another of pistachios.

You'll have to erase these boring descriptions from your book. Nobody's interested in what you shove down your gullet—unless they're feeding you worms and mouldy bread.

7:00: I'VE BEEN READY for hours. Red nose is powdered but slitty-ness of eyes remains. Never mind, my goal is not to seduce but to enlighten. Having so much time to think is really a precious gift.

Fuck me.

Yeah, fuck you. 'Preciate if you could shut up while he's here.

I sit in yearning, and don't care whether it's pathetic or not. The only human contact I've had all day is two minutes with Sami. I used the abundant time to think about how to help Kassem. If he doesn't come, the whole day will be wasted.

A soft knock on the door and I leap to my feet, casting my eyes around for the best place to drape myself. There aren't too many choices.

He comes in and stands, smiling down at me while Sami puts the tea things on my bedside table.

I smile back. Tall men make one feel so delicate and feminine. I've always felt huge next to my bantam husband (it doesn't help that he calls me "elephant-y," as though I'm too large rather than him being too small).

Subdue flirtatious gaze and focus on saving the world.

"What did you do today?" he asks, and I'm no longer annoyed by this question because it's natural to ask that if you care.

"I wrote, meditated. Nothing much. What did you do today?"

"I did no harm," he smiles. Then the smile fades. "Unless I'm harming you?"

"Harming me? Of course you're not..."

He fucking is.

"Umm, do you mean psychologically? Well..."

He reaches forward and takes my hand, causing an instant rush of gratitude and pleasure. What happened to the fear? Simple. Yesterday I understood one thing, and today I understand another. There is no need to fear. It would be foolish.

"I would do anything at all to make you happy."

"So let me go."

"Just a little bit longer. Please. I need you."

I almost feel sorry for him, he looks so woebegone. If his conscience is so bad over this, how could he have killed thousands? "It's okay; we have an agreement. One month. Stop worrying about it. Really."

"But are you happy?"

Delirious.

"I'm fine with our agreement. Truly. Especially the part about... you know." I feel embarrassed; it's so presumptuous.

"About...?"

Shit. I take a deep, brave breath. "If there was a reason for my captivity, I'd feel much better about it. For example, what we discussed last night. The idea that every human being is immersed in their own perspective so utterly that it's hard for them to know when they're doing wrong."

I don't remember that discussion.

"Do you remember we discussed living each day without doing harm to others? And if, because of a war, we have to do harm, then first we must look desperately for alternatives. Then we acknowledge we are doing harm. That's how we miserable egoists can attempt to lead virtuous lives."

Does he have to do that for everyone he pops? Or can he do it once per thousand murders?

"Look, you either really want to be a decent human being or you just want to appear that way."

"I want to be a decent human being."

He stares straight into my eyes, conveying sincerity. I stare straight back. "Causing death is doing harm, even if it's a terrorist. Your goal is not to win this war against an enemy. Your goal is to end this war by offering real democracy, which you believe in."

He places his hand over his heart. "I have done that."

I look away from him in irritation. I notice that Sami has placed a dish cover over the treats tonight. Instantly, my curiosity is aroused.

Focus, Sieve-Brain.

"You haven't done that. You've got to stop thinking in terms of bad people and good people—every Syrian has the right to vote and unless you hold real and honest elections for all your citizens then you're not really interested in democracy. And your people are stuck with another Mugabe-like madman who clings to power against the will of his people."

"There are a few things I need to tell you before…"

"That's the deal. That's the definition of doing no harm." I lean back and fold my arms, precluding the eyes' tendency to slide toward the covered dish.

"What deal?"

"Well…" I feel a little confused. My stomach is rumbling. "I guess it goes back to whether you want to truly be a good person or not."

"Yes."

"So that's how you do it. Move steadily toward the goal of real elections."

Not to mention how much better you'll feel about your incarceration.

He sits back and laughs. Uh-oh. "You are so simplistic—it's marvellous! You remind me of myself before I came to power."

Then he catches sight of the annoyance in my face. "I agree with you, but it's more complicated than that."

"Which part do you agree with?"

"Elections for all Syrians is my goal too. But you remember what you told me about perspectives? You must hear a little more of mine before you start to insist that this process happens immediately. You are missing information."

You did say that about perspectives. That one has to listen to many to understand.

That's true. My solution probably is simplistic. My solution for Israel was pretty simple too. Offer the Camp David peace accord every five years. It's the best deal the Palestinians are going to get and eventually they'll realize that. The problem is that both sides are idiots, but that's the solution.

If only they'd listen to you.

"At what point did I end my narrative last time?" Kassem is asking. "I was explaining to you my position in the war, if you remember."

"I'm pretty sure we were finished that bit about the war."

He smiles indulgently. "Not at all. If you are to help me, then you must know everything."

Sarcasm?

"You're right. I'm listening."

So he starts to talk. I focus really well for the first two minutes, searching frantically for connections between what he's saying and the impossibility of launching a democratic process tout de suite, but he seems to be going on about his father, the differences in their dealings with the enemy, nothing to do with democracy, seemingly again proving how relatively good he is, and then Sieve-Brain starts to yawn, and those covered dishes start to cavort and frolic on the periphery of my vision. Of course he must be getting thirsty, talking like that, so I lean forward and pour him a cup of mint tea, holding it to the light to admire its colour— just like the new leaves on Canadian trees in spring.

Then finally, when he's sipping and vying with my history teacher at school to transform history into humdrum, I lift the cover off the dish. Chocolate cake with vanilla icing; a bowl of salted almonds and another of Turkish delight. As nice as, but no nicer (perhaps that would be impossible) than any other day. So why cover the dish?

"The people see me as a gentle person. Do you know what they call me?"

I shake my head and smile. Sami is trying to please me. He knows I enjoy lifting the lids and discovering their secrets. Every covered dish is like a little present to open.

How does he know?

Telepathy. Because everybody likes presents.

I sample a little of this and a little of that and sip my delicious tea. And Kassem talks and talks, every detail of the five-year war, what they did, how they did it, how he tried to respond. I can't see the relevance to the question of when to implement democracy, so I can't focus.

I have a cigarette and zone out, studying his face. Every detail.

His hands gesticulate; his eyes swivel from face to air to tea—their serious hues aren't alleviated by even a glance of admiration.

That's why women don't rule the world: Sieve-Brains AND sexpots.

I'm not a sexpot. It just amazes me that I possess something that can give such pleasure. You'd think he'd be aware of it. That there's a little ol' vagina right over here. Like I was aware of the cakes.

Finally, he's winding up. "Do you understand a little more of where I come from, Charlotte?"

"Yes, I think I do, Kassem."

"That is good. First you listen so we are on the same page, as you say, and then we start to create an action plan."

"Sounds good."

He stands up. Despite the fact that I've just been dying of boredom for over an hour, my heart drops.

"I have to go."

My whole body screams NO! I wrack my brains for ways to keep him here. He's standing up, brushing some imaginary lint off his suit. Couldn't be crumbs, because he never eats anything. How to keep him?

Stroke his ego.

Hmm; screw that. "I have a list for you," I say in wounded tones. "Have you sent the video to my family yet?"

Murder if he says no.

"Of course."

Joy! "How did you send it? By air? Courier? When do you think they'll get it? Did you tell them they can send me one back? How will they do that?"

He provided an address, idiot.

Doubt!

My hands tremble. This is what "hanging on an answer" means.

"We sent it electronically, of course. Don't worry. You will probably have a return video very soon. Why do you worry? I promise you."

He looks down at me fondly, and then raises an index finger to stroke my cheek. "Silly girl."

My stomach clenches with pleasure and I flush, dropping my eyes. His finger stills on my cheek, a circle of human warmth. I incline my cheek ever so slightly, so his finger presses more firmly.

"Charlotte," he says softly, but I don't lift my eyes. Then both his hands are encircling my face, gently, inexorably, raising it up. "Charlotte." I glance up into the blue depths and without thinking I yank my head backward out of his hands, pushing him at the same time. He stumbles a little, then rights himself and walks out the door without looking at me.

Shit.

Shit.

NOVEMBER 14: 11:30 P.M.

I can't believe myself. Why do I always do that? It's happened a half dozen times in my life; an instinctive reaction that can't be controlled. Man shows a little amorous inclination, and I bash him to kingdom come. I was fifteen the first time it happened, with my family at the bar in the King David Hotel in Jerusalem. A probably very intelligent and handsome drunk journalist was trying to dance with me, and I shoved him so hard he fell over. As far as I can remember he laughed uproariously and pursued me gallantly (from a distance) for the rest of the evening. Entirely his fault, therefore, that I'm doomed to repeat regressive behaviour until death. On the other hand, I might also attribute the fact that I've never been sexually harmed to Drunken Journalist. I've travelled through Africa, the Middle East, the Far East, and South America all by myself. Men have pushed their hard-ons against my bottom in crowded buses, "accidentally" cupped breasts during team sports, walked tentative fingers down hills and valleys: they all got the same treatment. On the ball field or in crammed Turkish buses, I'd fling myself backward with elbows flailing, as intent on contact with offending member as member had been intent on contact with me seconds before. So I've never been hurt sexually, and lucky for me a couple of them persevered. Drunken Journalist and Husband.

Shit, though. What if he doesn't come back?

What do you care? Maybe he'll let you out before the end of the month if you piss him off enough.

I sigh, then do my end-of-day routine. I read my journal out loud. I pull my calendar from under my bed and cross off one more day. Too many more to go.

NOVEMBER 18: 11:00 P.M.

He came back. Every night he's been here, blabbing on and on about history, the war, the Syrian people, his vision. It's so boring I can hardly remember why I'm listening politely.

Because you're delusional.

Right, I knew there was a reason. I'm going to influence the history of Syria, if I can get a word in edgewise. Am I gaining a clearer perspective of his point of view through listening to him rant day after day? It doesn't feel like it. I can't grasp the relevance. Whatever atrocities have been done, on both sides, are in the past. We can only control what we do from here on in. That's the bit I want to help him with—not the past. And I can't help him unless he genuinely wants to help his own people. All of them, including those who hate him. So is my acquiescent ear…

Seemingly acquiescent, Sieve-Brain.

Why seemingly? How am I not acquiescent?

You're not listening to a damn thing he's saying.

If you'd just shut up and let me finish. Is my totally 100-percent acquiescent ear paving the way to an open dialogue about what he needs to do to help his country? Or am I just boring myself shitless for no reason?

If you can incorporate his viewpoint into the dialogue, you might shock him into listening, because he's totally aware you're sitting here glassy-eyed …

Okay. That's it.

I've just started, actually.

You don't need to continue. You're right; I concur. I've realized there's no point spending the whole month talking exclusively about him. It's not encouraging him to behave better and I'm sick of the subject. Have you noticed how often in my relationships we talk about the other person exclusively?

No.

Well, we do. I'm always sitting there amazed at the other person's lack of awareness, how they can yak away about their latest love affair or kid issue…

Are you admitting you're really a selfish ego-centric?

Yeah, I am, duh. But I learned years ago that it was one of the ways to get people to like you. When they're talking about themselves, they're happy and they think it's because of you. You know me, always pathetically pursuing the hope that others will like me.

Oh good. I thought for a moment you were saying that you're selflessly interested in others. Such a dramatic change would surely signal the first step on the rocky road to insanity.

Nope. I talk about them for entirely selfish reasons. But I've listened to his perspective long enough. I'll launch into a monologue as soon as he comes in, otherwise it'll be too late. Did you notice how I tried to bring up the psychic stuff again, just to change the topic for two minutes?

He said his sister was the spitting image of Rana in A Hero.

Yeah man, he's nuts. Who even knew he had a sister? What chance do I have of influencing a nut to do anything?

And yet.

Yeah. He does seem to care about my opinion. So weird. So the psychic stuff was just an excuse? An excuse for what?

Maybe it was real initially, but now he realizes you're not psychic.

So what does he think of me? I can't tell. I don't understand why he cares what I think. It's not even sexual—have you noticed he hasn't even looked at me recently?

You pushed him. That might have done it.

Well, when he comes tonight I'm going to behave differently. I'll launch into a diatribe about me and tie it into the main theme.

How?

I'll talk about my tendency to violence.

He'll identify with that.

And how I struggle. How we must all struggle to do right. How hard it is. But how I learned to say hello to my anger when it flared up, and think about where it came from. So it didn't feel unwanted, so to speak.

But it IS unwanted.

No, it's part of me. We need to love *all* our parts, even our faults, and then maybe we can have a dialogue with them. Then we figure out what made that anger flare up and work together with our beloved part—our anger—to solve the root.

Lightbulb moment! I love your Sieve-Brain, your laziness, your immaturity, your low EQ, your sexual incompetence...

Okay. Shut the fuck up. I'll ask Kassem what he struggles with.

Back to him?

I don't mind if he talks about himself, so long as there's a point. If I'm here to influence him to do good, then I need to make a plan. Not let him rule the coop every meeting.

So long as there's a will, there's a way.

What?

So long as you think there's a purpose for your being here, you won't try to cut your wrists.

I GET UP AND PUT ON some music—at least betwixt and between his ranting, I managed to slip him a few more lists. I received a CD player and a bunch of CDs with specific dance-able music. I crank it up to full volume and dance madly at least once a day, which is much more fun than those awful exercise routines I was doing in the beginning. I also got some Arabic books for beginners and an Arabic-English dictionary. Every day, I painstakingly work out a simple sentence or two to say to Sami.

Every day is planned down to the smallest detail. Routine = sanity.

And every day ends the same way. I read my journal out loud. I cross off another day in my calendar.

Twenty-four days to go.

NOVEMBER 18: 8:00 P.M.

Where is he? I've got my new list; I've got several ME topics ready. Where is he?

8:30

I bang on the door to get Sami's attention. It opens to his wide, startled brown eyes.

"Where he?" I demand in Arabic.

Sami launches into a complicated reply, obviously labouring under the impression that my two-word question really masks total fluency. I cut his gibberish short.

"Not here?"

"La."

"Emta... hozer?" I know the word for *when*, but Sami's slack jaw tells me that the word for *return* is different than the Hebrew word, which I stuck in there just in case. I step (twice) to my dictionary and flip frantically to the word *return*. Sami shuts the doors before I get to the "r"s. It takes me minutes to figure out what the letters of the alphabet spell, even though I memorized the alphabet on the first day. And even when I figure the sound that the letter corresponds to, I still only have the root of the verb *return* and have no idea how to conjugate it. But who cares? The goal is only to make oneself understood. It's something like rajaa. Close, anyway.

I bang on the door again. "Emta rajaa?"

Sami opens the door, looking puzzled, and I worry that my pronunciation is so bad he can't understand me. I had asked for tapes in my list, but although Kassem had agreed that it was necessary to listen to a language in order to learn it, the tapes hadn't materialized. I'll certainly give him an earful when he appears!

Sami beams suddenly and rattles off another few sentences. I understand the words thalatha, arba'aa.

Three or four what? Days; weeks? Obviously not weeks. He wouldn't go away and leave me here to rot without reason.

So days.

How am I going to get through three or four days without human contact? Sami barely counts; he never talks to me long. What's more, I can tell he doesn't like it. Always looks nervous, as though he wants to get away.

He's doing it now, shifting from foot to foot, trying to nudge the door shut imperceptibly. I want to ask why Kassem hadn't told me he was going away, but I only know the word for *how* in Arabic. I pick up my dictionary with a sigh and begin to look up the word for *tell*—if I say *why no tell me?*, there's only one word to look up. I'm great at bastardizing the Arabic language. Again, the door shuts before I get to the "t"s.

Don't bother. How would Sami know?

I sit looking at the closed door, a tide of misery rising slowly over my heart. There is only one solution to fight despair; I roll a joint. Within minutes, the smoke rolling through my lungs does its work; all anxieties and voices are silenced.

chapter five

I lie in bed, staring at the stick man on the wall. The blanket is wrapped around my head; only my nose is sticking out. It's the only position where I feel completely comfortable. Wherever the camera is located, it's almost certainly not behind my bed, embedded in this smooth plaster wall. So if I lie with my back to the room facing the corner with my blanket over my head, nobody can see me. Sami can only see a lump in the bed. Or whoever else is out there. Is there anybody else? It's odd that I've barely seen any other guards; doesn't Sami ever get a day off? I'd ask him, if I cared enough to spend half an hour looking up the words.

My face can do whatever it wants, without self-consciousness.

Right now, it's crying, softly, so nobody can hear.

I'm not getting up today. There's no point. Miserable thoughts trundle through my brain; tears seep from my closed eyes. I picture my children, crying at my absence. I wonder if they've seen the video yet? The possibility that they haven't is intolerable. If they have no idea where I am or what I'm going through. If I'm even alive. The suffering and misery they must be experiencing! That bastard Kassem. If he had an ounce of compassion, he would have communicated with them immediately. This is going to be a really bad day.

Stop wallowing. Get up already.

Fuck you.

Start your routine. You're already late—you should have started your exercises half an hour ago.

Without Kassem, my routine is fucked anyway.

What about those perfect thighs you wanted to present to your husband?

Who sees thighs? Thighs only appear in the summer when swimming. It's completely useless to work like crazy in order to achieve halfway decent thighs just before the binging and boozing at Christmas.

What about your book?

The one you call really boring? The one that meanders around an empty head when it's not itemizing every dish for every meal? It's crap. Fuck you!

So this is going to be another "fuck-you" day, is it? What about making friends with the "fuck you" and figuring out where it's coming from. Unblend from your "fuck you"!

No, it's not, it's *not* another fuck-you day... can't you just...

There is a tentative knock at the door, and Sami comes in. What's the point of knocking if you're not going to wait for an answer? Oh right, I'm just a prisoner, what was I thinking? There's the sound of rustling as Sami moves a couple of things on my bedside table, then a mild clatter as the metal tray is placed on the table. Then silence. Rage jolts through my body. How dare he stand there, looking at me.

Anxiously.

Who cares how he's looking? Isn't it obvious I want to be alone? It's not like that clod can say anything to make it better, is it?

"Get the fuck out of my room," I hiss venomously.

There is another scrape of metal and a whiff of fried eggs and toast. Sami has lifted the cover off the dish so I can smell the contents. If he doesn't get out of my room in two minutes, I'm going to smash his fucking face in. What can I use? Fists won't inflict the necessary damage. What would happen if I knocked him out? Is there somebody else out there, watching the camera to make sure Sami emerges safely? Surely not. Even if there are more guards, even if they have instructions to watch all the time, when the cat's away the mice do play. I bet they're enjoying these

Kassem-free days immensely. If I knocked Sami out and burst from my room like a demon out of hell, how far would I get?

"Get out," I say again, raising my voice. If he remains there one more second, I'm going to blow. I'll scratch his eyes out.

But the door clicks softly, and he is gone.

The smell of the eggs is killing me, but I don't want to give Sami the satisfaction of seeing me eat, in case he's still watching anxiously from a place of safety.

And your point is?

Everything's got to have a point? A desire to create worry and anxiety in another human being. Is that a good enough point? Maybe if I stop eating, he'll let Kassem know and he'll come back.

So pathetic. All this childish behaviour because Psycho isn't here.

I repress another *fuck you*. No, because I'm a prisoner.

Poor you. Great food, great scenery, great books. What could be worse?

That's what you always say when I feel down. There's never any reason, I *know*. My children are wonderful, my husband is bearable, I live in a lovely house and have everything I want, when most of the world is either starving or at war. Lucky, privileged me. What right do I have to be depressed? None. But it doesn't matter; I can't help it and I never could. Surely now, when there's just a smidgen of a reason—despite wonderful conditions, this is still a prison—you could cut me a little slack. Why don't you just go away and let me indulge in torture scenes with Sami?

If you manage to modify a single aspect of Kassem's behaviour, this might turn out to be the most important month of your life. Don't you see? You have to embody the values you're trying to convey to him, else you haven't got a chance in hell. Do no harm. Including to yourself. Remember?

You have a point. Plus the smell of the eggs is killing me.

So I sit up and eat. Wondering if this rotten feeling is all because he's not here. I don't even like him, yakking on about politics ad nauseum every night. But he was part of my routine. I hate disruptions to my routine. That's all it is.

So I spend the rest of the day adhering rigidly to those parts of my routine that I control. I meditate, wash, exercise, study Arabic for an hour, eat lunch, write for three hours, eat dinner, smoke. Gaze hungrily out the window, pretending I'm not in a tiny room, for hours at a time. I don't talk to Sami, though he asks me how I am. Not talking isn't doing harm. Not talking is the only way a rights-less prisoner can pretend her feelings matter.

Another virtuous, empty day.

NOVEMBER 22: MORNING

His eyes slide down to the outline of my breasts and linger there. My heart starts to beat strangely, but I continue to talk as though his eyes aren't glued to my tits.

"You've spent days comparing the state of your people during your father's reign and during yours, emphasizing the security, riches, education, and freedom they enjoy."

"Charlotte."

"You've even compared modern Syria to other states in the Middle East, stressing the relative peace and security your people have enjoyed."

"Charlotte."

The way he says it. Slowly, deeply. With such desire. Surely he can see the palpitations of my heart?

"And I've listened really carefully. I understand your viewpoint, I really do. And for the most part I believe you."

His eyes meander reluctantly back to my face. "For the most part?"

"Yeah. I don't have access to anyone else's viewpoint, but I'm sure they'd bring up facts that prove the opposite. But the point is, it doesn't matter."

Now his eyes are on my lips. I think I need to pee.

"Why doesn't it matter?"

"Because the past is the past. Perhaps wrongs were done, perhaps not. It's what happens now that's important."

"Yes." His eyes are ransacking my body, staring boldly here and there. I wish I didn't feel a pleasurable twitch in my vagina, but I do. I wish there wasn't a heavy, warm feeling spreading throughout my abdomen. But there is. I swallow.

"Are you listening to me? This is important. I'm about to get to the nitty-gritty."

"The nitty-gritty," he murmurs, as though it were an erotic word, and in one fluid motion he slides off his chair and is on his knees before me, his hands raised in supplication.

"Please Charlotte."

"What?"

"Please let me touch you."

"Certainly not."

If my husband were here, he could have told him that it's pointless to ask, that I'll always say no. The trick is to just go ahead and do it. Not politically correct, I know, but thank goodness not all Middle Eastern men are politically correct. IMHO I'd still be a virgin if I hadn't left Canada.

Then, like a good alpha male, he clasps my thighs on either side and buries his face in my lap. I can feel his hot breath through my thin skirt, encasing my whole sex in heat. My mind knows this is wrong and stupid and a mistake, but my body quivers, desperate for him to touch, and rub, and lick, and penetrate. My poor, neglected body. Untouched for days. I rest my hands lightly on his head, feeling his hair, the vulnerability of his nape. I close my eyes, focusing on the sensation of his skin sliding under my fingers.

His hands travel along the sides of my thighs and over my hips, kneading, stroking, his head pressed firmly against my skirt. I slacken my tightly clenched thighs a tad and he responds immediately, thrusting his whole face into the widening crack, pushing and yearning toward the desired place, which waits with aching anticipation. Despite the admonitions of my head, I spread my knees more, and his hands sweep down and under my tent-like skirt and I'm lifting myself off the bed so he can push it over my hips and of course there's no underwear and the warm, firm thrust of his tongue—oh my God. My legs swing open in utter abandonment, willing him to suck and lick and thrust. My whole body is trembling with pleasure; his hands and lips feel like they are everywhere and I've never been touched like this. All self-consciousness is gone and I groan sensually as the pressure starts to build and my hands hover over his head, ready to direct but not needing to because he knows exactly where to touch and how much, and I'm not worrying about whether I should touch him back or whether there's too much hair down there or whether it's clean enough because his lips and tongue and fingers are everywhere and every thought is driven out of my head as my body jerks in climax.

Then his hands are traveling further up, under my dress, and they cup my breasts as gently as if they were porcelain, and I figure I'd better initiate some action on my own, even though I'd really like just to be tied up and helpless so I wouldn't have to worry about what I should or shouldn't be doing, and he would do it all to me, but I'm not tied up so I reach out and undo his pants and ease them down, then his underwear, and his penis is long and thin and purple and I'm not taking that into my mouth—the colour is most peculiar—but it doesn't matter because he's pushing me backward onto the bed and I'm thrusting my hips up to meet him and I can feel the length of it sliding in and I watch his face because I love the expression on a man's face when he's penetrating, and the knowledge that I'm giving him such pleasure without the slightest effort on my part, and his face contorts and he cries out and falls on top of me.

I open my eyes and peer cautiously around the room, then down at myself. Thankfully, my body is completely covered with the blanket so any watching eyes haven't seen whatever my hands have been doing. I roll luxuriously over in the bed so I'm facing the wall, and explore my nether regions surreptitiously. I feel heavy and moist. It doesn't take more than a few strokes to reach orgasm, but it's nothing like the waves of pleasure in the dream.

Never mind; at least you won't have to tell your husband you lasted less than nine days before capitulating to a mass murderer.

Every cloud has a silver lining.

Plus fantasies are always better than the reality. So stick with those.

Well, duh. It's not like I'm about to ravish Kassem. Sheesh, it's just a fantasy.

With him.

Naturally. He's the only human being around.

Since when do you need a living human being? Add Leonard cohen tapes to your list and listen to him non-stop; won't take long before he's fucking you instead.

His voice is much sexier than Kassem's.

And he's probably had a lot more women.

And he's probably much better in bed.

And Arabs don't do oral sex.

Don't generalize.

Even your husband, who loves you...

I know! Fuck him, man; every time I think about that, it pisses me off. What is the matter with these people?

well, he'd claim you never wash.

That's an excuse. Really, it's because my vagina grosses him out.

Because it's filthy.

NO! Because...

He's a backward, nasty little Arab.

Adam hates it when I call him an Arab. The truth is, his family comes from Morocco and obviously I'd perceive masses of differences between Jewish Moroccans and Muslim Moroccans if only I wasn't Canadian. But since I am Canadian, damned if I can tell the difference.

what?

If you're from a different culture you miss the nuances, you know? It's like, we Canadians feel that we're utterly different from Americans—we have a totally different value system, for starters.

Please, not the superiority-of-canadians-over-Americans speech again.

All right. The point is, do you think Europeans can differentiate between Canadians and Americans? Of course not. So, there you go, my failure to differentiate between Arab Jews and Arab Muslims is not connected to my Sieve-Brain.

Those little nuances, you know.

Whereas the difference between Canadian men and Middle Eastern men...

canadian men probably prefer oral sex to real sex. You'd be like, stop it already, I've already come ten times, it's your turn now, and they'd be like, no please, I can't stop, it's like eating candy.

A giggle erupts, quickly followed by a pout. It's one of my great regrets, the fact that I've only made love to three men in my life—all of them Middle Eastern.

Don't die with regrets.

Sometimes it's a question of weighing one regret against another. I'd regret it a lot more if I made love to someone else and my husband left me (which he certainly would) and then my children would suffer the horror and destabilization of a broken home. Meanwhile, he'd probably link up again within a year, and then they'd spend half their time under the influence of the Other Woman, while he'd spend his time pouring bitter hatred about me into their little ears. I brought them into this world and I have to try to bring them to the age of eighteen without fucking them up if at all possible. Giving up Canadian men is a small price to pay.

Shame you can't lie.

I know. Sucks. Hate my Little Looney-tunes.

Because it might be bullshit, and you'll never know.

What?

Perhaps all men are exactly the same. So you're regretting something that doesn't even exist.

It's not likely, is it? I mean, name an area where Canadians and Arabs treat women the same?

Generalizing.

Really? Do I have to specify "most Arabs" and "politically correct middle-class Canadians" every fucking time I open my mouth?

Fine, so your point is, canadians do oral sex because they've been brought up that way, not because they actually enjoy it.

I picture my husband's face when he slithers down about once a year to do his duty.

Yeah.

But if the importance of giving pleasure has been engrained in you from birth, then wouldn't the giving of pleasure become as important as the receiving of pleasure in the end?

Well, yeah. I do it to give pleasure, certainly not to get pleasure. Triggers my gag reflex.

And you wouldn't feel happy if you weren't giving pleasure. I mean, you've been with Adam for over twenty years and you still give him that pleasure.

Reluctantly. And it's not quite the same.

Why not?

Vaginas are grosser than penises. I wouldn't suck a vagina if you paid me. All those slimy crevices…

Oh stop.

And putrid secretions.

You're just being disgusting.

I begin to laugh. Rancid emissions! Oozing discharges!

I fall off the bed and onto the floor, shaking with laughter.

It feels good to laugh.

NOVEMBER 24

Where the hell is he?

How many times have I wished to go away to a desert island for a month; maybe this experience is a classic "careful what you wish for." Maybe I'm being punished.

Yup, it's your fault. Sane thinking.

Why? It sounds plausible to me.

Because, Voice says with heavy sarcasm, *you were heavily interacting with nature on your desert island, with long walks and swims every day.*

Oh yeah.

NOVEMBER 25: 7:00 P.M.

There's a knock at the door but I don't look up. Entry doesn't depend on my acquiescence in any case; a knock is almost more insulting than no knock at all. It's like a loudspeaker proclaiming that everything is a pretence.

Even the promised month? A thought to avoid at all costs.

"Hello Charlotte."

The deep voice makes me jump. I look up, and there he is. A huge, unbidden smile spreads across my face. As soon as I'm aware of that unwitting grin I try to tamp it down—determined to play it cool. Nevertheless, it is imperative that I go to the bathroom immediately and check my face; what if there are crumbs stuck to my chin from the dinner I practically inhaled?

"Excuse me for a minute," I say and escape.

Are you kidding me?

What? I'm just checking my face.

You're putting lipstick on.

Yeah, well, I'm determined to do what you said. Focus on my goal and make this internment meaningful. I feel there's more chance of that if I look presentable.

Bullshit. Are you trying to kid yourself? Because you're certainly not kidding me.

You are me. I think. Oh no, am I going…

Insane? No—I'm not you, I'm the best part of you. So I'm very small.

Ha ha. You're hysterical, you know that?

I slam out of the bathroom with unnecessary aggression, causing a raised, perfectly sculpted black eyebrow. Kassem hasn't sat down yet; instead he stands right in front of me and raises my hand to his lips. "I have missed you."

I feel the tickle of his moustache and a hint of moistness. The heat of the dream rushes back and my face goes hot. He smiles, watching me. Thank God he can't see inside. The inappropriate and pathetic desire, born only of these weird circumstances and lack of human contact. Born of desperation. I *hate* his weak little chin.

I withdraw my hand and sit on the bed, awash in self-consciousness and suppressed excitement. I despise the violence and absurdity of my emotions. "Where have you been?"

"I have a war to run, you know. I would have come to see you, but I was called away for a few days."

So says every man to every kept woman.

I leap to my feet and begin to pace. This is such a crazy situation.

"What's the matter?"

"Nothing! What on earth could be the matter? I'm just imprisoned in Damascus, spending day after day utterly alone in bloody isolation. They don't isolate violent criminals in Canada anymore, you know. It's too psychologically hard on them."

A note of alarm creeps into his voice. "Why do you pretend to know where you are?"

"Oh, fuck you! It's cruel to isolate me!"

"Charlotte, please!" In one stride he has grasped my shoulder and pulled me into his arms. My face is pressed against his warm shoulder and tears begin to leak onto his clean white shirt. "Tell me what you want, my dear. I will give you anything you want. Would you like a companion for a couple of hours a day? Some nice woman who can speak English? Would you like an animal, perhaps? I know you love animals."

His hand is circling my back, soothing and exploratory at the same time. A feeling of surprise and joy sidles under my confusion; he just wants me to be happy. I rest my head on his warm, broad shoulder and think about what would make me happy. A companion? Perhaps not. In nineteen days, I'll be plunged back into 24/7 companionship and be desperately searching for ways to be alone. So, what is it? Just the uncertainty of the nineteen-day deadline?

Nature.

I lift my face up and back so I can see Kassem's eyes. "Is it possible to go outside for an hour or so every day? I think the lack of... outsideness... is depressing me."

Kassem's eyes cloud over "I will think about it, okay? It's a difficult request, because your presence here is a big secret to most of the people on my compound. Do you understand?"

"Yes."

He lifts a finger and touches my cheek. This must be a standard lead-on with him. "Why do you think you are in Damascus?"

I shrug and pull away from his embrace. "We must be near your home, or you wouldn't be able to visit me all the time. Do I get the slot after the bedtime story with your kids?"

He smiles, relaxes. Goes over to the chair and sits down next to the table. I watch as he adds cream and sugar to my coffee, knowing how I take it.

"You're very wise."

Oh fuck off.

"But perhaps I have several residences?" He holds out the coffee and I glide over, cursing my adolescent self-consciousness.

"Shukran," I say with great vehemence. Bizarrely, the word for *liar* in Hebrew is the same as the word for *thank you* in Arabic.

"Several residences, huh? Does it bother you that you're so rich when there's so much poverty?" I ask without preamble.

"My wife and I are very generous."

I blink, surprised. He doesn't mention his wife much. And I only remember reading one thing about her—that she bops around, buying like crazy while her people suffer from deprivation. "Generous to clothes and jewellery stores?"

I guess your soothe-and-amuse period's over.

I guess so. I don't even remember why I wanted to soothe and amuse. I'm not Scheherazade from *One Thousand and One Nights*. My life isn't in danger if I fail to amuse. Whatever danger it's in—and it's impossible to know if it's in danger or not—my behaviour is going to have very little impact on the outcome.

You're a bit variable, changing your mind every two minutes.

Prisoner's prerogative.

But Kassem is simply smiling, somewhat patiently. "No, to those less fortunate. Aren't you interested in what I've been doing for these past few days?"

I eye the covered dishes as I weigh my answer. The determination to try and influence this man to do good hasn't abated. But is this ridiculously pretentious? If he'd been interested in my input and advice like he *said*...

Did he say?

Perhaps not. Wishful thinking. Same type of thinking applied to guessing the contents of the covered dishes. It is so sweet of Sami to cover them.

Yes, let's switch abnormally grateful emotions to Sami.

It's actually abnormally intuitive of Sami to sense how much pleasure I get from revealing my food myself. Do you think it's because our family hardly ever eats out? Or does everyone feel the same amount of pleasure when their food is a surprise?

Maybe it's because you're abnormally greedy.

Maybe it's because I'm bored out of my mind in prison. Dinner is the highlight of my mother's day too, and all her friends there in the nursing home.

A small cough brings me back to myself. Kassem is looking at me quizzically. I smile apologetically. "I don't want to hear what you've been doing in great detail," I say. "The only important thing is—umm, obviously you've done harm because you're in a war. But you are either conducting this war in an honourable way or you're not. Your goal is either to bring the entire country to a place where democracy can happen, or it's to prolong your own power."

He launches into a spiel about how he's trying to bring the country to a place where democracy can happen, but it's a bit difficult when his poor country has been divvied up between ISIS and the rebels.

Everybody else is to blame. He is faultless.

Meets our definition of insane.

More's the pity. There is a very definite smell wafting from those covered dishes, but surely it couldn't be.

I can't resist; my hand inches forward, even as he rambles on, and lifts the cover. It is! Cinnamon buns!

I give a little cry of pleasure and hold one to my nose. Warm and sticky.

Kassem's voice trails off, and I open one eye to peek at him. He's watching me indulgently. I wish he wouldn't; I'd enjoy it much more if I wasn't being watched.

"I love how much pleasure you get from food," he says.

It's like my brain gives a little reminder beep every time I see an opportunity to fulfill my destiny: to make an honourable man of him. "Do you know why I enjoy nice food so much?"

Kassem shakes his head, still smiling.

"Because it's a treat. Why? Because I never have food like this. You can't really appreciate something you take for granted. So if you have nice food all the time, you can't enjoy it in the same way." I take a bite of my sticky bun and chew slowly, to emphasize my point. "So I could put the exact same plate of food in front of two children and one would feel happiness, while the other would feel indifference. Which is better?"

I pause for effect, sticky bun gripped between thumb and forefinger. He doesn't answer, so I prompt him. "Is it better to feel happiness or indifference?"

"Happiness."

"Of course. That's why money can't make you happy. Perhaps when you first get it, if you've been poor, you think it spells the end of your woes. But actually, happiness has just been denied you. Treats become commonplace, and no longer treat. So the amount of satisfaction your wife gets from shopping sprees is negligible. Now if, instead of that, you and your wife believed in something passionately—like the environment for example—and donated your money to a green organization fighting climate change rather than buying another unlived-in, unloved house, you'd actually be happier."

I take a defiant bite in conclusion, remembering to chew mindfully.

Kassem looks at me blankly. I know without asking that he couldn't care less about the environment. For a second, my enthusiasm flags.

You're the teacher. Teach him.

I put my bun down and lick the sugar off my fingers. Damn, it's good. "Do you believe in climate change?"

"I am in the middle of a war. Do you want to hear what's happening or not?"

You can only do good if he gives a shit.

Right. Stop thinking global issues and focus on Syria.

"Did you do anything morally reprehensible while you were away?"

Kassem looks taken aback. "No."

"You did no harm?"

"It's a war. No *avoidable* harm."

"Did you weigh all your options before doing unavoidable harm?"

"Much more so than I would have done before I met you." There's no mistaking the warmth in his voice, even though he's patently lying through his teeth.

"Good. Did you negotiate with the rebels, and let them know they'll be able to vote in the next elections, which you'll hold within six months because the last ones were a joke?"

"Negotiate with terrorists?"

"Well, duh. Do you think murderers with life sentences can't vote in Canada? You have to let everybody vote if you're a democracy."

Kassem takes a sip of his coffee. Glances at his watch. Guess it's not so fun when you're not allowed to yak on about yourself. I know how to get his attention.

"The reason I'm in prison is because you think I'm psychic, right?"

Eyes skitter back to me. Glob on.

I lean forward with a portentous expression (I hope).

"I'm sure about one thing. If you behave honourably, you'll be treated honourably. If you live by the sword, you'll die by the sword."

Bullshit.

You're telling me. If only God existed…

He can behave as honourably as he likes, millions will still want to string him up by the balls.

Kassem is leaning forward in his chair, fixing me with a distinctly puppy-dog-waiting-for-treat expression.

"Plus, if you behave honourably, you'll have a greater sense of self-worth, so you'll be happier."

"Bah, happiness!" Kassem throws himself back in his chair. "If I give money to climate change, I'll be happy. If I behave well, ditto. It's a Western obsession, happiness. It's not my goal in life."

I backpedal quickly. "No, of course not. Human beings aren't even programmed for happiness, so it's futile," I say, thinking of the black depression that has shrouded me for the past two days. "But we have to behave honourably, else there's no point at all to our lives."

Kassem fiddles with his cup. "You think the way we live impacts the manner of our death?"

I nod solemnly, hating my own hypocrisy. Anything touching on religion makes me uncomfortable; it seems crazy to believe there's some almighty being out there. But unbearable to think that we flawed humans are the highest there is. God help us. But looking into those beautiful eyes, nodding solemnly, I am willing to say whatever it takes to help this one man behave honourably. Just like religious people have been doing all along.

When they weren't molesting choir boys.

Haha, one of my father's little poems:

Religion isn't really my pigeon.

My higher joys depend on choir boys.

Kassem clears his throat. "We were defending one of our cities, which the terrorists were trying to take from us. But we didn't do anything I'm ashamed of."

"No chemical weapons?"

"No. Let me show you." He yells something to Sami, who rushes in with pen and paper. Kassem begins to draw some type of diagram; it looks like he's marking out positions—or something. Is he serious? I'm his moral, not his military, adviser.

I wiggle to my feet just as my eyes start to glaze. "Today's subject is the environment," I announce firmly, remembering my resolution to talk about things that interest me. Let his eyes glaze over for once. "You never answered my question. Do you believe in climate change?"

He abandons his paper with obvious reluctance. "I suppose it's a fact."

"Some stupid U.S. Republicans are still in denial, so good, I'm glad you're not one of them." I begin to pace up and down the room. "So here we are, eight billion and rising. We'll hit eleven billion by 2050. You talked about the crowded Syrian cities. Where will all these people go? They'll spread over even more of the earth's surface, displacing trees and animals as they go."

I stop to take a bite of my cinnamon bun. "Who will feed these hordes? Where will we put their trash? How will we control their pollution?" I'm trying to put as much *oomph* into my speech as I can, punching the air with each point. Still, his eyes are glazing. I drop down on my knees before him and gaze into his face. "All these stupid wars, we don't have time to wait while you break your teeth on democracy. There isn't *time*."

Kassem looks perplexed. "I don't understand what you want me to do."

Neither do I.

"Okay, so you're in the middle of a war that seems really important to you, so it's not like you're going to start implementing green strategies right now—but while you're waging your war you can still give three quarters of your fortune, which we've already established is useless in terms of adding anything significant to your life, to a solid environmental organization who can use your desperately needed money for research." I stop to gulp for air. His eyes are well and truly glazed now.

And here you thought he was going to resign and give up his fortune.

Only three quarters of it.

"I have to go, Charlotte."

"But I haven't even finished my sticky bun!"

He stands, holds out his hands to me. "I hate to go. But you have given me food for thought."

I take his warm, dry hands, desperation seizing my throat. I can't be alone for the next twenty-four hours. I can't! "Don't go!" I babble. "I'll shut up. I won't talk about the environment. Fuck the environment, who cares about that? I sound preachy, don't I? And it's totally stupid to talk about the environment when you're in the middle of a war. Of course you're so worried about your own people it's impossible to see this threat to the entire human race. I just want you to be a good person. I want you to do right."

Infantile.

Kassem raises my hand and brushes it against his lips. And my whole body goes hot. It's fucking insane, but that's what happens. If he lifted up my dress right now I'd plunge him in like some wanton whore. My body begs to thrust against him, feel the length of his body hard against mine.

That would be disastrous.

It's only because I've spent almost two weeks in isolation. There's nothing *wrong* with me. I've always had this problem with inappropriate sexual thoughts. I've gyrated on the penises of practically every man I've ever met, but it doesn't mean I'd actually...

There's no doubt in my mind. Of course you wouldn't press your body against his. You wouldn't even move it fractionally in his direction.

I keep my body rigid, shooting a quick glance upwards. He's smiling at me. "I know that, Charlotte. And I want to be a good person too."

He turns to go. I feel desolate, but at least he's thrown me a crumb that will uphold me for the next twenty-four hours. He must mean because of me. He wants to be good because of me.

Then he's turning back, and my heart gives this whoop of joy. "I almost forgot," he says, pulling a tape from his pocket and handing it to me. "'It's from your family. I wish you wouldn't view it. You will be sad."

My heart starts to beat as I take the tape in my hands. My family has sent me a tape. I am going to see my family. Everything else is forgotten. Nothing matters except this. I just wish he'd go already, so I can view it.

Instead, he puts his finger under my chin and raises my face to his. "I do care about the environment, Charlotte. But I have to sort out the issues of my country before I can think about anything else."

And then he's gone, before I can tell him that by the time everybody's stopped focusing on their own issues—which will never be sorted—it'll be too late.

chapter six

NOVEMBER 26: 6:00 A.M.

I slept like crap. I knew it was a mistake to listen to you.

You'd have slept just as badly if you'd seen it last night.

I'm not waiting another second. With unsteady fingers, I shove the tape into the video camera. I feel slightly sick. What had Kassem said? *"It's from your family. I wish you wouldn't view it. You will be sad."*

Take your time.

What's the worst it could be? Imagine the worst and the reality won't devastate. The worst... the children have been kidnapped by terrorists as well!

Give me a break.

The children are weeping. The entire video will be one long distress call begging me to come home. That'll probably cheer me up. Remind me that I'm loved and needed and will soon be enveloped in those needs again. But instead of resenting the lack of "me time," I'll revel in every minute with my kids!

For a week.

This video has no fears for me. My trembling fingers press the "Play" button.

Three beloved faces, beaming at me bravely. They take turns to speak, telling me how much they miss me, how they watch the video that I sent them every day. "We watch you...," begins Jonathan, and then there's a funny blip in the video; his voice is cut off mid-sentence and chimes in again on a different subject. I pause the video and replay it, approaching the screen to peer myopically at each face, but I can't figure out the reason why the video might have been cut. My little boy looks like he's been crying. I touch his face on the screen. My daughter's sweet, anxious eyes.

They tell me what they've been doing. They assure me they're spending tons of time with the goats, practising their instruments. All the things I nag them about on a daily basis are now achieved without a word from me.

Duh.

My husband stands close to the camera. "I worry about you so much. Kassem's a fucking terrorist."

If this was censored, how come they left that in?

And what did they take out, that was worse than that?

And does everyone know I've been kidnapped by Kassem?

Perhaps he signed his name by mistake when he sent the video.

My husband's chin wobbles as he struggles to control himself. "Be careful, Charlotte. This is a man who doesn't hesitate to use chemical weapons against his own people. Barrel bombs."

'I'm not so sure it was his army who used chemical weapons,' I want to say to him. 'And don't swear in front of the children.' But of course I can't say anything.

They don't say a word about whether Canada or Israel are doing anything to get me out. Well, obviously they wouldn't on a tape that my captor is going to see, but it stands to reason that some type of negotiation is going on at least. Visions of Entebbe and the Sabena Flight dance through my head. Come on Israel!

My children tell me that my mother and siblings want to speak to me too. They start to say their goodbyes; "We miss you, Eema, we miss you!" they chorus. And then it happens; first my son's face crumples, then my daughter's.

"You promised you wouldn't," cuts in the irritated voice of my husband, himself fighting tears. "We're fine, Charlotte! You mustn't worry about us. We are counting the days until you come home, but we're fine!"

"We're great," call the voices of my children, as tears stream down their faces and mine.

Then my mother comes on. At least she won't cry; her tear ducts dried up long ago, "from all the crying I did when I was young," she claims. She says the same sorts of comforting things that the others said: that I mustn't worry, everyone is fine.

I must include a message to her on my next video, my beloved mother. Then my siblings, one after the other, with the heads of their children poking above their shoulders. They are all thinking and praying for me.

I play the video again and again, all day long. Frame by frame, watching the faces of my children crumple.

Then I make another video for them; I direct the camera at the television so they can see their own faces on it. "See?" I tell them. "I got it and I watched it a hundred times. Even though I'm being treated so well I still miss you terribly and your video is going to help me so much! There's only seventeen days left to go. By the time you get this, it'll only be a couple of weeks. Just enough time for you to make me one more video." I smile widely at the camera, nodding my head vehemently. Will the videos still evoke the same concoction of grief and happiness when I watch them in a nursing home at the end of my life? Perhaps. They will certainly be amongst my most-prized possessions.

Inshallah.

It is harder to know what to say, second time around. I've told them all about my routine and showed them my digs. I tell them there's a reason why this has happened, that perhaps destiny spawned my imprisonment. I am here to help with the situation. Worried about censorship, I choose my words carefully: "My captor really seems to listen to me; I believe I can shift his perspective just a little. He is open to it, which is pretty incredible when you think about it. How many dictators would be capable of listening to different perspectives? Perhaps I will help to influence him to hold real elections and to abide by the results."

Flattery, in case he listens to the video before sending it off. But truth also.

I talk to my mother, knowing it is worse for her than it is for me. I would ten times rather be tortured than know my child was. I assure her again and again that I'm happy. I send love to my siblings, ending with a complicated structure of blown kisses and love, which I have to redo and edit several times, to make sure that the amount of affection and kisses is exactly the same for each person. It's exhausting. It's therapeutic. It brings home the bottomless-pit demands and needs of my large family. How everyone wants a piece of me, with barely enough pieces to go around.

That's how you feel.

Yes. It's just my feeling.

KASSEM COMES PRECISELY AT 7:00. He is wearing a white t-shirt instead of his usual suit, and it contrasts with the darkness of his skin and stretches over his chest enticingly. He holds out his arms. "Isn't it a Western custom to hug? That is a good custom."

I hesitate. It might not be such a great custom if the majority of one's time is spent in sordid fantasies where potential hugger's penis is rammed into every existing orifice.

"Come Charlotte, we're old friends now, aren't we?"

I give him a peremptory hug and retreat. I have to stay away from that broad chest.

He smiles at me, his eyes flicking down my shapeless dress. "I wish I hadn't brought you those dresses. You never wear anything else."

"They're totally comfortable and airy and I love them."

Plus they keep you safe.

"Don't you want to look attractive for me?" He's still standing about two feet away, his chest at eye-level.

"Why do you ask that?" *And all the ladies go moist...*

"You act like you do." He hesitates, peering at my face. Which possibly looks horrified at the idea that my current pervy train of thought might be written there.

Pathetic.

Textbook ordinary, actually. Many prisoners lust after their captors. So fuck you.

"You make up your face. You... look at me sometimes..."

My mind jumps about in search of a safer subject. Despite the content of my daydreams, any hint that he wants *real* sex with me is scary.

Logical.

Mm-hmm.

Sane.

Shut up.

"Today I suddenly remembered something I heard on the CBC. About barrel bombs. You're dropping them all over the place and killing tons of civilians."

He rolls his eyes and drops into his usual chair. As if on cue, Sami appears with a tray holding two steaming cups of Nescafé, sugar, cream, and a covered dish.

"The army uses bullets, missiles, bombs. I haven't heard of barrels or cooking pots either."

He smiles as if this is a good joke. It's not.

"Kassem," I say, leaning forward and gazing directly into his eyes. "I'm not going to ask you if you're telling the truth, because that would be futile. But *you* know whether you're telling the truth. *You* know what type of person you want to be. *You...*"

Kassem shrugs irritably, leaning forward to pour cream in the two cups. I sniff surreptitiously, to divine what's hidden in the covered dish.

"Truth," he sneers. "There is no truth. The rebels have one truth, and I have another. Didn't you say it's all a matter of perspective?"

The covered dish loses its appeal. "Whether you're dropping barrel bombs or not isn't a matter of perspective. You either are or you aren't. I just wish you wouldn't lie to me. What's the fucking point of lying to me? I'm going to find out the truth in a couple of weeks anyway..."

unless he's lying about...

He's not. Not about that. Shut up.

"Calm down, Charlotte. To your knowledge, have I lied to you?"

I shake my head.

"So you must give me the benefit of the doubt."

"But you once said everyone lies."

"Of course they do." He hands me a mug of coffee and I sip. It has exactly the right amount of sugar and cream.

"You're probably right about that. The only reason I tell the truth is because my internal filters are aberrant."

Kassem looks puzzled.

As well he might.

"You know, internal filters—the ones that let you know what's appropriate to say and what's not. Mine are aberrant. So out comes verbal vomit."

Now he looks totally bewildered, so I explain about verbal vomit.

"Also, I don't see the point of lies. What's the point of communication if you're going to lie? What's the point of having a relationship with someone if you can't believe anything they say?"

"It seems to me that you're lying right now when you say that. Nobody tells the truth all the time."

"Unless they're always caught when they lie, like me." I smile at him, even though he's pissing me off.

Because he should understand you after these intimate weeks together.

"It's not a *merit*; I can't help it. There's this Little Looney-tunes…"

Puzzled again, but I can't be bothered to explain. "I *know* everybody lies sometimes. The point I'm trying to make is, one shouldn't lie mindlessly. There has to be a good reason, just like when you do harm. So if you're using barrel bombs, why would you lie to me? It's just you and me. You can explain why. Maybe your explanation will convince me that you have to do it. Alternatively, maybe your explanation won't convince you; then you can either stop, or continue, knowing that you're doing harm without justification. That's the point of using our brains and thinking about what we're doing and why—to ensure that it makes sense. Or not. At least if we're doing something terrible we're not lying to ourselves."

So long as we're not insane.

"That's the difference between us and the animals."

"I'm not using barrel bombs, Charlotte."

Fine. I lean forward and lift the cover off the dish. Ten squares, each one different. Chocolate, vanilla, carrot, nut. I pick one up and nibble. Raisin?

"You've heard so much about the terrible things I'm doing; do they also tell you what ISIS is doing?" He launches into a diatribe against ISIS, reeling off stats about their victims and other crimes. A blow-by-blow account of a recent battle, where his troops were apparently victorious. I nibble a coconut square and watch his animated face.

As soon as he pauses, I slip in. "ISIS is totally nuts. Do you think hurt pride plays a role in all this—the Arab world wants to rise up and stake out a huge caliphate because the West has had the power for too long? Like the Germans in the Second World War? Humiliated by the First World War and seeking to restore pride?"

Kassem thumps his own chest. "I am the Arab world. They are fighting their own. ISIS are wicked animals."

"Still, wouldn't it be nice to hear their perspective? I mean, there must be some intelligent, rational people who support ISIS."

"There are none," he bellows. "They are all insane."

I feel it is wise to drop the subject. I offer him a cream cheese square, assuring him that they're absolutely delicious. I don't think I've ever had one before.

"What did you do today?" he asks, mollified by my attentions.

I proudly present him with the edited/censored/oft-viewed video.

"That was quick," he says and glances at his watch.

NOOOOOOOOOOOOOOOOOOOOOOOOOOOO.

"I must go."

How to keep him?

Stick your tongue down his throat? NOT.

I run to him and hug him, burying my face in that broad chest. "I'm so lonely," I say.

He squeezes me back. Tightly. "Charlotte. Let me bring in a woman companion. Or an animal."

I draw back. "Sorry. I know it's not for much longer. It's good for me to be alone like this—I'll appreciate my family infinitely more than I did before as a result."

He pulls me back against his chest and presses his lips against the top of my head. "Charlotte. Charlotte."

I can feel heat spreading up my neck. He smells so good.

And he'll love fucking you. He won't want to let you go. Then he'll get sick of fucking you. So he'll bring in some friends because it's

89

titillating to watch them fuck you, and after all you're just another western whore who spreads her legs to anybody...

I slide my hands up his chest, preliminary to pushing him away. He slides his hands down to my bottom at the same time and squeezes gently.

I still push him away, but gently. More a nudge, really.

"Charlotte."

I shake my head and turn away.

He leaves quietly. I read my diary. Mark off another day in the calendar.

NOVEMBER 28

"Show me your cunt," he says, sitting in his usual chair, coffee cup in hand.

"No fucking way."

He leans forward, smiling. "I'm afraid there's no choice, this time. We can do this pleasantly, or by force."

"Do what pleasantly? Display my cunt? It looks the same as every other cunt. Look at your wife's cunt, if you want to see one."

"But I want to see yours," he says. He stands and smiles down at me. Leisurely, slowly, never breaking eye contact, he unbuttons his shirt and lets it fall to the ground. He unbuckles his belt. Unzips his pants. I keep my eyes rigidly on his. He stands there, proudly. "Look," he says, and glances down. As soon as my eyes are released, they skate down his tall, muscular torso. His jutting penis. A languid, heavy throb pulses between my legs.

"Now you," he says. "You never wear underwear, do you? Just hitch up your tent a little, and spread your legs."

Slowly, incrementally, I begin to inch the fabric up. His eyes are riveted below; his penis yearns toward the sky. He is so beautiful. My sex convulses as I expose it to his eyes, as though it's a bashful, yearning virgin. I lift the tent up, pinching my nipples to make them hard as I pull the dress over my head.

For a second he gazes at all of me; then he's on top of me; his hands and tongue travel and burrow; my own fingers glide over his body, caressing the smooth muscles. He pushes in and groans, pausing for a second with eyes closed. It always surprises me, this demonstration of the intensity of a man's pleasure. They must be feeling something a lot fucking better than what I'm feeling.

Then he's thrusting and that delightful little spot inside kindles to life, and I forget my penis envy and hold my breath and focus. His thrusts become stronger, and I feel a familiar tug of anxiety.

Oi va voi if he comes before you do.

Suddenly I jerk awake; the sheet is twisted around my body, holding me down. Sweat coats my skin. I tentatively touch my wet vagina and come within minutes. God almighty. These fucking dreams are killing me.

NOVEMBER 28: LATER ON

Getting a little obsessed here. Probably because I'm in solitary confinement.

You're probably ovulating.

But why shouldn't I make love to him?

What?

What difference does it make? It will only make him like me more. It feels like years since anybody's touched me. It'll calm me down.

Not as well as dope. Stick to dreaming your foully sexist fantasies, where the men are rapists and...

Oh, shut up. But you're right, what am I thinking? Practise what I fucking preach. I'll do harm if I make love to Kassem—harm to my husband. My marriage will fall apart, and then my kids will be harmed. And for what? For a transitory desire? What am I, an animal, locked mindlessly to my biological urges? Use the old brain and control yourself. If it causes harm, there is no question.

None.

NOVEMBER 28: 9:30 P.M.

Kassem has just left. ISIS has launched another offensive and he talked obsessively about it the whole time.

"Don't you see I'm the only reasonable option here?" he roared. "You bleat about barrel bombs: American atrocities are the reason why ISIS exists! You don't know how the Americans behaved in Iraq because your media lies. Indiscriminate killing of innocent civilians; trigger-happy soldiers who see every dark-skinned Muslim as the enemy. Midnight house raids, arbitrary arrests and detentions, unprovoked beatings. The Iraqis were glad to get rid of Saddam Hussein—for about six weeks. Then they realized that security and safety were worse under the Americans."

"Why are we talking about Iraq?"

"Because Iraq was the seed that grew ISIS. Because everyone does terrible things in a war. Maybe I have done terrible things, but this is my war and I am directly threatened. The only threat to the West is an interruption in the flow of their oil."

He is pacing back and forth. I have never seen him so angry. "It is the American's fault that the ranks of ISIS swell daily! What are they even doing here?"

Yeah, that's always puzzled me too.

"Who appointed them guardians of the Middle East? They're bullies, imposing their political system by force on the rest of the world. It's like colonialism all over again. We're better, be like us, or else. They're screwing up the entire region, just like they did in South America. They never learn. They cause chaos and mayhem and then turn around and blame it all on the Muslims."

He stops to pant for breath. I look at him with sympathy. Who do those fucking Americans think they are?

It's a terrible burden, seeing everyone's point of view.

You're telling me.

Especially if you're a Sieve-Brain and incapable of remembering the last point of view you heard.

Your point being?

Just don't forget that this is a dictator who massacres and tortures his own people without compunction.

"At least in America they don't murder...," I begin, then stop. They've already bopped off four of their presidents, and didn't I read somewhere that every president's life has been threatened with assassination since Kennedy?

"Are you listening?" Kassem has pushed his face so close I can see his blackheads. "What other option is there, besides me?"

I might be a Sieve-Brain, but I'm pretty sure there's a lack of candidates in the Noble Rebel Leader category. "If the choice was just between you or ISIS…," I begin.

"That is the choice!" he shouts. He stands straight, removing his blackheads from my perusal. He smooths his hair, trying to calm himself.

"I have to go now," he says. "I am sorry to get so angry. It is hard to watch a bully from the other side of the world destroy your country."

He exits with dignity.

"Typical hubris," I say conversationally to Voice, nabbing the last of the salted almonds before Sami arrives to clear away the tray. "Nothing that happens is their fault. One of the debilitating effects of too much power. Very common. Mussolini had it, Hitler, Margaret Thatcher, Woodrow Wilson…"

Yes, yes. I heard the same CBC program, oddly enough. At least his tirade meant there was no temptation.

Yeah, thank goodness. Though his blackheads did kinda turn me on…

I spend the last few minutes of the day working on another video for my family. I show them their own faces on my TV screen. Me watching them. I tell them I watch it every day. I kiss their faces on the screen, so they'll see me doing it on their screen. Kind of weird. Only a couple of weeks to go now, I tell them. No time at all! They've been at camp for longer than that.

I mark off another day in my calendar.

NOVEMBER 30: 10:00 P.M.

Kassem continues to rabbit on about ISIS. God, those ISIS people are nuts. But if I believe that in order to get to the truth you have to understand the perspective of the "other," then doesn't that mean that if I met a rational, intelligent ISIS supporter, his perspective would enlighten me? Nazis too? No, there's a limit to this perspective idea. If you have a leader who is a charismatic nut, then the crowd follows. Crowds don't think. So you have a nut and animals. Sometimes that's all there is.

I must remember to tell Kassem that the perspective idea only applies to individuals, not crowds.

So many new ideas popping out of that Sieve-Brain!

Well, there's so much time to think here.

But I can't help smiling. It's true; I've never spent so much time pondering the meaning of life.

And never hoped so deeply that such meaning exists.

DECEMBER 1

I've been smiling all day. The month has changed—it's December! Twelve more days!

On the 12th day of Christmas,
My true love bought for me:
Twelve family members,
Eleven in-flight whiskies…

Twelve family members?

Yeah, duh. One mother, one brother, one sister, one husband, two kids, two goats, three sheep, and a cat. Twelve, not counting the chickens.

Right. Duh.

DECEMBER 3

Kassem has just told me about another ISIS atrocity.

I listen to him with sympathy. It is terrible; I feel sorry, but also helpless. There's nothing I can do about ISIS, so I don't really want to hear about it. Why does he tell me? So that his own actions will be exonerated because theirs are so much worse?

"Charlotte, you are a thousand miles away."

"I'm listening intently, actually," I reply, miffed. I had been focusing on him completely for once—my mind hadn't slipped to gyrating-on-penis thoughts for a single second. "I just don't know what to say. I can't help, so I feel helpless. It doesn't sound like things are going too well for you." I lean forward to cover his hand with mine.

Aww, you care if he's ousted.

I don't want him ousted if he's going to morph into a good person.

under your tutelage.

Well, he wasn't doing very well on his own.

I stop abruptly. Kassem has taken my hand and is kissing it with great passion. I regard the usual rise in my body's temperature with indulgence. Silly body. Lucky brain's in control. He is pouring kisses along my arm, rising slowly to his feet as he reaches my shoulder; he pulls away the fabric of my tent so he can access my skin. I try to rise, but he pushes me back down. Panic balloons in my chest and I fling myself to the other side of the bed, scrabbling to my feet and facing him with clenched fists.

"Let me," he says, advancing steadily. I jump away and snatch up the nearest thing to hand: the remote control.

"I'll brain you if you don't stand still," I shout, in case he thought I wanted to watch a movie with him.

He stops. "I know you want me," he whispers. "I want you too."

He knows.

What's to know?

About your revolting dreams.

Oh bull. He can't see in my head, can he?

You read your journal out loud every night.

Shit. *Fuck.* No, you're wrong. He's running a war, for God's sake. The idea that he's got time to watch me doing nothing all day is preposterous. And Sami couldn't tell him because he wouldn't know what I was reading.

"I only want you in my head," I say, brandishing the remote control. "Not really."

Technically you want him in your body.

"Charlotte," he says indulgently, "what's the difference?"

"Sit down," I cry, and he hears the desperation in my voice and perches on the bed.

"Come and sit by me so we can talk," he invites, patting the sheet.

"Listen Kassem, I promise you the only thing I feel is fear when you do that."

"Do what?"

"Come at me like that." I sit in his chair, remote at the ready.

"Why? You know I'd never hurt you. I would only do what you wanted me to do," he says tenderly.

I try to think of what to say so he'll understand. "Whatever you think I might be imagining in the privacy of my own room," I say, quelling the sarcasm in the word *privacy*, "the reality is that I'm married and have no intention of making love to you. My husband would divorce me and it would fuck up my kids."

Good moral decision. But why the fear?

"But Charlotte, he would never know."

"I would know."

He hesitates. Rubs his knee. "Can we just lie here together, fully dressed? Will you let me stroke your hair?"

My whole touch-deprived body screams *yes*. That would be so very nice.

But why the fear?

"The thing is, Kassem, I'm a prisoner, and you're my jailor." I speak slowly, working it out in my mind as I go along. "It's only your feelings for me that prevent you from… hurting me. Making love might change your feelings."

"It will make them stronger!"

"I don't want them to be stronger! I'm leaving in two weeks!"

He jumps to his feet and so do I, waving the remote like a baton. "Sit down."

"Nothing will change your date of departure, Charlotte," he says quietly, sitting.

But why the fear?

"I hope you like and respect me, Kassem, but you also have absolute power over me. Even good human beings are poisoned by such power. Have you ever seen the movie *Quills*? It's about the Marquis de Sade and there's this priest looking after him." I wrack my brains to remember the movie. "The priest is a very gentle man, but he wants the Marquis to stop writing porn, and the Marquis is a prisoner in his power. The Marquis refuses to stop writing, so the priest goes to greater and greater extremes to force him to his will. He takes away everything, bit by bit, until he's left naked in his cell. But he continues to whisper his stories, so he cuts out his tongue. Because he can. Because he has all the power. Because it is infuriating when someone under your complete power refuses to do what you want."

As I say it, I realize how true it is. Power over others warps and corrupts. Look at Israel.

voilà, the reason for the fear.

"Do I look infuriated?" he asks.

"I believe that when one human being has total control over another, poison sets in. Terrible things happen."

"But Charlotte, because of a film?" he says indulgently.

"Are you kidding? There are a million examples when an authoritative body in power does terrible things to its people. Our Indigenous people. The Black slaves in America. Your regime with its torture. It's all the same thing."

And Israel.

I would never say anything negative about Israel to him, as he probably hates the country. But what better example of the corruptive nature of power? Israel, which started off with such exalted hopes and goals. But the defeated enemy in her midst refused to be cowed; refused to accept any deals, even fair ones, like the Oslo Accords. What are the chances of the Palestinians getting such a fair deal today, when the state of occupation has poisoned once-exalted minds? We have the power, but they still keep trying to kill us. So we show them—build another settlement, steal a little more land, let the poison seep in deeper. But I'm not going to say that to him. A wave of fury rises in me as I look at him. Who is he to criticize Israel? He's not worthy to lick the dirt off Israel's feet.

He's not criticizing Israel, idiot. You are.

Oh right, sorry, got a bit carried away there.

"I don't feel like I'm the one in power at all when I'm with you," he's saying, laughing. "You're the one in control here, I think." He stands up again and for a minute my heart thumps with anxiety, but he's looking at his watch.

"I have to go."

Really? Only time for a five-minute fuck?

He looks right into my eyes. "Even though all my desires are in this room, I have to go away for a few days."

My heart drops. It was so shit last time he went away. I try to keep my voice steady. "Do you know when you'll be back?"

If we'd made love, would he still be going? I walk over to him and place my hands on his chest.

He raises my hands to his lips again. So gentlemanly.

In and out was what he wanted.

I blink my eyes and give myself a little shake. He's sitting on his usual chair. Why did I imagine he'd stood up? I try to focus on what he's saying.

"Do you see how insane they are? Do you see the alternative to my rule?"

I feel discombobulated for a moment. He is still talking about the current ISIS atrocity. Did I doze off? Did I imagine his sexual advances?

Duh. You've been out for at least ten minutes.

So he never tried to fuck me?

Wishful thinking.

Am I going mad?

You just clocked out for a time; don't be too hard on your ovulating self.

I breathe deeply, focusing on his every word. I'm not sure whether this seamless segue into fantasy spells insanity or not, but I'm determined to control the remainder of our meeting.

"I have to travel north for a few days; there is heavy fighting in some of the northern cities and I need to meet with my commanders. Please don't get sad while I'm gone. Promise?"

But didn't he say already say that he was going away?

Nah. That was part of your fantasy. Maybe you are psychic.

Please God, just don't make me crazy. I focus on him with all my mediocre brain for the remaining minutes, as he stands and takes his courteous, completely unsexual leave.

There is no benefit in agonizing over potential insanity in aforementioned fantasy. He's boring, and I take little imaginative breaks, that's all. Ovulation causes those breaks to be sexual.

That's all.

Not mad not mad not mad, please God.

I continue with the rest of my evening routine as though my brain isn't fighting waves of despair at the thought that I might be going mad.

At the thought that he's going away.

Pathetic, I know. I read my diary aloud (omitting the naughty bits) and cross off another day in my calendar. Then I crawl into bed.

Don't think of the next few days. Think Today. Think This Minute, when we stick to our routine.

chapter seven

DECEMBER 5: EVENING.

Stop it already.

What?

Smoking. You've been stoned for two days.

Who cares? What difference could that possibly make to anybody?

You're stupid when you smoke. What about your routine? Learning Arabic? Writing? Exercises? You're eating all the time and getting fat.

Oh, fuck you.

Great, another fuck-you day—we love those. You've only got a few more days. You should be happy!

Just... just. There's only one thing to do when Voice becomes too insistent. Roll another one. Wish I had something stronger.

When I'm at home, Adam is the one who tries to minimize my smoking. Adam. A wave of homesickness engulfs me. We waste so much time criticizing each other over stupid little things, when really we share so many values. Not spoiling the kids. Not wasting. Nurturing nature. He keeps me sane.

I love him.

When I get back, I'm never going to be critical again.

DECEMBER 7: SOME TIME.

For God's sake, get out of that bed!

Voice is right. I feel like shit. Spending the days in a dope-haze isn't working anymore. I have to find another way to keep depression at bay. Back to my routine.

11:00: Wake up. I know it's a bit late, but the luxury of sleeping in—or simply lying there and dreaming—is too rare to give up. Wash face/shower.

11:30: Sami brings breakfast. Read while eating. Hopefully do poo after first cigarette.

12:30: Meditate.

1:30: Exercises—stretch routine and dance.

2:30: Sami brings lunch. Eat while writing events/ thoughts from previous day and up to this point. Do not write about fears of going mad. Little sexual segues are entirely normal when conversational companion is boring.

4:30: Time slot for learning Arabic, though Sami is such a reluctant conversationalist that my only incentive is worthless. There's only a few days left anyway—what's the point?

6:00: Sami brings supper. Start watching movie.

7:00: The Time of Kassem. Currently the Time to Toke. Though sometimes I toke as soon as I get up, in which case my whole routine goes to pot.

Rest of evening: Whatever I like. Write, read, do Sudoku, watch movies.

Fuck him. I hate him! I would have sent another video to my family, if he was here. Maybe I would have gotten one back.

DECEMBER 8: WHO KNOWS WHAT TIME?

It's hard to keep to the routine. I'm talking to myself the whole time like a crazy person. Perhaps I should just smoke and zone out.

or practise a conversation to have with Sami.

I don't feel like I have the energy. There is no energy at all; what if it never comes back?

You have to do something to get energy.

I repress my "fuck you." This *is not* a fuck-you day. This is a day when I'm sticking to my routine. There's only a few days left. Soon I'll be inundated with people.

Better practise talking to them, then.

I pick up my Arabic books diligently. When Sami comes in, I'll be ready.

He knocks at the door at precisely 6:00 and is greeted by a massive grin. Doesn't matter what I do, he always looks slightly apprehensive. But I'm ready for him; as he places the tray on my bedside table, I nip around his back and stand firmly in front of the open door, dictionary in hand. He whips around, sporting the same apprehensive expression he had when I was smiling at him.

"Kayf halik?"

"'Inna bikhayr."

"Kayf hal eayilatik?"

"Hum 'aydaan."

Great; he's well and so's his family. Riveting fucking conversation. No wonder he's trying to edge around me to the door, without touching.

"When is he coming back?" I ask abruptly (or some vague approximation of the question).

Sami shrugs and almost pushes out the door.

That went well.

DECEMBER 9

Two days left. Two days left. Two days left. Two days left. (What if he doesn't come back before I leave?)

DECEMBER 10

I'm going to persuade Sami to give me a special last meal. I spend all day wrestling with the dictionary and pounce on him as soon as he's set the tray down on my bedside table.

"Ahda eshr min Disambir," I enunciate slowly into his anxious face, holding up ten fingers and then one more, to emphasize the eleventh of December.

"Taem… for food," I pantomime eating.

Really, you've made so little progress. Pity. You'll probably never have such a lot of free time again until you're too decrepit to enjoy it.

I love it when Voice is nasty. It means I'm not depressed.

"French fries," I say in recently memorized Arabic. "Tabbouleh; humus; more salads; a whole fish—half fried and half grilled. For dessert: baklava, cinnamon buns, chocolate."

Sami looks a bit stunned. I hope he's getting this. I nod vigorously, indicating I've finished. He nods back, then opens his mouth to let out a flood of Arabic. It's my turn to be stunned—Sami is talking to me! Anxiously, I listen for the words I've just said, but he's not talking about fish. I get "Kassem yaeud": that means he's coming! And "yawm ghad"— doesn't that mean tomorrow?

My face breaks out in a massive grin. I can't help it. Sami grins back and continues to talk. I focus really hard, trying to understand. "Kassem 'akl maeak": Kassem will eat with me tomorrow? No way, man, I want to focus on the food for my special meal. Grab the fish with my hands and tear the flesh off with my teeth and not worry if the sauce smears over my chin.

I pantomime eating again, then hold up six fingers. "Sitta!" I say. I want to eat at six. Before he comes.

Sami looks confused. I bring my hands together in supplication. "Please," I say. "Min fadlik."

I don't know whether he understands. One never knows with Sami— hence my failure to learn Arabic.

Glad he's decided to grace us with his presence one last time.

So am I. Not going to analyze joy in heart.

Glad you still rate food higher than company. Wouldn't want your isolated incarceration to have changed you or anything.

I hate it when people watch me eat. Especially during special meals!

Every night's a special meal.

I have the grace to look sheepish as I lift up the dish cover. Goat kebabs, rice, and salad. Fruit and dates for dessert. Damn, I'm going to miss these meals.

DECEMBER 11

I try to keep to my routine, but I'm just crazy excited all day. When I try to meditate, my mind bops around like an inebriated rabbit. Tomorrow, tomorrow. But also tonight, tonight, let's face it. We won't have a lot of time. I need to clarify the important things that still need to be said, or reiterated:

1. One needs to identify one's basic values in life. For example, do no harm.
2. Once you've identified your values, you need to apply them consciously, every day, to both micro and macro issues. For example, do no harm to individual people nor to the environment.
3. If you try to live your life like that, your values will clarify the best route for you to take, even when the situation is most complicated.

Stop! I'm going to vomit.

4. You have to acknowledge your own limitations. For example, I'm not very sensitive toward others, so I do hurt people without even being aware of it. But I can only do the best I can—and the first step is to be aware of your limitations.

Kassem is so going to know how to apply this to the war. He'll phone up ISIS right away and let them know he's not going to harm them anymore.

5. Good point. What do you do when someone is harming you? How do you resolve this? You have to listen to their perspective.

Give me a break.

6. But you can only do that if their perspective isn't crazy.

That rules out ISIS.

I sigh. Who am I kidding? I'm not influencing Kassem in any way. There's no point searching for a reason why this happened to me. People are suffering all over the world for no reason. It's all crap.

Who cares? I'm going home tomorrow!

DECEMBER 11: LATER

All day, I move around in a fever of excitement. I pack, then unpack. I don't know what time I'm leaving tomorrow, so there's no point in packing stuff like wash things. I talk incessantly to myself, imagining the moment when I first see my children. I will hug them and hug them. All of us will turn into one big hug.

I kiss them. I mash my face into their soft necks. My teenager screams with delight instead of outrage, because she hasn't seen me in a month.

My husband is there too, transformed into an Admiring, Appreciative Partner because he never knew how much I actually did until he had to do it all himself. He'll never call me lazy again. And once I've kissed my family, I go into the barn and my goats rush at me, *meh*-ing in delight. "Abba was crap looking after us," they confide. "He just chucked us our food and didn't scratch us for a minute."

Even the hens perk up.

And that same evening my partner is suddenly transformed into an Endless Oral Sex Lover, because he missed me so damn much and is really grateful I didn't make love to anybody else despite great temptations and loneliness. And great temptations reminds me of all those lovely books, and I carefully select one or two to slip inside my case, just in case I have to lug my carry on over the desert or something. There's a dopey smile on my face; it's been there all day. I can hardly eat; I wish I'd ordered my special meal for an earlier day. Perhaps they will drug me so I sleep? Or blindfold me so I can't see where I am?

I don't care. I'm not frightened of anything. I'm going to see my kids, my kids, my kids!!

I take a long bath, trying to calm my fluttering stomach. I make up carefully and don't analyze my motives.

DECEMBER 11: 6:00 P.M.

Bless Sami. The most gorgeous repast is spread out on the desk by the window. No lying in bed with a book propped between my knees as I eat. I am going to eat in style, as befits such a feast. I pull up my chair and remove the covers, inhaling the splendid aromas. The fish is done to perfection; I clean every bone, meticulously.

Kassem must have consented to your eating alone.

Thank God for small mercies, I say, carefully piling a little salad, a ketchup-drenched French fry, and a chunk of fish on my fork. It's painfully delicious. I'm painfully happy. So fucking happy.

Replete, leaning back in the chair and holding my swollen stomach, I ponder the remains regretfully. Perhaps Sami could give me a little box for the desserts, so I could put them in my carry-on. Erase the last vestiges of worry or distrust as I produce it with a flourish in front of my family: This is what they fed me!

A knock on the door sends me flying into the bathroom to erase the grease stains; then out again, eyes downcast demurely, as he opens his arms for a hug.

"Charlotte," he says with great tenderness.

My heart flutters with pleasure and my tummy lurches with displeasure as Sami brings in yet more covered dishes. And... mint tea. That's the ticket—a nice cup of tea and a cigarette should aid digestion immensely.

"How have you been?" Kassem asks, sitting in his usual chair as I pour the tea.

"Not too bad. What have you been up to?" I pray he doesn't launch into any military details. States of intense excitement just exacerbate the sieve-ness of brain.

"I have been very bad," he says.

I look up in surprise. What has ISIS done this time?

"This is our last night together," he says. Then in one fluid movement, he is pressing his face into my lap and I feel the heat of his breath through the thin fabric of my tent, but it doesn't arouse me; I feel sadness, mixed with affection. I don't care if it's Stockholm syndrome or what, I'm fond of him. I caress his hair and bend down to whisper in his ear. "You are a man who is trying to do the right thing, even at great cost to yourself.

That is a brave thing to do. It is why I believe that you are destined to be a great leader who will bring an end to this war, even if it means the end of your reign over Syria.

He lifts a tragic face. "I can't do it without you."

"You can," I state firmly and tap my nose with my finger. "I'll be checking on you." Immediately, it occurs to me that this is totally possible, in this era of advanced technology. I give his face a little shake with excitement. "We'll keep in touch. We'll do weekly phone calls or something. It's not the end! It's the beginning of your reign as a great leader!"

He pulls back a little. Is he irritated? Why?

Maybe he's sick unto the back teeth with your preaching. As am I.

"You don't think I'm a great leader now? I've told you everything. Haven't you listened?" Tears are actually glistening in his eyes.

I place my hands on each side of his face, very gently. "Kassem, every minute another family is fleeing your country—to the tune of 3.2 million and rising. Over 500,000 men, women, and children have been killed. Why?" I point right in his face. "Because of one man."

WTF?

"I know that you have the seeds of greatness in you. I know you can be a wise leader and hold democratic elections and step down if you lose. But no, waging this war isn't wise. All this death and misery would end if you'd *just disappear*."

He gazes at me owlishly. "If I just 'disappeared,' as you say, complete chaos would ensue."

"The misery will end if you hold real elections, where every Syrian can vote, no matter who they're affiliated with."

"I can't do it without you."

I sigh. It would be so nice to be alone, indulging in fantasies about giant family hugs, rather than dredging up the energy to pretend he's listening to me. "We should work out the next steps, so I know when to contact you. Every time you take a concrete step forward, we'll get together for a chat about it. How does that sound?"

Sounds like a reward system for a dog.

Glistening eyes stare back at me.

"People will call you Saint Kassem—do they have saints in Islam? All you have to do is call elections and be prepared to step down. Then you can devote your life to the environment."

"I will certainly be elected again."

"I dunno, Kassem; every person that dies is one family less voting for you."

Perhaps a little less combative on your last day?

"And every family the rebels or ISIS kill is another one voting for me—and there's a lot more of them."

Yeah, yeah. Tomorrow I'll be googling this stuff, y'know.

I pick up my mint tea and go to stand by the window. I don't know why I don't feel more sympathy for him. Is the twinge of contempt his glistening eyes evoke sexist? God knows I cry enough.

But never to make an impression.

Such uncharitable thoughts. Perhaps fundamentally I'm a horrible person.

I light a cigarette and exhale into the balmy night air. I question him about the plans for the next day: what time am I leaving, what will the trip be like? He replies that he did not arrange the trip himself but entrusted his precious cargo (white teeth flash in my direction) to a commander. He doesn't know if he can come to say a final goodbye tomorrow (thank goodness for that) because the time of departure depends on several factors; I should be ready to go at any minute.

I nod enthusiastically, despite the fact that I'm no wiser than I was before.

Then Kassem is beside me, sliding the cigarette out of my fingers. "Where your lips have touched, so shall mine."

That would be romantic if his nose wasn't red from emotion.

"This is your last night."

I turn my face to his as he lowers it, infinitesimally.

A lurch of excitement churns my stomach as I reach upwards; how will his lips feel on mine?

They brush, gentle as gossamer. I stop breathing, focusing on the feel of his lips against mine. They caress my lips, moving slowly from one corner to the next, then opening slightly and deepening, and it feels so sensual; my lips part to accept him, and a shot of lust travels down my groin, but I don't move, I don't reject him when he moves, pressing the length of his body against mine. Wanting him to press harder and harder until he pierces through.

Then his long, delicate fingers travel under my shirt and up toward my breasts, and the straining contact lessens to make room for his fingers, and I step back.

"No," he murmurs and tries to pull me back, but it's too late; you shouldn't have gone for the breasts Romeo, they're just lumps of flesh and any woman who pretends she gets off when men caress them is just trying to please you.

"Charlotte," he whispers.

"It's enough," I reply, bringing my cigarette, clenched forgotten between tense fingers, to my mouth.

"Enough for whom?" he protests.

Enough to frustrate the hell out of both of you.

"Enough to show my affection and gratitude to you, and to indulge in my great attraction for you, without destroying my marriage."

You sanctimonious...

Kassem wraps his arms around me again, pressing his lips against mine. I don't feel frightened anymore; he would never hurt me. I don't think he is capable of it. So strange: a fundamentally gentle man, responsible for so much death and misery. I slip my hand between our lips, leaning away from him. "It would destroy my family."

"We are alone," he cries. "They will never know!"

He's forgotten about Little Looney-tunes.

"I would know," I say gently, and proffer him the half-smoked cigarette. Tears well up in his eyes again.

can he conjure them at will?

No, they're genuine, you uncompassionate shit.

"I think I love you," he weeps.

Love, desire; they can get so mixed up. I don't feel like I know him. He certainly doesn't know me. He doesn't even believe that I don't lie, let alone that it's not a virtue but rather the result of a mind challenge.

Well, hardly ever lie. I might not tell my husband about this kiss.

Eventually I am able to send him, weeping, on his way.

DECEMBER 12: 6 A.M.

I wake up at the crack of dawn. Didn't sleep a wink.

You snored for hours.

Did Kassem kiss me last night?

At what point does imagination become insanity, would you say?

I'm taking that as a no?

He bent his head toward you at one point...

That's it?

You hugged. Then you started spouting about not destroying your family. He must have realized you were nuts. If he hasn't already.

Man, I need some Adam cock.

I wash, then pack my wash things and dress in the clothes I'd laid out the night before. I sit primly on the side of my bed.

It's 8:00 a.m. Foolishness.

Maybe, but I'm happy sitting here, waiting. I'll wait for as long as it takes.

At 9:00, Sami comes in with my tray. I savour every morsel of the pita, salad, boiled egg, muhamarra, and the thick goat labane that's so delicious.

At 11:00, I take off my travelling clothes and put on my tent to do my workout. My thighs are looking pretty damn good from all this exercise, so the mirror tells me.

Time isn't moving today. The meagre remains of my dope stash beckon seductively, but it's easy to be restrained on the last day.

After lunch, I meditate, thoughts ricocheting off my firmly closed eyelids, and it's so boring I must have fallen asleep, because when I wake up it's almost 5:00. A twinge of anxiety in my gut, but it quickly subsides; obviously, it's better to travel at night.

keep those crazy thoughts at bay.

Gotta stop talking to myself all the time. That's totally looney. It's just because I have nobody else to talk to; once I get home, there will be so many damn people the last thing I'll want to do in my rare alone-moments is talk.

I feel a fuck-you day coming on.

What if Voice can't be shut off? What if I've actually gone a tiny bit insane in here? What if I keep hearing that annoying whine on and on in my head…

Don't worry; they'll pack you off to a shrink first thing.

At 7:00, he comes. My heart cavorts in joy and I smile and smile into his sombre face.

"Is it time to go yet? I'm ready."

For ten hours already.

He collapses into the chair, weeping. Okay, it's sexist, but I feel totally embarrassed for him.

This pathetic boob is running a country?

Where's my compassion? I stand beside him and rub his back. I wish I could fast-forward to when I'm gone already. Surely he's not coming with me? I don't have the energy for this—I want to save my energy for my long journey, for my children. Pull yourself together and act like a man, for God's sake.

"I'll never see you again," he weeps. "I can't do this alone."

Yeah, yeah, whatever.

It's important to hide my irritation and impatience; it's just another man, clutching the last remnants of my attention before he's inevitably shoved out of centre field. Much like he's doing in his country.

"There, there," I murmur mindlessly. Can't we just say our goodbyes already?

"There, there." Pat, pat. "There, there."

He raises his head, his eyes shimmering in turquoise undulations.

"What will I do, without your input into my decisions?"

Give me a fucking break.

I try to speak gently. "Come on, Kassem. Can you point to a single action you've taken as a result of my 'input'?"

Without lying.

"How can you say that? I've told you that I'm thinking differently now. You said that thinking about my actions and making it clear—clarifying—to myself why I'm doing them is a major step… and the result has been different actions on several occasions. If you'd shown interest in recent events of the war…"

"I've listened endlessly to you…"

"I'll show you!" he cries, shouting through the door in Arabic.

Within minutes, a guard has appeared with a laptop in his hand, closely followed by Sami with the tray. We're having tea? I'm not sure how much more of this bullshit I can take.

Kassem's slender fingers are slithering over the keyboard. I stand beside him, jumping a little as he shouts, "Look!"

"Kassem has finally allowed humanitarian aid into the besieged city of Eleppy," says the BBC reporter. "Thousands of near-starving people lined up in an orderly manner to receive food and medical supplies."

I could kiss the feet of that clipped, British voice.

But Kassem is already moving on, double-clicking on another icon; he has pasted these video clips to his desktop. But it's not like he could fake a BBC reporter, is it?

CNN. "Kassem has always denied the use of barrel bombs, but now he's promising to punish his own soldiers if they are used in any capacity…"

I restrain the urge to burst into song,

Hello to Nova Scotia the sea-bound coast,
Let your mountains dark and dreary be,
Since I've been away on the briny ocean tossed,
Have you ever heaved a sigh and a thought for me?

He's playing another video clip, so he doesn't notice my eyes fill with sentimental tears. I'm glad he's trying to be good, truly I am, but he's picked the worst possible hour to ask for my attention. He's already fading into my past.

He jabs toward the screen, and I try to focus. No way, is that the CBC? The silly tears spill onto my cheeks. "Kassem has been discussing the possibility of negotiating a cease-fire with the leaders of the rebels, through an American/Russian combined approach…"

This is truly remarkable, and little boys must be endlessly praised to continue to be good. My finger slides under his chin and urges his wet, turquoise gaze upwards. "I'm so proud of you," I whisper and bend to brush his lips.

He leaps to his feet (but not before carefully shutting off the video stream) and clasps me in his arms. "You see? Now you believe? You are changing me. Because of you."

I hug him back, full of affection and pride. I was right about him all along.

Yessiree, you never doubted for an instant.

"I am so glad to have spent this month with you," I whisper. "Thank you for your rare capacity to grow and change as a human being."

"You are changing me as a human being. I cannot lose you. I can't do the right thing alone."

I pull back a little, so I can gaze into those beautiful blue eyes.

Hopefully for the last time.

"First of all, you can do this without me. You've already started, and look at how the whole world watches and commends you! Second, why shouldn't we stay in contact? We just have to pick up the phone."

"It's not the same."

As when you're enslaved in a cell.

"What time am I scheduled to leave, anyway?"

"Charlotte," he says more insistently, "please listen to me. I have proved that your influence is making a difference—a huge difference. I need you. To stay on this path."

Suddenly, I get it. Was I being deliberately stupid? It's hard to describe this sudden feeling: like a python has wrapped its coils around my heart. It makes for difficult breathing, so I open my mouth a little.

Don't panic.

"Kassem," I say, as gently as I can, "I am leaving tonight. You promised. If you force me to stay, all trust will be extinguished, forever. And all influence with it."

"Just a few more weeks," he cries wildly. "You claim that you live according to your principles; can you forsake—can you harm a whole nation, by leaving too soon?"

Stay calm. Stay calm.

"It's not my physical presence here that's making the difference—it's our conversations. We can talk on the phone. Every day if you like. I will commit to meeting you once a year, or more if you feel you need it. We can arrange a neutral meeting place through the Russians. I promise it." I stare him in the eyes. "I never renege on my promises."

"I agree to that," he says. "I trust you. Now try and trust me. I swear by Allah that I will let you go in another two weeks. Two weeks is all I ask—is that so much? When we're making such headway?"

A rage of violence so intense that I clench my hands, so as not to bash his treacherous face, rip his flesh with my teeth, penetrate his eyeballs with the tines of my fork.

"I can't stay within these four walls a minute longer," I scream, shoving him away with all my strength, so that he stumbles over the edge of the chair and almost falls, casting him away so I don't try to kill him and lose any possible chance of escape.

He doesn't get angry. "I'm just asking for another two weeks; it is now that progress is being made—it took time for me to start listening. Really listening." He tries to insert a note of tenderness in his voice, but I'm rocking back and forth on my bed, fighting the panic, which burrows like a weevil into my stomach and cackles that I am here forever, forever, forever; I will never get out.

"Perhaps we could arrange for you to walk outside for an hour a day. Tell me what you need. Try to stick to your own values—helping the Syrian nation toward peace is an important task which Allah has given to you. It would be wrong for you to leave now. It would be a selfish act."

You hypocritical, lying shit.

I cast my eyes to the farthest confines of my prison, whimpering. "I'll go mad if I stay here."

"Two weeks. If you stay, I promise to begin the process of inviting the rebel leaders to talk tomorrow. I will contact the Americans and the Russians."

An image of him trussed like a chicken dances before my eyes. I am sawing off his penis with my dinner knife, and he is writhing and screaming. I shove the bloodied flesh down his throat while his screams morph into gags.

"I will go on the television tomorrow and swear to release you in two weeks. Before the whole world. Then you can believe me and focus on the important job we have to do together."

I eye the teapot that Sami brought in. If I move quickly, can I throw the hot tea directly in his face?

"Talk to me." He crouches beside me so his face is level with mine.

It wouldn't be long before the guards came. I just have one moment of surprise. Adrenalin and rage shoot through me and I jump up and knee him with all my strength—visualizing my knee smashing into his face and snapping his head back, breaking his neck and killing him. That would be as good a way to end the war as any.

But my knee pings off his chest, and he's on his feet in a moment, pinning my arms to my sides and gazing at me sorrowfully; then he's gone and I am all alone.

chapter eight

IMPOSSIBLE TO DESCRIBE THE AGONY. Nothing I've felt up until now compares to this. They were just minor blips of dejection. This is hopeless despair. What can I do? Is there nothing I can control?

control how you deal with this. Remain dignified.

You mean, don't beg? If I thought it would help, I'd beg.

What will help? What might help?

Nothing. Expect nothing from him.

I press my face into my pillow, beneath the sheet so nobody can see me. The pain inside is so bad that I scratch my arm until it bleeds; perhaps one pain will diminish the other. I don't know how I'm going to get through this hour, let alone the day, the week. Why even try? All this pain will end with my death.

That's not worth two more weeks.

It's not going to be two more fucking weeks, cretin.

You don't know that. You can't do that to your family, just in case.

That old argument that has always succeeded in staying my hand during depressions. Suicide is such a selfish act. When people love you, what right do you have to hurt them so deeply?

But that's not relevant now. My family must be suffering because they don't know what's happened to me. Remaining incarcerated will actually do more harm to my family than if they find out I'm dead. It wouldn't be suicide—the ultimate selfish decision to destroy other lives for my own sake. It would be murder.

Unless you'll be free in two weeks.

Despair and rage, rage and despair, course through me all day.

How could I ever have dreamed of this man? He is utterly despicable. I would kill him if I could. As for the Syrian people, I wasn't helping them anyway. He's a liar; I can't believe anything he says.

The anguish inside is unbearable. What should I do?

Take back control.

Then suddenly, I know.

THE DAY IS ENDLESS. Each minute seems like an hour. I try to meditate, write a little. When Sami comes in, I don't look at him, even when he speaks to me. Not even when he lifts the lid off the dishes and the smell escapes.

By mid-afternoon, my stomach is growling in protest. Do the aromas make it harder? Nevertheless, even though my stomach and tongue crave and beseech as though they were alive, it is not hard. The enemy wants me to eat. I can feel it in Sami's hesitation, when he brings in the dinner tray and sees the lunch untouched. In his gentle "mm-mm" as he whisks off the new covers. The anxiety in his voice is fodder to my will. People go on hunger strikes all the time—sometimes for tiny reasons, like keeping a school open or some stupid thing. Surely I can summon the willpower that so many others have rallied for lesser reasons. I'm not fasting in order to gain something; the fasting itself is its own end. I want to die.

At least drink.

And prolong life for weeks?

Two weeks. Just in case.

So when I'm not released in two weeks, I can continue to die?

You'll be halfway there already! Voice says in an encouraging sort of way.

Good point. Plus it seems to me that dying of thirst would be rather unpleasant. By the middle of the twenty-four-hour Yom Kippur fast, one always has a raging headache that effectively prevents one from really feeling sorry about one's sins. Which is supposed to be the point.

I totter into the bathroom and drink greedily. Only water. That's all I'll take.

The minutes tick by. My stomach cajoles. I wrack my brains for memories of things I've read about hunger strikes. Don't organs start disintegrating or being eaten by the body at some point? What point is that? Surely I've read that the first couple of days are the hardest. Just one more day than Yom Kippur. No problem.

My stomach rumbles.

Kassem doesn't come. I wanted him to come and beg me to eat so he would know that he no longer exists for me.

Apart from that, I don't care.

SOMETIME IN THE NIGHT I dig out my calendar and look at all the crossed-out dates. It is December 13th. If he lets me out in two weeks, it'll be after Christmas. My family will suffer through the holiday, because of him. My poor mother. It's so much worse, for those outside.

The crossed-out dates mock me. They are a lie. I shan't cross off the next two weeks, to prevent another lie.

Don't you want to know when the two weeks are up?

Who cares? Nothing matters. Especially my life.

It matters to your daughter. It matters to your son.

I'm one of billions. Human beings are like fungi, like disease. If God came to me and said, hey Charlotte, human greed is driving the climate crisis and the only way the human race can survive is if three billion are wiped out, pronto. I can do this (seeing as I'm God), but your children have gotta die too. I kind of like you, so I'll let you decide.

Would I hesitate? The survival of the human race in return for the insignificant lives of my children? Of course not.

Sorry, I don't get the analogy. Your death won't save anybody; it'll just cause pain.

Dunno what I meant, but it was still an excellent point, so fuck off.

I lower myself back into bed, thankfully. Could twenty-four hours of fasting have damaged my mind already? It feels sluggish and stupid. I fall asleep immediately.

THE NEXT DAY I have a killer headache, even though I'm drinking water. Sieve-Brain vaguely recalls from God-knows-where that the second day of a fast is the worst. One more day before my tummy stops writhing like a live thing, outraged at my indifference. One more day before it succumbs to the inevitable and starts snacking on delicious things like muscle reserves. Yum yum.

Perhaps the days will go faster when that happens. This day refuses to advance. I face the wall as much as I can, hiding from possible surveillance. Staring and staring at the spider cracks in the wall that resemble an armless stick man cavorting. I become intimately acquainted with Stick Man. If I half-close my eyes, his legs pivot back and forth. I derive huge satisfaction from planning every detail of my demise. I will break the mirror in the bathroom. Surely there's no camera in the bathroom; wouldn't Muslims respect a woman's privacy? And they don't even know that I suspect that there's a camera at all, so why would I . choose the bathroom to do something I'm not allowed to do?

And maybe the camera is narcissistic paranoia.

Exactly. So I'll smash the mirror into smithereens. Then I'll yell loudly and totter out of the bathroom, cursing the fact that I fell and broke the mirror. Tumble back into bed, hiding a small piece of mirror in my hand. Face wall. Cover head. Slit wrist. This bit is a little hazy; I hope aggressive sawing isn't required.

At this point, the visualization gets even more pleasurable (though I won't actually be present for it). Sometimes Kassem comes in to talk to me and rolls me over impatiently when I ignore him. Confronted with my staring eyes, he shrieks and tears his hair and rips his clothes, which might be a little Old Testament, but the depth of his grief parallels the depth of my satisfaction, so there has to be a lot of hair-tearing.

Or Sami finds me and screams for help and the entire room is filled with unknown people. And Kassem comes and tears his hair and so on and so forth.

But the dream always ends, and the present seizes my mind like an aggressive cancer.

It would help pass the endless day if I smoked. It would also shift the weight of misery.

But what if it makes me hungrier? Breaks my resolve?

Death frightens me.

I try to meditate; empty my mind. Food intrudes; how this or that would taste on my tongue.

Banish lobster; bring mind back to breathing.

Somehow, the day passes.

Sami brings in trays three times and takes them away untouched. He does not address my shrouded form, though he hesitates beside my bed; I can feel waves of anxiety rolling off his aura. The smells of his increasingly apprehensive offerings are killing me. My mouth fills with saliva. I hold my breath; I shan't make a sound while he's physically with me, even if he can probably listen to my mad mutterings whenever he likes.

Slowly, the room darkens. Then, at some indeterminate point in the evening, he comes. The scrape of the chair as he pulls it closer to the bed. The creak as he sits.

"Now, Charlotte, what do you think you are doing?"

Of course I could always pretend renewed lust, go down on him, and bite his dick off. Might not end the war, but it would certainly put him out of action for a while.

"Do you really think this is a reasonable response to a request for two more weeks?"

His voice drones on. I have no idea what he thinks he'll accomplish. That I'll roll over suddenly and say, "Golly gee Kassy, you're so right! Thank you for showing me the light once again, and please bring me a hamburger with the works."

Ouch. The thought of a hamburger is actually painful.

Then he's grasping my shoulders and trying to roll me toward him. My first instinct is to fight, to bury my face in the sheet and keep it there by force. But that requires a lot of energy, besides being ludicrous. So I go as limp as a ragdoll, and he rolls me over and pulls the sheet down.

"Oh Charlotte," he says. Feeling compassionate, are we? Or horror at the transformation from pretty woman to grey gargoyle? My eyes are lowered; I don't want to see his face.

"Why are you doing this to yourself?"

Right, I'm doing this to myself. Just like the Syrian rebels are destroying the country, all on their own. How to tune him out?

Hum.

He tries to smooth my hair away from my face, awkwardly. I can't stand it. My whole body recoils in disgust; I twist away and wiggle down under my sheet again. He lets me. He begins to talk. Under the sheet, I slide my fingers surreptitiously into my ears and hum softly, like I used to do during nasty bits in movies when I was a kid. It works. I can't hear a thing. I try to hum softly, so as not to aggravate him unnecessarily. I don't know if he can hear above the sound of his own voice. In any case, he eventually gets up to go.

Relief!

IT'S EASIER THE THIRD DAY. Easier still the fourth. It's hard to find the energy to write these few words. I lie here and time slips by, unnoticed. Going to the bathroom becomes an ordeal of planning and effort that wipes me out for several hours. Luckily, I barely need to go.

Next day. Same as yesterday. Can't write. Nothing to write. I lie here all day. There is little discomfort now. Just a sort of weak peace. Day entwines with night; my eyes are always closed. Even Voice is silent. Kassem has come. Once or twice. I lie with my back to him, face covered, hands in ears, humming inaudibly.

Days have gone by, I think. It is hard to focus. Maybe the mirror idea isn't going to work after all, especially if I have to saw. I don't even know whether the two weeks are up or not.

I think Sami has stopped bringing me food. It is very easy to meditate now. I lie here and think of nothing.

Sleep. I have always loved sleeping.

I didn't think I would die like this. It's not so bad. I'm not frightened. I *loved* life. But it does go on and on...

How many days have passed? I slip in and out of sleep.

TODAY I MUST RECORD. Something different. He turns me over by force and gets on top of me, straddling my hips.

Rape me, I think listlessly. I don't care. You cannot touch my mind, and my body's already fucked.

I note objectively that my breath must smell like rotting sewage. Nothing really matters anymore when you are dying. You regard the endless vanities of your previous life with fond contempt. If he releases me when the two weeks are over and I begin to eat again, will all the vanities return in full force? Or am I wiser now?

Wiser? Truly, all is vanity.

He mushes his wet face against mine and whispers things like "please Charlotte, don't do this." My mind meanders and I almost forget the moist cheek pressed against mine, until he mouths something so hideous I turn him off like a faucet. I begin to hum, even though I can't wiggle my fingers into my ears.

"Your children can see you."

How despicable he is!

Then his head rears up and he shouts down at me and my humming can't block his words. "You have to stop this! The Americans have upped the ante…"

I can't follow what he's saying. I hum louder.

"They're bombing me!" he shouts. "Thousands of people are dying."

Excellent. Hopefully I'll join the club.

"All because of you!" he screams. He's hurting my head.

He presses my face between his hands. "Do you understand what I'm saying? If you're unable to respond we'll have to force-feed you. Do you hear me?"

Yes, I can hear that. I can imagine that. Tied down, tubes. Horrible. After all this effort, to be force-fed? To have to start all over again with those awful first days?

Pretend interest.

Bingo. Then use the mirror as soon as he's gone. He's capable of anything; I see that now. I have always believed that if you speak rationally to a neurologically normal human being, they will be able to understand your point of view on any given topic (unless they have strong emotions about said topic, which unfortunately undermines logic). But too much power undermines the neurological soundness of a human mind. Occupation corrupts, just like in the movie *Quills*. This man has been corrupted by his own power and he would murder my soul without compunction.

Pretend interest.

"Why?" I whisper, my voice rusty and painful. "Don't they consider ISIS to be the greatest threat anymore?"

"Apparently not."

"What evil have you perpetrated," I hiss, my hoarse voice laced with venomous loathing.

He hears it too; I can hear the shock in his voice. "I have done nothing—nothing!"

I make an effort to open my eyes and look at him properly. "Then why? Tell me the truth."

"Because of you," he says. "Well, partly because of you. That's why you must eat. If you don't care that thousands of people are dying, then think of your children. Who are watching us right now."

You wicked fuck.

Pretend.

Okay. I'll pretend he's not insane. I smile at him indulgently. "That's nice. Can you see them? Aren't they good-looking kids?"

He leverages himself to a sitting position and frowns down at me. "I can't see them," he enunciates very slowly, "because there isn't a camera on them."

He's looking at me like I'm the one who's mad. I have to play this carefully; if he thinks my mind is gone, he'll force-feed me.

"There is a camera behind this wall." He indicates the wall behind him, where I have always imagined the camera to be.

"I know," I say, but he looks worried again so I hasten on. "I knew there must be a camera somewhere. Bound to be."

Relief flits across his face. I'm saying the right thing. Wish I didn't have to make the fucking effort, because I'm desperate to sleep. If hatred could spontaneously combust.

"Good," he says, levering himself onto the side of the bed and taking my hand in his. It looks so small and shriveled and wrinkled in his giant palm. "You're halfway there. Can I get you some tea while I explain?"

Oh—tea! With a little bit of milk and sugar. I'm not sure I have any saliva left to flow into my mouth, but something perks up in there.

"Sami!" he shouts.

Technically it's not allowed, but...

"What day is it?" I whisper.

"December 24th. Merry Christmas."

Two more days. If it had been the day of my supposed release, or after, I could have had tea to give me the strength to break the mirror. But if I have three more days, then what if the tea wakes my stomach up and it starts baying for food again? Unbearable thought, when we've finally come to an understanding. I feed it a bit of tasty muscle and it keeps mum.

"Just water," I murmur, and he holds the glass to my lips.

"So let me start from the beginning. There are people in my employ whose job it is to keep on top of everything that's written about Syria in the West. So they checked out your book and were immersed in a story of a Syrian family written by an author who had never been in Syria. Since most of the facts in your book seemed to be based on the truth, we wondered where the 'fictitious' elements came from. Why did Rana possess so many characteristics of my sister? And the death of the dictator. Could it be that you had some ability to see the future? I have known people with such power."

I fight the urge to close my eyes.

"I would never have followed up on this curiosity, except you conveniently came to the Middle East for a holiday, and it was so easy to arrange to have a chat with you. I thought a chat would be the end of it, truly. So I brought you to this nice room, where we keep our most important guests."

Prisoners.

"The camera is here for security purposes only, so the guards can glance at our... guests every now and then to make sure everything's okay. But then there was a massive international outcry."

He leaps to his feet suddenly and begins to pace. I close my eyes.

"The racism of the West! What happens to white people is so much more important than what happens to brown people!"

There he goes, off on a rant.

The next thing I know, he's shaking me by the shoulder. "Can you hear me, can you understand me?"

"Yes," I rasp, "I just closed my eyes for a minute."

You were snoring.

"I was talking of our first meetings, and how I soon realized you weren't psychic. So why didn't I let you go?" He pulls the chair close to the bed and leans over me. His breath on my face sickens me. "The reaction of the West when you were kidnapped angered me; all the speculations about the terrible things happening to you. I saw a chance to show them how racist they really are.

"So I uploaded some of the content of the camera onto the web, so they could see you were being wined and dined like an honoured guest."

There is a pause, as though he expects a reaction. He doesn't seem to realize I'm busy dying.

Or maybe he's finished. Excellent. Soon I'll be nipping into the bathroom and breaking Mr. Mirror.

Sami sidles in with the tea tray. It's pretty obvious that I'm not going to pour it, so Kassem waits until Sami has gone and then fills his own cup.

"I'm not sure how it happened, but there was... avid interest. Right away, many viewers. Within days, millions."

No wait, don't I have to wait three more days to use Mr. Mirror? I'm confused.

"At first, I just played them one clip to shut them up. But during my first few visits, you kept saying things that made me realize how falsely I'd been painted in the Western media. I wanted to set the record straight, and when I saw how many people had viewed the first video clip, I thought of a great way to insert my voice into millions of homes. My perspective, as you would call it." He smiles at me.

I smile back, still trying to work out whether I'm allowed to kill myself today or whether I have to wait.

"So I began to show them the tapes of our meetings, so I could convince them—and you—that I am the only way to peace. Are you still listening?" He shakes my arm gently.

"You showed them tapes," I repeat automatically, then stiffen as his meaning sinks in. I think of him talking and talking about the war, his role, his thoughts. I remember wondering why he cared so much for my good opinion. But he wasn't interested in my opinion at all. It was the world's opinion that he was aiming for.

Lies, all lies.

"I began to explain the situation as it really is, to counteract the lies their media are telling them."

I remember those conversations, bewildered at the trust he seemed to place in me. Filled with wonder that my opinion seemed so important to him.

"I also think your diaries kept them entertained." He smiles at me indulgently.

I stare at him blankly. "But I used to read my diary at the end of the day, after you'd gone."

He has the grace to look sheepish. "So many people were watching. So much interest. There was communication too, asking to see more. So I started streaming the video live all the time."

It's hard to grasp what he's saying. What he means.

"Eventually, I hired a professional to do the video. So it wouldn't always be the same view, the same angle."

"Right now?" I whisper.

"Yes," he says. He looks extremely sheepish.

It's preposterous. Who the hell would want to watch someone sitting in a fucking room all day when they have Netflix?

Lies.

Of course. He almost had me there. This is all an elaborate plot to get me to eat.

So that means he really does love you and wants you to admire him?

It makes more sense than millions of people choosing to watch someone in a room.

"I'm tired now."

The sheepish expression disappears. "Do you understand what I'm saying?"

No, unfortunately my stomach's been snacking on my brain.

"Have you been listening?"

And possibly my audial equipment too.

"You don't believe me, do you? Is that it? Look!" He fishes one of those clever phones out of his pocket and hits some buttons, then holds it in front of my face. I squint to focus; my eyes aren't working properly these days. There's me and Kassem.

"Do you see?" he asks tenderly, with a dollop of frustration. He reaches out to touch my cheek. So does the image on his cellphone. He calls out something in Arabic, and the camera pans onto my face. God, I look horrible. I stick my tongue out and wave it around. What a peculiar colour. I'm on his phone, all right, he's definitely proven that.

But millions of people? Mad as a hatter.

But then why spill his guts every night?

Because he likes me. I can't bear to let go of that belief, even though I'd kill him if I got the chance. Not that I really care; it's just, I don't know what the fuck's going on. I don't know if it's because I'm starving or because of Sieve-Brain, but I can't handle all this new information.

"I want to sleep." The face on the camera looks like it's going to burst into tears.

"Will you eat something now?" Kassem asks, and the camera pans out to include the two of us again.

I'm confused. What's changed? "I am going to eat in three days when you let me go." I can barely hear my own voice. Desperation mantles my chest. Why won't he go already? I'm so fucking exhausted.

"You need to eat now."

I watch him fearfully. Is he going to force-feed me?

"Don't you understand? Your children are watching you right now! How do you think they feel, watching their mother starve before their eyes?" His voice ratchets up a notch or two.

Silly man. As though Adam would let the children see.

"And if you don't care about your children," he says in a voice that implies I'm a rotten mother, "doesn't it matter to you that the Americans have upped the ante? Because you refuse to eat? They're bombing all our positions simultaneously."

I almost smile, despite my exhaustion. The face that launched a thousand ships.

More like the face that lapped a thousand gins.

"People are dying because you refuse to eat!"

His voice is getting quite insistent. Black spots dance on my vision. I long for him to go. Or at least shut up. Infinitesimally, in the absurd hopes that he won't notice, I begin to inch under my sheet.

"So will you eat now?" he asks again.

I wave a languid hand in the direction of the camera. "Because I'm on reality TV? What difference does that make?"

"Because you're starting a war."

What rubbish.

Now he's angry. "What are you not getting?" he shouts.

Ouch. Ouch. My fingers creep toward my ears. If I had the energy, I'd explain. It doesn't matter if he's telling the truth or not, I no longer care what's happening in the fucked-up Middle East. I could barely follow *before* I was half-dead; the U.S. and Russia supposedly allied against ISIS, while Russia continued to bomb Syrian rebels that the U.S. supports. Never mind the enmity between Russia and America's other ally, Turkey; and the fact that both those allies hate the Kurds, allegedly the best fighters against ISIS. So now the U.S. is bombing Kassem. Who cares? Even if a great, united Muslim caliphate rises out of the mess and joins forces to banish both West and East, I couldn't care less. Not because I'm dying and I'm selfish, but because we're destroying the world anyway with our pollution and our greed, and right now I hate the human race.

"Listen, Jonathan and Rebecca."

The names of my children give me a jolt. He's thrust his phone in front of my face again. I can see him looking at the back wall, but on the phone he's looking directly at me. "Your mother needs proof. Please send a video clip to us tomorrow by email. Tape yourselves watching her in this bed, starving to death. Show what you feel. We have the same goal right now, Jonathan and Rebecca. We both want your mother to live."

He gives an email address. Switches off his phone. Leaves the room without looking at me.

Thank God. I slide under the covers and am unconscious within seconds.

chapter nine

I WAKE UP, and for a second I gaze peacefully around my little prison. Then panic ripples through my body, before my mind even remembers why. He's nearing the edge. He's pulling out all the stops. I have to do it now.

Wait two more days.

He threatened me. He's going to tie me up and stick a tube down my throat.

It'll probably be a needle in your arm.

Whatfuckingever. I ponder for a minute, probing my languid tongue into the parched depths of my mouth.

Tied down. Helpless. I thought I had become a ragdoll, merging with my mattress, losing all desire for life. I thought I'd reached a state where nothing could hurt me, where indifference reigned supreme. But last night, he showed me that he could still hurt me, by preserving my body as long as he wanted to: ad infinitum. Oh, wretched existence! Death doesn't scare me. But the alternative…

The imagined alternative. If the whole world is watching, do you really think he'll break his promise again?

He broke it the first time. Such a waste of time, searching for some logic, some reason for my being here. Oh, it must be because he loves me. Oh, it's because God has decreed that my destiny is to end this war. Oh, it's because he wants to use me as his mouthpiece to the West. He's just raving fucking bonkers. There is no rhyme or reason. Trust that he'll let me go? I don't think so.

What if you're wrong? You can't undo it.

I lift a weak hand. Truly, it feels like a ragdoll hand. In another two days, maybe I won't be able to lift it at all. I have to do it now.

So break the mirror now, but hold off on the final act.

What good will that do if my hands are tied? He's mad. Nothing he said was true, not a single thing. He's not going to let me go.

Heaving myself into a sitting position exhausts me. I tremble on the edge of the bed and fight the blackness pressing on the edges of my vision. Surely I'll faint if I stand up? Take a sip of water. Force it down. Pick up my journal; focusing coaxes the blackness to retreat. I write some last words to my children, just in case they will receive them. I try to condense the reason behind this act in a few simple sentences, so that they will understand—because my life had been taken away from me; because I couldn't be their mother, and without that, life wasn't worth living. I jot down some last, loving words that I'll never read out loud.

Why should those be your last words? Try digging up some pithy phrases as your blood drains out. Make it interesting, just in case there really is an audience.

I cringe. If he was telling the truth. What a fucking violation. The enormity of it.

I place my journal under the covers and rise in increments, shuffling to the bathroom like an old woman. I run the water, supporting myself on the sink.

Don't give yourself time to think.

Glad you're finally on board; I smirk at myself before driving my forehead into the mirror.

The biggest piece is lodged under my armpit and I'm busily reaping the rest and throwing them in the wastebasket by the time Sami wrenches the door open.

"Sorry, I slipped."

He looks at me aghast, so I squint at myself in one of the remaining shards. It's just a bit of blood, Squeamish Sami.

He tries to flap me out of the bathroom without actually touching me, but I'm determined to gather the shards. First, if the mirror is in the garbage then nobody'll notice there's a chunk missing and second, my movements disguise the fact that a hunk of glass is stuck in my armpit. And Sami is watching me carefully.

"Saa'adini," I snap; *help me.*

A flood gushes forth; the moron still hasn't cottoned onto the fact that one word does not a bilingual make. But his gestures say *get back to bed.* Fine, elation is the only thing keeping me on my feet anyway.

I totter back to my oasis and slip with gratitude under the lovely covers. Sami bangs about a bit more in the bathroom and suddenly bolts toward the door, where someone hands him something. Please God, I know I only talk to you when I'm desperate—but good news! This is my very last request! Please make this fucker get out of my room right now.

What??? No requests that your children's lives will be happy? If they ever recover from the horrific video of their mother offing herself? Possibly in front of their eyes? And what about wishing humans would modify their lifestyles to avoid catastrophe?

But Sami is coming back and crouching by my bed, dabbing my forehead with iodine-soaked cotton wool. I close my eyes, willing him to keel over from an aneurism.

"Charlotte?"

"Mmmm?"

"Will be okay," he says in English. My eyes fly open in shock. He looks so sad. "Will be okay," he says again and gets up to go.

Yes, it will be okay, Sami. Joy and excitement course through my body. Not even a smidgen of trepidation. Voice was right; I'm already halfway there.

I snuggle under the covers, caress the nice, sharp piece of mirror as though it were a box of Thorntons chocolates. Investigate my wrist for a vein, momentarily mesmerized by the ancient appearance of starving hand. Veins stick out as though asking to be severed. I try to do it quickly, a vertical slash starting two-thirds of the way to my elbow, straight down to my wrist. I scream before I can stop myself. It's so fucking painful.

Not quite halfway there, then?

I lie rigid with tension for a few minutes, but the door doesn't open. Screaming must be chalked up to Typical Behaviour by this point in our acquaintance. I peer under the covers at my wrist. A thin trickle of blood. Are you fucking kidding me? Call me stupid, but it never occurred to me how hard this would be. I have to cut myself again, deeper. I'm not sure I can do this. Closing my eyes, I visualize my hands in restraints as they force-feed me. I have to imagine for a long time before I have the courage to cut again. I stuff as much of the pillow as I can get into my mouth, but it doesn't prevent the keening from my throat. Slicing into the existing incision is the hardest thing I've ever done. My eyes weep and my throat moans and I do it as quickly as I can and the pain is atrocious.

Afterwards, I pray for a second that the cut's now big enough to do the trick. And BTW God, I want this way more than I wanted Sami to leave. Obviously he was going to leave at some point so that was a totally wasted prayer.

Probably unheard. It's not like he's spending all day tuned into you.

Like the rest of the world, you mean?

I wait for a reply, but none is forthcoming. Absurdly, I now want Voice. I won't comment on your ominous silence when I most need encouragement.

I'm against this idea. Plus, the sight of blood makes me woozy.

I snuggle down further to assess the damage. A jagged trail of blood leaks out of the wound and gurgles steadily into the mattress. I'm mildly astonished by the speed and quantity. I certainly hope one arm does the trick, because there's no way in hell I'm doing the other arm. I press the wound into the mattress, so that the blood goes the right way and doesn't betray me, but not so firmly that it will stop the bleeding.

And then I start to grin.

Do you see the light at the end of the tunnel?

Just the end of your fucking endless carping.

Alas, enlightenment isn't for you, even at death's door.

Silence reigns for a bit. What are my thoughts as I die? I am sure it's a far, far better place.

Even if it's not a far, far better thing you do.

It's an okay thing. Under the circumstances. This, I control.

The darkness is pressing around the edges of my vision again. Not insistently, like before. Gently; beckoning; enticing.

I am not frightened. I am not repentant. I am exultant.

It's just like falling asleep.

chapter ten

THERE ARE LUXURIOUS HOUSES, filled with chandeliers and beautiful pictures; fireplaces in every room and silk sheets on the beds. There are simpler houses as well, two-storey erections with wraparound porches. There are rustic cottages, simple and basic; there are tin shacks, rough shelters made of pine boughs, tents with earthen floors.

"The house you get depends on the way you have lived your life," explains my father. "I currently have a rustic cottage, but one can work one's way up."

I'm full of love, as I look at him. Of course he'd be waiting for me, ready to show me the ropes. He looks just the same as when he died, except the yellowish pallor has disappeared from his skin. "But don't you prefer the rustic cottage?" I ask.

He laughs. "Every place is equally good, really. It's not like Earth, where the rich and the poor are segregated."

"So, the good and the bad aren't segregated?"

"No, not really. All the places are good," he repeats.

"I'm so glad to be here," I say.

He smiles and holds out his hand. I remember his hands; sturdy and delicate at the same time. I am glad he is in heaven with me.

There is a light behind my eyes and I'm more comfortable than I've been in a long time. Just as heaven should be.

PARADISE IS A PASTORAL scene of beauty. Animals dot the landscape; water shimmers in the distance. I know people who prefer the city—I wonder if everyone gets to be in their favourite place in heaven. I turn to ask my father, but he's no longer there.

I'm lying down, eyes closed. The light still pulsates against my eyes. Little too much heavenly radiance. My nose itches and I want to scratch it but my arm won't move. I peer down at it. The conviction that I loll in pastoral magnificence is so strong that it's impossible to register my surroundings right away. White bed. White walls. White everything.

Someone speaks in Arabic beyond my head. *Surely we all speak the same language in heaven*, my brain muses sluggishly, before dread morphs into a train whooshing down the track of my mutilated arm as I yank against the restraints. The train chugs over my lungs, crushing them and restricting my breathing.

A hand on my arm. "Is all right," says a gentle voice. "You in hospital. You fine."

My heartbeat ratchets up a few miles and I struggle for breath.

"Is okay!" insists the voice, but I ignore it, eyes skittering down the length of my bound body in disbelief. It's not okay. I'm alive. It's a fucking disaster. My worst nightmare… hysteria chokes me and I thrash back and forth, wrenching against my restraints. I can't feel any pain.

My peripheral vision glimpses the needle dropping toward my arm, and I scream and twist away, futilely.

And when I wake up again I lie very still, my area of control shrinking to the pretense of sleep. My worst fear has come to pass. I'm trussed like a fucking chicken. Tears slip from the corners of my eyes. I bite the inside of my cheek so as not to make a noise. They might be listening.

"Please, no cry. You all right. Everything all right." Not only listening but obviously peering at my fucking face. I open one eye, straining to see through the blur of tears. She's standing right there. A middle-aged woman in a white nurse's uniform.

"Are you my… guard?" It's hard to talk.

Back from the dead and those are your first words?

Thank God, Voice. I thought I was alone here.

"I Nurse. You all right?" pleads the gentle voice.

That's the only English she knows: "You all right? You all right?"

Maybe no English; maybe no brains, I retort. What a relief, to have Voice here! Something that can joke and poke, no matter the circumstances. I glance around the room. It's small and bright; the window stares onto other buildings. It certainly *looks* like a hospital room. Are there cameras here too?

I look down at my body. Tubes protrude from my arms, leading to bags attached to IV units. Feeding me, against my will.

"You all right?" repeats the Nurse.

They've appointed a parrot to look after you.

No, actually I'm not all right. I am alive. Bound. Helpless. Helpless. Helpless.

Panic surges through my body. I fight the urge to thrash from side to side, to jerk the needles from my veins. That would only bring more needles. I'm not in control of anything anymore. I close my eyes and try to breathe deeply. Focus on relaxing my body on my out-breath.

Breathing in, I smile.

Breathing out, I relax my body.

Living in the present moment.

The present moment is a wonderful moment.

But it's not. The present moment is the worst fucking moment of my life. My eyes fly open. The woman is still looking at me. She has a compassionate face.

"You be all right."

Is she repeating a mantra too?

I close my eyes again. Hot, bitter tears seep from the corners and glide down my temples, dampening the pillow. I can't scratch them, even though it tickles. This must be what Samson felt like when they cut off his hair.

Her warm, dry hand covers mine. "Don't cry. We make you healfy, then you go home."

I open my eyes and look at her dispassionately. "Do you have information that I don't have, or are you just talking bullshit to make me feel better? Because the problem with bullshit is that you actually feel twice as bad when you find out that it's bullshit."

My voice rasps like a creaky door, but the effort of speaking doesn't exhaust me. Food is being pumped through the needles, building my strength. For what?

You know what Samson did when his strength returned.

Maybe that's my destiny: to bring down as many of the enemy as I can in my own death. Maybe that's why the suicide didn't work.

Hope surges eternal in the human breast.

I'm not supposed to die quietly and selfishly in my bed. I have to bring him down with me. How?

Maybe you should practise on her. If you could somehow get her head under your strapped arm, then press down really, really hard into the mattress...

Oh, shut up.

"Kassem wants you healfy. Then you go home."

"That's wonderful news." Like I believe you, Nurse Parrot.

"So you do relax, and better soon. Then go home."

"Are there cameras here?" I ask, trying to silhouette a camera with one trussed hand.

"No. No cameras."

But I don't believe her and the impossibility of hiding my face under my sheet overwhelms me.

"Is okay, why you cry?"

Is she serious?

"I don't want to be tied." I keep my eyes tight shut, the interminable tickle like water torture.

"That because you try kill you. Not good."

Oh, you're judging me, Parrot? Maybe you're right. Perhaps suicide is always, ultimately, cowardice. Could I have sliced his jugular with the mirror instead?

You're a pathetic fighter.

What if he were asleep? Post-coitus or something?

Another woman comes in and bends over me without preamble. I shrink away from her hand, but she laughs like I'm amusing her or something and wipes my face with a warm flannel. She whips out another object and I cringe again, but it's only a brush. What the fuck is

137

the point of that? I roll my head from side to side on the pillow to deter her, but she takes my chin in one hand and brushes determinedly with the other. Anybody can do anything they want to me. The tears start again, seemingly in endless supply, rather like my misery. The tears seem to annoy her; she regales us with a lot of Arabic tut-tutting and holds my chin even more firmly. I hate her with a passion.

Another object flying toward my face without so much as a "by your leave." Makeup? Are you fucking joking? I become still and she lets go of my chin, smiling at my collaboration, even patting me on the head as though I were a good dog. She begins to apply lipstick to my lips, and I lie motionless and count slowly in my head: one, two, three, before I lunge my head forward and grab two of her fingers between my teeth. She yelps and I bite down viciously, holding on like a bulldog as she attempts to wrench her hand away. Oh yes, my strength has returned, bitch. Her yelps turn to screams as I grind down, intent on breaking her fingers so she can never apply makeup again.

Now Parrot's got in on the act, pinching my nose and forcing my head back, trying to open my jaw. Bitch howls and pummels my chest, then punches at my face. Nurse speaks to her sharply. I don't let go, even though I can hardly breathe. For one minute, I control what's happening to me. Then I feel the prick of a needle in my arm and barely have time to wonder why they waited so long.

WHEN I WAKE UP, Parrot is standing beside me, looking at me compassionately. Does she have a life? Does she leave to piss occasionally? She presses a nurse call button and speaks into it. Bitch is nowhere to be seen. Bet I won't be seeing her little makeup brushes any time soon. Hope she's lugging a cast that prevents her using her hand, like I can't use mine. Parrot is moving deferentially to the end of the bed, where she picks up a chair; Kassem has swept into the room and gazes down at me with the same compassionate expression she has. Perhaps that's the expression reserved for failed suicides. Except on him it looks sheepy and fake.

The chair materializes behind him and we are alone.

He takes my trussed hand. "Charlotte, Charlotte, Charlotte."

Bile rises in my throat. The feeling of hatred is so strong, I'm not sure I can hide it.

Imperative that you do.

I close my eyes so I don't have to see him.

"What are we going to do with you?"

Truss me like a chicken, apparently.

"Why did you do that?"

It's unbearable. Didn't I once read something about a particular people who used to die in captivity, through sheer willpower?

"Don't cry, Charlotte. As soon as you are stronger, you are going home."

My eyes fly open. "How can I believe you?"

"I am not a monster," he says with great dignity.

Plenty would differ with you about that.

"If you are so determined to go..."

IF you're determined? Do you think he's a bit stupid?

"When?" I ask.

"As soon as you are better."

"Can you be more specific?"

He hesitates. "When you are eating independently."

"I can do that now. Bring me a sticky cinnamon bun and watch." My voice gains strength with each sentence. Can't he hear the vigour?

He smiles indulgently. "I will talk to the doctors. Already, you are stronger."

I raise my trussed hands. "Please, untie me. I can't bear it."

"Maybe you can come home for a few days before your departure, rather than staying here. But you must promise to eat and behave."

Home? "You're not answering my question."

"There is no more trust, Charlotte." He raises his hands in the air as though it's out of his control.

Pure loathing clutches my heart. "*You* don't fucking trust *me*?" I shout.

Now he can hear the vigour.

"Do you think I wanted to do this?" he snaps. "What type of person are you, to die right in front of your children?"

"My husband wouldn't let them see," I hiss, searching for the most insulting Arabic swear word I know, and I know them all, because

Hebrew doesn't have any swear words so they borrowed the Arabic ones. "Coos emek. Coos emek!" Then I spit, right in his face.

He jumps to his feet. A muscle twitches in his cheek. "You shouldn't have done that, Charlotte."

You could say that again.

"No, *you* shouldn't have done this." I pull against the restraints, feeling the straps dig into chafed skin. "Are the cameras on now? Are they? This man is a fucking monster. He's killed and tortured thousands of his own people. And now he's doing it to me."

"Charlotte, calm yourself."

"You're going to rot in hell, Kassem, you know that? For all eternity."

"I don't believe in hell," he says with dignity. "I forgive you because you are not yourself. You don't know what you say."

"Coos emek!" I bellow after his retreating back.

And then Parrot is beside me, needle in hand.

When I wake up, misery lies on me like a thick blanket. Under its weight, I feel curiously resigned. Perhaps this quiet despair is the first, necessary step along the path to extinguish the soul.

Alternatively, you could control your anger and emotion and try to think. What's in his mind?

Been there, fucking done that.

Try to think rationally for a minute. First, is there a camera or not?

What difference does that make now?

You need to understand him. Knowledge is power.

Okay. So first let's say there's no camera. If he's lying about the camera thing, then why does he want me here?

He wuvs oo.

Is there any other explanation?

Perhaps he thinks that you'll help him bring peace to Syria?

Fuck off. Seriously. To think I actually thought that. Seems I've my own personal hubris issues.

Hubris is so much worse in people who actually have power.

Lucky me that I don't, then. So if he has strong feelings for me, my focus should be persuasion: if you force me to stay, you get nothing from me. I don't talk to you. You don't exist for me. However, if you let me go, I will communicate with you on a regular basis and commit to meeting up, say, once a year.

But you'd be lying.

In the circumstances…

Obviously. Lie your brains out.

On the other hand, all the reasons why I don't like lying apply here. One more nail in the coffin of his mistrust of the West. In humanity itself. Whereas, if he knows we're going to have regular check-ins, he might modify his behaviour, in order to earn my approval. If he cares for me.

Or…

Or he was using me as a mouthpiece to the world, and the world really is watching. In which case he'll let me go because the world is also judging. And it's essential to him to see himself, and be seen, as a good person. Either way, it looks good, don't you think?

So bye-bye black despair?

Until it comes again.

And bye-bye childish temper tantrums?

It disgusts me that I have to metaphorically kiss his ass. But I'll do it. Not just to find out his intentions but to cajole him into taking off these fucking restraints, because I will literally go crazy soon.

Soon?

IT'S HARD TO KEEP TRACK of time here, what with the stream of medications knocking me out every time I make a peep. Parrot is often by my side, slipping bedpans under me when I need to go or washing me with a warm, wet sponge. I tell her it feels amazing, so she does my back for a long time. She's not a bad old bird, Parrot. There couldn't be a camera here; I'm sure they wouldn't show me half naked like that to the whole world. Was it all just a lie? But why?

Despite the untrackable passage of time, I'm pretty sure he stays away for a while. Maybe a couple of days. I know he's coming, because Parrot comes in with a little bag.

"Just hair," she says, obviously petrified, watching for my reaction.

When I see she isn't moving without my say-so, I graciously incline my head. So they see the difference between forcing and asking politely.

After brushing my hair, she rummages in the bag and holds up a powderpuff.

"Just nose," she says, and waits for my permission again.

Next comes a tube of lipstick. "Just mouth," she says.

"No," I say, and she puts it away immediately.

When he comes, his expression is more wary than compassionate.

I smile tremulously, anxious to put him at his ease. "Sorry for the other day," I say, even though I'm not.

He smiles back, relieved. "I knew you were not your normal self. You have never behaved like that before."

If only he knew.

"It's these restraints," I whimper. "Please. I can't stand them. Can't we take them off?"

"How can I do that, Charlotte? When you are prepared to do such dreadful things to yourself?"

Let the tears seep. Use any ruse to persuade. Just free me.

It's not really a ruse. You've been leaking tears since you woke up in hospital.

It's still a ruse. Hatred dries tears like hellfire.

"But you said you were going to let me go."

"I have always said that."

Fear clutches my heart.

Don't lose it.

"You said you'd let me go as soon as I was stronger. I'm stronger already."

"Charlotte, you are not strong. Look how you screamed and spat last time I came. Is that how a strong woman behaves?"

I'll gouge those pale blue orbs…

Focus on the restraints. The other, later.

I speak carefully, hoping the loathing doesn't leach into my words. "If you're truly going to let me go as soon as I am stronger, then there's no reason to kill myself. But these restraints are driving me insane. They're the reason I lost it the other day. I beg you, release me."

He considers me for a long time. I try to make my face sane and piteous at the same time.

And loving.

Don't push it.

"You can choose between restraints or 24/7 surveillance. A woman, of course."

A hard choice. Still, if my hands were free I could pull the sheet up and block out everything. "Okay," I whisper. "Surveillance."

He smiles and nods. Reaches over to undo the restraints himself. Looks at me expectantly. Does he expect gratitude? Sees himself as some Semitic Santa Claus?

Say that ten times quickly.

Careful not to disturb the needles (which might be misconstrued), I lift the sheet over my face.

"Why, Charlotte?"

"Cameras," I whisper through the fabric.

"There are no cameras here."

Like I believe you, fuckhead.

"Safer," I murmur. In the privacy of my cocoon, exhaustion strikes.

"Do you remember that we asked your children to send a video the last time we spoke? I have that video. You should see it."

I don't answer. *Don't think about the children. Don't think about the children.*

After a few moments, he gets up to leave.

I lie under my covers and focus on my new freedom until the painful images of my children exit from my thoughts. I can't bear to think about them. Exult in new freedom instead. Why, I could pull out the needles under here and they'd never know.

Don't do anything stupid. Your IV is probably communicating directly with the nursing station, letting them know how much you're eating every minute.

I'm not going to. I'm just *revelling* a bit, if it's all right with you. I scratch my nose vigorously, just because I can. My arms look like they've been through a war. In addition to the long, white bandage encasing my arm like a cast, the needle is immersed in a mountain of tape (as though they suspect my desires to wrench it out), and there are angry red rings around both wrists from chafing against the restraints.

It's wonderful to rub my wrists. Wonderful to turn on my side.

Reminds me of the Rabbi's advice.

Yeah, I used to think that was really clever, but now I see it's totally bonkers. This guy comes to see the Rabbi, complaining about how small his house is with five kids and the wife, how everyone's tripping over one another and arguing and he needs some advice.

"Do you have any animals?" asks the Rabbi.

"Yes," says the guy. "We have chickens and goats."

"Bring them into the house," says the Rabbi.

I guess the guy is one of those weird religious nuts who blindly trust other religious nuts who happen to be higher up the hierarchy, so he goes home and brings the animals into the house. A week later, he's back. "Rabbi, that was terrible advice you gave me. The chickens are shitting everywhere and the goats are eating the furniture. It's even worse than before!"

"Take the chickens out of the house," says the Rabbi.

The guy comes back a few days later. "It's a bit better without the chickens, but the goats are still chewing on the bedposts and the whole house smells like a barnyard."

"Take the goats out," says the Rabbi.

A few days later, the guy comes to see the Rabbi. "Thank you so much for that wonderful advice, Rabbi. The house seems so big and spacious without the animals! We are all so grateful for the extra room, we aren't arguing at all!"

There is a short silence.

What's bonkers about that?

What, are you stupid? I should be grateful that I'm not trussed like a chicken anymore? Great! When I get home, maybe I should ask Adam to tie me up for a couple of hours every day, just so I can appreciate the freedom afterwards. I'll beat the fuck out of my kids for a week so they'll appreciate how good they've got it when I stop. Some things are supposed to be taken for granted. Basic human fucking rights, for example.

All right, stop hyperventilating. Return to revelling.

But before I can revel a bit more, the sheet over my head twitches and flips down. I stare up at Parrot in outrage. "What the fuck are you doing?"

"I like see," she says.

"I don't give a fuck what you like. The sheet stays up."

"I no see if... sheet up."

"And you have to see because? What do you think I'm going to do, stab myself with the mattress?"

I don't think she understands me; compassion and obstinacy battle in her face. "Sheet down," she commands.

I promptly draw the sheet back up, and a sort of sheet battle ensues, both of us pulling in opposite directions. Rage overcomes me; I measure the distance to her nose as she tugs. If I thrust upwards with all my strength, mightn't that kill her?

It'd definitely stop her tugging on the sheet.

And then Voice begins to laugh and I'm a fly on the wall looking down at this ridiculous spectacle—two grown women tugging at a sheet—and my rage dissipates with a smile.

Immediately, Parrot smiles back and releases her end.

"You haven't won, Parrot. Call Kassem."

"Sorry?"

"I want the sheet over my head, all the time. Call Kassem."

"Why?"

"He'll let me. He'll make you let me," I explain affably.

Parrot has a really expressive face. I can trace the uncertainty and worry flitting across as she tries to decide what to do. "Okay. You can."

I smile smugly. "Thought you'd say that."

Ensconced beneath my blessed sheet, I sleep.

NOW I'M EAGER TO SHOW them I'm "healfy." Ignoring Parrot, now stationed in perpetuum at my side, a compassionate expression painted on her face as though she were a marionette, I heave myself to my feet and totter to the bathroom, dragging my IV drips behind me. She leaps to help, but I don't even glance her way. There is a moment when a black tightness encircles and squeezes my vision just as I get to the door, but I take deep breaths and ignore that too.

145

So long as you don't crash to the floor in a faint...

I don't. But I'm thankful to collapse on the toilet. She comes into the bathroom with me, for fuck's sake. I think about demanding Kassem again, but I feel too sick from the three-second walk. She stares discreetly at the corner. I wonder briefly what she's feeling.

Shock at the enormity of your farts.

Back in bed, I accept a cup of tea. Possibly the most delicious tea I've ever tasted. I savour it slowly, trying to focus only on the tea. It's important not to think. The same thoughts swirl around so often, they're boring even me. Is there a camera or not? Best plan of action if he's lying; best plan if he's not. What do you think?

I think we've agreed not to think.

True. SHUT UP ALREADY, MIND!

Live in the moment.

The present moment is a wonderful moment. Not.

KASSEM VISITS AGAIN. "Do you want to come back to your room, or would you prefer to stay here until your release?"

"Here."

"I thought you liked your room," he says in a wounded voice.

Give me strength. "No cameras here," I say, though I don't really know.

"Well, you see. The world wanted to know…"

Right, another lie. I don't care. I spend most of my time under my sheet anyway. I shrug. "Whatever. When am I going home?"

"The doctors say you will be strong enough by the end of this week. It's Tuesday, by the way."

I don't ask what month. What difference does it make? "So, is the end of the week Thursday? Seeing as Friday is your holy day?"

"I suppose so," he says, looking at me sadly.

There is a silence, during which I try to control the hope billowing around my heart, tugging at the corners of my mouth, during which he tries to convey his sadness. At first I'm astounded that I even notice what he's trying to convey, then that he imagines I give a shit.

Pretend you care.

Nope. Done pretending.

"Would you like to see the video your children sent?" he asks.

My children. That I'm going to see so very soon. Elation is swept away by the desire to weep instantly. I'm still hanging by an emotional pendulum, apparently.

He holds up his device in front of my eyes, and the faces of my family fill the screen.

"Charlotte," my husband says, "he is definitely going to let you go. Please just hang on for a little while longer. It won't be long now. We love you."

"We love you," chorus the kids, and then Rebecca holds a photo close to the camera. Me in my teens, with my horse, Muchacho. Jonathan swiftly pushes her photo away and holds up another one in front of the camera: my arm looped over the shoulders of my guide, with a massive bull elephant looking over our heads. Literally.

"Where is that?" asks Kassem.

"Africa."

Rebecca covers the elephant with one of her as a baby, with me cuddling her, of course.

Transparent intentions or what?

"Stop it, Dumbo," hisses Jonathan, thrusting his own baby picture to the fore.

"Your mother is watching this," Adam says in Hebrew. "Behave or no movies for a month."

I start to giggle. It's like I'm there. The children's escalating naughtiness over the stupidest things. The father's extreme threats, always involving outcomes that punish us twice as much as them. No movies for a month—great! That's about the only time I'm guaranteed quiet.

Worse still, his threats are never upheld. Rebecca's only response is to pinch Jonathan; photos flutter off-screen as he belts her. I dissolve into hysterics. It feels *amazing* to laugh.

Adam seizes both their arms. "That's it! You're grounded for a month. No electronics! Bread and water only! Now we'll have to make another video."

The children subside immediately and meekly hold up photos, waiting so long that Adam has to tell them to switch: photos of my wedding, photos of Christmas and Passover. A recent one of the whole family, Mum in the middle clinging to a mugshot of me. She looks so old.

"Imagine all the future photos, of you and us," Adam is saying. "You at your children's marriages; you with the grandkids." And the video ends with a kissing spree—the screen, the photos, each other, all strife forgotten. "He is going to let you go very soon," Adam shouts over the hubbub. "Hang in there, just a bit longer."

I wipe tears from my eyes. "Are they watching right now?" I ask Kassem, who is looking at me with a delighted, bemused smile. He nods.

So they're watching you on a screen, watching them on a screen.
Adam can see me laughing.

"I'm glad they didn't redo the video," I say loudly.

"Since it made you laugh, so am I," Kassem replies.

"It's weird so many humans only want to show what's perfect to others, when only the imperfect is interesting," I tell him. "It's just like Tolstoy's quote about happy marriages all being the same, and unhappy marriages all being different. Happy marriages don't have books written about them, because they're boring. So why do people persist in sending those Xmas updates about how wonderful their lives have been over the last year, and neglect to tell us about Hubby's affair or Teen's dabble in drugs—which is a thousand times more interesting than where they've travelled and their tedious renovations?"

Why is Kassem staring at me like I'm incomprehensible? He's the one destroying his country because power's gone to his head.

It's been a while since your voice hasn't dripped loathing.

"You see?" says Kassem. "How wicked your death would be?"

"Would have been," I say. "But to be imprisoned forever is worse than death to me."

"That was never going to happen!" he insists.

I look at him. Even now, I'm terrified to hope. My life, like so many, is dependent on him. What if he changes his mind about letting me go?

"You have no reason not to trust me."

Apparently, my giggle dams have burst open. I stifle my hysterics in the sheet, while he looks offended.

"What reason have I given you?"

My laughter is nipped in the bud. "You broke your promise," I say quietly. "You don't understand the implications of a vast imbalance in power. One day, perhaps, you'll understand."

"What do you mean?" he asks anxiously.

Surely not still pondering your psychic ability?

"He who lives by the sword, dies by the sword. I am not psychic, but I predict a comeuppance."

He doesn't know what *comeuppance* means, but his male pride prevents him from asking. He's getting uncomfortable. "I am doing the best I can in my situation. We had these conversations. I explained to you that I am in a trap, just like you. I'm not making choices all alone."

I don't want to get into this again, but I let him regurgitate his old spiels: the viciousness of ISIS, his role as protector, the lies of the West. "I have transformed your life," he says. "The whole world knows you. You are famous; you will be rich beyond your wildest dreams. Now people will actually read your books."

This is an attractive thought. "Really?"

He thinks I doubt him. He half-sits beside me on the bed and chooses select footage of international media to show me. It's all about *me*—how exciting! If this is true, won't he definitely let me go? Famous—and possibly rich as well!

"Think how much I can give to charity!" I say.

"You can buy a bigger house. A second house in France."

"I don't want a bigger house, when so many have no houses at all. I'll give every cent to environmental organizations. I can actually make a difference!"

How amazing life is going to be. In just two days.

"I think I'd like to eat something now."

"A cinnamon bun?"

"Perhaps some chicken soup. And toast."

He smiles and takes his leave.

THE SOUP TASTES AMAZING, and for the first time Parrot is absent, which I take as another sign that I'm really getting out. The sudden privacy doesn't make much difference, though, if there's a video recording my every move. There is a self-consciousness to each movement, plunging me back into the self-obsessed world of my youth. It would be awful, if it wasn't so finite. Just two measly days. I feel cheerful enough to harangue Voice a little.

Did you notice the language in the video? "Hang on" rather than "don't kill yourself." That means the children don't know. I told you; Adam probably started censoring what they watched as soon as he heard me talk about suicide.

Or as soon as he saw you rolling about masturbating, busily constructing disgusting fantasies about your captor.

Please never mention that again. It shames me, now. The point is, Adam is protecting the kids. They don't know about the despair.

They'd have known if you'd succeeded though, wouldn't they?

They'd have known I was dead, rather than being tortured in prison.

Which do you think they'd prefer?

Listen. Every year my does have kids, and the goats cavort together all summer long, going on walks and gorging on the best. Then in the fall, I take them to the butcher and give them something nice to eat while the butcher slits their throats. And every year, watching that blissful death, I think: if only I could be guaranteed a death like that.

Your point?

My point? My children know there's nothing to fear in death. It's only the manner of death that can fuck you up.

Your "preferred manner" would certainly have fucked your children up.

But they wouldn't have seen it. Jeez Voice, open your ears, wouldja?

My eyes were certainly open to your filth in those photos. Always dressed in those dirty overalls. Couldn't the kids find any photos of you clean?

Well, I guess I spend quite a lot of time... filthy. I do run a farm, you know. Animals shit. No point wearing high heels in shit, is there?

And you were filthy in Africa because?

Well, I explain slowly, when I travel I stop washing, because I don't really like washing that much, and a holiday is a holiday, n'est-ce pas?

So basically you're saying that you're filthy all the time.

Uhhh...

Why does Voice always seem to get the best of me?

SAMI COMES, AND I AM delighted to see him.

"Kaf halik, Sami!" I exclaim.

"Good, good," he says, nodding and smiling, but he can't tell me what he's doing there until Parrot explains that I'm going back to the room in order to gather my belongings before my departure the next day.

Everybody I meet is talking about my departure as though it's a done deal. I'm in a state of excitement and trepidation so powerful that I can barely eat or sleep. I try to convince myself not to be hopeful, but it's useless. Hope springs eternal in the human breast.

They blindfold me for the short trip back to my room. Even so, I breathe the fresh air, feel the warmth of the sun on my face, want to dance and shout—this is the most wonderful moment—blindfolded and captive as I am!

It is even good to see my little room again, useless to remind myself that he might not let me go. He will. The whole world is watching!

"Hello Armless Stick Man! Hello Books! Well, hello Little Baggie of Dope; methinks we can sample from your magic freely today. Bring on the munchies with a vengeance!" I turn slyly toward the wall opposite my bed and raise my hand. "Hello World."

I know about the emotional pendulum, and it's crap when you're down but oh-so-lovely when you're up. I never did unpack from the last time I was supposed to be leaving—from the moment I knew I wasn't going to leave, I didn't wash or change my clothes. The sight of the bag doesn't depress me. Second time lucky.

Isn't it supposed to be third time?

Shut up.

I peer at myself in the mirror, mesmerized by the differences in my face. So much thinner. Paler. Wrinkles more pronounced. Sadder.

151

But not wiser.

Shut *up*.

I pore over my Arabic-English dictionary with my former enthusiasm and request a sumptuous last meal from Sami: a spread of Middle Eastern food including tabbouleh, labane, hummus, fresh pita, hot peppers, goat skewers.

This feels like déjà-vu.

Shut up.

All that rich food will give you indigestion; you've only been eating for a few days.

Why can't I ever turn you *off*?

Kassem comes to eat with me, puppy-dog misery palpable. Unlike the first last meal, the semantics of enjoying food under scrutiny don't apply. I'm hardly wolfing; just picking. My stomach seems to have shrunk. In any case, I was never without scrutiny, apparently. Thank goodness I didn't know—none of my pleasures would have been so pleasurable. A permanent actress on the stage, without a holiday or even a break. Makeup always, even when free of Kassem-lust. Eating daintily, even when I wanted to shove it down my throat willy-nilly. How horrible, had I known. Now, it's irrelevant. One bite of goat. A smattering of salad and labane. Kassem maintains a hangdog expression throughout.

"I will never see you again."

"Yes, yes," I say, "I'll see you again. We'll find a way—neutral territory, through the Russians or something."

"Has our time together meant nothing to you at all?"

"It has. I will be watching you, Kassem. No chemical weapons or barrel bombs, all right?"

He wipes away a tear. Scoops some hummus and pita into his mouth. How did I ever desire this man? I only desire to get away from him now. His presence is a burden to me, an interruption of my excitement.

"What is the itinerary for tomorrow?"

"They will come for you around 10:00 in the morning. They will blindfold you and take you to the plane. I am sorry for the blindfold, but it must be done."

I couldn't care less about the blindfold. I smile and smile. "Am I flying directly to Canada?"

"Yes, it has all been arranged. To Toronto. Your family will meet you there."

I feel like my face is going to split in two. Silence falls.

Finally, he gets up to go.

"I won't see you tomorrow," he says. "This is our farewell."

I stand and face him. He holds out his arms, and I hug him. He tries to find my lips, but I peck his and turn away. I don't feel like titillating the whole world.

He looks into my eyes for a long time. "Shall we meet again?" he asks.

I nod, but somehow I think not. I never did figure out what his real feelings are. Or my own. The unnatural circumstances of our relationship make it impossible to decipher.

He kisses me quickly, one more time, and departs.

Sami comes in to clean away the dinner things, and then I am left alone. *You and the world.*

Yes. Either I'm hyperaware or I totally forget.

I lie in bed, but I cannot sleep. I feel the whole night is passing me by, and that I will never get to sleep, but at some point, I dream. A nightmare. I am being tortured by all the guards, even Sami. Kassem watches as they apply burning cigarettes to my torso, chanting: "Death to Western decadence and hubris."

And I supplicate them to stop, and there is Kassem, and I beg him to let me go, but he goes out the door, and I weep and weep, and wake up weeping.

chapter eleven

A CRAP NIGHT. I sit, washed and dressed in comfortable, clean sweats, exhausted and exultant at the same time. My bag—the same one I packed so long ago—sits by my feet; I am ready to go at a moment's notice. I ignore the sense of déjà vu, because this time it's really happening. I even dab a little makeup on, conscious that I'd like to look nice for my family. Allay any residual fears.

Two soldiers come to get me. They hold up a blindfold, and I practically leap into it. Holding my arms firmly so I can't fall, they guide me down some steps and outside. I raise my face to the warmth of the sun. My other senses feel heightened by my lack of sight. I smell the rocky heat of the desert. A whiff of flowers. The sweat of my right guard. I feel the crunch of sand granules on concrete beneath my feet.

"Steps," one says, and I am being guided upwards, then pushed into a seat. I wonder if they'll take my blindfold off in the plane, but they don't. I feel the clasp and click of my seatbelt. The roar as the plane engines kick into action. I wonder if I'm on a tiny jet plane or a regular passenger plane. I touch my surroundings; the rough fabric of the seat, the hard plastic of the armrests. I smile and smile as we lift into space, relieved that nobody can see me.

At some point, they place my hands on a little dinner tray, with its individual wrappings like a regular airplane meal. I sample, although my stomach won't allow me to eat normally yet. Just bites, then it claims it's full. Pasta, with a salad on the side. Cake for dessert. Water.

I smile and smile.

I doze on and off, and the flight drones on and on, but I am not bored in my dark little world. I have been in a single room for so long that my own mind has become an entire entertainment system. It occupies itself with imagining the reunion with my children, over and over. We run toward each other, in slow motion, and they leap into my waiting arms.

Soon the whole world will embrace me.

Hours go by; I doze and dream. Finally, we begin our descent. I only know this because my ears pop.

There is a great bump as we land, and then we're coasting along the runway.

"My blindfold?" I ask, but nobody answers me.

My hands are free, so I reach up to untie it myself, but hands push mine down. I subside, although it's impossible to imagine why I'm still blindfolded in Canadian territory. I refuse to entertain the possibility that it's not Canada.

The plane jolts to a stop. Hands pull me to my feet and guide me toward the door.

"Steps," they say again. Talkative chaperones, these.

There's only one step, and then there's carpet beneath my feet. They stop me, and reach up to untie my blindfold; the sudden light blinds momentarily. My guards have reentered the plane and the door has already closed before my eyes adjust. I would have liked to see their faces. To thank them. To kiss their feet. Gratitude and love well up and fill my throat. I take tentative steps forward, down the tunnel-like jet bridge attached to the plane. Suddenly a man is striding toward me, hands held out and his eyes crinkling above his mask. Ah yes, I had completely forgotten about COVID during my time away. Nobody was wearing masks in the room.

"Welcome home," he says simply, reaching out to pump my hand. "We have been waiting for this moment for a long time." A web of laugh lines sprout around his brown eyes. He is looking at me as though I'm his dearest friend.

How amazing that this stranger—and apparently others—care.

My eyes drink in my inauspicious surroundings as we amble along the jet bridge; there are clever travel-related ads pasted to the walls. I read every one. Savour every free step.

"My name is John Whisty," the man says. "I have been involved in the negotiations for your release since the beginning." He hands me a mask to wear.

As we emerge into the stronger light of the airport, a gaggle of reporters starts to snap away to my right.

John notices the direction of my eyes. "We did let a few reporters through; as you can imagine, there is great media interest in your return. However, the room where your family is waiting is private."

"Is it true then?" I ask. "Was every moment in that room filmed and released to the world?"

He hesitates, scanning my face. "Not at the beginning. For the past few weeks, yes."

I smile and wave at the reporters, who surge nearer. Thank goodness I put some makeup on.

"But why would people watch someone doing nothing in a little room?"

Before John can answer, the media gaggle converges in front of me and microphones are thrust into my face. "How are you feeling, Charlotte?"

"Can you describe your state of mind?"

"My name is Peter Reynolds, and I work for the CBC. Would it be possible to request an exclusive interview with you?"

My body is still weak and I've just been on a plane for hours; exhaustion strikes. I take John's arm, leaning heavily against him, smiling pleasantly the while. At once, he shoos the reporters away and leads me toward another door. To my surprise, they acquiesce silently. Perhaps there was a prior agreement. Bless them for abiding by it.

My focus hones in on that door. Is my little family waiting behind it? Will my mother be there too? My heart starts to palpitate as we draw nearer. Exhaustion retreats and exhilaration takes over. This is the moment I've dreamed of for weeks. This is the moment I was terrified would never come.

Then the door opens and bodies launch themselves at me and I'm practically knocked to the floor as my children engulf me. "Be careful," shouts Adam, himself beaming and trying to hug any exposed bits. I laugh and laugh as masks fly in all directions, kissing frantically first one face, then the other, as they smother me with love. Out of breath, I grasp their cheeks and hold them away from me, scanning their faces for any changes. Rebecca is wearing a touch of mascara and some eyeliner. I want to tell her that thick eyelashes don't require mascara. It's as if I've never been away, I fall so quickly into the motherly role. Apart from the makeup, she looks exactly the same.

Jonathan looks pale, as if worry has drained his vitality. His eyes are red-rimmed, although he's grinning like a hyena, and scrutinizing me intently right back. "My darlings," I say. "My sweetest little children."

Adam pushes his way in and is hugging and kissing both them and me, one big family squish-up, just as I'd imagined. Better than I'd imagined.

"We missed you so much," he says. "We've been so worried."

I can only imagine. So much worse for them than for me.

Then the barrage starts, both children vying for my attention, attempting to pour out every detail about the missing weeks instantaneously. A jumble of personal details, mixed with lurid details about their suffering during my absence. I stagger to a chair, as Adam bellows at them to leave me alone, to stand back, to give me air. I wave him away, sharing my children's desire to be as close as possible, Jonathan draped over my knees and Rebecca pressing into my side.

"I got ninety-nine percent on my math test yesterday!"

"We watched you every day while we were eating dinner."

"But you were sleeping a lot..."

"And we'd watch you at lunchtime on the weekends."

Scrabbling frantically in memory to figure out what I might have been doing at that time in the room.

"You sounded crazy sometimes, muttering away to yourself..."

"That's because she was locked up all alone, stupid."

"I know that! We liked listening to you, though you often got sad..."

"That made us sad. But sometimes you were happy too."

"Abba watched it all the time. He'd record the best bits for us, so we wouldn't just see you sleeping or something."

Thank goodness he censored.

You still here, Voice? You can bugger off now.

"Eema, are you listening to us?"

"Intently."

"We liked the talks with Kassem best."

"You sure told him how to behave!"

"We missed you," they chorus, and Rebecca strangles me in a hug while Jonathan burrows into my lap like a little animal.

I smile above their heads at my husband, who is gazing at me with moist eyes. "How are you?" he mouths.

"So good," I mouth back. "Mum?"

"She can't wait to see you tomorrow in Nova Scotia."

John is sitting in a chair in the corner, discreetly looking away. He reminds me of Parrot. Suddenly I want to be away from all other human beings—even discreet ones. I stand up, tumbling children on both sides. "I want to go home," I say to Adam.

He shoots a questioning look at John. Why? Can't we make our own decisions?

John turns toward us and smiles. "I'm sure you want to get home as quickly as possible, but we'd like to do a medical examination first. Of course, we're also anxious to ask you some questions, although that can wait."

"Can I be examined in this room?"

"It would be better in the hospital. There's a taxi waiting to escort you there now. It shouldn't take very long. Your family can come with you to the hospital."

I shrug. I'm not sure whether I have a choice or not, and it doesn't really matter. The best part of coming home has already happened.

As we enter the taxi, more reporters flash cameras at me, but John keeps them at bay. In any case, I am deep in conversation with my kids and barely notice.

"Abba was horrible while you were gone," says Jonathan. "He never let us do anything."

"Did I ever yell at you?" Abba bellows at him.

"Did you read to me? Did you let me have a snack at night?"

"Did you let us have chips with our movie?" Rebecca pipes up. "Did you let us have a friend over *once*?"

"Glory be," I say, in a high state of enthrallment. "Not a single friend, once?"

"You were kidnapped by terrorists," he says, "so they should be inhaling chips and living it up with their friends?"

"No, they should be suffering every minute, just because you are. They're kids, Abba. During hard times, parents are supposed to make them feel better."

Yay—I missed your constant criticism.

So true. I'm always yakking away at my husband, poor guy. He's just taken care of the kids solo for weeks. They survived.

"Abba never yelled once?" I ask.

"He tried really hard to be nice," Jonathan concedes reluctantly.

"We had to make our own breakfast and lunch, every day," Rebecca says.

"What an excellent habit. Let's keep that up, shall we?"

"NOOOOOOOOOOOOOOOOOOOOO!!" they both yell.

When I'm not drinking in my children's faces, I gaze at the scenery flying by the taxi window. It feels like I've been given new eyes. Everything is fascinating; everything is magnetized. So many people.

There is another gaggle of reporters at the door of the hospital; if they know my itinerary, that's more than I do. This new ability to observe everything intensely is exhausting. I don't know how much longer I can hold out.

My family stays behind in the waiting room while they check me. Doctors prod and poke, take blood, urine, ask so many questions that I start to feel ill. They leave me alone for two minutes and I'm dead to the world when they come back. I have no memory of how long it took or what I said, but by the end I no longer want to fly home. I want to dive into the nearest bed and sleep for ten hours.

The disappointed faces of my children change my mind, but why wouldn't they want to stay in an exciting city like Toronto for a night?

"We just flew up for the day," Adam explains. "We didn't arrange for anyone to look after the animals."

Ah yes, the downside of the farm; it's so much more complicated to get away.

"Plus, we have stuff to show you at home," the children whisper mysteriously in my ears, as I totter past the reporters, no longer caring what my tired eyes look like above my mask as they snap away. Smiling pleasantly, always smiling, to show that I'm not ignoring their questions; simply the flesh is weak.

I sleep the entire two-hour flight to Halifax and feel outraged when they wake me, as though it were the middle of the night. I cover my face with my hand as we emerge into a firework display of camera flashes, no longer able to smile, fatigue enveloping me like a straitjacket.

As the taxi extricates us from the bevy of reporters, Jonathan begins to relate what each teacher had said to him about my kidnapping, one after the other (how many could there be in Grade Seven)?

I look at his beloved face and smile. Once upon a time, I would think: *could you just shut up for two minutes? I can't think!* Not now. It's as if I've never been away, except love is managing to triumph over irritation. Quite a significant difference.

Bravo... not. It's only the first day. Last for a week without screaming and impress me.

I feel like I can last forever.

As the taxi approaches our house, I devour every detail hungrily. Piles of snow tower above our heads on either side of the driveway; winter has arrived in my absence. It's like driving through a white tunnel. "Did you let the goats out every day?" I ask.

"Most days," they answer. Bull.

"How did you manage extracurricular activities?"

"Neighbours helped a lot," said Abba.

"We hardly missed any," said Rebecca, a note of disgust in her voice.

"They missed at least half," said Abba. "They stopped going to music lessons and Scouts."

Every creature's life has shrunk in my absence—goats and children. I enrich their lives.

I smile and smile.

We go into the house. I inhale the familiar smell of woodstove and books. Jonathan tries to pull me outside. "You must come and see the goats—you'll find a surprise in the barn."

Rebecca tries to pull me upstairs. "You have to see the cards and presents. So many people sent us stuff! Abba tried to throw it away, but I made him wait until you saw it."

My legs begin to tremble and I feel an absurd inclination to cry. Happy tears, but also exhausted ones.

"Leave her alone," shouts Adam. "Can't you see she's tired? She can see everything tomorrow."

"Are you sick?" Jonathan asks me anxiously.

"No, my darling. Remember how many hours' difference there is between Israel and Canada?"

"Six."

"Exactly. So I'm on Middle Eastern time; what time is it for me?"

"Three in the morning. Poor Eema. Are you going straight to bed?"

"Maybe a cup of tea." And a bloody cigarette; first one since my brekky cig in the room. Seems like a different life already.

Seems like a dream.

chapter twelve

IN THE MORNING, I'm not sure where I am. Until I open my eyes, and there's Adam's grinning face, inches from my own, waiting with bated breath for me to wake up. I stretch luxuriously, bumping inevitably into his erection, which seems to traverse half the bed.

"Where are the kids?" I ask.

"They went to school."

"Really? On my first day back?"

"I want you all to myself." And then he's on top of me, and pushing inside, and all the touching that I dreamt about is happening…

But fantasies are always so much better.

And it's been so long that he comes right away, but then he brings me to orgasm several times, loving me with his tongue and his fingers, and he didn't even ask me to wash first.

Then we cuddle, and he tells me the agony that was his during these past weeks.

"But you could see me whenever you wanted," I say. "You could see that I was all right."

"That was a great relief," he admits, sitting up and cupping my face in his hands. "Also a great relief that you kept your fantasies to… fantasies."

He's smiling, but I realize how awful that must have been for him. Watching me salivate over another man, while I believed that every word, every action was private. Rage punches through my body and I jerk up to a sitting position in the bed.

"That bastard. What the fuck was he doing? What was his motivation?"

"He was using you as a mouthpiece to the world, spouting his propaganda through you in the hopes that people would see him in a more sympathetic light."

"Yeah, so how does fucking around with a prisoner evoke sympathy?"

"I don't know. Perhaps he knew that the millions of people watching you were beginning to respect you, even love you."

"Really?"

"Yes, really. You should go online and google your name."

"That will tell me that people love and respect me?" I pull his head onto my shoulder and begin to scratch his scalp. He closes his eyes in bliss; he must have missed his Giver of Pleasure in so many ways.

"There are people claiming that you're wise. There'll probably be a queue of sufferers hoping you can heal them."

Wise? You spent most of the time stuffing your face and fondling your clit.

"You're lying," I say to Adam, poking him.

"No, I'm not. People are having academic discussions around some of your ideas. All that stuff you were telling Kassem about perspective. Here, I'll show you."

"No, we're talking," I snap. I could never stand it when Adam took online into bed.

I grill him on the details of life-without-me: what had they eaten; how worried the children had been, my mother. I am astonished to learn of the flood of support flowing from neighbours and strangers alike. Food arriving on the doorstep, mounds of cards and emails expressing sorrow and support. I decide to wait until the kids return before looking at this stack of correspondence, but it does pull my heartstrings, this human wall of support, reaching out to a stranger.

"They think they know you," Adam explains. "Some nutters watched you obsessively. I hope they'll leave us alone now you're home."

"Did you watch me obsessively?"

"Of course."

Thank God I didn't do anything to be ashamed of. It's *not* the thought that bloody counts.

I SIT IN MY FAVOURITE PLACE in the sitting room while Adam makes me breakfast.

The only place he lets you smoke.

One of the cats settles itself on my lap as I gaze around the room, with the same curiously heightened observation powers that I possessed yesterday. I love this room, with its ceiling-high bookshelves and wooden walls. I love *every* room. I turn my eyes to the window. It's a fairy-tale scene, hundreds of branches covered with a thin layer of snow; so beautiful. A blue jay alights on a branch beside the window, twittering and cocking its head at me.

"Did you feed the birds while I was away?"

"Yes."

Bull.

"When is my mother coming?" I ask, digging into a plate of freshly laid eggs.

"Your brother is bringing your mother later on in the afternoon, when his kids get home from school. They all want to see you. Your sister is coming around that time too."

"That's perfect. I can have a quiet day meditating and catching up on my emails," I reply, sipping on my tea. Why does he never put enough sugar in it? Does he really think his annual proffering of bitter tea will change my sugar habits?

Missing Kassie already?

Fuck off.

AFTER BREAKFAST, I PUT ON my winter gear and go outside to visit the animals. It's probably -5 Celsius, not too cold for the end of January, which is just as well because I haven't had the chance to adapt to winter temperatures. I look at everything intensely on my way to the barn. The green of the fir trees pokes through the white snow; the grey-brown branches of the leafless trees stretch toward the blue sky. How many colours, after the yellowy browns outside my room's window. How wonderful to have more than one type of weather!

If only there weren't nine months of winter...

Look on the bright side. The shit winters keep the population in Nova Scotia low because nobody wants to live here.

And there's no spring. The weather veers drunkenly back and forth between winter and rain right up to June, when it plunges into the sticky temperatures of summer.

But our autumns are fantastic.

There are indeed two new kids—white with brown splotches. Neither of them show much interest in me, and the female is positively timid—proof that my children haven't spent much time with them. But my two old girls, Willow and Lilah, push each other out of the way in their eagerness for attention. And Lambie, fat old thing. I scratch them and their eyes half-close in ecstasy. My heart is full of happiness, as I stare around their woody enclosure, noticing every detail. The pile of branches and trunks plonked beside their shelter hasn't grown any bigger. I used to cut down a tree for them (conscientiously choosing overcrowded saplings) every day that I had to work so they'd be entertained in my absence.

Giver of Pleasure.

To every living thing in my vicinity.

While you bubble with resentment.

Not anymore.

Make sure it doesn't come back. Give until resentment comes knocking, then stop.

I'm going to live my life differently now. I look around, noticing every detail. I chose this place based on its privacy: I can walk around the entire house naked, apart from a two-metre stretch crossing the driveway, which is visible from the road. Seven acres spread back to join an unknown neighbour's property, eventually ending in a dirt track that meanders to the lake in one direction and to the road leading to our house in the other. I do this circle walk several times a week with the goats, gathering greenery for their delectation. They love fir trees, so even the winter provides. How I love my little slice of forest!

The chickens are next, hurtling toward me when I call, in the hopes of food. I make sure that each one gets some bread, even the shy ones who hang back, intimidated by the bullies. I check my bird feeders; both full—which either means that they've been feeding the birds regularly, or they hastily filled them for my homecoming. I hope it's the former. The deer I know they haven't fed, because Adam resents throwing money away. But he doesn't seem to get that it's not thrown away if pleasure is derived. Surreptitiously, I fill up a bucket with cracked corn and place it within the woods, out of sight of the house.

It's when I'm crossing the driveway to return to the house that I notice the gaggle of reporters. Their cameras point right at me, and when they see me looking they call out. I rush into the house.

"There are reporters here," I tell Adam.

"I'm afraid so," he says. "They'll get over the novelty eventually."

I pull down the shutters and peek at them through the slats. I don't like them here, in my private place. I want to wander around with unwashed hair and filthy clothing like I always have. This is the one place in the world where I don't have to wear a mask.

"What's the quickest way to get rid of them, do you think? Ignore them or offer them a few interviews?"

"I think you should talk to them." As he speaks, the phone rings and he picks it up. "She's busy right now, can I take a message?" He grabs a piece of paper and a pen, listens and writes.

It goes on like that all morning. The phone rings. People wanting to talk to me. Exclusive interviews. Any interview. A quote. An offer to appear on television. It throws Adam into a state of excitement, and this confuses how I feel. Is this good or irritating? It certainly wasn't what I expected.

"Shall I begin scheduling for next week, to give you a week off?" he asks, as though it's a job.

"No. I'll do them right away, get them over with. One after the other. Say the same thing to everyone until they lose interest." I peek through the slats of the shutters again. The gaggle is still there. For my strategy to work, I should talk. Endlessly, until they leave.

So I put on a makeup mask, don reasonable clothes and march up to them with a fake smile. Cameras blind my eyes and the questions pound from all directions. "What was it like there," / "What was it like seeing your children again," / "How did you feel when he..." / "How did you cope with..." / "What was the worst..." / "How does it feel to be famous?"

"Famous? A flash in the pan isn't fame; it's replaced by the next piece of news."

They laugh at that, as though I've said something funny. They laugh often, in fact. Were people laughing at me while I was in prison?

You've always wanted to be a comedian.

Yeah, but it'd be nice to be *intentionally* funny. So I know what they're actually laughing about.

I answer and answer; then I begin to point out that I'd already answered the same question. Finally, utter exhaustion coincides with their denied inability to think up new questions, and I stagger back to the house.

"Your family is coming," Adam informs me. I glance at my watch. It's 2:30; the children will be home in half an hour and I haven't meditated or done my exercises or checked my emails—God knows how many of those I'll have to wade through. The old malaise overcomes me—I can never get my own stuff done in this bloody house!

Oh shut up, you whiny old biddy.

True. God, human nature. Bottomless pit. I'm totally happy.

And I am. When I stop focusing on the gaggle outside (why don't they go away now that I've talked to them?) or on what I assumed I'd accomplish this day, I'm outrageously happy. Smiling and smiling like a jack-o'-lantern all the time. I just have to let all that other stuff go; it's not important.

I must have dropped off, because Adam's voice startles me as he leans over my supine bulk to look out the window. "The children are coming." I look, suppressing a surge of irritation at the sight of the kids pushing their way through the gaggle to get in their own driveway. They are talking and smiling at the reporters. Maybe I shouldn't have brought up my children to be so polite. They rush in, leaping on me and kissing me exuberantly. God, how I love their smell, their sweet little faces. What pleasure to hear the details of their day.

"Guess what I got on my test?"

"Eighty percent?"

"No."

"Ninety percent?"

"Nope."

"Eema, do you know what the teacher said about your return?" Rebecca interrupts.

"Shut up, I'm talking to Eema," snaps Jonathan.

"You're boring her to death!"

"Behave or I'll send you to your rooms," yells Adam.

And whip you until you scream for mercy.

Yeah, really. I must remember to ask him when he's returning to work. I'm here—discipline is my domain—butt out!

Especially since his discipline's so shit.

Exactly. Hey Voice, no offence or anything, it was really great chatting with you when I was in solitary confinement but right now there's a million fucking people vying for my conversation, so could you shut up?

"You haven't guessed yet!" says Jonathan.

"How long do I have to wait?" asks Rebecca. "We don't care about your stupid test. I bet you got a hundred percent anyway."

"Shut up!" yells Jonathan.

"*Upstairs!*" bellows Adam.

I wish I'd meditated. Really. It keeps me calm in these situations. If the meditation session is reasonably successful (a few five-second stints of uninterrupted thoughtlessness), its tendrils of calm weave throughout my day.

But alas, I didn't, so I'm on my feet and screaming at Adam to let me handle it and it's so sudden and so aggressive that they're all silenced.

"Sorry," I murmur. "Jonathan, I'm going to guess your test first. Then I'm going to hear what your teacher said, Rebecca. We're going to speak one at a time, in quiet voices, like reasonable people."

NOT.

"So Jooney, did you get more or less than ninety percent?"

"Not telling. You have to guess."

"Ninety-five percent?"

"No."

"Seventy-five percent?"

"No, Eema, of course not!"

I used to find this excruciatingly boring. How many random numbers do I have to make up before they deign to tell me something I haven't the faintest interest in anyway, since they always do well and I don't live vicariously through my children?

unnatural mother.

Hey, all you mothers who naturally dote on your kids, they're still going to blame you for the rest of their lives for all the shit life throws at them.

You're just jealous.

Yeah. Why couldn't I have been a naturally good mother, instead of just pretending? But hey, maybe I've morphed into Good Motherhood while I've been away, because right now everything they say is bloody riveting.

"A hundred percent!" Jonathan crows.

"We already said that," says Rebecca indignantly and launches into the story her teacher asked her to write, about what this whole experience had been like for her, and then she told us what she had written, and it was very long, and Jonathan was seething with impatience, but he kept quiet, thank goodness. And it was fascinating, hearing the whole story from her perspective: the anxieties and fears of a teenage girl, mixed with excitement at the special attention she had received throughout, tangled with embarrassment at her mother's outrageous thoughts made public.

"Did your classmates watch me on the internet?" I ask.

"Well yeah, duh."

Christ. I must watch those clips.

"Have you been... teased?" I ask hesitantly.

She looks incredulous. Thank God.

Then it's Jonathan's turn, and he launches into a vivacious description of his own friends' reactions, and the teachers—was everybody really watching me do nothing in the room?

"Now let's show you our surprises!" they say.

"I've seen the baby goats—they're adorable," I enthuse, guilty to have discovered their "surprise" instead of waiting for them to show me.

"Awww," says Jonathan. "But there's something else, something you're going to love."

169

They lead me to Rebecca's room, where they have hidden a massive box full to the brim with missives and presents. They begin to show me one by one, sure my delight will match theirs. Indeed, tears do begin to seep from my eyes as they take polite turns to read the wonderful, loving, supportive messages.

"And these are only the best ones, because there were too many to keep," explains Rebecca. "There were so many letters, it would have filled a whole room! You should check your social media; I bet it's full of messages too."

How much love people have sent me, a stranger. How they identified with my suffering. Human beings are truly incredible, with their immense capacity for both good and evil. The children read, delighted with my weeping. They couldn't have hoped for a better response.

After half an hour, a tiny, niggling anxiety sprouts in the back of my mind. How long will they keep this up? Two or three already supplied the gist.

Meditate.

Oh, wonderful idea. I lie on my back and close my eyes ("To listen better," I tell the children) and focus on my breathing. *Living in the present moment. The present moment is a wonderful moment.* I'm lying here with my beloved children, listening to hundreds of strangers sing my praises while I meditate. How could any moment be more wonderful?

We are interrupted by the entry of my extraordinarily loud family as they burst through the door downstairs.

"That was a wonderful surprise," I tell my children, helping them heap the cards and letters back into the boxes. Then we go downstairs to join the hullabaloo. My siblings envelop me in a maelstrom of hugs and kisses. My nephews and nieces gaze at me in awe. "You're famous, Auntie Charlotte," they say.

"It seems so," I reply.

Then Jonathan leaps into their midst to drag them upstairs, and my new prestige is never mentioned again.

My mother looks so frail. She sits beside me on the couch and gazes at me. I am barraged by questions—almost the same questions as the reporters had asked. It's boring, but I answer again. At least I understand her interest.

Adam brings tea and a plate of cheese and crackers and pickles. I restrain the urge to help; the kitchen is too small to hold us all.

God, how tired I am.

Missing the room?

Don't be stupid; I'm happy! Look at all these dear faces. My beloved family.

The plate of crackers disappears in minutes, and Adam trots out some more.

"This stuff tastes weird," says my fifteen-year-old nephew, Jake.

I nibble the cheese. It's strong cheddar; the kids only like mild. And the crackers are an unknown whole wheat brand. Thinking to add some cookies to make the snack more palatable, I sidle to my feet.

"Am I looking after things or not?" Adam snaps.

Not well.

"Oh, I'm here, dear Adam," coos my sister, Liz. "When I'm here, you can take a break." She's obviously dying to supply her own kids with cookies.

"No way. Your kids eat even worse than ours," Adam replies, retreating to the kitchen for the third time to return with some cut-up fruit.

He's health-conscious. That's a good thing, right?

I urge the children to go outside to play. It's getting colder and the older cousins demur, but Adam leaps in with his usual heavy hand and out they go for a game of soccer in the snow.

Even so, the house is still full of voices. How often have I listened with pleasure to the animated bellows of my family, as each one strives to be heard over the others. Both my brother and sister talk without pause, claiming that they can't get a word in edgewise; I love the feeling of being part of this group. As long as nobody shouts or gets unpleasant, no group in the world gives me such a sense of comfort.

But something has changed. They're not talking amongst themselves, they are talking to me. Even after the first onslaught of questions and answers, their curiosity rages unabated. I begin to feel quite ill with exhaustion. Finally, my mother notices and orders me to bed. I'm too excited to go to bed, but at least her notice buys me refuge in silence. The debate rages on without me; I am attacked for my ridiculous sentiments toward "that murderous monster Kassem," and then defended for the same feelings because of the "unnatural circumstances" of my imprisonment. A subdued shouting match ensues (out of consideration for my exhaustion) about the definition of *unnatural* ("I wish I could have a month of peace and quiet." "What an unbelievable thing to say. As though you have any idea what such an experience would be like!")

And so on and so forth.

My mind drifts. Adam brings in more crackers and cheese. "Do we have anything more substantial?" I ask him in Hebrew—luckily, because he launches into a stream of outrage, based on his determination not to provide a single morsel beyond common decency to my family.

A pox on cheese and crackers! Where's the baklava and the cinnamon buns?

Once, I would have battled the point. I would have leapt to my feet and brought them food myself, and drink, which they like so very much.

I want a joint.

"Who has been milking the goats?" I ask, apropos of nothing.

"We stopped," Adam replies. "I couldn't manage it with work and everything."

"That's fine," I say. "They've just had kids. I can start milking at any point."

I resist the urge to start today.

He rests his hand on my shoulder on his way to the kitchen to make more tea. "You do a lot," he says. "It was hard without you."

I am astounded and delighted. He has always undermined my contribution. Perhaps it's human nature to notice only what we ourselves do, to always think we do more. I run a small farm, drive the kids back and forth to their daily extracurricular activities, cook, do half the cleaning, teach three times a week, and write a novel every couple of years, but according to him I've always been lazy. Could this have changed? Glory be!

"I thought the different ideas she came up with were interesting," Liz is saying. "If human beings had more time to think, we'd obviously be doing massively better."

"Interesting ideas? She didn't come up with a single thing that wasn't completely obvious," shouts my brother, Ben.

My mother smiles at me and squeezes my hand, which she has been holding tightly the whole time.

"Do you want to go for a walk with the goats?" I whisper to her, but Adam overhears.

"You're not going for a walk," he states. "You're exhausted."

"Would you like to go for a walk, darling?" Mum asks. "Or are you doing it because you feel you should?"

"They haven't been walked since you left," Adam interjects. "They're not expecting a walk."

As if to belie his words, both our cats walk right into the circle of people and sit down, fixing their catty gazes on me. I glance at my watch. 7:30—their usual feeding time.

"The cats," I whisper at Adam.

"What?"

"They're looking at me."

"So?"

"They expect me to feed them."

"I'll get the kids to do it when they come in."

I sigh. "The point is, I'm back and they know it. The cats look to me for food and the goats are expecting a walk."

Adam erupts. "The animals are fine! Do they look ill or unhappy to you? You have to relax for a few days! God, your entire family is a bunch of crazies."

My mother is nodding her head sagely at me. "He's right, I'm afraid," she murmurs.

Am I crazy? For the first time in my life, my husband is telling me to relax and take it easy, and I'm raring at the bit to shoulder the heavy burden of endless responsibility as soon as possible.

Practise what you preach. Remember? You told Kassem that one should invest thought into each move one makes, to ensure that every action adheres to one's values.

What's the war in Syria got to do with walking the goats?

The trick is to THINK.

Oh right, mind over emotion, or sense over sensibility as Jane Austen might say.

No she wouldn't.

Whatever. The point is, of course the whole household can continue to run without my input.

And the goats aren't really wondering why you're not taking them for a walk, since you're back.

Miraculously, Adam seems to have shelved his usual expectations as well. So all I need to do is focus on myself. Luxury!

My mother is looking at me anxiously.

"Okay," I say firmly. "First we'll have something more substantial to eat. Then I'm going to bed."

chapter thirteen

All the time I was away, my little home seemed like a faraway dream. Now, after just a few weeks, my time in the room feels like a dream. I try to conjure Kassem's face, and the details jumble. Did he have lines on his forehead? Mindlessly, I sketch the cavorting armless stick man that had been on my wall. Can't get him exactly right.

I have become a little obsessed with the video clips from my incarceration; there is something addictive about watching oneself. Sometimes the videos make me laugh, but usually they make me cringe. I sound like a mad woman, yakking away to myself all the time.

Actually, to me.

Oh right. That's okay then.

At first, I flip from one clip to another. Then I settle down to watch it chronologically.

Oh, the desert of egotism men call life.

I watch myself grasp Kassem's hands, gazing into his eyes. "Do no harm," I tell him earnestly. "And if you want help, of course I'm here."

I want to puke, it's so embarrassing. God, where did I get off, thinking that I could transform the Middle East with my wisdom? What fucking hubris.

Still, I can't stop watching. Oh, here I am, having hysterics at my own vulgarity.

"Putrid secretions. Rancid emissions! Oozing discharges!"

175

Did my daughter see this?

"Remember you have two interviews today," Adam calls.

Did I say I "settled down" to watch the clips chronologically? Wrong phrase. I slip my obsessive viewing betwixt and between what feels like a madly hectic schedule.

"You'd better hurry up; we need to leave in an hour."

"I need to meditate," I say firmly.

"You told me to set them all up right away," he replies, equally firm. "To get them over with."

"Yeah, but damn. I feel so rushed all the time."

"It's a TV interview, so you might want to put some makeup on."

Adrenalin and excitement sweep through my body; no chance of calming agitated mind now. That is a problem. There is no calm alone-time in my current life. Adam hasn't shown signs of going back to work. He's around all the time, a large presence tut-tutting over every unwashed dish. Incapable of understanding that alone-time is not a luxury, it's a need.

I have a quick shower and apply makeup carefully. I hope the camera faces the left side of my face, where my teeth are straighter.

Everyone's seen every side a million times.

It's weird how hard it is to remember that, especially since we have to push through a hedge of reporters every time we exit our driveway, snapping straight and crooked teeth indiscriminately.

"Why is the Gaggle still here?" I grumble to Adam. "How long will it last?"

"Don't worry," he says, patting my hand. "The Gaggle have already left."

On the way to Halifax, we practise the questions they might ask me, so I can answer succinctly. I'm still terrified of questions that I'm not prepared for—even though I can no longer count the number of interviews I've done—I'm still crap at quick ripostes.

"You can stop and think," says Adam. "You don't have to leap in with a quick response every time."

"You've never been on television," I snap.

"If the silence is too long, they'll fill it up," he says. "They're not going to allow any dead time."

When *A Hero* came out, I was on television for five minutes. These interviews seem to go on and on; it's incredible to me that their interest continues; the questions repeat themselves in one continuous loop, even though there is nothing more to learn.

"So, Charlotte Mendel, was it a shock to realize that your imprisonment had been taped?"

Fucking A.

"You knew that Kassem was a merciless dictator capable of torturing and killing his own people without compunction. It's hard to tell from the tapes: how much fear were you really experiencing?"

I take the time to think. "Human beings are incredibly complex and multifaceted. So you might say that Kassem is a merciless dictator, and I might say he's fundamentally a good man, albeit a weak and fearful one, and we'd both be right."

"Fundamentally good?" the interviewer asks doubtfully. We are sitting at right angles to each other, six feet apart, unmasked.

"It's like when you read a horoscope. If they say 'you're a very sensitive person,' you think: that's true! I am sensitive. But if they say, 'you're an insensitive person,' you think—hot dog, I am pretty insensitive sometimes. Because we can be both; we're really complex. So yes, Kassem has done terrible things, but I really do believe that he thinks of himself as a good person."

"But we could say that about anyone in history. Hitler probably thought of himself as a good person as well."

"I don't know, I didn't meet Hitler. But one major difference between them would be that Hitler was totally convinced that the Jews weren't fully human, not like him. Just like white Americans thought Black people weren't like them, in the time of slavery. You can't harm an entire people if you believe that they are suffering in the same way that you would, in the same situation."

And how many Israelis think the Palestinians are "not like them?"

"So Kassem has convinced himself that the rebels aren't really human?"

"No, I'm saying the opposite; he's fighting his own people, so he can't dehumanize them in the way racists do. But Kassem does believe that his own survival depends on winning the war. He's convinced himself that the rebels are wrong, that they'd destroy his country and slaughter the Alawites if they took power."

"Does that absolve him from responsibility for the horrific things he has done?"

"No, but once I understood that he saw himself as a good person, I believed it was possible to decrease the gap between this view of himself and his actions."

"By making him identify his values, and whether his actions corresponded to them?"

"Yes."

"And do you think it worked?"

I take a sip of water. Surely, that's incredulity at my arrogance shining in his eyes?

"I don't think I made the situation worse. He genuinely thinks that he's been a good leader..."

"Except to those who disagree with him...," the interviewer interrupts.

"And that his country will be destroyed if he releases the helm. Certainly, the fate of the Alawites might be grim."

"He's got his trillions stowed safely in some foreign bank; he'll be fine."

I look at the interviewer for a minute. "He was kind to me," I say finally.

AFTER IT'S OVER, I AM EXHAUSTED, mentally and physically. But there's another one to do. Thankfully, the next group—Americans, I think Adam said—are coming to my home with their cameras.

I try to rest and meditate in the too-brief interval, but my mind whirls in mad excitement; I can hardly eat. Impossible to stick to my five-cigarettes-a-day regime. I light one from the previous butt. The goats *maa* loudly, and guilt pummels my heart. I must walk them today. So many living things demanding my attention.

Finally, the crew arrives. The interviewer introduces himself as Craig; he might be well known, but we don't actually have a TV, so I wouldn't know.

Another well of woeful ignorance.

They set up, making small talk and admiring the property while Adam makes another round of endless tea.

"Can we see the animals after the interview?" one asks.

"Of course," I say. Can't he see that I'm exhausted?

I point my straight-teeth side toward the camera and begin to parry the avalanche of questions. It's so fucking repetitious—why can't they compare notes and share? Maybe I should film myself answering every question I can possibly think of and post it on Facebook. Then, when they come asking for another interview, I could tell them to check whether their questions have been answered already. Because I simply *can't* keep doing this forever.

Eventually, inevitably, Craig begins to disparage Kassem.

"If he wasn't fundamentally good," I enunciate slowly, "he wouldn't care what the world thought of him. Why would an evil man be desperate to explain his perspective to the world? His entire interaction with me revolved around his desire to reveal his hand to the world, because he thinks it's a good hand."

Do you have an agenda?

Oh God, I hope not.

"But if I understand what you said to Kassem about perspectives correctly, the fact that he perceives himself as good doesn't necessarily have anything to do with reality. He could be absolutely certain that he's good and still be completely evil."

That's another thing; they keep dredging up shit I said during my incarceration as though it's worth repeating. *I'm not very intelligent*, I want to explain to them. *Please don't expect pearls of wisdom from swine.*

Yup, a nice, ignorant misquote would convince them.

"I think the only segment of society who are convinced murder will propel them directly into heaven are the extremely religious. Kassem is secular." I feel rather pleased with this point. Half the time I'm terrified that my mind will go blank during these interviews. There's a certain amount of knowledge in there—not a lot, but a certain amount—but it's never available on demand. Most of the time arguments leave me groping for thoughts while my adversary plows his way through a list of facts that prove his point absolutely. So thank goodness I remembered Kassem's main claim to sane trains of thought: his secularity.

But Craig just looks perplexed. "So?" he says.

"So he's not justifying his actions because God told him to do it," I explain. "Unlike ISIS."

He's still scratching his head, metaphorically.

"We're not dealing with a gap in logic that's impossible to bridge. Like if a person *truly* believes that the Bible or the Qur'an is a revelation from God, and it tells you to make war on the infidels, you're actually a very good person if you bump off a few Westerners. This monstrous lack of logic—the belief that God himself wrote or inspired all of our holy books, and therefore everything in them is the absolute truth—makes it impossible to reason with religious people. Same with the religious Jews, right? It's fine to build settlements in Palestine, because it says in the Bible that that land is ours. The extreme religious are usually illogical and can't be reasoned with."

He shakes his head with a smile. "But I'm still not sure what you're saying. Obviously evil isn't restricted to the religious extreme. All the worst wars our world has experienced have been secular."

Please don't bring up Hitler again. What is it with these guys and Hitler? *Always wanting to compare your darling Kassie to that fucker!*

"I don't know what was in the minds of the people who initiated the world wars…"

"The desire for more power and control, just like Kassem."

I feel my face flush. "I don't think he wants *more* power and control…"

"He just wants to maintain the status quo, regardless of the wants of his people. Swimming in money, while they struggle."

There it is again. That little rush of irritation. Stop fucking interrupting me, it's hard enough for my brain to adhere to its train of thought. I wish this was over.

It's not your job to whitewash Kassem's image. All he did was let you go after you tried to off yourself.

"I'm not trying to…" I stop, confused, aware that I've spoken out loud. "My perspective coincides with his on this; I don't think he's evil. I think he's a human being, striving to judge his own actions with reason, instead of emotion. Isn't that the most we can ask of anybody, including ourselves?"

"Not if our actions include horrendous torture, imprisonment, and murder of anyone who opposes us."

Deep breath. This irritation can only mean that I'm more emotionally attached to Kassem than I thought, because it's a reasonable question. "The fact that he was swayed by my influence isn't necessarily a good thing. Kassem is a weak man, in my opinion, swayed too much by the advisers and military which surround him."

Craig leans forward with a kind smile. "Do you feel you're completely objective, where Kassem is concerned?"

Why are you fucking asking me, then.

well, given his manly torso and beautiful blue eyes...

"I think that power has gone to his head, as power is wont to do," I say carefully. "I realize that millions of people are dying, fleeing, and suffering because of this one man. But right now, the whole region is in chaos. It doesn't look like the West will succeed in booting him out by force anytime soon."

"Because they're occupied with ISIS, not to mention COVID."

"Yes. So Kassem is actually the most reasonable player on the stage right now. If I'm forced into a situation where I have to hobnob intimately with him for a month, I'm going to put my energies into something useful—inducing him to think about his behaviour, which might result in modifying it—rather than something useless, like convincing him he's evil."

Why are these strands of irritability coiling around my heart? Shouldn't I be feeling grateful for the attention? Wasn't I always griping and complaining at the lack of media attention in my previous writing life?

Awww, you're missing Kassie.

I try to smile. Visualize a yellow halo emanating from Craig's head for the rest of the interview, to thwart negativity.

Finally, it's over. I gesture vaguely out the window: "The goats are back there," I say, astounded by my own rudeness.

Adam gives me a strange look and escorts them out himself. I hover, unsure how to use these five minutes my rudeness has bought me.

What is the source of your discontent? You should be revelling.

I revelled for the first few days. Human beings aren't built to revel.

If they were, the entire west would be revelling in its privileged existence.

Some of them don't feel privileged.

That doesn't mean they're not, compared to ninety-five percent of the world.

True. Yet instead of revelling, they spend more time bitching and complaining than the other ninety-five percent put together. Proof that it's human nature to be discontented.

So you're just being a privileged, spoiled bitch?

Noo-o, not exactly. Something's not quite right. I'm not centred. I'm off-kilter.

Why?

Dunno.

Practise what you preach; think!

Right. Before incarceration (I'll have to start dividing my life between BI and AI), I was alone most weekdays. I would get up, make everyone breakfasts and lunches and see them off. Then I'd deal with the animals, eat my breakfast, meditate and settle down to work for a few hours until the children got home again. Now, I have no idea what's going on and every second is inundated with people. There's no *order*.

Now you know what to do.

I smile. The five-minute reprieve from people hasn't been wasted after all.

I shove my journal into a knapsack, along with some cookies, fruit and a bottle of water, and am ready for Adam when he comes in. "Let's go to the river for a talk."

He gives me this new, worried look of his. I thought at first that it was the result of his terrible anxiety during my imprisonment, but I think he's just more… focused on me or something.

Time to get you both back on track.

I take his arm as we move toward the goat enclosure. "Do we have to go with the goats?" he asks.

"Of course." How many times do I have to remind him that we got the goats because he refused to let me have a dog? People think it's amazing that my goats do tricks and come on walks, but it's really just so I can pretend they're dogs.

Poor deprived child.

Oh, piss off. Of course, a goat's capacity for learning depends on their level of greed. Plastic baggie of treats in hand, I entice them past the barn door and into the driveway, where I'm confronted by the Gaggle. There seems to be other people too, a little crowd of onlookers. Some neighbours. I march forward purposefully. "How long do you guys plan to camp out here?"

Microphones stab toward my face. "Where are you going?" / "What interviews are coming up?" / "You take your goats for walks—so cute!" / "Would you say you have a special affinity with animals?"

"*How long are you going to be here?*" I shout. Adam links arms, smiles placatingly, propels me forward.

Among the hubbub of voices, I hear one answer: "For the foreseeable future."

I turn toward the voice—a young, bearded man. "But what for? I've already talked to you. There's nothing left to say."

"People want to know what you're doing now."

Adam edges me onwards, holding tightly to my arm. Only vigorous shaking of the plastic food bag induces the goats to brave the newshounds.

"There must be a way to reverse this," I say to Adam as we walk forward. Neighbours trail on my periphery, calling greetings. I nod and smile, wishing them in hell. It's not like they just happened to be walking by my house at the exact moment I decided to take a walk, is it?

A *ma-aa* from behind and I glance back. "Adam," I say anxiously. "They're following us. Are they allowed to do that?"

"It's a public road."

"But they'll discover our secret spot on the river. Then the whole world will know about it."

Turning to face them, I strive for a reasonable voice. "You have to leave me alone. I'll go mad if you follow me everywhere."

Their faces hide behind implacable cameras.

They are people too.

So it must be possible to appeal to them on a human level. "If I can't go anywhere without being followed, questioned and photographed, then my house will be the only place I'm safe from scrutiny. My house will become like a prison. I've just got out of prison. Please leave me alone."

"This is our job," the bearded man says, as if that trumps all humane considerations.

"Shame on you," one of the neighbours trills toward the journalists. "You're no better than *him*."

I ignore her ingratiating glance. She has never liked me. Why? Because I'm insensitive, offensive, and weird. I haven't changed, why has everyone else?

I push back past them and stride back home, confused goats trailing in my wake.

"We can talk inside," says Adam.

"I've been inside for a long time," I reply, dropping my voice to a whisper. "They never come on the property, so it must be against the law. If we go through the woods behind the house to the lake, they won't know." I skip ahead, happy again.

Sunlight dapples the snowy forest floor as we meander along the property lines that lead to an empty expanse of lakeshore, discovered during our first year of exploring. The snow is less than ankle-deep, so the going isn't difficult. The goats amble along behind, finding God-knows-what to eat in midwinter. Lambie sticks to our side; if she were clever enough to do tricks, she'd make a much better doggie.

"What did you want to talk about?" Adam asks.

I link my arm through his. "When are you going back to work?"

Miss Subtlety.

"You've just got back. I want to spend some time with you. Why do you ask?"

Willow decides the best firs are in front of us and pushes past rudely.

"I need to get back into my regular routine."

"You can't do that right away."

"I'm not doing any more interviews. There's nothing more to say."

I practically fall over Willow's ample bottom, planted firmly in the middle of the path as she scoffs up a low branch of fir tree, poking its green needles through the snow. I try to push her aside, but she resists mightily. It's a goat's nature to resist mightily. Now, if he'd allowed me to get a dog...

Adam lends his shoulder and we basically lift up her haunches and shift them to one side.

"You should look at the media interest like a job. If people stay interested in you, they'll read your next book, which you should be writing, by the way. If your next book is a bestseller, maybe I won't have to go back to work at all."

I glance at him sideways. "It's great that I might finally make some money," I say, nudging him playfully, "but you've still got to go back to work at some point, don't you? Ouch!"

Now two ample bottoms are planted in front of us. The goats are determined to set the pace and it obviously includes a lot of snack breaks. The fact that we keep smacking into their behinds doesn't faze them a bit. Dog, not.

"I'm like your manager," Hubby explains as we edge past the goats on the narrow path, which is especially difficult as Lambie is determined to edge by at precisely the same moment. "It's not a small job, you know. You live in your own little world and don't even notice, but I'm answering dozens of emails and phones every day. You're crap at publicity and your first three books flopped. It's up to me to make sure the next one won't."

The goats shove past us again and take the lead. "What do you know about the publishing world?"

"Book agents are already knocking at the door; remember how hard you tried—and failed—to get an agent? Two minutes with the media today and you practically bit their heads off. You can't possibly do your own publicity."

I'm confused. "But why don't we just choose the best agent and they'll handle all that?"

"And give them a huge percentage from every sale when the books will sell themselves?"

Before us, the vista brightens as the trees scatter. We are approaching the lake. The goats pick up their pace in anticipation of lusher greens along its banks. Perhaps they've forgotten it's winter.

"You have to go back to work," I say firmly. "Maybe I won't answer every phone call, but it'll all get done. You said yourself the books will sell themselves."

"You don't understand," he snaps. "I've supported us ever since the kids were born; now it's your turn."

This is familiar ground. The old "you're not making enough, why don't you get a proper job" routine.

The lake springs into view suddenly as we come through the trees, a glistening panorama of sparkling liquid. Always takes my breath away. I stand quietly, breathing deeply. But Adam can't shut up.

"We have to follow up on every glimmer of interest that every peon shows in you, if it helps sell your next book. The interest probably won't last so we have to cash in on this right now."

I have to adjust my perspective to accommodate this new information. "So I'll respond to every peon's interest, Adam."

At least for a couple of hours every morning, between milking and meditation. On the days you aren't stoned.

"This is temporary, your job's forever."

We find a nice flat rock and sit down. "This could be forever too," he says.

I frown, pulling our snacks from the knapsack. "Don't say forever. I want to return to anonymity. The less I encourage publicity, the quicker that'll happen."

He bites into an apple. "Do it until your next book comes out and you'll be able to retire with enough for the rest of your life."

"But we have enough for the rest of our lives. You've been working your entire life so we'd have enough when we were old."

"It's never enough," he barks. "You don't understand anything about money."

"We have several hundred thousand saved," I say gently, mindful of the years of money-related arguments behind us, "and you have a pension."

"Anything could happen," he says. "More is always better."

I take a bite of a cookie, wash it down with water. This is an ancient argument. When we first married, he said he'd relax about money once we had a house and a car paid off. Then he said he'd relax once we had enough for our old age. For me, that meant about $40,000 a year to spend from sixty-five onwards, with a little extra for the end in case we had to move into one of those expensive retirement homes. For him, it meant factoring in the distinct possibility that one of us would suffer a debilitating disease at the age of fifty-five and would have to be installed in aforementioned pricey retirement home for the next fifty-five years. While the other one popped themselves from grief, presumably, to explain why no money would be coming in from fifty-five onwards.

I've let him scrounge and save and deny many little pleasures; I actually think fewer pleasures enable you to enjoy the ones you have much more. I love that he doesn't spoil the children and buy them rubbish. But I hate the selfish hoarding: "Jews are supposed to give away ten percent of their income," I've said to him many times—the only time I've ever used the religious card. "We're rich compared to ninety-five percent of the world. We don't have the right to keep it all to ourselves."

Judging by his ballistic reaction, I might as well have punched him in the face. "I've worked like a dog all my life so you could do your hobby!" (Hobbies are, according to him, something you like to do that doesn't make money—i.e., my writing.) "Now you want to throw my hard-earned money away?"

"We're not throwing it away. We're giving unwanted excess to a dire need, like the environment."

"You laze around all day doing bugger-all while I'm working my ass off…" And on and on.

I always capitulate, because it's always been his money. This time, patently, it will be mine. I have to be strong, set clear boundaries from the beginning.

"I will respond favourably to every sign of public interest in me, on condition that eighty percent of the money from the next book goes to an environmental organization of my choice."

He begins to laugh—never a good sign. Willow realizes that we're eating something more interesting than dead, snowy leaves and lumbers over to investigate. She has her lips wrapped around his apple before he's finished his fake laugh, and with a bellow he throws it away and strikes her in the face simultaneously.

She leaps away in shock. I am paralyzed with anger. You do *not* strike goats. They are nervous little creatures, primed for flight, not fight. A move like that could undo years of gentleness. I struggle to breathe, fury constricting my lungs.

"First, I'm sick of these stupid goats," he says. "We don't have time for them anymore and I think we should get rid of them. Second, not a single cent of that money will go anywhere. We will buy my brother a house. We can pay the mortgage on your sister's house. I'll get a nice car, for once in my life. There are so many things we could do with that money."

My voice comes out in a high-pitched wail. "First, you ever hit my goats again and I'll fucking kill you. Second, if I don't have a say in my own money, then I'm not going to make it. Third, unless you allow me absolute freedom with my money, then I will leave you as soon as Jonathan hits eighteen."

"It's impossible to talk to you," he sneers. "Look at you, practically crying because we disagree. Always shooting your biggest bullet right at the beginning. Why wait until the kids are eighteen? You can go right now."

I feel waves of violence beating up from my chest, heating my face. If I could wish him dead right now… "I would, you little shit, but divorce fucks kids up, so I have to stick with the biggest mistake of my life for another few years."

We're both yelling now. "You want a say in the money? You don't even know where it's invested! You have no idea how much I make, how taxes are done. You want a say? You do it. Your turn."

keep calm.

But I lost it the moment he struck Willow in the face. "You're a fucking controlling bastard! Why did I marry such a small mind?"

"Nobody else would have you."

I go for his face, claws extended, but he sees me coming and blocks my blows easily. He doesn't hit me back, to his credit. I want to hurt him. I try to gouge his eyes out, and he grabs my hands. I try to maneuver his hand, holding mine, up to my mouth so I can bite it.

This is insane.

I know. I know it's insane. Even as I focus on inflicting pain, part of my brain knows that I'll regret it.

It's only when he releases my hands, leaping backward at the same time, that I desist, watching him stumbling back down the track to the woods, cursing me with all the hurtful words he can conjure up: "You're certifiably insane. You should be locked up. You're not fit to be a mother."

chapter fourteen

I pace backward and forward on the beach, until misery replaces the rage; then I begin to cry, wails that reverberate over the water. Coming home wasn't supposed to be like this. But I have returned to a different world. Nothing is the same.

I want my old life back again, now.

Excuses.

I know! I'm no better than an animal. Here I am preaching the importance of thinking and as soon as something upsets me… I raise my face to the sky. "God help me!"

Good thinking.

What?

What could be more logical than asking for help from a made-up entity?

My eyes drop from the skies and scan along the coast. Then I see them. A group of people, walking in my direction along the shoreline.

Drawn by your infernal noise.

My eyes are bad at long distance, so I can't tell whether they're neighbours or strangers, and I don't care. Calling to the goats and Lambie, I plunge back into the safety of the woods, departing from the path in case they try to follow me. I half-run until I have a stitch, until the *maa*-ing of the goats beg for respite, and then I turn, entice the animals to me with food, scratch and stroke away the memory of the blow. Willow responds

190

as always—eyes half-closed unless I hit a sensitive spot, whereupon she twitches irritably and menaces me with a butt. Perhaps she realizes it was a nasty man who hit her and won't blame me for it.

I move forward again, more slowly, trying to aim in the direction of the path and hoping I don't get lost. Every so often I stop and listen, straining to hear above the clomping and chomping of the animals. I think I lost them. Probably neighbours then, embarrassed at the idea of running after me. Strangers have no such shame.

By the time I get home I'm exhausted, but there is no rest for the wicked. Adam is nowhere to be seen, but the children are home from school and they vie for my attention.

"Will you make us a snack?" they ask.

"Sure." Children in third-world countries are already working full time at your age.

Unnatural mother.

I rummage in the cupboard and select some cookies and apples. A snack only takes a few minutes. No grounds for resistance.

Like sex with Adam.

I'm never letting that piece of shit touch me again.

"Guess what happened today?" Jonathan asks, nibbling his Granny Smith apple.

I wait for a second, but obviously he means it literally. "You got an A in a test," I hazard.

"No. I didn't say I had a test today, did I?"

His confidence in my memory is touching.

"I had a test today," says Rebecca, pulling her cookie apart to eat the cream first.

"Oh, how did it go?"

"You haven't guessed my thing yet!" Jonathan says indignantly.

"You had a substitute."

"No."

"I don't know."

"You have to *guess!*"

"It could be a million different things, Jonathan. There's no point guessing if there's no way to get the right answer."

"Please! Pretty please!"

"Your teacher threw up. Your friend Jamie farted in class. Somebody kissed in public."

"You're getting close!" he crows.

"Don't you want to hear about my test?"

No, I want to have a nap. "Yes I do, darling. I want to hear about that more than anything. As soon as Jonathan tells us what happened, I want to hear all about your test. Okay, Jonathan, I'm not guessing anymore."

"A girl in my class was suspended!"

This tidbit grabs even Rebecca's attention. "Who? Why?"

"Katelynn Williams. She pushed someone down the steps because they were teasing her about her boyfriend. He just broke up with her."

This is better than a soap opera. Not that I've watched any since I was fifteen.

"Aiden was her boyfriend, wasn't he? Why'd he break up with her?" asks Rebecca.

"He said she did drugs and stuff."

"She sounds like a screwball," I say firmly. Why is my son playing infantile games with his mother while his peers are kissing girls and smoking dope? Is he backward or something?

"What drugs?" asks Rebecca.

Drugs! That's what I need!

"She was smoking marijuana."

"In Grade Seven? That's terrible," I say, a ring of joints dancing a jig in my head.

"Do you want to hear about my test or not," Rebecca asks testily. "It was a disaster."

I wrench my thoughts from cavorting cannabis and focus on my daughter's face. "But you memorized the whole thing. How could it have been a disaster?"

"Because my stupid teacher told us to study the outline, but half the questions on the test weren't even on the outline." She has finished her cookies from the inside out.

"Were you only supposed to study the outline?"

She picks up her Granny Smith apple and satchel. "That's all she *told* us to study. Bye, I'm going to my room."

"Wait!" This is the point where I'm supposed to give sensible, motherly advice. "Did everybody just study the outline? Do you know what you got?" I call out, following her up the stairs.

"Seventy-five percent," she answers through her closed door. This is a really bad mark for her. I open the door a crack. "Did everybody do badly?"

"Most people."

So some people did better. "You're a wonderful student and you study really hard, but it's always possible to learn, right? So perhaps it wasn't a good idea to stick to the outline; maybe you should have read through all the material."

"She *said...*"

"I know, to only study the outline. But obviously..."

"She's a stupid teacher."

"Who only studies the outline?" pipes up Jonathan from behind me. Our heads swivel as one and we both shout at him to mind his own business. He retires to his own room, affronted.

"I expect she is a stupid teacher," I say, knowing that you're not really supposed to say stuff like that, but this doesn't seem to be one of my wise days. "But I only care about you. Everyone has to learn how to study. It's always a good idea to read through all the material, even if you only memorize the outline."

Rebecca gets off her bed and comes toward me, her voice ratcheting up a few degrees. "You don't read through everything if the teacher tells you to only study the outline. Now get out of my room!"

And then she's pushing the door shut in my face and unbelievably rage sprouts anew and I'm pushing back and shouting, "Don't be so bloody rude," and then Adam is yanking me away and I stumble back and the door slams shut and Jonathan is looking at us with a stricken face.

"What is wrong with you?" Adam's voice is dripping with wrath. "Do you need help? Do you need to see a psychiatrist? Perhaps you have post-traumatic stress disorder or something." But he's using the same voice he always has after a fight. Furious, not concerned.

And I feel the tears threatening and run to the barn as fast as my legs will take me. The hen with the new chicks fluffs herself up to an impossible size in response to my entry and a small smile pushes through the unhappiness. I take a couple of deep breaths, marvelling at my own lack of control. Does every human possess such Jekyll-and-Hyde characteristics?

Calmly now, I rummage through every shelf meticulously, but I can't find my stash. I must have it. Now. That fucking useless husband must have hidden it. With a husband like that, who needs enemies? I've been through the most terrible experience...

You're always like that.

Only when I'm in bad shape!

You're always in bad shape.

Oh right. It's my fault. My horrendous incarceration...

The endless supply of cinnamon buns was particularly horrendous.

I sink to my heels and rest my head in my hands, to the indignation of the anxious hen.

It's true. I'm not capable of happiness. I have everything and look at me. But at least I know how to hoist myself out of the doldrums. I'll have to swallow my pride and ask him.

He's not receptive to my question. "We've discussed this. I don't want you smoking before the kids go to sleep. They're not babies now; they know what you're doing. And you'll reek of dope."

If he were a thoughtful man, he would weigh the benefits (outwitting insanity) against the disadvantages (the remote possibility that the children will know I've smoked dope). But no, he's leaning on good old-fashioned prejudice. I could bear a man incapable of self-awareness, if he was gentle. I could bear a controlling man, if he was a thinker. But this combination of stupidity and control...

You do know you're insanely negative about your perfectly reasonable husband, don't you?

"Did you throw it away?"

"No."

"So either you tell me where it is right now, or I'm going to drive past the Gaggle to spend unnecessary money, risking my name being splattered across the headlines tomorrow. The children won't know anything, other than that I've calmed down. I'll chew some gum so I won't smell."

He still won't tell me. It's not until I've made a couple of phone calls and am sitting in the car ready to go that he approaches the window, his face a visor of dislike.

"You're addicted, you know that?"

Yada, yada, yada, can we skip past all the insults your hurt ego needs to launch before capitulation?

Joint in hand finally, I enter the goats' enclosure and wade through the snow to the very back, deep in the trees. They are delighted to see me again—what an exciting day they're having—and stand with me as I inhale slowly, anticipating the inevitable change of mood. Even as it comes, relaxing the muscles along my shoulders, my mind churns. To be a good wife and mother, I just need to be left alone for a couple of hours a day. I'm a giver, not a hurter.

You're incapable of dealing with the continuous onslaught of people.

I can if I get some fucking time to meditate and smoke.

You're certainly successful at the latter.

I giggle; this reminds me of one of my mother's stories. A little boy at school was asked to give two sentences about Queen Elizabeth I. He stood up nervously, his soprano ringing out bravely. "Queen Elizabeth was known as the Virgin Queen. As a queen, she was a great success."

The goats sniff the air in an interested fashion. Bump my pockets to see if I'm hiding anything edible. Lambie plasters herself to my side, eternally hopeful that I'll plunge my hands into her thick, greasy wool and rub.

You must meditate. Carve out your own space.

My shared bedroom has a pool table in it, because it's the only room in the house big enough to accommodate it. My smoking couch is the centre of all traffic.

There's a room in the basement.

It's only got one window, so it stinks if I smoke there.

So?

Yeah, get my priorities right, right? If I'm frightened of losing it, the onus should be on finding it.

What?

But the dope has taken over, finally imparting relaxation to my mind. I sigh, scratching the animals, who, in turn, sigh.

How marvelous to focus composedly on the present. So much quicker than meditation! Losing it? Oh well, maybe, but never mind.

I saunter back to the house, calling up the stairs to remind the children to practise their instruments, as though nothing has happened. They respond in kind. Perhaps nothing *has* happened.

The downside to smoking is a great resistance to any type of work, which is a shame, because resentment curls its fingers around the periphery of my brain as I prepare the evening meal.

My awful conduct is my fault, totally, but still my anger is ignited by others. If only I was alone, I'd have time to think. Thinking modifies behaviour. I mutter to myself, scraping carrots into a container so the animals can eat the peel later.

Alone like in the room. What a shame we had to leave!

That's so absurd I start to laugh, but then it trickles away in the middle. Do I miss the room? Confusing real loss of control with imagined loss of control—that's delusional.

So take control.

The missing piece is being by myself, in my own room.

Even though you weren't really.

Ignorance is bliss.

AT DINNER, JONATHAN AND I keep the conversation going. I just have to throw out a question and he's off for the next five minutes. "We haven't had tacos since you went away," he enthuses.

"I hate tacos," grumbles Adam.

"I love them," exclaims Rebecca, and we exchange small smiles. Children forgive quickly, either because it's expedient or because they have short memories.

They practise their instruments after dinner. I love hearing them play, even though half the time Jonathan gets frustrated at the difficulty of the songs and begins to vilify the teacher. I wash the dishes and then gather my cigarettes and laptop and head downstairs.

"Where are you going?" Adam asks.

"To the basement."

"Don't smoke down there; you'll stink the whole place up."

"Where else in the house can I can smoke and be alone?" I ask sweetly, still under the blessed influence.

"Outside."

So, build me a room outside. Meanwhile, fuck off. "I'm happy to sit outside in the summer, but not when it's -14."

He's still protesting as I continue down the stairs, about the smell, about the unnecessity. Does marriage mean that every action involves compromise? How many times has he tried to control my actions today, when they don't impact him at all? The money is one thing; that's an ongoing issue sprouting from deeply different values. But using the unused, downstairs bedroom? Get out of my face.

Poor Adam. Living with your incessant negativity.

I know. I *know*. It's like I blame everything bad on him. I've *got* to stop.

The basement is chilly, but I crank up the heat and climb into the bed, connecting to the internet on my computer, sinking mindlessly into the curious pleasure of self-observation.

"If a human being is rational, I will understand how they arrived at their conclusions, even if I don't agree," I am telling Kassem on the video. "So yes, I'll listen to you."

How earnest I was! Later I say, "If you truly want to be a good person—and you're not just bullshitting me—then you don't want to do harm, right?"

Mirth overcomes me: what a gap between my words and my actions! Who am I to judge Kassem? Who are any of us, to judge anyone else?

when you torture, kill, and displace millions of people, I'll let you know.

I'm destroying the happiness of those closest to me for no reason whatsoever. At least he had an enemy.

First, you're not destroying their happiness.

Okay. They're destroying mine. Just by *being*.

I take a cigarette and blow smoke defiantly at the ceiling. I don't really believe that my family is destroying my happiness. Of course not. It's my responsibility to figure out my needs and fulfill them.

When Rebecca was first born, I had this beautiful baby girl—I was supposed to be happy. Instead, a sense of incredulity ruled my days: all my basic rights were gone. Really, I can't shit in peace? No more sleeping two consecutive hours? No more sit-down meals? No smoking, except snatched inhalations with the door ajar, her mewling nudging my blood pressure back to pre-cigarette highs within minutes. No idea how long this would last—possibly eighteen years, until she left home, for all I knew. Then I got the brilliant idea of putting her with a sitter for a couple of hours a day. How amazingly industrious I was, writing away for those two hours rather than smoking or sleeping. How I loved those hours.

I reach for my journal and pen.

Needs

1. Time alone.
How much? Unknown. Start with two hours a day.

chapter fifteen

MARCH 17: 2 P.M.

Breathing in, I smile.

Breathing out, I relax my body.

Living in the present moment.

The present moment is a wonderful moment.

I lie on my bed in the basement, trying to empty my mind of all the pointless thoughts that enter unbidden at microsecond intervals. The value of this time is incalculable, since the rest of my life refuses to accommodate my needs: the children still pelt me with every minuscule detail of their days; Adam still hasn't returned to work; the Gaggle is still ensconced at the end of the road; the phone still pierces the serenity with its strident call twelve times a day.

Adam is trying to communicate better. The day after our fight, we sat down over a cup of coffee on the porch. Sitting outside has become an almost manic craving since the room. The main difference between summer and a "good" winter like this one is the amount of clothing one must don. Instead of slipping on Crocs and dashing outside, you have to wrap in so many layers of protection that walks become waddles, but you can still indulge in outdoor activities like sledding and skating. Other winters, months of intermittent snowstorms and -20 temperatures make your snot freeze in your nose and your eyes sting and appendages go numb within minutes, no matter the thickness of your mittens. So you stay inside; my craving for the outdoors existed before my incarceration, though that has exacerbated it.

Today it is a balmy seven degrees—lovely for March. Adam and I sit on our porch for our post-fight talk, winter coats slung loosely over our shoulders. Fir trees hide the Gaggle from view, though I can hear the murmur of their voices.

We try to listen to one another, our fingers curled around the tea mugs for warmth.

"I'm sorry I'm such a difficult person," I begin, although one doesn't have much perception about one's own levels of difficulty. "I've been trying to think about what's making me go off the deep end. Basically, it boils down to a need for solitude."

"Solitude?" Adam repeats.

There's an interesting difference between first- and third-world attitudes concerning the needs of the individual. Generally, Adam and his family plow through life without really thinking about their own needs at all. His mother probably doesn't know what the word even means: she slaves away all day, a little old woman of seventy-six on her knees scrubbing the spotless floor. But she's not dissatisfied. Adam views me as spoiled, a person born with a silver spoon who's always bemoaning trivial things.

Actually, that's how you view Nova Scotians.

Yes, all right. I see his point. Except it's more complex than that.

It always is, with you.

If it was just a matter of the more you have, the more you want, the more dissatisfied you are, then my sojourn in a Syrian jail would have made me more appreciative of what I've got here. But I also believe that thinking itself is incongruous with happiness.

Why?

Just because. Intelligent people suffer more.

Oh, so Adam is both third world and dumb.

Exactly.

Perhaps you should refrain from informing him of his deficiencies.

"Yes, solitude," I say to him. "I want to behave like a rational human being, and obviously you want that too. That's why you need to go back to work."

His fingers tighten around the cup. "I've already explained why I can't go back to work. There's no way you could cope." As if to emphasize his point, the phone peals its exasperating tone. He itches to answer it, trembles on the edge of his seat, but we have promised to give each other our undivided attention. "That could be an important call," he mutters.

"Then they'll phone back." His anxiety is a mystery to me. If everybody is so goddamned interested, what difference does our response time make? It's not like they'll say—oh, she's not answering, let's call that other author who's been incarcerated for a month.

"So how do you propose that I get my necessary solitude?" I inquire brightly over the urgent voice on the answerphone. Adam strains to hear. It occurs to me that he's in a state of wild excitement. All the time.

"Can't you just do without solitude for a couple of months?"

"A couple of months?" My heart soars. Is the end in sight? "Are you proposing to put an end date on this 'catering-to-strangers' period? I think that's a great idea!"

Why does this sound like déjà-vu?

"I've already explained why we need to continue until your next book comes out. I meant that it'll be easier to carve out more time in a couple of months."

Fucking **lame**!

Breathing in, I smile. It doesn't help to accuse him of lameness. Focus on the goal. Solitude.

"Do you think it's more important to be a good mother or a bestseller?"

"I don't see why it has to be either-or."

I lean forward. "I need several hours of unbroken, sacred solitude every day."

He gazes at me in silence. Suddenly, I become aware that the murmur of the Gaggle has stopped. I can almost hear their bated breath. Those bastards. We need to speak more quietly.

"How many hours?" he asks incredulously.

"As many as possible. So I can meditate and stay sane."

"Do you mean to tell me that I've been going to work at the crack of dawn my entire life, while you sit around *meditating* for hours?"

"Yes, I just sit around, teaching three days a week, running a farm, shuttling the kids…"

"All right, we've heard the list of your numerous chores about a million times. You're not teaching anymore though, are you? But okay. You need some time to yourself."

A wave of relief drenches me; how silly to be unaware how vital Adam's support is. He needs to be on my side. If not him, who?

"Thank you Adam," I say joyfully, and he grins.

"Two hours a day, tops. Can we go in now? I'm freezing."

Wait! There are six more things on my agenda.

SO I GET MY TWO HOURS A DAY. I lie on the bed in the basement and try to meditate and work. The peals of the phone rip through my focus, and Adam seems incapable of respecting the sanctity of those two hours.

"Do you want to be part of a panel discussing the situation in the Middle East next Tuesday?" he bellows down the stairwell. "I don't think you should; it's not like you're an expert or anything."

Is it too much to ask for two fucking hours of non-communication out of twenty-four? Not to mention the ludicrous continued presence of the Gaggle at the end of the driveway, filling me with hatred every time I leave my home.

I close my eyes and try to re-focus on my breath. The phone screeches again. Forget it. I'm out of bed and leaping up the stairs to reach the phone before Adam does. I place my hand over the receiver. "Don't answer it."

"Why not?"

"I want to talk about the Gaggle. I hate them," I yell over the strident peals of the phone, following Adam into the main room as he all but drapes himself over the wood stove.

"What gaggle?"

"The reporters at the end of our road."

"The ones that were here your first week back?"

I look at him, confused suddenly. "I want to talk about... this continued absurd interest in me."

"Use it to influence people," he says in an encouraging voice. "Teach them the importance of decreasing their footprint and how to do it. Tell them that what they do today will have an impact on their children's future."

Sudden distrust paralyzes my smile. Adam doesn't give a fuck about the environment. This is exactly what Kassem did. He pretended to seek my counsel to mask his real agenda—communicating to the world through me. Adam is enjoying the excitement. He's even pretending there isn't a Gaggle at all, no doubt to sow seeds of doubt about my own sanity. Thank you for tossing me a bone to shut me up.

You're equating your poor husband to a murderous dictator? Are you listening to yourself?

He's either with me or against me, by God. I had sworn to myself that I would not talk about money, under any circumstances, but… "Giving away my money to important causes would be a brilliant way to showcase my values to the world."

His face tightens immediately. "Showing them your little farm where you produce your own eggs, milk, and meat is showcasing your values best. Giving away your money doesn't reflect your values; it reflects your insanity."

Luckily, I am prevented from replying by my mother's voice on the answerphone. I rush to pick it up.

I have only seen my mother a few times since I came back; every time I go out, I'm followed.

"Mum," I yell joyfully down the receiver.

"Darling! I thought you were out. Don't you answer your phone anymore, darling?"

"The phone rings constantly, Mum; sometimes, I don't even bother to look to see who it is."

"Are you all right? You sound a little down."

Mum knows. She always knows. "I'm fine, Mum. The constant attention is driving me nuts."

"You need to get away," she says firmly.

"Mum, I've just been away. Remember?"

"Very funny. I'll meet you at Liz's place at 4:00; Ben will take me. Leave as soon as the kids get home from school. There's no need to prepare anything; Liz had a friend over for dinner last night and she has tons of leftovers."

Immediately, a sense of mutiny. Seeing too many bloody people. Want to be alone.

You always think you want to be alone when you're depressed.

What have I got to be depressed about? Only that I'm never alone. "Hey Mum? I don't really feel up to it, but maybe you could convince Adam to come?"

"Nonsense. You need to get out."

"They'll just follow me, Mum. They're everywhere."

She laughs. "Put Adam on the phone. He'll give them the slip."

I watch Adam nodding his head, smiling. Plans are being made for me, without my input. Again.

"There's nobody to give the slip to," he says. "She's imagining things."

Why would he say that? Is he trying to paint me as insane?

The children crash in as he's replacing the receiver; he calls out instructions while I sit on the sofa like a ragdoll. Perhaps I don't exist.

"I don't want to go," I say.

"You're going," says Adam.

LIZ LIVES ABOUT AN HOUR away and Adam takes the back route, speeding along so ferociously that, when I risk a glance back, nobody is there. Perhaps they never were, except in my head. When we arrive, the teenage cousins rush out and hug each other passionately. We did something right there. Liz tells me Ben's family is bringing Mum within an hour.

We sit around the kitchen table and Liz's husband Joe cracks jokes until my face aches from smiling.

"You see?" Adam informs me triumphantly. "You need to get out more."

He's right; the reluctance to go outside is becoming a phobia that must be conquered.

"Let's go for a walk," says Liz.

The familiar reluctance clenches my gut, but she isn't taking no for an answer. So we don our winter gear again and troop out of the safety of her house, the kids splotched together behind us, reluctant because they're teenagers; but we have always gone for walks since they were little and they don't refuse to come.

We meander along a backroad, but people still cross our path. "Hello Sam," Liz calls out cheerily; living in a small town, she knows everybody. "Hey, Liz. Could that be your sister? Hey, how's it going?"

We meet four people. They'd all heard of me; they all wanted to talk to me. After the second one, Liz said firmly, "We can't chat now; we're going for a walk."

"Do you mind if I just take a quick photo... we'd be so honoured."

And I watch the uncertainty in Liz's face. The struggle between her desire to protect me and her desire for good relations with her neighbours.

"Now you see?" I tell her, safely back in her kitchen with my wine glass clenched in my hand.

"See what? That you hate friendly neighbours?"

"Snapping photos is normal friendly neighbourliness?"

Liz walks over to me and fills my wine. "I thought it was sweet. They wanted to capture a big family walking in the sun during COVID."

"Oh, come on, this isn't the crazy early days when nobody was going outside. They wanted to photograph me."

Liz leans over me and strokes my cheek. "Now why would they want to do that?"

Oh, these ever-more frequent frissons of rage. "Mon Dieu," I quote, "donnez-moi la médiocrité!"

"What?" says Adam.

"I know what she means," says Liz quietly, bending over me and giving me a hug. "She is what she is, even if she'd prefer to be otherwise. Oversensitive, paranoid, manic-depressive, obsessive..."

"All right," I interrupt, "we get the picture."

"I don't," Adam grumbles.

"It's a prayer for mediocracy, assuming that intelligence increases the capacity to suffer. She's saying she'd prefer to be dumb."

Adam stares at me incomprehensibly. "Keep inhaling pot the way you are and you soon will be."

Joe is cooking and delicious smells waft in our direction. "But you do see, don't you, Liz? One can't get away politely. They don't let you."

"So get away impolitely. Speak firmly, smile and ignore. Who cares if your neighbours think you're a snob?"

I don't say that she'd been pretty reluctant to antagonize her neighbours less than an hour ago.

"Alienation from my community isn't the issue anymore. When I go out, I'm basically incapable of achieving what I went out to do."

"What do you mean?"

I lean over to scoop up some chips. "If I want to watch Jonathan play soccer, I can't. If I shop, it takes me ten times as long."

Adam snickers. "That's because you can't do two things at once, despite your alleged brilliance."

Then the door thumps and Ben's family fills the kitchen, laughing and talking. Mum sits down next to me, accepting a cigarette and a glass of wine, despite the fact that Ben's wife Leah promptly pulls her sweater over her nose and begins to cough.

"How rude," Mum whispers to me. Mum was brought up in a different era.

We mobilize the kids for a tobogganing excursion. As they rush hither and thither, locating snow pants and the always-lost "other" mitten, I realize that I'm happy. The children love their cousins, and I am free to sit and sip and puff without anybody shelling me with expectations. She always makes me feel good, my sister.

Once the children have departed in the direction of the tobogganing hill, the noise level actually ratchets up a few more decibels as the adults relax. This is what I love, watching my family seize life by the balls: arguing, knocking back wine and food, wringing the last ounce of enjoyment out of every moment.

Except when they're depressed.

Well yes; we're prone to that.

"The only reason you think the CBC is any good is because every other radio program is total rubbish," Ben is saying. "The CBC is so bleeding heart I can hardly bear to listen to it anymore—always giving air space to some whiner or other."

"Many of your so-called whiners have valid grievances, and the CBC is the only venue where they can access the ear of the nation," Liz replies. "I bet a lot of wrongs have been made right through the CBC."

"Bull!" shouts Ben. "The only people that listen to the CBC are the same bleeding hearts that agree with them anyway."

"I listen to the CBC all the time and I certainly don't always agree," Mum says in her quiet voice.

"Plus they pretend they're neutral, but they're not really," Ben bellows right through her.

Joe places a huge plate of shrimps and garlic butter on the table.

"This is really living," Mum and I exclaim at the same time and laugh. Dad used to say that.

There is a few minutes of contented scoffing. No saving the best for the kids in this family!

"The CBC uses language that shows complete prejudice. Like when they suggested that Israel treats Palestinian minors in prison badly." Ben douses a shrimp in butter and washes it down with a swig of beer, hardly pausing for breath. "In fact, the opposite is true—but even if there was a grain of truth to it, that focus ludicrously ignores the fact that Hamas groomed these kids to do horrific things in the first place."

"I heard a program about a group the other day, I don't remember which group...," says Mum.

"The CBC airs information that supports whatever cause they happen to be championing at the time," Ben plows through her again.

"I think you have to look pretty hard for those types of examples," says Liz irritably.

"I'll give you a million of them," Ben shouted. "On the radio the other week, the CBC was interviewing a First Nation guy about a bunch of money they'd just gotten from the government. This guy was complaining that they weren't being given complete freedom to dispose of their own money the way they see fit."

I grin and grin, looking from one animated face to the other. This is my tribe, all right. They'll always interact with me in exactly the same way, ignoring me and yelling over my head, no matter what's going on in my life. How comforting.

"The residential schools are the biggest blot on Canadian history!" my sister is yelling right back, smoking and scoffing shrimp simultaneously. "They should give them as much airspace as they can, anything that can restore the pride we destroyed..."

"The CBC program I heard was about some group that had been placed in an institutional school in the '40s and '50s, I think," says Mum.

"So, in the interest of restoring their pride, we should ignore the truth? Why didn't the CBC interview someone who could explain that the reason this First Nation group wasn't getting control over the money was because they'd done a crap job controlling their money in the past, misspending, misappropriating, lining the chiefs'..."

"I can never get a word in edgewise," Mum murmurs in my ear.

"*Shut up!*" I cry, then whisper into the sudden silence: "Mum wants to say something."

Another plate appears, bearing baby quiches. Ben and Liz set to with gusto. "This group that I was listening to on the CBC had been in an institutional type of school," Mum says quietly, "I think they were mentally challenged or something. Anyway, they were describing the treatment as though it were the most terrible thing. I went to a posh British private school, and we got more or less the same treatment, as far as I could tell."

Outraged "Oh Mums" fill the room. "How can you say that?"

"What was similar?" asks Liz.

"They complained on the CBC that they were forced to finish the food on their plates and were punished if they refused. In my school, I remember one time the girl beside me couldn't force her sausage skins down, and she began to retch. The teacher made her crawl back and forth under the table and bark like a dog."

We all stare at Mum. "What's that got to do with our discussion?" asks Ben.

"Weren't you talking about the CBC having an agenda? It's the same thing. Giving voice to the victim without a balanced voice from the other perspective. Schools were very different back then for all of us. Children were simply treated differently. Corporal punishment was applauded. Sexual abuse was not, obviously, but it was still rampant in the private boy schools."

"But they're not all fucked up as a result, are they Mum?" says Liz. "Those same boys that were beaten and raped throughout their private school lives are now running England."

"Oh, that's what's wrong with England," cries Ben, dissolving into laughter at his own wit.

"And why aren't they fucked up?" continues Liz. "Because their culture wasn't ridiculed and disdained, and that's why it's not the same as what you experienced, Mum…"

"Because raping and beating is British culture," howls Ben, falling off his chair in a paroxysm of infectious mirth that has us all giggling.

The children burst in, red-cheeked from the cold, and discard a waist-high pile of outdoor clothes in the entryway.

Dinner is delicious: leftover cold cuts of lamb with reheated mint sauce. Salad and potatoes. I enjoy every bite, marvelling at the hubbub of children's voices added to the mix. Adam and I should eat better; food is a great source of happiness.

And company.

In moderation.

LIZ PUTS HER ARMS AROUND me when it's time to leave. Adam is already sitting in the car, beeping. "Are you okay though? Are you still… sad?" she whispers in my ear.

"Not when I'm stoned, which is usually. Makes me like Adam better too."

She withdraws her head so she can look me in the face. "He's really trying. I hope you appreciate that."

"Amazing! Liz supporting Adam?"

"You're so down on him all the time."

"Really?"

She envelopes me in a hug again. "Sorry. I don't mean to criticize. Just do whatever you need to get through this. Create a routine. If two hours aren't enough, carve out four. I just wish you wouldn't avoid everybody—even me—when you smoke."

"It's a serious downside."

Human interactions are so complicated, even when you can grasp what's going on. Which you unfortunately can't, Looney-tunes.

chapter sixteen

MARCH 30: 11 A.M.

Finally, I have carved out a routine. Sticking to it has made a big difference, though even when I think I'm relaxed, weird, unpredictable mood swings still overwhelm me without warning.

The first item on my routine is to prepare breakfasts and lunches for the kids, while Adam stays upstairs. This has all been worked out; if he's not in the kitchen, there's no running critique on the health of my food.

Next, I walk the children to the school bus at the end of the road. BI (before incarceration), I used to enjoy this part of my routine, but now the remnants of the Gaggle, including a neighbour or two, stake out the end of my driveway. Rebecca insists that I don a clean coat and pants, when she used to suffer my goat-y clothes in silence.

I am grateful for the steady stream of Jonathan's chatter as we walk along the road, because it condones brevity with the neighbours. Every single car slows down so its owners can spew meaningless pleasantries through the window. This is new. It fills me with resentment.

Mountains out of fucking molehills.

Look, I want to walk quietly down my own road, chatting to my children, without being interrupted every five minutes. Why do I have to exchange pleasantries with every fucking neighbour every time I step out of my house?

Listen fruitcake, dope makes you pathologically anti-social. Friendly neighbours are normal.

"Why is your face all red, Eema?" asks Rebecca. "What's wrong?"

"Nothing's wrong, sweetie."

I take deep breaths, trying to calm my ridiculous, thudding heart. I'm trying to figure out my needs and look after myself. But what if I go insane anyway?

You've always walked a thin line.

I stand with the kids at the bus stop, smiling at the other mothers, thwarting their desire to interact by talking in Hebrew.

"It's fun that we can speak a language nobody else understands," I say to my kids, tempting them into the game, "plus it's good for you to practise."

Once they're safely on the bus, I wander home, gathering grass and other plants for my goats on the way. Every time a car passes, I'm busy in the ditch. Still, they beep, waving frantically, even though I'm obviously busy...

The gall!

Exactly! Look, I just want to be left alone. I don't want layer upon layer of human beings encircling me, enclosing me, waiting desperately for any piece of attention I might throw their way. The kids and Adam. The animals—yes, I know they're my choice and I enjoy them, but they're still more sentient beings wanting my attention. My mother and siblings. Neighbours. Friends...

You haven't seen a single friend for months.

It's true. In the first few days, I posted on Facebook and wrote to everybody in my email contacts: I am overwhelmed. Please forgive me, but don't contact me.

It's like you want the world to disappear.

Crazy, eh? I mean, if I really did want that. Of course, I don't. Grass always greener and all that bullshit.

My mind begins to swell with trepidation as I reach the last turn before the Gaggle, toting an armload of greenery for my goats.

To pass through captivity with mind unscathed and then to lose it here. No, don't think like that! Arrange your face in a neutral expression...

Martyr-like, more like.

A few half-hearted questions as I pass; they already know I'm not going to speak to them, but they keep going, just like the ads for Duracell batteries.

I walk stiffly with my green burden up the driveway, enduring those eyes boring into my back. Then I'm around the corner of the house and into our backyard, my whole body slumping in relaxed relief. Only then do I realize how tense I'd been.

The goats fall on the greens, practically tearing them out of my hands as I try to get the load into their hay rack. I entice Willow onto the milk stand and feed her some grain to keep her busy while I milk. Pressing my head into her warm flank, I recite all the wonderfully positive aspects of my life. This gift of warm milk squirting through my fingers is definitely one of them.

I feed the wild birds and the hens, who have also given me gifts. Carrying milk and eggs, I totter back to the house. Adam is having breakfast.

"I want to build a wall around our property," I announce, straining the milk through a filter into the milk jug.

"Good morning to you too. Why? Because a neighbour occasionally lurks at the end of our driveway in the hopes of glimpsing our menagerie?"

"What an odd question. The end of our driveway is crammed with idiots every day."

"Is that what you think?" He looks at me strangely. "Would you say that there's less and less of them?"

"Fewer and fewer," I correct him, popping my toast into the toaster.

"Sounds weird."

I begin to wash the filter, so it can be reused. "So what about the wall?"

"How are you feeling, anyway?"

"I need to feel protected, or I'll go mad. What are your reasons against building a wall?"

But as usual, he has no reasons. He's taken a stand without any thought at all.

A Looney-tunes and a non-thinker making the decisions. Great marriage.

"I'll think about it," he concedes, "but be careful how many outrageous requests you make."

"Thank you."

It's been hard on him too, this rupture in our status quo. He's still clutching at his receding dream to make millions from my next book.

The next part of my routine is four glorious, uninterrupted hours by myself, armed with my companions in the cold, smoky basement room I've labelled as mine: books, Sudoku, my journal and computer. It might be the coldest, yuckiest room in the house, but my happiest moment of the day is when I enter it.

"I cannot live like this," I had told Adam plainly, the day after I'd spoken to Liz. "There has to be a quiet time in my day."

"I'm only asking you to do this for one year. Why should you live a life of indolent luxury, just because you're an introvert?"

He has a point.

"I know I'm privileged. But since I *can* choose how much I work..."

"Who put you in that position in the first place?"

Yes, yes, because you worked so hard all your life, yada, yada, yada. You'd have worked full-time no matter who you married, because you're a nose-to-the-grindstone kinda guy. And I would *never* have worked full-time, so our current positions aren't co-dependent.

Of course, I didn't say this. I kept to the script, partially written by Liz, and circled again and again to my original point: I cannot live like this. I could see the dollar signs extinguishing in Adam's eyes as I explained my need for peace and quiet, but we finally agreed to four hours of uninterrupted work. Victory!

FOR THE FIRST HOUR I read and eat breakfast and then I meditate, punctuated by naughty dreams in which Kassem's tongue usually collides with my clit, though I expect time will soon introduce another's phantom tongue. Still, he creeps into my thoughts several times a day.

After my meditation, I go online, searching every day for news of him. So far, I have been amazed by the efforts he's been making since I left; he is in the midst of peace talks, attempting to reach out to Syrian rebel groups, dangling the carrot of real elections, trying to find common ground in their fight against ISIS. I'm so proud of him. Perhaps I will contact him and tell him.

Then I search myself; this has become, unfortunately, almost as tempting as watching the clips from my imprisonment. I read and reread everything that has ever been written: skim the positive; seethe and ponder over the negative; blow fuses at the lies.

There are new form entries on my website every day. Adam created the website for me when I published my first book; I dimly remember the excitement in the beginning when my inbox informed me of a new entry. Now, it's inundated with messages, ranging from praise at my courage to pleas for help on various personal issues (as though I was successfully dealing with my own!) to a spate of fan mail about God knows what because who has time to read it? Adam suggested I hire someone to respond, but I don't want to respond. I want them to go away. Their idea of me is so wrong. Can't they hear how moronic I sound on the video clips? Are they so desperate for heroes?

Then there are the people who "know" me. A Facebook message from someone who was in Katimavik with me. Don't they remember that they all voted to kick me out of Katimavik, while I sat in their midst weeping? Many messages from old school colleagues. For most of junior high, I spent my lunches in the bathroom, meting out my pee dribble by dribble so that the rotating occupants of the neighbouring stalls would think I was doing my business, rather than being totally friendless. What do these people want from me now? We've already established that we don't like one another.

The online bombardment invariably kicks off a state of excited irritation, so I always end the session with a particular video clip, which calms me.

It's our last night. Kassem has hugged me, and I suddenly push him away and say it's enough.

"Enough for whom?"

"Enough to show my affection and gratitude to you, and to indulge in my great attraction for you, without destroying my marriage."

He must have thought you were insane, preaching morality because he hugged you.

Yeah well, I *thought* he was driving his tongue down my throat. Fuck off. It wouldn't be the first time I'd fantasized about a despicable human being. But I don't watch it to remind myself of his duplicity. It makes me sad to realize how our entire interaction was based on a lie. No, I watch it because it reinforces my belief in myself. I am a person who defines the values that are important to me and tries to live by them. My greatest flaw is my beast-like, uncontrollable anger.

well, you're also pretty lazy, insensitive to others, unaware, disorganized...

Shut up! Right now we're focusing on my *worst* flaw.

I am doing everything I can to eliminate this flaw, such as carving out this space so I can reflect on it. That's the best we can do.

Finally, I write. Sometimes it comes easily; usually, it's like pulling teeth. Whatever the session's like, it ends when I hear the children's voices upstairs. "Eema!" they bellow. "EEEMMMMMAAAA!"

Repressing the nudge of dismay that my four hours are up for another twenty, I rush upstairs to simulate happy motherhood, the job which comprises the rest of my routine.

"Gross," Jonathan says, falling back from the basement door as I exit. "It stinks down there."

"Oh my God, close the door," Adam freaks, thankfully on his way out to check on his bees, who might be out on a now-sunny, +9 day.

"You know that you're killing us with your secondhand smoke?" Jonathan accuses.

I ransack the cupboards for a snack. "I have to do a shop. Your father never buys any treats."

"Are you listening?"

"Yes, darling, but I don't think my smoking in the basement while you're at school is going to kill you. Would you like a cheese stick and a yogurt tube?"

You know individually wrapped treats aren't environmentally friendly.

"My teacher is an idiot," Rebecca chimes in conversationally and launches into a story about the teacher chastising the whole class for talking, but Rebecca hadn't been talking; in fact, she hated those stupid boys who talked and made it hard to listen, and she didn't appreciate the teacher lumping everyone together.

Jonathan tries to interrupt several times, which makes Rebecca's story infinitely longer, so he attempts an elaborate eye-rolling exchange with me, but I daren't participate because Rebecca's eyes are fixed on my face.

"Is it my turn yet?" he interjects and is subjected to two icy stares.

Eventually, she can think of no more to say on the subject, and Jonathan leaps in with a list of all the one hundreds he got that day—seven quizzes, no less, and every question must be examined individually. I wonder if it's too early for a joint.

"I have a soccer game today at 5:00. Are you taking me?"

"Isn't Joan taking you?"

"She always takes me. How come you don't take me anymore? Don't you want to watch me play?"

"Of course I do!"

Bull.

"I'm one of the best in the team, Eema. Come outside and watch my new moves."

Swathed in my winter jacket, I listen to a play-by-play description of each move, trying to figure out when I'd stopped attending extracurricular activities.

The bright sun on my cheeks, I applaud Jonathan, then join him in a game of soccer, ignoring the headlines running across my vision: "Mendel Indulges in Game of Soccer with Son."

We call the chickens, who come running madly from all directions and are rewarded with little chunks of bread. The goats *maa* for attention.

"Shall we take the goats for a walk? We haven't done that in a while," says Jonathan.

Surely I haven't avoided that too? "Sure."

"Do you want to take them to the river?"

"Nah, let's cut through the back of our property to the lake."

"But we haven't been to the river in ages."

The animals rush out of their enclosure as though they'd been suffering from claustrophobia in their acre of fenced woods. I entice them into the woods with a handful of Cheerios.

"The Gaggle might follow us if we go to the river."

"What Gaggle?"

"Haven't you noticed there are always people at the end of our road?"

"Do you mean the neighbours that walk on the road?" Jonathan asks. "I like talking to them."

Sanctus Simplicitus. He thinks they're just walking there by chance. "But if we see one, I'd have to talk to them, and you hate it when I do that."

"That's because you never stop talking, once you start."

"Let's be quiet for a bit now." My good little boy finds a stick and begins to participate in some imaginary war game with a lot of whoops and thrusts; the animals become his retinue, eyeing him suspiciously as he rallies them with a war cry.

I am left with my thoughts. Just the way I like it.

JONATHAN ALWAYS INSISTS on arriving at his soccer games half an hour before they actually start. He is jubilant that I'm there to watch him, so I hide my anxiety and pray for calm.

A chorus of "hellos" as I reach the bleachers. "Hello," I call back jovially to the entire group, eyes searching for Joan. The least I can do is sit by her, to thank her for taking my kid to all the soccer games.

But everyone is talking at me. "How are you doing? It's been a long time since we've seen you here."

None of you gave a shit whether I was here or not BI.

Just justify your son's jubilation.

I try. I smile and answer, even though my head starts to ache from swivelling backward to look at my interrogators.

"I'm so glad you're here. I've been meaning to ask you—what was it like? I mean, really?"

How am I supposed to answer that in a nutshell? "It was... pretty similar to what you saw in the video clips." Like fucking duh, every second was documented, what more is there to ask?

"I don't know how you survived, not knowing if you'd ever see your kids again."

"Well, technically, as soon as I believed that I wasn't going to see them again, I ceased to survive." .

They all laugh uproariously at this.

Another woman says, "I think about it all the time—what I'd do in that situation."

I smile and turn back to the front, but there seems to be a line of people passing, almost like a queue. As soon as I'm facing them, several stop. "I thought it was you. How are you? You must remember me. Our kids go to the same school."

"Hello," I reply brightly. "The game is starting."

But there's a little ring about me, blocking my view. "I know it's kitschy, but do you mind signing your book for me? I loved *A Hero*, I couldn't put it down."

"Sure. But I really came to see my kid playing soccer."

"Of course you did." The bodies part like the Red Sea, standing in two solid columns while I peer out through the tunnel. The kids are racing after the ball like a flock of chickens after a piece of bread. Jonathan seems to control the ball rather well, and he's fast.

"How are you settling in, now that you're back?" someone is asking. It's always been hard for me to focus on more than one thing at the same time. I want to concentrate on my son's game; who are these people?

Oh, come on.

I vaguely recognize their faces, but I've certainly never talked to any of them before.

"I'm doing fine," I say. "Wow, we've got a goal. I've got to watch this!"

"Sure, sure," they say. But it goes on. People pass in front of me and wave, every minute. Each wave fans a core of irritation. It's like they're thrusting themselves onto my attention.

Fixing my eyes on Jonathan, I respond as automatically as possible.

"He's a great little player," a soccer mom says.

"Mmhmm."

Someone actually pokes me in the back. "How come you don't come to any of the games? The kids need all the encouragement they can get."

There are these rushes of rage, like electric shocks, that jolt through my body sometimes.

"He's playing twice as good today because you're here."

I turn around and stare at the man. Why can't we just be honest: hey, the fact that you want to talk to me doesn't mean it's reciprocated.

Yeah! Ask them how they can be ignorant of the massive intellectual gap ...

Well, isn't it a bit weird that people recognize physical differences, but not intellectual? No hideously ugly men have ever dared to approach me, but stupid men—oh my God! When, in fact, I'd much rather fuck an ugly genius.

"We're all busy, but they're not young forever," the man was saying.

I rub my sore neck surreptitiously, pinching it to allay the foolish sting at the back of my eyes. Turn back to the game without answering.

"Hey, I hope you're not offended."

I throw a smile over my shoulder, shaking my head.

Headline: "Mendel Bursts into Tears at Kid's Soccer Game."

It's like some kind of nightmare that I can't escape. Person after person, determined to stop me watching the game, while astounded that I don't watch more of them. Eventually I get up, pretending to need the washroom.

Headline: "Mendel Pees."

I walk to the other end of the field and try to watch from there. Jonathan's at the centre of every tussle, and the ball invariably pops through the melee of limbs in the direction Jonathan wants it to go. I'm glad that I had time to notice this before the tide of people alter direction and flow toward me again, as though I were a magnet.

Finally, it's over. I hightail it out of there with Jonathan in tow, complimenting him.

"Did you see that big guy? He kept on trying to stop me, but I just dodged around him. David and Goliath!" he laughs happily.

"You were great."

"Hey Eema, you said we'd go to the shops."

"I meant to, but I'm so tired."

"Aww, c'mon Eema. Abba never buys treats."

"Who can say no to a soccer star?" I gather my energies to enter the fray again. In any case, a roast chicken will save me making dinner.

Every salesperson in Superstore finds a reason to hang around the produce section as I pick my fruit.

"How's it going?"

"Do you know I watched you online every evening? I'd skim through the hours until I found a good bit, and then I'd listen to it while I got dinner ready."

Still, I struggle to stay polite, exchanging a word here, a smile there, a sentence or two with the plump lady who always offers Jonathan sliced meat to taste. The problem is, I can't do these things and check the fruit for bruises at the same time. I have to stop checking the fruit and wait until the exchange has finished.

"Can you stop talking to people? I'm starving," says Jonathan.

I bend my head to whisper sotto voce in Hebrew: "Say that every time somebody stops to talk. Say it urgently and pull on my sleeve."

The first person ignores him, dangling firmly from my other sleeve.

"My son is tired," I point out, moving on.

The next person exclaims, "Oh, the poor little boy!"

Headline: "Mendel Drags Exhausted Kids around Store."

People keep talking, Jonathan keeps complaining, I doggedly try to finish the shop. I stagger out of there, shaking, and suddenly bend down to retch beside the car.

"Are you sick?"

"Maybe. Let's get home."

Safe in the barn, I try to roll a joint between my tremulous fingers. It's the only way to get through the rest of the evening; an instantaneous and desperately needed mood swing. The black hen Miss Muffet decides to bully Nonny, sidling along the roost in order to peck savagely at Nonny's head. I grab the broom handle to poke her backward, but Nonny has already jumped to the next beam. That's what dope's all about, bringing your focus to the immediate present.

Feeling better, I run into the house to chop up some veggies to go with the chicken.

The children are upstairs, but unfortunately Adam is in the kitchen unpacking the bags, criticizing each item as he lifts it from the bag: "Why did you buy this? It's like feeding the kids chemicals"/ "We already have one of those"/ "Didn't you check the fruit for bruises?" And on and on; it's like a script. It would make a funny movie, a caricature of marriage.

"Have you smoked?" he asks, sniffing around me like a dog.

"Yes."

"You reek. Chew some gum or something so the kids don't smell it. The rule is no toking until the kids are in bed."

"You have a lot of rules," I say.

He bristles, but luckily dinner is ready and the kids come down and he subsides.

Rebecca picks out the things she likes and Jonathan is silent, filling the hole in his stomach.

After dinner, the children practise their instruments and indulge in their one hour of electronics while I give the animals their supper. Then I come in, feed the cats, and empty the lunch bags so they're ready for tomorrow. Rebecca has a test, so I go upstairs to ask her questions. Then it's snack time. It feels like I'm lurching from one need to another, praying there are only ten leaks in the dam to stop with my fingers. More than that and we shall all drown.

One of my favourite parts of my routine is lying with the kids before they go to sleep. I always read to Jonathan, giving each character different voices to inject life into even the most mediocre books. By this point in the day, my entire being aches to lie down. But there's Adam, lying on Jonathan's bed, reading the news on his iPad. Every day, it's the same scene: "Abba," Jonathan murmurs with the sweetest hug and kiss, "Eema is here to read to me."

"You want Abba to read to you today, don't you?"

"No, Abba, you have to leave now."

Abba drops his iPad on the floor and promptly buries his head in Jonathan's armpit. "Abba wants to stay. There's room for Abba!"

I stand there, wondering what would happen if I keeled over right then and there.

"There isn't room," Jonathan points out, beginning to shove. This is my cue to get in on the act. Resisting the urge to pummel and pinch (because Adam loves this bit and prolongs it as long as possible), I drag him by force on to the floor. Invariably, he brings all the blankets with him, clutched in both hands. This infuriates Jonathan, who had arranged them carefully.

"You're an idiot, Abba!"

"Don't be rude to me. You're not using the iPad for a month, do you hear me?"

Every day, an acerbic ending.

I begin to read.

"GOONDAREEOOV," howls Adam from the bathroom.

"What, Abba? I'm reading," snaps Rebecca.

"GOONDAREEOOV!" Now he's laughing hysterically at his own wit.

"Shut up, Abba!"

"Don't be rude. GOONDAREEOOV!"

They say that there must be five times as many positive interactions as negative between two people in order for a relationship to be successful. There was actually a period where I marked checks under the headings "Positive" or "Negative," in order to count them at the end of the day, but it became too confusing. Does an irritable eye roll count as a negative? Adam's nightly ritual springs from pure affection. He's interacting with his beloved kids—by annoying the hell out of them. Is this positive or negative?

Once Jonathan has drifted off, I head into Rebecca's room. I lie beside her and massage her back, her feet. She is like a cat, luxuriating in my touch. I love my kids.

After they're both asleep, Adam usually retreats to our bedroom with his iPad and I have a wonderful hour to myself; usually I do Sudoku and Wordle and smoke on my sofa until I'm sure Adam's asleep, but my sortie to the soccer field has tired me, and I crawl upstairs earlier than usual. It's fine when he wraps his arms around me and pushes in; I don't even know why I resist it, it takes so little effort and gives such pleasure. And it puts him in a harmonious mood. Afterwards, I pull his head onto my chest and begin to scratch. "We have to build a wall around our house, Adam. I've done some research and it's expensive, but we have money, right? It'll be around $35,000 for a wooden fence per acre." I rush on, despite his incredulous expression. "But we only need a wooden fence around the front and sides of the house for privacy—the rest can be chain link, which is much cheaper. I figure we can do the whole thing for like, $100,000."

Adam undergoes a coughing fit.

"It won't take more than a few weeks. Six or seven max."

Adam appears to be choking to death. I thump him on the back. There's a long silence.

"Hamood, you want to spend hundreds of thousands of dollars to blockade ourselves in like rats?"

I tell him about the soccer game. The shop. I will him to understand. The horror at the unwanted attention. The fear that I'll say something rude and damage my relationship with the community, or worse, my children's. The oscillation between depression and the numbness of being stoned.

"Are you saying that you're never happy?"

"How hard it must be, to be married to someone like me."

He lifts his head away from my scratching fingers to look at my face. "What are you talking about? I love you."

"I know you do. So I really need this wall." I feel suddenly hot and reach behind me to open the window a notch. Cold March air cools my forehead.

He laughs, dropping his head onto my chest for further ministrations. "Don't use love to manipulate me."

"Haven't you been listening? I need an oasis of space where I'm not being scrutinized. It's imperative for my sanity."

"You can't use your sanity as an excuse every time you want something," he says, pulling his head away. "You claimed your sanity was in danger when you insisted on four hours of privacy, where you do fuck-all as far as I can see…"

"I'm writing!"

keep calm.

"And now you claim that sanity insists on enclosing us in a cage. Try to think of the children—will they have to get down to unlock a gate every time they want to ride their bikes down the road? You haven't thought it through."

"The reporters at the end of the road aren't going away. Every time I'm outside, I can hear their ears straining for any tidbit of information. Prowling the line of trees for a chink. They'll fuck off if there's a wall, and even if they don't, I'll have seven acres of freedom in this whole world, and I need that."

He sits up and pulls off the condom with distaste, dropping it to the floor, to my distaste. "I wish you wouldn't talk like that. You sound crazy. There are no reporters at the end of the road and you already have seven acres of freedom. I won't be caged in my own house."

"You're compelled to argue about every single…"

"Your wants are a bottomless pit. You've got your four hours of privacy and now you…"

Our voices clamber up the hill of decibels; God knows what energy reservoirs I'm draining.

"I'm doing exactly what *you* want…"

"It's me that wanted you to make nothing for a living?" he asks incredulously.

Every married couple in the world, bickering in just this way, the classic power struggle, each trying to shove their POV down the other's throat. But thanks to the miracle-worker, I compromise instead of murdering.

"What about half a wall?" I interject.

"You're crazy."

"Basically, you *think* you'll feel like a rat in a cage, and I *know* I feel like a rat in a cage right now. Everyone is gawping at me. I can't stand it, Adam. I need to draw a curtain around my cage or I really…"

That bloody stinging behind the eyes again.

He lies back, scratching his pubic hair contentedly. "Can you close the window? It's freezing. You see, the problem is that you were spoiled as a child, and now you have too many expectations and are never satisfied."

It's funny that someone can love you and still interpret your feelings in a negative way when they don't understand them.

I take his hand. "I don't 'have it all'—I have less than I used to. Can't you see? Every life choice I've made has embraced solitude: refusing to work full-time after the kids, living in the boondocks. For me this is like a nightmare, except I can't wake up." Now the tears begin to seep. He might think it's manipulative, but I can't help it. I massage his hand with all my strength. He's not looking at me; perhaps he won't notice.

"These spurts of rage mean that I'm not centred. Because the phone rings too often and life is so damn exciting." I laugh, and snot sprouts over my upper lip. I grope for a tissue on my bedside table, still massaging furiously with my free hand.

Adam peers up at me. "Are you crying, Hamood?"

"Sorry. This rage—it's very strong, Adam. I'm frightened."

"That you'll hit the kids?"

"That I'll do harm." I lower myself against him and push my head into his chest, staunching my tears on his hairiness.

"You won't, Hamoodi."

"The room downstairs is my sanctuary in this house, but I've always been an outside person. I need an outside sanctuary as well. This is my last request, I promise."

"How are my bees going to get through your wall?"

"We can make it a chain link fence in front of the hives."

"And the rest?"

"Thick. Soundproof."

He laughs. "You're insane," but then the laugh catches in his throat as I lift my face to his and he sees my expression.

"I'm going insane, aren't I? Help me!"

And I'm crying and he hugs me and hugs me. "We will build a wall," he says. And then a moment later. "We don't have the money to build a wall."

"I will pay for it. Every dime I earn will go toward it until it is paid off."

"You donate all your spare cash to environmental organizations. The wall is more important than the environment?"

I hesitate. "Nothing is more important than the environment, but no value is worth suffering for—especially when the impact of one little family is so negligible. I can't fight for the environment if I'm insane. I need a wall."

MARCH 31: 10 A.M.

Headline: "Mendel Breaking Up with Husband!"

It's such bullshit. I thought they'd gone last night, but they must have been at the end of the driveway, straining their little eardrums as we bellowed out our bedroom window. Even so, they got most of it wrong, chucking money issues and sex problems and God knows what into the mix. They even had a photo of me looking grim—I always look grim when I have to pass their horrible cameras, so that wouldn't have been hard.

"Can't we sue them?" I ask my husband.

The phone freezes halfway to his ear; he is in the middle of phoning contractors and negotiating prices for the wall.

"There are no reporters at the end of our driveway," he says firmly. "Why do you keep saying that?"

I bring my laptop over to show him.

The weird thing is, I can't find the article straight away. I key in various possibilities: "Mendel Breaking Up with Husband"; "Mendel, March 31, 2023"; the names of all the media outlets I can remember. My fingers start to judder against the keys.

He grasps my head between his hands and tries to raise it from the screen. "Do you see people at the end of our driveway all the time? Is that what you're telling me?"

I look into the moist carapaces wrapping his eyes.

I pull my head away and jab another name into Google.

Nothing. *There is no article.*

"Oh my God," Adam says, grabbing my face again. "Don't go crazy on me."

"I won't. Of course not. There's no Gaggle. Got it." I smile reassuringly, and after a few minutes he smiles back and releases me.

That night, once I'm sure he's asleep, I press my head into the pillow and cry. If I'm mad... if I'm mad... I'm fucking terrified... I'm seeing things that aren't there. I *remember* reading that article.

So you are insane. Damn, I was hoping it was just typical delusions of grandeur.

I bite the scars on my wrist to stifle the sobs. Voice, this isn't funny. Not even a smidgen of humour.

You're not seeing things all the time. Not when you're stoned, for example.

Is that true? I'm not sure... I don't remember... my mind is confused. But it's a straw, and I grasp it firmly with both hands. Stoned, in perpetuum.

chapter seventeen

APRIL 6: 10 A.M.

The builders are out there right now, making a godawful noise even as I write. It's hard to focus with that racket going on. This period of construction is hard, not just because of the noise but because it's impossible to go outside. I hurry back and forth to the animals, head down against the avidly curious eyes of the builders.

In your head.

It doesn't really matter if it's in my head, or if they're really avidly curious, does it? Either I'm mad or they are.

Preferable if it were them.

Not really; their madness ruins my life as much as my own would. Plus, my madness might be cured in time, but madness feeding off mob mentality doesn't have a chance.

Until they lose interest.

Inshallah.

I find excuses to avoid walking the children to the school bus in the morning, but they know.

"Just once a week, Eema. On Wednesday. That's my favourite day, so you have to walk with us on that day."

"Wouldn't it be better if I came on your worst day?"

"No. What good would that do?"

So Wednesdays become my worst mornings, hunching with irritation against the rabid curiosity of the Gaggle, newly energized by all the excitement, shoving microphones in my face as though I'd just come home.

"Why are you building a wall?"

I want to scream: because of you fuckers, what do you think?

Adam shows me examples of the gutter press, predicting the divorces and betrayals of celebrities, depicting horrible photos of beautiful stars' cellulite. Seemingly, the media can do what they want, so long as they bung in words like "allegedly" every few sentences. It's outrageous; they are like leeches. Just like the people pulling oil out of the ground even though we know it's environmentally suicidal. Just like the people who stay in power long after their nations stop wanting them. Where power and money is concerned, humans usually behave abominably. Fuck, I hate everybody.

But mostly, your own leeches.

If they can write what they want about me, it's imperative that I remain civil. Adam emphasizes this as we venture out to the porch for lunch, screened by the trees, whispering like criminals.

"But why do I care about being civil if they write horrible things anyway?"

Adam takes a huge bite of his omelette, watching me carefully. "Probably your neighbours' curiosity will continue, because neighbours are curious about everything anyway. The reason you have to be civil is because your position in the community is important to you, not to mention the kids, and everything will get worse if you antagonize people."

I'm not sure that he's right, and I'm not sure that I care. I have to whisper on my own porch. I'm imprisoned in my house. "What community? They're in cahoots."

He looks at me. Crumbs adorn his beard. "Hamood, try to think rationally, okay? Don't let yourself get paranoid."

Bit late for that.

"Okay, there's a workman coming up the driveway right now," I say to Adam in Hebrew. "There's a gap in the ivy around our screened-in porch; watch that gap."

Adam looks obediently.

The workman's head bobs past the gap, turned at a ninety-degree angle as he tries to peer through. I resist the urge to give him the finger. The strength of my wall depends on this guy.

Adam turns back to his sandwich. "Well, humans are curious. I'm not saying they're not. You have to find a way to ignore them."

"Ignore them? Every single human being is prying…"

"You have to try."

I take a sip of tea. "Most famous people have presumably pursued fame. I didn't choose this life. If fame means I can't swim in my river…"

My voice catches as I realize the enormity such a loss would mean. "Fame is anathema to me," I whisper.

Adam pushes away from the table and rubs my neck. He's being so fucking nice, despite the fact that I've whittled public engagements down to zero. "Just for the time being, so I have time to write my book," I had assured him. "Which you said will be a bestseller even if it's crap, remember?" To my astonishment, he hadn't said a word. And now he's rubbing my neck.

Headline: "Sex, Sex, Sex, That's All They Think about!"

"Hamood, I've been reading a bit about… depression, and I'm thinking perhaps you should see a counsellor."

"What?" Is this my husband talking? The Adam who thinks shrinks are just another proof of Western self-indulgence?

He rubs harder. "Your behaviour reflects certain symptoms."

"What behaviour? Depression? I was born that way."

"Avoiding certain situations. Reacting strongly to small stuff. Delusions of grandeur."

Being relentlessly negative about your long-suffering husband.

"You think what's happening is small stuff?" It's hard to whisper angrily.

"A few gossipy neighbours are curious. So what?"

He must be talking a foreign language.

"The websites say people with depression may withdraw from family and friends. And that we shouldn't take this personally; it's about the illness."

who'd have thought potheads and depressives have so much in common?

"Are you quoting from memory?" I whisper sarcastically.

Hey, milk this new angle.

"Perhaps I do yearn for more time to myself."

"Exactly. You spend hours a day by yourself and you want more."

My mouth literally drops open. "You used to work; you'd fuck off for about ten hours a day. Now there's something wrong with *me* because you never leave the fucking house?"

He takes his rubbing fingers away. "Keep your voice down. Your anger is a symptom too."

"Oh well, if every character flaw I've always possessed is suddenly a *symptom…*," I snap, standing to gather the plates. My little room calls to me. My tiny, smoky sanctuary.

"Keep your voice down, will you?"

Headline: "It's Official: Mendel's Gone Insane."

"Why not talk to someone? There are support groups if you don't want one-on-one counselling."

Milk it.

"Maybe you're right. Meds might help. Or mushrooms." Arms cradling the dirty lunch dishes, I push the door open with my foot.

"No meds. You don't need chemical crap to get you through this."

Damn.

Adam and a new idea are like a dog with a bone. Every day, he digs it up and flourishes it about. Have I thought about counselling? Have I googled depression?

Then one day he suggests that maybe I have post-traumatic stress disorder.

I'm glad it comforts him to give a name to my madness, but I was in a top-notch prison facility—rather like now—nothing "post" about it.

Bingo, you like being miserable!

I stay in my house all day, housebound; mostly roombound. Day after day, meditating with increasing desperation as the phone peals overhead. I google famous people, to see if there's a bunch of rubbish about them too. There is, which is strangely comforting. I find some boring articles examining the quality of my inner life. *Mendel likes to be alone because she's never bored. Her rich internal life occupies her, even when she's doing nothing.*

Most infuriating of all, people believe this crap. A spate of courses spring up as a result of the articles: "How to Enrich Your Inner Self."

Why are people so stupid? Human leaders are mostly extroverts, often with brilliant qualities, even if rich inner lives aren't among them. Besides, it's not a *choice*.

why do you care what rubbish unknown people believe?

I wrest my attention away from the present to ogle videos of myself in the room. Yakking away to myself all the time; how crazy it sounds. I even use different voices.

My voice is deeper and sexier.

Often, I feel great pity for this sad, lost little person, reading the words out loud as she writes in her diary. Trying to find meaning in random tragedy. Just like religion.

Except the religious think everybody is going to hell, except them.

While I wish humankind in general would go to hell. A heat wave that killed off a billion might enable the West to pull their selfish heads out of their arseholes and do something about climate change. I'd sacrifice myself as one of the billion, if I thought it would wake the rest of the world up. Everybody flying and driving as though their footprints weren't destroying the lives of their own kids. And they're calling *me* looney?

Milk it. Pull your head out of your own arsehole and do something to help the world.

I could make a video explaining that the value of time-spent-alone-to-think was precisely for that—learning how to think. Think about the fact that the scientists and experts tell us our actions this decade will cause or avert catastrophe. Tell them that my value is to be part of the solution in the fight against climate change, not part of the problem. Tell them how I had modified my life, and that they could too. Less meat, less travelling, less driving, less buying.

It doesn't matter what individuals do, if the corporations continue to pollute.

Collectively, people have power over corporations. We can choose to consume from eco-conscious companies and invest our money in renewables, not fossil fuels. We can attend protests and demand our governments slash emissions. Couldn't I turn the current interest into something good, just like I tried to turn Kassem's time with me into something good?

Hey, you could start a religious cult.

Or maybe I could change our political system. Instead of just letting anybody vote, wannabe voters would have to fill out a form, identifying which of their own values were reflected in their choice of candidate. To prove they've thought about it.

Wouldn't that be discriminatory?

How? Somebody would help them if they couldn't read or something. Why should the non-thinkers get to choose who runs the country? It's democracy's great flaw.

My little elitist.

We should force wannabe parents to fill out a form too, proving they've considered every aspect of childrearing before they're allowed to get pregnant.

Think—or lose all basic rights! I love your thinking, you fascist, you.

It's about living your life a certain way.

Rule #1, don't fuck psychos. That could help a lot of people.

At least I didn't fuck Kassem. It relieves me that I consciously decided not to harm my family. Especially since, increasingly, I feel like I'm damaging them now.

The builders bang away outside. The kids don't ask me to take them anywhere anymore, except to the Wednesday morning bus. No soccer, no extracurriculars. Adam does it all. They know. They are my wall. Protecting their crazy mother.

"Do you want me to kick them, Eema?" Jonathan asks one day.

"Who?"

"Those nasty neighbours?"

I hug him hard. "It'll be easier for us if we're polite to them."

APRIL 17: 1 A.M.

That night, Adam spoons me from behind and I press my bottom against him, but he doesn't slip inside like he usually does. Instead, he flips me over and begins to kiss my breasts, moving downwards.

"No," I say, placing my hand over my vagina. "It's not clean."

He pushes my hand away and begins to lick the inside of my thighs.

"I don't want to, Adam. It's not clean. I'm not in the mood."

"Shut up." His tongue slides over my labia and, despite myself, I arch toward him, willing his tongue to probe that tiny, miraculous knob. He teases me, lapping on either side, refusing to touch it even as it yearns toward him. I groan, my inhibitions forgotten. And then he's sucking, right there, at exactly the right spot, and a sigh slips through my lips, my eyes tightly clenched as I focus on the delightful sensation. His fingers push inside me, rubbing against that sensitive place inside as his tongue continues to stoke the mounting lust. But I cannot focus entirely on the sensation. Always, I am conscious of the amount of time my orgasms take, his tiring tongue. To speed it up, I have to fantasize. I am a third-world girl playing naked with my peers in the sea. I am beautiful. Three American soldiers watch us, their hard-ons pressing against their pants as our unconscious breasts glisten in the sunlight. We bathe in the sea day after day, until one day they take my clothes, and I search frantically while my peers get dressed, circling farther and farther away from the group. One of the soldiers appears before me, holding my clothes. I reach for them, and he holds money in his other hand. "I will give you this money, if you let us take some photos of you."

I want the money and the clothes.

"We won't hurt you," he says. "We just want some photos, because we think you're beautiful."

Photos aren't so terrible. I nod, trembling as he leads me toward the small building where they are stationed. There are two other men there; one holds a camera. The first man slides his hands over my smooth body, arranging me so that I am leaning back on a chair with my legs spread-eagled, my breasts jutting toward the sky. I am embarrassed, and my hands sneak down to cover my sex, but they push my hands away. They take photos, then ask me to stand up, turn around and bend over, spreading my legs and peeking through them. I tremble with both excitement and embarrassment. There is also fear, but they keep their word. They just take photos, and then they give me more money than I have ever seen. "My name is Tom," the first man says. "This is Jeff and Terry. If you come here tomorrow, we will give you even more money."

I argue with myself. I know it is wrong. But so much money, for so little! I go there the next day. Tom shows me an even bigger wad of bills than on the previous day. "Just for photos?" I ask.

"Yes. But for this extra cash, can we touch you?"

"No. I am not having sex with you."

"Of course not. We will remain dressed, just like now. But you are so beautiful, we want to touch you. Just with our hands. And maybe some kissing."

All that money, for a bit of kissing? Why not?

"Lie down and close your eyes," Jeff says. I feel soft lips trace the contours of my face, then move toward my breasts, circling the nipples with his tongue. Hands part my legs, then there is another tongue on my sex. Nobody has ever done this to me before. I try to reach down and cover myself with my hand but someone's face half-pushes, half-kisses my hand away, and a head burrows between my breasts, more flesh between my hand and its goal. I can't believe the sensations reverberating in my vagina. A gasp escapes my lips as tendrils of pleasure intertwine and build. My legs begin to shake. Something is inside me, and my eyes pop open in accusation, but they have kept their word. They are fully dressed; Tom is sucking and licking my whole torso, Jeff is kneeling between my legs. He has slipped his fingers inside me. Terry is snapping his camera, kneeling down for a close-up of Jeff's tongue on my clit.

I focus on what Adam is doing to me, but I am not Charlotte being pleasured by her husband, I am this third-world girl being exploited by three American soldiers. The third visit is similar to the second one, except this time Tom says to me as I climax, wide-eyed with amazement at the miracle my own body has achieved, "You liked that? It would be so nice if you could do the same for us." And Jeff positions himself over the top of me in a 69 position, and continues his cunnilingus as Tom slides inside. Terry takes close-ups of Tom's thrusting penis. And I want it, I ache for it, I come again as I look at Jeff's erection trembling over my face. Then Jeff pushes his penis gently against my mouth and asks if I can pleasure him, since he is pleasuring me, and then I am sucking his cock and Tom is contorting in climax and Terry is taking wide-shots of the entire scene. Then Jeff and Tom trade places and I suck Tom to hardness again while Tom sucks me, and Terry throws his camera on the table and shoves Jeff aside because it's his turn and he can't wait any longer. They penetrate every orifice, and some days later bring more men in to fuck me as well, charging them exorbitantly and paying me a fortune while Terry takes close-ups of huge penises sliding in and out of my slick cunt... displayed on huge screens to entice more soldiers...

My legs begin to shake uncontrollably and I cry out as I come, convulsing and trembling, unbearably sensitive immediately afterwards. And then Adam is inside me, sliding into my wetness and moving on top of me, and it feels great.

Afterwards, I scratch his head, feeling each finger scraping away the layers of possible resentment, from trying to be too good, from being married to someone too difficult. I feel so grateful for the spent relaxation of my body. "Do you think it is fucked up if you have to fantasize about violent sex in order to come?"

Adam lifts his head and looks at me. "Would you like me to pretend to rape you?"

"No. To experience violent sex would be the most terrible thing in the world. So why do I fantasize about it?"

"Maybe you watched too many porno clips in your adolescence. They're all violent. They're all about the pleasure of the men."

I scratch with renewed energy. Sometimes Adam hits the nail right on the head. "But why aren't there porno shows for women? Featuring three men baptizing every orifice with their tongues? So that the woman's orgasm is actually real?"

"Maybe waiting for the woman to come would slow down the action too much."

I ponder this. Watching the men thrusting until they come is pretty bloody boring too.

Then he says to me: "You realize that you've stopped all interaction with the public."

My fingers become defter, massaging across his scalp and down his nape. He groans with pleasure, arching his neck toward me like a cat. I hope that's done the trick.

236

But no, a few minutes later he asks, "And what's happening with the book?"

I sigh; fingers decelerate. "I'm so sorry, Adam."

He props himself on an elbow and looks at me. "Let me try to set up a couple of engagements, to put you in the public eye until your book is ready. I'm hoping that I can still whip up a bit of interest in you, even though you haven't published in a few years."

"No."

"If this book sells well," he says slowly, "I don't have to work forty hours a week. Ever again. Do you understand?"

Big incentive.

"People will leave me alone if I disappear."

He looks at me carefully. "I'll play the fame game if you like. Believe me, I want you to be as famous as you're pretending to be." He lays his head back down on my chest. "Public engagements will lead to selling more copies of the book."

He nudges me with his head. My fingers rise to his scalp in relief. We can't have a really nasty argument if I'm scratching his head. "Maybe you didn't hear me. I don't have to work forty hours if your next book sells well. It'll sell well, if people remember who you are. They'll only remember who you are, if they see you once in a while on social media."

"Fame will kill me."

He pulls his head away and sits up. "Cut the drama. If you ever did sell your books, we could buy a plot of land on the sea in some remote third-world country where nobody's heard of you. Money frees you."

I press my fingers in my eyes. "We can't just gallivant around the world; the children are in school. And I don't want to fly more than once a year. Or own two houses when others can't afford one. More stuff means more work and more stress."

He turns his back to me and swings his feet onto the floor. "We'd hire people to look after things."

"Oh great, then we'd be employers; that would cut our workload for sure."

"Okay, then we'll just rent. Is renting too much work for you?" he asks tetchily.

"No, and I think it's a great idea to take a holiday once a year, just as we've always done. More than that and you stop appreciating them."

"I think I'd appreciate a yearly six-month holiday very much."

"Flying all over the world increases our footprint, which harms the environment."

He shrugs irritably, as always when he hears the word.

"Look at me, Adam. I love you. All this attention makes me utterly miserable. If I withdraw, it'll go away. We don't need the money; you said this book will sell copies even if I don't do a thing to promote it."

He bends down and gives me a kiss. *Thank you God, thank you God.*

"You're still an idiot."

I hold my breath.

"You're suffering twice as much as a normal person would." He grumbles into his goatee for a while, apparently listing all the wonderful things we could do if only I'd leave the house. Phrases like "mad as a hatter" and "married into bonkers" waft toward me, and I reach up to rub the back of his head as he sits on the bed. Finally he snaps, "The fact that you're nuts is driving me nuts."

I hold my breath.

"Maybe I can go back to work part-time."

I reach for his head and pull it tenderly onto my chest. "I think that's a great idea."

APRIL 24: 11 A.M.

Warmer weather beckons and I want to go outside, but it's a week or two until they finish the fence. And my forced internment has a silver lining; namely, I'm writing! It's an easy book—all I have to do is wade through the material in my diary, select and edit. Tweaking, adding, cutting—all this makes me feel that I'm working. I waste fewer counterproductive hours online.

But the biggest and best change is...

Drum roll please.

Adam has gone back to work!

It was supposed to be part-time, but within a week he was swept back into the fast, exciting rhythm of his hi-tech company. He looks happier, and I'm fucking delirious. Six hours alone—not in the smoky little room downstairs but anywhere in the house. And in another week or so— anywhere on the fenced-in property! Everything is going to be all right. I can feel it.

APRIL 30: 2 P.M.

The workers have departed! It's the first time I've been outside in weeks and I dance around the property, giggling madly. I squat down in the middle of the garden and pee. I moon the animals. The wall protects me. It is miraculous to be outside, under sunny skies, safe from prying eyes. My little oasis.

Your seven-acre oasis, you privileged bitch.

If privacy equals privilege, I was a lot more privileged before this fame-thing ruined my life. Now I have to hide behind walls; my river is denied to me.

Oh this desert of egotism men call life.

I'm not a bottomless pit, destined to endlessly want more. I'm truly happy now.

MAY 5: AFTERNOON

I am content. I write, I smoke. I get stoned, well before Adam is due home in the hopes he won't notice. Doesn't always work.

"Are you stoned?" he snapped at me once when I had asked a stupid question.

"A little," I admitted.

"You're an addict, you know that?"

He wants the word to shock me, but all I can think is: *you're worried about that?* Okay, psychologically I probably am an addict. But so the fuck what? I'm managing, aren't I? Everything gets done. The kids are fine.

Until one day, they aren't. I hear them come in from school and call out to them. Jonathan goes immediately to his room and closes his door, which is a little unusual, but he's getting older.

"Do you want a snack?" I call through the closed door.

"No thanks, Eema," he replies.

"I don't either, Eema," Rebecca calls. "I have tons of homework."

I go downstairs and start to make dinner. Eventually Adam comes in and I call the kids to the table.

Jonathan plops down in his seat; I can see his eyes are swollen from crying. I put a plate of chicken, potatoes and salad in front of him. "What's wrong?"

"I'm never wearing these pants again," he says quietly, and the tears trickle down his cheeks.

Immediately, my own eyes fill. "What happened?"

Jonathan slips off his seat and curls into a heap on the floor, so Rebecca answers, "The kids were teasing him about his clothes."

I try to hug his rigid back, but he jerks irritably. "Why would they do that?" I ask the air. "They've never done that before."

Rebecca shrugs. "They say, how come he wears crap, secondhand clothes with holes in them?"

"Your pants have holes in them?" roars Adam, spraying bits of chicken across the table. "Let me see your pants, Jonathan."

Jonathan rolls over, still covering his face. Both knees are ripped. "Kids were teasing me," he sobs.

"How could you let him go out like that?" Adam shouts at me.

"He's a big boy. I don't monitor what he wears."

"It's your job to teach him what's appropriate. Jonathan, don't you have any unripped clothes?"

Rebecca finishes her salad and begins on her potatoes; she always eats one thing at a time, saving her favourite for last. "They also laugh at us because our clothes are secondhand."

I know why she's emphasizing that; she resents my insistence on thrifting our purchases.

"Why are you buying secondhand, ripped shit?" demands Adam.

If I don't smoke a joint right now, I'm going to smack his stupid face, lashing out at me because he needs someone to blame. "I don't buy ripped shit," I say carefully. "I buy good clothes that fit, and I go to secondhand stores because I believe in reusing and recycling. Everything we buy ends up in the landfill…"

"Fuck the environment!" yells Adam. "My kids are being bullied and teased because their crazy mother wants to save the world singlehandedly."

"I hate non-thinkers," I tell him conversationally. "They're not being bullied and teased because I care about the environment, but because most people have stupid little brains like you."

Apoplectic, he shouts a string of abuse about my mothering skills, and I feel a rising surge of fury in my own breast. But then I look down at the heap on the floor. This isn't making things better for Jonathan. I crouch down beside him, ignoring my husband. "Don't you worry, Jooney; we'll take you shopping this weekend and buy you whatever horrible brand names you want. We'll go through your clothes and throw out anything that's looking a bit ratty. I'm so sorry that people are being mean, and that I didn't notice what you were wearing this morning."

"I noticed," interrupted Rebecca. "I told him he had a hole in his knee. He never cares about things like that."

"That's your fault too," Adam bellows at me. "You go around looking like a farmhand..."

"That's what I am..."

"How are they supposed to know how to dress when you look like a slob?"

I look pointedly at our immaculately outfitted daughter and remain silent. He continues to huff and puff, but I focus on my son, rubbing his back, coaxing him back onto his seat, feeding him little nibbles of food as if he were a baby. Does the mother tiger urge to protect rage unabated until we die?

Later in the evening, I go online and I see it A petition. "It's disturbing to see a child suffering from neglect. Mendel must have millions and this is how she dresses her kids?"

What if social media hurts my child? This has happened because of me.

I spend the evening with Jonathan. We pick out non-holey clothes for tomorrow.

"See, Mum?" he tells me, holding up a shirt and pointing to two overlapping C's on the front, "this is how you know something is good quality. This is the logo for Under Armour."

"Having a brand name doesn't mean it's good, it just means it's popular. The secondhand clothes we bought are good quality, too."

Rebecca sticks her head in the door. "It's popular because it's good, duh."

"Don't be rude, Rebecca. Popularity has little to do with quality; it's usually just a fad for no reason. Uggs are ugly, Crocs are ugly—what's high quality about a rubber monstrosity? People are like sheep; they want something because others have it."

Jonathan focuses on his Rubik's cube—he can solve it in just over a minute. "But then I should refuse to wear brand names, so I'm not a sheep."

I hug him sorrowfully. "You're right, but people are looking at us more now, judging with their sheep-like minds."

"Stop indoctrinating the children with your bullshit superiority complex," Adam shouts from the office.

I didn't think he could hear us. I lower my voice. "I think we should conform, because we don't want you to be upset again. That's more important than making a stand against the sheep."

Jonathan giggles. He likes me calling them sheep.

I get into bed with him and read. Then I lie with him until he falls asleep. I lie with Rebecca and rub her back as long as possible, but eventually I have to go to my own room.

He's waiting for me. "Are you saying that the environment is more important to you than our kids? Did you see Jonathan's face?"

I pull my nightie over my head and slip in beside him. "We're on the same page here, Adam. We both agree he needs some new clothes; we both abhor the fact that he's being teased..." I stop for breath. It makes me so angry. "You can take him into Halifax on Saturday and buy him whatever the hell you want."

He rises slowly from the bed, like a stallion rearing up before the attack. "I am working full-time while you sit around doing nothing all day. You will take him shopping. It's your job."

My heart sinks. "Can't you do it?"

He flings himself down on the bed with his back to me. "No, I can't. Start being a mother again. If you weren't a pothead, maybe you'd notice the holes in your kids' pants."

"Good to know that whenever there's an issue with the kids, you'll be blaming instead of supporting."

"What type of mother lets her kid go to school in holes?"

I take a deep breath. Why does negative thinking come naturally, while positive thinking requires effort?

"I remember going to school with hay twine holding up my pants, while Liz dressed in the latest fashion. Sometimes it's the kid that drives these things."

"It's your job to teach them what's appropriate, if they don't do it naturally."

"You either notice these things or you don't," I murmur.

Who wants to fight? Not me.

I want to be held.

SATURDAY: 4 P.M.

It is done. Jonathan has appropriate clothes that will satisfy the sheep. It would have been impossible to go into a secondhand store and pretend the clothes were new, though the thought did cross my mind before I got there. Fucking zoo. There were people everywhere, commiserating: "That petition is so stupid. Your kids are lucky kids." And me trying not to cry. Hard to tell who was more embarrassed, me or the kids. It was a nightmare. We went home after two stores, but we did purchase some new clothes. Now I shall sit on my porch and get stoned, listening to the staccato patterns of the rain against the roof.

"This is a good start, but you need at least two more pairs of pants," Adam is saying, banging out the front door and stopping dead in front of me. "Are you smoking? In the middle of the day? We have rules…"

"I couldn't wait until the kids go to bed. And I'm never going shopping again."

He leans over me, his hands gripping the edge of the table. "I've been patient for a long time. You have to pull yourself together. See somebody, do whatever you have to do, but stop destroying our family."

I just look at him.

He leans closer, hissing in my ear so the kids won't hear. "My kids won't have a pothead for a mother, do you hear? Pull yourself together."

He marches back into the house. I smile vacantly at the trees and listen to the pattering rain. This I can do, thanks to blessed marijuana. Carry gum in my pocket so he can't smell. Become crafty and devious. Hopefully, this also I can do.

Adam comes out with Jonathan and they begin to play basketball together. I watch him with dislike.

Give credit where credit's due. He plays a lot with the kids.

I must try.

MAY 10

I broke my vow to ignore media coverage and surf online.

Don't get obsessed about that petition.

When you only see people on screens, do you forget they're actually people? That's the only explanation I can think of, to forgive the woman who started the petition.

So stop visualizing ripping her face off.

The bitch hurt my kid. I wish her harm.

I read articles about the damage a parent's fame can do to a child. I read about how this ten-year-old was dubbed a lesbian because she liked to wear pants, or how the parents of this two-year-old were vilified because they hadn't brushed the kid's hair. I read how easy it is to be obnoxious when you're anonymous, and how social media has given birth to "an unprecedented brand of cruelty." So long as my status only hurt me, it was bearable. But my kids?

Stop it. Read something positive.

The internet is like an entire world; you can get lost in it. Flattery brings a smile to my lips as I read words about my wisdom. Country real estate has shot up all over North America, as people try to produce their own food. Goat sales have quadrupled.

I google Kassem, and the news dissipates my sadness like pollen in the wind. It's only been a few weeks since I stopped going online, but so much has happened! My mouth gapes open as I read that Kassem has actually held elections. Real elections, including the rebel factions. Why didn't Adam tell me? I sit up straight, jumping from screen to screen. I read that Kassem lost the election. He was voted out; he ceded power without bloodshed and has gone into exile in Iran. Articles predict how long he will stay there and which country he'll ultimately choose to live in. He can pick and choose—he has been granted immunity from prosecution for war crimes as part of the deal he forged with the international community prior to the elections. I begin to laugh. "What a man!" I yell to the room.

He's a murderous bastard responsible for the death and destruction of God knows how many lives.

"Really? Then it must have been my influence!" I crow.

I consume every bit of news I can find, inhaling the words until I hear the children's voices yelling for me.

I rush upstairs, enveloping them in a joyous family hug.

"What's up?" Jonathan asks.

"I just feel you had a good day today, in your spanking new clothes."

"Actually, I did." He smirks. "The principal talked to the whole school about bullying. But I hate unlocking that stupid gate every time I come in."

"Or go out!" yells Rebecca. "Abba curses it when he's in a hurry."

All the more reason to appreciate his compromise.

I feed the animals and spend some time scratching their backs as they push one another out of the way, then I bustle around the kitchen making dinner.

As soon as Adam gets home, I accost him with my new information. "Why didn't you tell me?"

"I didn't want you to waste time online. I want you to finish your book."

I want you to be less fucking controlling. "But don't you understand what this means to me? I've been down, and you had a piece of news that would totally cheer me up."

He sits at the table, knife and fork already in hand. "I didn't know you still cared what was going on over there. You're always focused on the present; you never mention Syria."

I yell for the kids and dump spoonfuls of pasta and meat sauce onto each plate. How could he imagine I'm not interested in Syria? I just spent six weeks there, trying to convince its evil dictator to do the right thing. Less than six months after my return, he does. And Adam thinks I wouldn't care?

Suspicion casts its net.

"When I look at Kassem now, I can't believe I ever found him attractive."

"He's disgusting," says Rebecca through a mouthful of pasta.

"Abba is way better looking!" I exclaim, watching him carefully. But he continues to shovel pasta down his gullet as though starving.

"I want to contact him," I say. "Let him know how proud I am."

"Don't you think he'd contact you if he wanted to be in touch?" Adam asks.

MAY, SATURDAY

It is a warm day and we're going swimming in the river. Jonathan has devised a way to shimmy up the majestic oak tree in our front yard so he can peer over the gate and see if anyone's there. I wonder briefly if every outing for the rest of my life will be preceded by military-like measures. No enemy in sight—proceed.

I am psyched to be going to the river, even though the water's probably freezing. Swimming releases happy endorphins.

"Can we take the animals?" I ask Adam. "They haven't been outside the wall for ages."

"No."

"Let's take our bikes," says Rebecca.

The bikes whoosh past the gate and along the road. A car passes and slows down as if to stop, but I pedal by smiling, prevented from waving by my bike's determination to capsize unless controlled by both hands. Jonathan starts a race—do all male children have to turn everything into a competition?—and we're giggling by the time we reach the entrance to the park. We prop our bikes against trees and walk through the woody path to the river. As always, it is beautiful. The water is cold, but we swim vigorously until our bodies acclimatize. We start a game with the huge rock on the other side of the river: whoever manages to sit on the rock for a count of ten wins. Jonathan and I team up; I grab Rebecca's ankle and pull her by brute force into the current, hoping it will take her far enough for me to hurtle back in time to save Jonathan from Adam's clutches. Grabbing Adam's arms, I yell for Jonathan to get on the rock and claim victory, but Rebecca is already back, fishtailing through the water to lie spread-eagle over the submerged rock, gripping it desperately with both hands while Jonathan butts her with his head. We are all shouting with laughter.

"Hello!" calls a voice across the water.

My face and voice freeze and I dive underwater and stay there for as long as I can.

When I come up, Adam and the kids are still wrestling.

"Hello," comes from the opposite shore again. "Is that you, Charlotte?"

I look, unsmiling. Several neighbours, dressed in swimsuits. Nobody in NS *ever* swims in May.

"Hello," I say coldly. "Fuck them," I say to Adam in Hebrew.

"It's not your river," he says.

"Our neighbours prefer pools to sharing the murky depths with leeches, eels, and catfish."

"Not these ones."

We continue our game, without the same zest as before. Then they swim up to us.

"What a lovely game." They simper. "Can we join in?"

Are they fucking joking? "I just want to be with my family. Do you want to be over here by this rock? If so, we'll go to the other side, so as to give you privacy," I say and motion to the kids.

"We'd love to talk to you for a few minutes," one says. "We've hardly seen you since COVID."

"Why should you see me? We're neighbours, not friends."

Adam grabs my hand. "Okay, let's swim back."

"There's no need to think you're better than us."

I can hear their reproachful tones morphing to disapproval as Adam tows me across the current. "I just want to be left alone," I shoot over my shoulder.

"Hamood, we are all that matter," Adam whispers, looking into my eyes.

I try to relax.

As we are climbing out, another couple approaches with a camera. Now I'm not in bad shape, but I haven't done any exercise since returning to Canada and I'd prefer close-ups of my dimpled thighs not to be strewn over the internet. I sit back down in the water.

"Charlotte! How wonderful to see you! Do you mind if we take a photo of you?"

I don't even know them. "Do you mind waiting until I have a towel wrapped around me?" I ask.

They accede enthusiastically, but I still ask Adam to watch them while I climb out self-consciously under a stream of flattery about the impact I've had on their lives.

"And you're impacting my life too," I say, trying to quell the bitter rage in my heart.

"Do we have to get out too?" shouts Jonathan.

"Stay as long as you like," I reply.

"You could stay too," Adam says in Hebrew.

I look at him in astonishment. "I want to swim with my kids, not converse with idiots."

"It's not that big a deal; just be polite and monosyllabic. Let's continue our game."

I gesture across the water. "They've taken over our rock."

One of them shoots me an angry look. A sudden visualization: I'm banging her head against the rock again and again, screaming, *Just fucking leave me alone!*

I push past the other couple, who look hurt that I'm not posing for a photo. "I just wanted a quiet swim; do you think I enjoy seeing you here?" I shout at them.

Incredulous affront sweeps across their faces like wildfire.

"Don't upset the kids," Adam calls in Hebrew.

I run through the woods to my bike and get home as fast as I can.

MUM PHONES TO ARRANGE a meeting at Liz's house and ask if we can pick her up en route. When the day arrives, Mum doesn't feel well enough to come, but she certainly feels well enough to phone and hound me out of the house.

I assure her that I had no intention of not going, even though it was the first thought that entered my mind when she told me she had a cold. "How do you know it's not COVID?" I ask.

"Because they test you the minute the first symptom arrives."

I listen to how she is doing and commiserate. She says she feels a bit down, not to be seeing me. I promise I will visit her tomorrow. "Were you depressed when we were kids, Mum?"

"Often," she says.

"How did you know?"

"If I cried every day, it meant I was depressed."

Only once a day?

WHEN WE ARRIVE, Liz bubbles out of her house with arms outstretched. Soon I am reclining on her couch with wine in one hand and a cigarette in the other. Adam has disappeared upstairs with Joe while the kids are outside, climbing onto the roof of the shed and leaping from there onto the trampoline. It's totally dangerous and they're loving every minute. How much does their happiness depend on mine?

Not at all. Did you notice your mother's happiness when you were a kid?

The house is silent. No phones ringing here.

"So how have you been?" Liz asks.

I tell her. About the unbearable attention. About the arguments with Adam. About Jooney's holey pants and the petition.

Her reaction is a bit weird. "Do you remember that phase a year or so ago when Joe was videotaping all our conversations?"

I do. A really annoying phase.

"I found one the other day that I'd like you to listen to."

Liz settles on the couch beside me with her laptop. Curious, I lean forward.

Flashes of animated faces shoot past as Liz fast-forwards—mostly of Liz, because it's her husband videotaping and so he naturally finds her

249

more interesting. The kids briefly pop into the screen at intervals. Liz stops on a shot of her peering at me anxiously, rewinds for a couple of seconds, and there I am, sitting on the couch in the video, just like I am now. Liz is rummaging in the fridge. Joe must be standing to the side, taking a wide-shot.

"How's the writing going?"

"Crap. Now that I've finished *A Hero*, I've got serious writer's block."

Liz is pouring two generous glasses of wine. She approaches the couch and sits beside me; now our past positions mirror our current ones. "So what do you do all day?"

The camera moves around so it's facing the couch, filming us head-on.

I am swishing my wine gently back and forth in the glass, looking embarrassed. "I daydream a lot. Insane waste of time, I know."

"Really? Give me an example of a typical dream."

"It's pretty much the same dream since I started writing *A Hero*."

Liz downs half her wine in one gulp and grabs a handful of nuts at the same time. "You've been dreaming the same thing for years? What? Do tell."

"It's so stupid; there's literally a voice in my head telling me not to *dare* tell."

"Go on, I'm your sister."

"Well, *A Hero* wins the Giller and... well, the Booker too, so Kassem hears about it and reads it. He's kinda superstitious, so when he reads about his own death, he's consumed with the idea that I might be psychic and that I foresaw it. So he kidnaps me. Then..." I notice a grin spreading across my sister's face.

"I said it was stupid."

"No, it's interesting. Go on."

I spit it out in a rush. "Basically, we fall in love. Lot of imagined fucking while I wrestle with morals. End of story."

Liz sips her wine, staring at me speculatively. "There's gotta be more to it than that."

"Well, I try to off myself and stuff, but we usually get to the fucking bit pretty quickly."

"And then…"

"Lots of fucking. Starts with Kassem, then this other guy that brings me my food and another guard join in, one in my mouth, one up my…"

"Okay, 'nuff detail," Liz interrupts, holding up her hand.

I turn to the table and scoop up some nuts. Liz's eyes continue to bore into my cheek.

"My libido is a bit high at the moment," I offer into the silence.

"This daydream might be the basis for a new story."

"You want me to write porn?"

She giggles and finishes her wine. "No. You'd start with being kidnapped and see where it takes you."

"I could explore the themes of imprisonment and sanity."

"Exactly."

"With a lot of fucking in-between."

Her gaze turns on me again. "It's strange that you think about sex so much. I never do."

"I have phases where I imagine fucking practically every man I meet."

Liz glances toward the camera. "Even Joe?"

"I've mentally fucked every man you've ever had. Often all of them at the same time. One in my…"

"All *right*! Turn the fucking thing off, Joe."

I FEEL MY SISTER'S EYES on the side of my face; I keep mine trained on the computer, even though the video has stopped. My reaction is held in check, as though I'm waiting to find out what's going on.

"So are you writing this elaborate fantasy, or is it just in your head?"

"Of course, I am writing it!"

Otherwise, you'd just be plum crazy.

Now it's my turn to take the computer, accessing Google Drive and opening up my latest document. I read aloud.

Consciousness seeps around the edges of my brain. I try to ask my husband for water, but before I can open my mouth exhaustion overtakes me again.

"Great," Liz interrupts. "So have you finished?"

"The kidnapping bit, yes."

"So how does it end?"

"It's still going. She gets home and she's famous and… her husband is annoying her and she craves solitude…"

My voice peters out and I glance sideways. Liz looks worried.

"So you're writing that now? Right now?"

"Umm, kinda?"

Liz just waits, so I press <Shift+End> to jump to the end.

"I'm so sorry that people are being mean, and that I didn't notice what you were wearing this morning."

"I noticed," interrupts Rebecca. "I told him he had a hole in his knee. He never cares about things like that."

"That's your fault too," Adam bellows at me. "You go around looking like a farmhand…"

"See? I'm right up to date. I'm totally writing it," I say proudly to Liz. "It's practically finished!"

Liz takes my hand. "When you came in, you were telling me about the unbearable attention. And the arguments with Adam. Dearest, there has been no kidnapping and no media attention. You know that, right?"

I blink. "Yes, I do know that. Of course I know that." My mind focuses wholly on what she might say next. Thought is suspended.

Liz strokes my hand. "So why were you talking as though it were actually happening?"

Because you're totally bonkers.

My heart is thudding in my chest. "I'm just getting into my book. Most of that stuff is completely true; Jooney *was* teased because of a hole in his pants and Adam *did* say those exact things and I *was* exhausted after a day of shopping. I'm just embellishing a bit to make it more interesting." It's hard to describe the feeling creeping around my throat like a tight band. It's like when Kassem told me of the constant surveillance. As though Adam has just spilled the beans about an extramarital affair he'd been having, complete with two bastards that he loves as much as our kids. As though my entire worldview has been a lie. In the book, it was just embellishing, but in my mind…

I like her stroking hand. Focus on it.

"Do you think you are projecting your fantasy onto real life because you yearn to be widely read? Has your lack of success resulted in an unhealthy obsession with fame, and the blurring of reality with fantasies about fame?"

"I'm not very happy being famous," I say uncertainly. "And what about all that stuff with Adam?"

Liz turns my hand over and traces the palm. "Don't freak me out. What do you mean, that stuff with Adam? None of that stuff is happening. It's in your head."

I struggle to keep the panic out of my voice. "Perhaps my imagination and my... sanity... are overlapping."

"If you can't distinguish between reality and fantasy, you might need help."

I feel a sudden flare of fury and snatch my hand back. "It *is* happening. He was home for months—he's only gone back to work recently. He's *still* in my face all the time."

"I'm on your side. You know that."

I jump to my feet and walk away, my back to my sister, so she won't see my fingers creep up to my temples and press viciously. I am *not* mad. I *can* differentiate between reality and dream. Obviously, the fame isn't happening, but imagination can be insidious.

Yeah! Post that on social media: "imagination is insidious"— it'll go viral!

My sister's quiet voice behind me. "He was home all the time because of COVID."

"Everyone else went back to work ages ago."

"Not if their work didn't make them," she says gently.

"I need a joint," I say with a note of desperation. Wordlessly, Liz gets up and fetches Joe's stash. I roll a joint with shaking fingers and lean out the window to light up. Inhale.

"But that doesn't matter—it's normal for an introvert to feel overwhelmed by the constant presence of extroverts," Liz is saying behind me. "It's fine to extend your irritation out to comprise the entire world and weave it into your current writing. It's a neat idea and there's nothing wrong with that, so long as you understand what's actually happening."

Yup. Actually, you're just another unsuccessful writer.

Yeah, fuck you, Voice, it's not like you've been *reminding* me that this shit isn't real.

I've only just heard about it!

I finish my joint and sit back down on the couch, letting my sister take my hand again. In her trusted presence, the entangled strands in my brain loosen a smidgen. The dope meanders its way through my panic. It will be okay, because if I focus, of *course* I can distinguish between truth and embellishments. Now that I know, I can be vigilant. I can ask others what's really happening if I'm not sure. "I guess... I'm so into my book that I'm living it... even when I'm not writing."

Liz looks earnestly into my face. "That's fine, so long as you *know* that."

I close my eyes. Focus. Wrest the fictional strands from reality. Divide and conquer. Of course when I focus like this, there's no issue. It's natural for writers to get involved with their characters, especially when they *are* the main character.

completely natural. And that's not the dope talking, either.

The kidnapping might have been fiction, but I really *am* in prison. The trapped, sick-unto-death-of-husband feeling is *real*. I'm weaving this reality into the return of my protagonist and embellishing it with the fame stuff. Writers do that all the time—isn't all writing autobiographical? Of course I'm not mad.

Not madder than usual, at least.

I smile at Liz reassuringly. "Maybe it's because I'm... my main character is stuck. If this were really happening—which of course it's *not*—what would you advise me to do?"

"I would advise your *protagonist* to stop talking to the media. Give them zilch, and people's interest will die. If film stars stop filming for a while, you stop hearing about them."

"That's the opposite from Adam's advice; he said giving them what they want would eventually dry the well."

"You're the one that decides what will work. Is giving them what they want working?"

A tweak of anger. "No, and I've been home for weeks! Is he deliberately lying?"

Liz pinches my arm. "It's a novel, so he's giving advice, not lying. We still on the same page?"

I nod vigorously.

"So, when your protagonist first came home, Adam was probably right; denying them interviews could have whetted their determination. Plus it wouldn't have been fair; it sounded like many people lobbied for her freedom and they deserved to see her happy at home…"

"And now he's enjoying the attention; it's giving him a rush—so interesting compared to his boring day job."

"You mean in the book, right? Don't let your obsession with this book let you get all negative about your husband."

I sip my wine. "What about our fights about money?"

"I think you're coping with a lot right now and that isn't a problem that needs to be solved immediately. Put it on a back burner and stop worrying about it."

"But do you think I'm right?"

She gets up to stir the pot simmering on the stovetop. "Doesn't matter what I think, although obviously your ideas about what to do with your joint money are just as valid as his."

"Especially since I'm making it."

"Fuck me!" Liz shouts, slamming the spoon down on the counter so droplets of soup spatter over the counter. "You don't make any money and you never have."

"So if he's making it…"

Liz's voice crescendos to a screech. "*If* he's making it?" She wrestles her voice down to gentle. "I need to know you are all right."

I wave my hand dismissively. "Don't get stuck on words. Perhaps I am inhabiting my character to an unusual degree, but authors do it all the time."

Oh, all writers are schizophrenic?

"Getting angry with Adam because you think you're making money when you're not isn't an author trait—it's a looney trait."

FFS—does this mean there's three of us now?

God, how existential can you get?

"I'm angry because he's controlling the money. You've always said it doesn't matter who is making it, it's equally both of ours."

Liz stares carefully into my face. I strive to look utterly lucid.

"Marriage is a balancing act of compromise and money always plays a role. But given the stress of COVID, it's stupid to fight about that *now*."

She's right. Ludicrous to get all hot under the collar for something that isn't time-relevant, especially during such a weird time.

"But the solitude thing is something you need to solve right away. If you aren't getting enough time, take more. Go away for a week's retreat. Figure out exactly what you need and make it happen. Adam will understand that this is a need, not an indulgence. He loves you so much, you know."

Then the kids flock around and we shoo them out again and bring the food to the table in the fenced-in yard, because we love eating outside in the summer. Simmering pots filled with rice and stew, a large salad and a plate of fresh bread slathered with butter. I'm spooning food onto plates and Jane is asking for more cucumbers and Rebecca's explaining that I'm doling out the veggies because Jane always takes all the cucumbers, while I whisper to Jane that her Mum's in charge of the stew because Rebecca picks all the meat out of the stew. The noise level is joyous. At least my family is behaving normally. At least with them, I can act as I've always done.

MY SISTER HUGS ME HARD when it's time to go. "Come as often as you like," she whispers in my ear. "We always love having you."

"It does me good to see you," I whisper back. "You always give such good advice. Which means I hate Adam a little less right now." I smile to show I'm joking. Not.

I totter out into the night, drunk and stoned and contented.

MAY

The kids will soon be home from school. I stare at myself in the mirror and think positive thoughts about my lovely life and beautiful home. Day by day.

I think these little pep talks with my reflection do some good.

The front door bangs. "Eema!' shouts Jonathan, and there is an element of panic in his voice that sends me flying down the stairs.

Jonathan is out of breath; he's obviously run all the way from the bus stop. "Rebecca is coming. She's crying."

"Why?"

"The kids have been nasty to her too," he gasps.

I dash down the driveway and catch her as she enters the gate, enfolding her red-stained face in my arms.

"Eema, it's all lies," she cries.

"Of course it is, Hamoodi. Of course it is."

Plying her with cookies and goat milk, I draw out the story in dribs and drabs. She was just standing by a boy on the playground; she barely knows him, and what she knows she doesn't like. Some kids started singing "Rebecca and Tyler in a tree, k-i-s-s-i-n-g."

And of course some reporter snapped them together and then emblazoned the headlines: "Rebecca Mendel Finally Gets Boyfriend."

Just between us, this is your protagonist in the book talking, and there's not really any article.

I know it's my protagonist, no thanks to you, so shut up.

It doesn't seem as bad as the ripped pants, because there isn't even a grain of distorted truth in this one. But my daughter's miserable face says otherwise.

All afternoon my mind probes and delves, turning over rock after rock in search of help, finding only slugs. That evening, while the kids are practising their instruments, I look through some of the video clips of my incarceration.

That only exist in your increasingly addled mind.

Okay, I re-read the parts of my manuscript that seem to calm me; perhaps they can help me find a way forward. The scenes where I contemplate suicide upset me. They suggest life is not worth it if you're in prison.

And if your death won't harm anyone.

Yes, I know; not the case now. It's interesting to follow the track of my mind as it performs a volte-face in regard to Kassem. *He's capable of anything; I see that now. I have always believed that if you speak rationally to a neurologically normal human being, they will be able to understand your point of view on any given topic.*

And that gives me an idea.

"I HAVE TO DO SOMETHING," I say to Adam that night in bed, after he's slipped in and out like an eel while I grit my teeth because he's not being nice to me lately and why should I pleasure him?

So demand pleasure yourself.

I ask for a foot rub. He says he'll scratch my head. I say I don't like my head scratched; I like my feet rubbed. He says they're filthy and I have to wash them. I say scratching his head makes my whole hand itch, never mind forcing us to sleep on a pillow cover of dandruff. He is adamant. I wash my feet.

"There's nothing you can do, except explain to the kids that the world is full of bullies."

"That life is a series of choices; do we choose to be decent, conscientious..."

"Yup," Adam interrupts, pushing one foot away and grabbing the other. I hope he doesn't think that one's finished yet.

"If you really agreed with me, you'd make all your decisions through an environmental lens. If everybody simplified their lives just a smidgen— fly less, eat a bit less red meat—then the lives of our children will be massively easier."

"Bull, it's the corporations..."

"That's just an excuse to do nothing. Absolutely we should lobby corporations and governments to change, but as consumers, the choices we make matter very much; where we buy, where we invest our money. Ouch. You're rubbing my foot too hard."

He pokes his finger between each toe, digging in and then flicking his fingers over the side of the bed. I know I'm not overly clean, but I'm pretty sure there aren't flecks of grime between every toe. "If you ever do make any money, I'm going to fly everywhere."

A wave of despair washes through me. Adam would do anything for his kids. Except the one thing that really matters. How many times had

I told him that the scientists and experts say that the next few years are critical? That if we make change now and keep warming below two degrees our kids would have full and reasonable lives? If we just stop consuming so much—it's not even making us happy!—our kids will have enough to consume.

I can already see his eyes glazing if I try to say it again. He's already digging between my toes very roughly.

Try a visual.

In a bit. I'm getting a foot rub.

It's about sacrificing a bit now to preserve the future.

I sit up and tap www.seeing.climatecentral.org into Adam's iPad, repressing regret about the terminated foot rub. "Look, Adam. Do you want the BIO building and Wallace Heights to be an island, or still part of Dartmouth? Do you want our entire coastline to be eroded, or just a few bits? That's the difference between 1.5 and 3.5 degrees of warming. That's the difference between you flying less or flying more. It's that simple."

"Oh shut up about the environment. It's too late anyway."

"I've just showed you that it's *not* too late." I throw myself face down on the bed.

"Don't yell at me."

Ditch visuals. Try poetry.

"I wish I loved the Human Race;
I wish I loved its silly face;
And when I'm introduced to one,
I wish I thought 'What Jolly Fun!'"

There's a short silence, and I try again. "This one is my father's:

I dislike the great majority,
They're so alike, and yet so unlike me.
And when I'm dead, I'll be laid underground,
But they're all dead and they're walking around."

No wonder you grew up with a superiority complex.

I doubt Adam caught the point, but he heard the poem as a cessation of hostility, and when I inch my feet back onto his chest, he begins to knead. "Since you don't make any money, this is all hypothetical."

"If I did make money, it would go to environmental..."

Do you like fighting?

"Over my dead body!" he yells.

I continue to speak calmly. "This seems to be a make-or-break issue for us. I have researched the detrimental effect of divorce on kids, and for their sake, I will stay with you until Jonathan reaches eighteen. At that point, I am giving half of everything I've made away, and if you don't like it, you can lump it."

He grabs my feet and throws them off his stomach. "You're threatening me?"

"Money poisons just like power. People who have it begin to think they deserve it."

"You don't know what the fuck you're talking about!"

I struggle to remember some of the articles I've read.

Sieve-Brain.

"Billionaires, dictators, and corrupt leaders—across the spectrum, the rich ferret money away to benefit themselves or to avoid paying taxes that benefit people poorer than themselves. It's horrendous. Those people are disgusting."

I can see the struggle in his apoplectic face.

"Okay, Adam, let's not discuss this now; we have enough problems on our plate."

No Shit.

"Don't give me fucking ultimatums. Ever."

I want to say that it's not an ultimatum. He's done what he wants with his money, and I intend to do what I want with mine. Divorce would only happen if he felt compelled to pour resentment over my head ad infinitum. Instead, I try to pull his head onto my chest, but he resists.

"I want a new SUV."

"Buy a Tesla," I say. "Your happiness and mine are co-dependent, and I've always wanted you to spoil yourself more." His head drops to my chest, and I begin to scratch.

"I didn't actually want to talk about money," I say.

"Can't we just shut up for a while?"

I scratch vigorously. He subsides.

I take the plunge.

Of course you do.

"I'm also going to arrange a press conference."

"What?"

"Most people see themselves as decent, conscientious. I am going to appeal to their humanity."

He jerks his head away from my ministering fingers. "Are you joking?"

"Don't you believe that if you speak rationally to a normal human being, they will understand your point of view? If I can convey the terrible impact of their attention..."

"Are you out of your mind? You can't do a press conference. Nobody wants to interview you."

"Adam, I have to show them my truth. It can't make things worse, and it might do some good. At the very least, there will be an element of shame in their persecution."

He jumps to his feet. "You've gone totally bonkers, you know that?"

A quavering little voice wafts from the hallway: "Eema? Why are you and Abba shouting all the time?"

I thought the kids were asleep. I get up so my fingers can minister to another needy scalp.

"Just make some money already," Adam calls after me.

JUNE, WHO CARES WHAT DAY?

I am walking the kids to the bus stop.

"See how it sucks to stop and unlock the fence every time?" Jonathan asks.

Not really.

Rebecca and I walk on one side of the road, throwing a ball back and forth to Jonathan, who walks along on the opposite side. I intentionally throw wide, forcing Jooney to lurch back and forth or dive into the ditch. Any energy expended now is a bit less energy at the end of the day. Jooney howls with laughter or frustration at my wayward balls.

"What are you and Abba fighting about all the time?" Rebecca asks conversationally.

"Mostly about money."

"Do we have enough?"

"Yes."

"So what's the problem?"

"We have too much, so now we have to argue about what to do with it." The ball whizzes past my head and Jonathan howls that I'd missed a perfect throw.

"Sorry," I say.

"It's your fault," says Rebecca.

"I know, I wasn't watching for the ball."

"No, I mean the fights with Abba."

I stop in my tracks. "What?"

Rebecca takes my arm and propels me forward again. "It's true, Eema. Whenever you're being weird or angry, you always want us to forgive you. You say every person has emotional triggers and... what do you say?"

"That we have emotional triggers that prevent us from being rational in certain areas."

"Yeah, exactly. So when Israel is doing something bad, Jews still defend her, because they love her, so they can't be rational about her."

"Yeah," Jonathan pipes up, joining us on our side of the road. "Like when you try to give Auntie Liz advice on her children, and she gets mad, even though it's good advice."

"How does that apply to Abba?" I ask carefully.

"Safta was telling me about her childhood," says Rebecca. "She and Saba weren't rich. They probably worried about money a lot. Abba is frightened about money because of his parents, so he can't be rational about it. Give him a break."

From the mouths of babes.

We reach the postboxes where the bus picks the children up. I watch them climb the steps, immersed already in their school world.

I am chastened by their wisdom.

JUNE

Sweat beads my upper lip as I gaze out over the up-thrust microphones; it's hard to see past the lights blazing in my eyes. I glance down at the speech that I've prepared. That's all I need to say; they've been told that there won't be any questions. There have been too many already. I just read this paper out loud and leave. It'll be easy; the hard part was working out what to say.

The room goes quiet. Someone introduces me. I take a deep breath.

"Thank you all for coming today. I am appealing to you as one human being to another, because my life is spiralling out of control. Before my incarceration, I was a free woman."

I take a deep breath. I can't see very well through the lights, but the room is silent except for the snap and whirr of cameras. "Now, people hound me every time I go out, so I barely leave my house. I'm trapped, just like I was in Syria. My marriage and my kids are suffering. Most of what is written about me is wrong. I am not worth emulating. I'm just a normal human being trying to lead a decent life, like most people. You extol my ability to be alone—but you don't allow me to be alone."

I look into the lights. Water burgeons in my eyes, but I can still talk. "I feel like I'm losing the ability to cope. If you have pity or compassion for what I went through in Syria, please have pity for what I'm going through here. I know the hordes won't just disappear if you stop printing articles and photos, but it would help. You can help me get a normal life back again. I appeal to your compassion. Please leave me alone."

JUNE

Headline: "Mendel Falls Apart."

Headline: "Mendel: Truth-teller or Liar?"

Headline: "Mendel Gallivants around Despite Appeal for Solitude."

The appeal didn't work. The kids are off for the summer, so yes, I take them out "gallivanting" every day. And I'm hounded every day.

The press didn't believe me and they were angry. I only kindled the malice that breeds like maggots in non-face-to-face relationships. It's almost as if my appeal pissed them off. "We're doing you a favour. Without us, you wouldn't exist," one blurbed online.

Well bud, we have different definitions of existence.

Luckily you, me, and the protagonist all agree, though.

Can you shut the fuck up? I'm trying to write here.

S'long as you remember it's a fictional story.

Well gosh, I hope every fiction writer has an indispensable voice, reminding them that they're really writing bullshit every two lines!

KING LEAR

Why, thou wert better in thy grave than to answer
with thy uncovered body this extremity of the skies.
Is man no more than this?

Hey Shakespeare, honey? Don't forget you're not the one who's mad.

Shakespeare: Oh thank you; what would I do without you? Now I've completely lost my chain of thought.

Bull. He wasn't a Sieve-Brain like you, Miss Hubris.

Just shut up. Please.

ADAM WAS SO ANGRY when he found out I had arranged a press conference that his vindictive flow hails me whenever our paths cross: "I told you" / "I was totally right" / "You've made it worse" / "Why didn't you listen to me" / "If the negativity affects our children…" and on and on.

I had to admit that he had been right—the whole thing had been a waste of time.

Anger and desperation lead to thoughts of retaliation. Another appeal, directly to the people this time.

"Don't you dare," says Adam. "It's a bad idea. I was right the first time, wasn't I?"

Why is the press doing this? Perhaps it is impossible for them to believe me. If they admitted that fame was a burden, then their whole profession would be called into question.

It's only a burden to you.

Exactly; most famous people worked hard for their fame. I got mine by fraud. I'm only trying to work out what it means to be a decent human being. Probably most humans are striving for this, but my ramblings were listened to because I was a prisoner—so I became a real person to them, struggling in exactly the same way that they struggle. If people identified with me as a prisoner, I can appeal to them.

Nobody's gonna identify with the second half of this book, MS. Fruitcake. But at least you've reassured a lot of readers about the brilliance of their parenting compared to...

At least my writing reflects the importance of thinking and setting values for oneself, instead of religion doing it for you—or worse, just blundering through life without thinking at all.

Beware of pontification. Oh, too late.

YET, DESPITE SUCH RATIONALIZATIONS, I still hesitate. First, there is Adam's implacable anger every time I go against his wishes, and I go against them so often, it seems, these days! But even more important is my growing distrust in my fellow humans. Are they basically good or basically bad? The thought distresses me inordinately—I want to believe people are good, because otherwise I feel suicidal. But I've been wrong twice. Once with Kassem, once with the media.

And negative media could affect the children.

That thought galvanizes me to add a video clip to the soap opera of video clips already in existence. I sit on my porch, with the sunlight shining through the ivy on the screened-in porch. Adam is at work. I explain to the kids what I'm doing and why.

"But what if the people listening are emotional?" asks Jonathan.

"What?"

"You said that emotional people can't be rational."

Both the children are looking at me attentively. "Everybody feels emotional about certain subjects," Rebecca reminds me.

"And the best we can do is acknowledge that, remember?" Jonathan asks. Damn, I like to have vague ideas about things, but my kids always force me to qualify and quantify.

"Umm, not exactly. It's more that we can recognize the subjects where our rationale might be compromised."

"Then it means the other person's right?"

"It means you should think carefully about what they said, if you can. But I don't think that's an issue here. People won't feel emotional over my reaction to the gutter press."

Rebecca yawns and inspects her fingernails. "I'll do your makeup. Jonathan can film you."

"Makeup?"

She looks at me incredulously. "You can't make a video looking like *that*."

I submit, gnawing at my fingernails and glancing at my watch until she's finished. Then I make a big fuss over her talents, which are not inconsiderable.

Jonathan wants to show the viewers our ivy-covered porch and the chickens underneath, taking dust baths where the flowers used to be. I let him. I can edit it out afterwards. Finally, he sits down and aims at my face.

"Was I lying then?" I say. "Has everything been lies? If anyone can explain why I beg the media to leave me alone, when really I love being famous, then let me know. I truly want to be left alone, but when I appealed to the media, this was their response." I read out some of the nastier comments: aspersions on my looks, my behaviour, my mothering; claims that my appeal is really a ploy for more attention.

"I know a lot of people think fame must be wonderful, and for some people, it is," I continue. "But most people who lust after fame are just ignorant. They have no idea what it's actually like. I want to be left alone. Truly. Please help me stop the media's persecution."

JULY

"Did the video work?" Jonathan asked me about five minutes after we'd posted it. For the next few days, I pore over the tsunami of online sympathy and support. I quote the best to the children.

"Wow," says Jonathan, "these strangers really love you." And he looks at me in a bemused sort of way.

The press immediately stops writing negative things; more, they even make a public and contrite apology about the negative things they'd written.

Perhaps the success of this appeal will neutralize Adam's anger over the first appeal.

The press leaves me alone for a few days, but then they start to trickle back. Somehow, despite their sympathy, people are still interested in reading about me and seeing photos. Somehow, after that first tidal wave of support, nobody follows up. Somehow, the situation reverts to the status quo and people turn their energies to other issues near and dear to their heart.

Somehow, nothing changes.

Except that Adam maintains a frigid silence. Except it's summertime and I have to do something with the kids every day. Beaches, strawberry picking, playdates, a half-smile plastered to my face because the kids get upset when I'm not sickly nice to everybody. "These people supported you when you asked them to," says Jonathan, pulling the corners of my mouth up in a ghastly caricature of a smile as yet another fan approaches. "They really like you. You have to be nice to them."

I don't tell him that their niceness is useless. I don't point out that swooping down on me in public is exactly what I asked them not to do. That they are stupid non-thinkers whom I'd as soon stab in the face as... no. Take deep breaths and control the barbs of rage lacerating my heart. For the sake of the kids.

If it weren't for the kids, where would I be? Every day, on my way home, I look at trees, signs, cars we pass on the road. I think: if I drive viciously into that obstacle, it would all be over. This endless, difficult existence.

If it weren't for the kids, I'd be dead.

Rebecca says, "Abba told us that you're not famous and people just thought that video was crazy."

I laugh nervously. "I am writing a book and the heroine is famous, and at the same time she is me. So she experiences everything I do—including the bullying of her kids—but in the book there's media attention."

"But I really took the video. Did you really post it?" asks Jonathan anxiously.

Had I really posted it? Surely this type of nitty-gritty is irrelevant—remembering every puny detail—the important thing is to distinguish between reality and fantasy in general.

Oh good, so you do know you're a failed writer and a manic-depressive?

"Abba says you suffer from delusions of grandeur," Rebecca says conversationally.

THERE IS SOME RELIEF in the evenings, when the kids are watching their summertime nightly movie. I sit with the animals and inhale my joint, waiting for that subtle shift in mood and perspective. Sometimes it works; Lilah shoves her soft little nose into my chest and I scratch away as though her pleasure is the only thing that matters. In that stoned minute, it is.

But sometimes I cry, reliving an encounter from the day; perhaps my plastered-on smile didn't satisfy someone, who demanded more, then launched accusations of snobbery, while I looked at my kids' anxious faces, mentally gouging out the person's eyes with my fingernails.

If the dope affects me negatively, I pop gum into my mouth and trail back to the house to watch the movie with the kids. It is impossible to wallow in misery when you're stoned and watching a movie. The plot is your entire world.

Sometimes Adam knows, despite the gum. Or he infers, because I'm stupid. "I don't want my kids to have a pothead for a mother," he hisses at me.

Too late.

WEDNESDAY. MONTH?

A normal day in the life of Charlotte.

1. Willow steps on my big toe and I have to kick the wall to stop myself hitting her. I almost break my foot, and the goats are petrified anyway. Anger is my worst enemy, my biggest fault. It has always been so, and I have carefully constructed a life to

control it: meditation, marijuana, plenty of alone-time, and a manageable workload. But then fame happened, and I'm too angry to meditate. Summer came, and I'm never alone. It's a downward spiral.

It's still the wall you're kicking. You're still in control.

2. Rebecca talks back to me, and I find myself yelling, as though she'd pressed a button to activate rage. I apologize, devastated when she cries. Rage and depression, back and forth.

3. Smaller things, not remembered much beyond the moment of happening: a cross voice or a contemptuous one; a put-down. "The house is filthy," Adam says every day when he comes home, as if on cue. Impossible to count all these tiny interactions, but if there must be five times as many positive interactions as negative for a relationship to be successful, then my marriage is doomed.

These little things add up. These little puzzle pieces create a picture called Depression.

4. I sit at the dinner table and cry. Not loudly. Silently. Tears roll down my face. The children glance at me once or twice; I smile and say to ignore it, it just happens sometimes.

"You just feel a bit low, right Eema?" says Rebecca.

"That's right. Nothing is wrong, really; it just means that tears come out a lot. I'm not even sad."

But I am.

Rebecca puts her hand on mine and says, "Poor Eema."

Jonathan gives me a hug. I try not to cry harder. All I can think is: I am making my family unhappy. How is that being a successful mother?

SUMMER

I take the kids to the lake. Liz's kids are with us for a couple of days, which is helpful. Unless they're arguing and can't solve it by themselves, they entertain each other and I'm left to my own devices. We do this every summer—she takes my kids for a few days to give me a break as well. On the beach, the usual bright smiles trip in my direction and I turn and bolt into the lake, swimming far past the buoys until I am all alone in the vast water. I take a deep breath and relax my whole body, every muscle loosening against the soft mass holding me afloat. I stay out for ages, emptying my mind into the silky expanse as I calm my body.

WHEN I RETURN, I FEEL BETTER. Half-smile plastered on, I only nod to the woman who claims she had been "keeping an eye on the kids while I swam," instead of resenting the slur on my mothering skills or pointing out that they're too old to need a babysitter.

I half-smile and half-shake my head at the man who asks if I received his message on my website.

"You should read your messages, if people take the time to write them. We're all busy."

I half-smile, as we stop for an ice cream on the way home, and the cashier simpers and giggles at me.

We sit on the picnic tables to eat our ice creams, but when the group beside us look over for the umpteenth time and a pick-up parks smack-dab in front of our table even though the parking lot is empty, I tell the kids we'll eat our ice cream on the way home.

"Excuse me, can you stop for one second? I just want to say one thing," Pick-up calls as I usher the kids into the car. Then, "Fuck you!"

"Why don't you talk to them, Auntie Charlotte?" asks Liz's eldest, Aaron.

"Because I don't want to."

"But you make them mad. That man just wanted to say hello."

"I can't talk to everybody all the time. If you can think of a way to avoid talking without offending, let me know."

Jonathan pipes up. "You could stay at home."

"That wouldn't be very fun for you, would it?"

We're passing a lovely oak tree that would definitely kill us all if I accelerated hard right into it.

Stop it.

I take a deep breath. Is that a little pain in my lung? I'm smoking a lot more now, plus all those weeks in that smoky little room downstairs, breathing nothing but smoke for hours a day. Now if I had lung cancer, that would solve everything. I could die guiltless—a victim rather than a selfish bitch who committed suicide. Everyone would love me, instead of hating me, and the end result would be the same. Oh, please God, give me cancer!

For shame! cancer is a horrific death.

It's 2023; surely pain's a thing of the past. I bet I'd love being high on morphine.

Maybe they'd cure you.

I won't be diagnosed until it's spread everywhere. I'll insist on staying at home.

Adam will want you to live. He'll force you into hospital, where they'll take control. Away goes freedom or privacy—once you're there, you can't get out.

Who is to say that my sudden death won't be a secret relief, as it might be with relatives who have Alzheimer's? I pull out my cigarettes as soon as I get home and have three in a row, holding the smoke in my lungs as long as I can, visualizing the spot growing bigger, the cells multiplying and increasing.

The kids come out on the porch. "Eema, you're killing yourself smoking!"

"My dear son, how many times have I told you that everything is okay in moderation? I only smoke five cigarettes a day."

Liar.

"I told my teacher at school what you said about moderation, and she said it wasn't true. You should see some pictures of smokers' lungs."

I carefully tap my ash. Smoking three in a row has made me feel slightly sick. "Think, Jonathan, which is something your teacher probably hasn't done with smoking. Most smoking stats focus on heavy smokers, not light ones. Now here I am, living in a relatively clean environment…"

"Even one cigarette a day is bad for you!"

"Perhaps you're right, my lungs would be even happier if I didn't smoke at all. So I weigh the very slight health impact of smoking a few cigarettes a day against the enormous pleasure. Just like I'm sure you do when you guzzle chocolate."

Hypocrite!

I believe every word I just said.

And when you die of cancer?

My kid will conclude that I wasn't able to be entirely rational in connection to cigarettes because of my emotional dependence. Either way, my teachings are reinforced. Now shut up, I want to think. Jonathan has given me an idea.

If you can't beat 'em, join 'em.

DAY? MONTH? SEASON?

Adam is so furious he can't even look at me. He has yelled for so long that my own mind has become confused. Was it a good idea, or the stupidest thing I've ever done? Since my conversation with Jonathan gave me my idea, I've been plugging my mouth with cigarettes every time I spot a camera. Instead of backing away with a half-plastered smile, I grin directly into the camera and tell kids that smoking is very enjoyable and they should certainly do it, along with many other vices like drinking, toking, eating crap, and lots and lots of sex.

Living vicariously, are we?

Yes, I'll die regretting not enough sex. "The trick is to do these things in moderation. So don't get addicted," I exhort into the expressionless eye of the camera. "This only works if you can keep to five a day!"

"Are you for real?" the reporter asks me.

"Aren't you happy? Now you can print negative things about me without compunction."

It's not like you're abandoning your values or anything. You really do believe that.

Yup. Just spreading my ideas, like I've always done.

I google the news for new ideas. There's always sexual stuff.

"Why does society pretend that girls and boys are the same?" I pontificate to the camera, cigarette in hand. "If you come to my farm, you'll see that most boys want sex a whole lot more than most girls. We are *not* the same, and the onus is just as much on the girls as the boys to deal with those differences. Enroll your girls in karate so they learn to defend themselves. Teach them reactions other than passivity. Teach your boys to do no harm."

"Her first, right, Eema?" chorus Jonathan and Rebecca when they see this video clip.

"What?"

"That's what you told us, when we were learning sex ed. at school. You said the entire subject could be dealt with in two words—Her First."

"Well... that's true. Her machinery takes a little longer to warm up, so it's gotta be primed first."

what??

Those two words solve the world's sex problems. Girls learn their sexuality should come first and stop putting men's pleasure above their own; boys learn to be decent lovers.

You should be teaching sex in the schools.

Damn right.

Online news informs me of the spate of African American deaths at the hands of police in America. "It is true that all the Blacks I know are middle-class," I preach to the camera. "But if middle-class Blacks have fewer unpleasant encounters with the police—then isn't the issue really about class more than race?" This is especially outrageous, because I don't know anything about the U.S., and in any case, racism is obviously preventing Black people from achieving middle-class status in the first place. But I don't care. "Ditto First Nations!" I shout at the camera.

If I get death threats from enraged minorities or females, will I be more in prison than I already am?

Headline: "Has Mendel Gone Insane?"

"What are you doing?" screams Adam.

"I'm trying something new. If people are interested in me because I'm so fucking wise, then I'll stop being wise."

"You sound like an ignorant racist," he says.

"Don't forget misogynist."

"I don't even know you anymore. You're paranoid and insane."

I almost feel sorry for him. If only he didn't pound away at my dope-smoking as though that were the worst thing happening right now. If only he didn't discharge words like "paranoid" and "insane" like weapons, while I quietly descend into lunacy.

If only you stopped to appreciate how he sticks by you, no matter how crazy you get.

That night he rubs my feet and tears course down his face. "What's happening to us?"

I am stoned and indifferent. I want to focus on his hands against my soles.

"It's like you don't care anymore, about anything. It's like you're detaching, even from your own family."

Quite possibly true. Marijuana is—for me—a very anti-social drug.

"Nothing seems to make any difference. Whether I'm yelling at you or bringing you to orgasm, you're floating in this… I don't know. Do you even care? Do you still love me?"

I open one eye and peruse his miserable face. It must be hard. He has always loved me unreservedly. I'm grateful. It's been wonderful to be so loved.

It's just not enough.

SEPTEMBER

The kids have gone back to school. I thought it would be better, but I've totally stopped going out. Madness looms, as I swing between rage and depression like a monkey in a tree. I know that I am paranoid, but I cannot stop it. Everyone is out to get me. Although people were kinder in their reactions to my attempts to turn the media against me than I thought they'd be. Of course, many decimated my "ideas," but most speculated about my mental health. Endless speculation. Perhaps there is more negative reaction than I'm aware of; I've stopped going online. I am stoned all day, every day. It makes me heavy and uninspired. I cannot write.

THURSDAY

I break a plate and rub a sliver against my scar until it breaks the skin.

It's a hot day and I want to swim in my river. I'm burning with resentment because I can't. I cried when Adam suggested that we put in a pool. I cannot believe what I have lost.

What the fuck are you doing? Is this part of entering your own book?

My paranoia grows with my smoking. People are trying to peer through the fence. The restaurant chef has poisoned my portion of Thai take-out that Adam brings back from work.

"What did you do today?" he asks.

"I'm writing," I lie.

He doesn't believe me.

How is my existence adding to anyone's life?

Says your protagonist.

Would you shut *up*? Of course it's my protagonist.

So you're not really considering suicide? Sorry, paranoia must be an inherited trait.

Very funny. No, I really am depressed out of my mind and contemplating suicide. But unlike my protagonist, I don't have a good reason; I wasn't kidnapped. It's just good old first-world problems. People are dying of starvation, while I want to die because I don't live alone.

Suicide for white privilege? I won't let you. The trick is to remind you every two seconds that this misery is all in your head. Get meds or I'll be buzzing around your brain all day like a gadfly.

You're going to ruin my novel.

Saturday

Adam doesn't want me to smoke while the kids are watching their movie. But I must, I must. I spent all day in Halifax, taking them to dentist appointments followed by a snack in a restaurant. All day, fending off idiots. I'm wound tighter than a drum and my misery is palpable. Dope dispels all of that.

He sits down opposite me on the porch, a serious expression on his face. "You're spiralling out of control," he says.

"Already spun."

"What can we do?"

"Smoke dope."

He flings my little tin, where I keep my stash, on the floor, but his voice remains calm. "You need help. How many times have I told you?"

"They'll give me chemicals. How many times have I told you?"

"Maybe it's time to do whatever they think best. You're out of control—saying stupid things…"

I wave my hand to dismiss him. "To the media? That was a phase. It didn't work."

"Our life isn't working."

I look at him. It's hard to care about our joint life very much when I've ceased to care about my own.

He raises his hands in despair. "So, are you going to see someone?"

I shake my head.

"Then what are you doing to help yourself? When is your book going to be ready? How long are you going to *be* like this?"

I hear his "like this" as contempt. "My book is going to be ready soon. Instead of always wanting me to do better, why don't you appreciate that I'm not worse? Every day, I struggle not to smash your head in, and I don't! Fucking kudos to me. And to this." I bend down to pick my little tin of dope off the floor, but he snatches it from my hands and leaps to his feet.

"I'm burning this, and all the stuff you keep in the freezer as well."

"That is the only thing keeping me sane," I shout, pointing at the tin in his hand.

"I don't want my kids to think it's okay to do drugs," he roars. "They're only twelve and fourteen years old!"

Within minutes, the smell of burning dope fills our yard. I can hardly breathe; rage chokes my throat.

Just get some more.

I get it from a friend of a friend who likes to talk; every visit swallows half the day. I don't want to go to my doctor, with her inquisitive questions. I don't want to see anybody, even my family. Liz and Mum know I withdraw when I get down; they always wait patiently. They don't know how bad it is this time. They don't know I'm on a precipice, the abyss beckoning seductively.

Tuesday?

I'm lying in bed, like I do most days while the kids are at school. I used to have energy, but it's gone somewhere.

There are still days when I try to be a good mother. But when you're insane, normal things fuck you up.

A normal day in the life of an insane person.

1. I decide to make a cake as a treat for the kids, to compensate for never going out.

   "Eema, it's Tuesday soccer practice," says Jonathan.

   "Phone Rick's mum and ask her to take you. Tell her you need a drive every Tuesday, and that you'll wait at the end of the road so she doesn't have to go out of her way."

   Jonathan looks at me incredulously. "Can't you phone her?"

   "You're getting older now; you should learn to do these things yourself."

   Yeah right, that's the reason.

   "Every other mother drives their own kids and *stays* to watch them play." And he launches a flow of recriminations until I stomp upstairs, having remembered that I have Rick's mother's email, so I don't actually have to talk. One email to ask, one to thank, and my kids disappear to their extracurriculars without me having to leave the house.

   So here I am, making a cake to remind them that I'm still capable of motherly actions. As I lift the flour out of the cupboard it somehow slips from my hands, spewing a white avalanche onto the floor. I quietly bend down and begin to smash my forehead against the counter, again and again.

2. I go out to check the new chick. Despite the lateness of the season, Nonny is eternally broody. Although I put ten eggs under her, only one hatched, which spells the death knell for our current rooster. He has two functions, to protect our chickens and to procreate. Instead he bullies the chickens and is apparently impotent. I find Nonny crouched under a bush; she is bleeding from the head and both eyes have been pecked shut. A blind chicken can't forage for food or teach her chick to. I get what I need from the house, then gather her up and imprison her between my knees, dabbing her wounds

with alcohol-soaked cotton wool. I try to handfeed her, but she refuses to eat. Her chick peeps miserably. How has this happened? The rooster must have held her down and pecked her viciously; that's the only explanation I can think of. I grab him and shut him in the cat carrier. I will leave him in the woods tonight, in the hopes that a raccoon will eat him. Then I sink onto the hay and cry copiously and hysterically. *It's just a chicken.*

3. When the kids get home from school, Jonathan talks and talks. I am trying to make dinner and find it hard to focus on two things at the same time. "Are you listening to me?" he demands several times. And suddenly my voice ricochets off the ceiling, "Can't you shut up for two minutes?"
Later, in bed, he turns his back and says he doesn't want me to read to him. Ever since he was a very little boy, I've lain beside him every night and read. I love doing this. Liz says once they hit teenager-hood it's only a matter of time before they stop rituals like this, but Jonathan has always seemed to like drifting off to the sound of my reading. "Don't be angry with me for yelling at you earlier," I say to his back.
"I'm too old to be read to."
"What age is too old? I like it, and you like it, so why stop?"
"I'm too old!" he shouts.
"Okay. I'm sorry for my bad temper."
"It's not just that. You don't do anything other mothers do. You don't come to parent-teacher interviews; you don't come to soccer games. When are you going to get back to normal?"
"I love you, and I'm here for you when you have problems, but I can't face the rest of the world. I'm sorry." Go away, tears. The last thing my son needs is to have to comfort me when I'm causing him pain.
"I don't understand why you can't ignore everyone. They're just being friendly. Why do you have to go crazy?"
"I'm sorry," I whisper and rush from the room so as not to burden him with my tears.

I rock back and forth on my bed. I'm never going to be a
normal mother. Or wife. I'm crazy.

You're not being violent. You're still in control.

I'll have to bite the bullet and visit my contact for more dope. I
can't cope without it. I thought I'd give it a couple of days, see
if my crazy feelings would diminish. But, no.

DAY? MONTH?

In my first jail, I was alone all the time. In my current jail, never.

My contact is only available on the weekend, unfortunately. As soon
as I get it, I have to smoke, desperate to feel that subtle shift from misery
to the immediate present: the warm breath of the animals, the book
I'm reading. I meander back to the house, determined to play a game
with the children, knowing that I will focus only on the game, having
temporarily banished those eternal tears which distress them so.

Adam meets me halfway. "Surely not," he says in a quiet, menacing
tone. "Surely you aren't smoking in the middle of a weekend day when
the kids are home."

I look at him blankly.

"I'm asking you one thing," he says, stabbing his index finger toward
my face. "One thing. You don't cook anymore, you don't clean, you don't
do anything for your own children. You're not writing and you refuse
to see anyone. The one thing I'm asking is Not. To. Smoke. In front of
the kids."

It's not supposed to happen when you're stoned. But it does. A little
bubble of rage bursts in my brain. "I'm asking you one thing," I reply,
"to think intelligently instead of reacting predictably. I am going through
a bad time. Sorry about that. And I am going to smoke to help me get
through it. The kids don't even know, and you're just being a Controlling.
Fucking. Asshole. Like you've been all my life."

"I'll burn it again. And again and again."

"There are real problems and you choose to focus on the one, utterly
trivial, non-issue, because you're a stupid non-thinker..."

He tries to grab my tin and a tug-o-war ensues. He's stronger; I
feel it slip through my fingers. That's two hundred dollars' worth of

necessity. A spate of rage-bubbles burst in my head. "Leave me alone!" I shout at him.

"Eema, Abba, stop it!" shout the kids, pounding over the yard toward us.

"Your mother is a pothead," Adam cries, holding the tin with one hand and fending me off with the other.

His stupid, controlling face. His inability to help me. Now trying to turn the kids against me. *He is my enemy.* Fury explodes in my chest and I punch him with all my force. He drops the tin and tries to grab my hands as I pummel and bash, scratching, hitting, intent on hurting.

Dimly I hear the kids yelling at me to stop, but I've lost control. I'll teach him to turn my kids against me. I'll teach him to take my props away.

Then my arm is grabbed from the side and I wrench it away with all my force and there's a kid on the ground and Adam is screaming at me to stop, that I'm crazy, that I should be locked up, but I'm still intent on hurting him, kicking with all my force as he pinions both my arms. Then my face is grasped between two hot hands and turned toward Rebecca's stricken face. Even then, I continue to battle: his arms, her hands.

Stop! It's insanity! This is not you—think!

And I stop so suddenly that I stumble backward from Adam's resistance, fixated all the while on my daughter's tragic face.

Tears are coursing down her cheeks; Jonathan is sobbing hysterically behind her.

I have done this. My violence has created this devastation. Seeing it, they too will become adults who react violently when times are tough. Learned behaviour.

I turn and stumble toward the house.

"You need to be locked up!" Adam shouts.

"Stop it, Abba," weep the children.

I don't look back. I hate him. Though he's right. I've been violent.

Faults are like emotions—you can't wave a magic wand to dispel them.

And that helps, because?

Violence is a fault, like any other.

Not like any other. More detrimental. And I don't know how to control it.

SOME DAYS LATER

I lie on my bed. The desire to die has become all-consuming.

You yourself have called it the most selfish act a human being can commit. .

"I am no longer a good mother. I am harming my children."

There is a silence. This fact is undeniable.

"So basically my choices are these: I can remain perpetually stoned, which places me in perpetual conflict with my husband's will, while he perpetually pours scorn and abuse on my head…"

We get the idea: in perpetuum. Second option?

I haven't finished the first option yet. Perpetual Potheadedness seriously impacts my ability to mother. And even if I go that route, I can still lose it if he riles me enough.

He doesn't want to rile you. He doesn't want the kids to be hurt, either.

I am weeping. It's such a normal state by this time, it should be assumed.

I do assume it. Second option?

I remove Problematic Me from the equation. Children and Adam are really sad for a while, but Adam steps up to the plate and becomes a loving and patient father…

Huh!

And my siblings give a lot of support as well. They're almost adults, my children, and life could be so exciting for them, if they were free of this Yoke of Fame.

You mean your protagonist's Yoke of Fame.

I'm unable to honour my first value: Do. No. Harm. If I'm not capable of living my life according to my most important value, then do I even deserve to live?

Oh, come on. Most humans don't even identify…

So that makes me even *worse*. If I'm not living according to my values, then in what way am I better than someone like Kassem, who doesn't identify his values to begin with? In fact, if I'm incapable of adhering to my values, then essentially it means I could become a Kassem, in the right circumstances. Therefore I shouldn't live.

LATER ON, NIGHTTIME

After reading with Jonathan, I lie down beside Rebecca to stroke her back. "Do you mind if your brother comes here for a minute?"

"I don't want him in my bed."

"Just for a minute. Look, he can wedge in on my other side; you won't even know he's here."

"When's the last time he washed?"

"Yesterday," calls Jonathan from his bedroom.

She acquiesces gracelessly, and he leaps into bed beside me and cuddles up.

"I just wanted to apologize to both of you for my behaviour lately. Violence is an utterly abhorrent fault, and I thought I had it under control. But somehow I have lost control of my life. Of myself. I'm so sorry that you have a mother like me."

They hug me from both sides. "My teacher yelled at Shawn today by mistake at school," Rebecca says. "She never apologized, even when she found out that he wasn't the guilty party."

The guilty party. I can't repress a smile.

"Yeah," Jonathan chimes in. "The people I know who do bad things never admit it. You always say sorry."

Children are so forgiving. Go away, fucking tears.

"How can we help you to be calm, Eema? We can help!" says Rebecca.

I can't stop the tremour in my voice. "You are the best children in the world. I am so blessed with you two. But you are not blessed with me. I was thinking of going away for a while."

"What?"

"No way." Jonathan props himself up on his elbow so he can look into my face. "Eema, it's crap that you don't take me anywhere, but I'm cool because I know that if you can't take me to a game, it means you can't go away either."

"But what difference does it make if I go away? You've just said that I don't drive you anywhere anymore. I'm not doing most of the things mothers are supposed to do."

Rebecca gives my face a little push. "What are you talking about? You do a lot more than other mothers. Jenny's mother never goes into her bedroom. You lie with us every night."

"And you make us great food," adds Jonathan.

"And you play games with us. And take us out in the summer, even if you don't want to."

They both shout together, "You're the best mother in the world."

I do not trust myself to speak.

Adam's head suddenly appears around the doorframe. "I'm sorry too," he says to the kids. "I behaved badly too."

He enters the room and throws himself on top of me, hugging the kids on both sides.

"Abba, get off my bed! You're hairy," yells Rebecca.

Adam is looking at me. "You drive me nuts, but you're still my life. You know that, don't you?"

"How can I still be your life, if every interaction ends in a fight?"

"Every interaction? What are you talking about? We get along great most of the time. Every marriage has rough spots. Please don't think of going away." He lays his head down on my chest.

I am safe within the arms of my family, held tight in a cocoon of love. A glimmer of sun breaks through the gloom in my heart.

Acknowledgments

I would like to thank first and foremost my dear sisters: Tessa, without whom I certainly wouldn't have penned this book, my sister Anna, for her dependable honesty in loathing this book, and my sister Susie, to whom this book is dedicated.

Thank you to all the folks at Inanna whose input and contributions are so integral to the success of our books, and especially for their invaluable editorial input—thank you Rebecca Rosenblum, Meg Bowen, Renée Knapp, Beate Schwirtlich, and Ashley Rayner.

Thank you to Val Fullard for their creative and eye-catching cover.

I would like to thank my writing group for their thorough reading and suggestions—thank you Gwen Davies, Joseph Szostak, and Nick Sumner!

I am often amazed by the support of my readers—especially my family, friends, neighbours, teachers at my kids' schools—many of whom have gone out of their way to support my events and promote my books through word of mouth. Thank you for enjoying my writing.

Credit: Bruce Murray

Charlotte Mendel is a traveller, an author, a parent, a farmer, a teacher, and an environmental activist. Her two published adult novels have both won prizes; her first YA novel, *Reversing Time* was published by Guernica Editions in 2021. Charlotte has lived in Nova Scotia for 20 years and raised two wonderful children; this year she left her partner of 32 years and is in transit—her first destination is Europe. www.charlottemendel.com